Crimes and Misdemeanors
New and Original Stories
of Love and Death

"Showcases the different possibilities
offered by short fiction."
—*Publishers Weekly*

"Something for everyone."
—*Winston-Salem Journal*

Celebrating the fiftieth anniversary of Signet Books, this stellar collection features new and original stories by some of the greatest literary talents of our time. These beloved authors have given us countless hours of reading pleasure with stories that startle, provoke, terrify, touch the heart, and portray us at our most human. They have moved and entertained us; forced us to think, to question, and ultimately, to understand. And always, they share with us their unique vision of the world. We at Signet Books would like to thank not only all the wonderful storytellers, but the readers as well, for fifty years of success.

A portion of the proceeds from this book
will be donated to Literacy Partners, Inc.

Crimes and Misdemeanors

New and Original Stories of Love and Death

Edited by Elaine Koster
and Joseph Pittman

PUBLISHED IN A HARDCOVER EDITION AS
The Best of the Best

A SIGNET BOOK

SIGNET
Published by the Penguin Group
Penguin Putnam Inc., 375 Hudson Street,
New York, New York 10014, U.S.A.
Penguin Books Ltd, 27 Wrights Lane,
London W8 5TZ, England
Penguin Books Australia Ltd, Ringwood,
Victoria, Australia
Penguin Books Canada Ltd, 10 Alcorn Avenue,
Toronto, Ontario, Canada M4V 3B2
Penguin Books (N.Z.) Ltd, 182–190 Wairau Road,
Auckland 10, New Zealand

Penguin Books Ltd, Registered Offices:
Harmondsworth, Middlesex, England

Published by Signet, an imprint of Dutton NAL, a member of Penguin Putnam Inc.
Previously published in a Signet hardcover edition under the title *The Best of the Best*.

First Mass Market Printing, December, 1998
10 9 8 7 6 5 4 3 2 1

Copyright © Penguin Putnam Inc., 1998

Authors' copyrights to these stories can be found on p. 396.

  REGISTERED TRADEMARK—MARCA REGISTRADA

Printed in the United States of America

PUBLISHER'S NOTE
These stories are works of fiction. Names, characters, places, and incidents either are
the product of the authors' imaginations or used fictitiously, and any resemblance to
actual persons, living or dead, events, or locales is entirely coincidental.

BOOKS ARE AVAILABLE AT QUANTITY DISCOUNTS WHEN USED TO PROMOTE PRODUCTS
OR SERVICES. FOR INFORMATION PLEASE WRITE TO PREMIUM MARKETING DIVISION,
PENGUIN PUTNAM INC., 375 HUDSON STREET, NEW YORK, NEW YORK 10014.

Contents

Introduction

The reading experience is a deeply personal one, a bond between you, the reader, and the author, brought together by the genesis of an idea, and the power of words. You read a book, enjoy it, place the author's name in the corner of your mind . . . and wait for his or her next novel. Or you rush to the bookstore in search of previous titles by the author. In either case, it's the author who has grabbed your imagination, and the relationship seldom goes further. Rarely is thought given to the behind-the-scenes part played by the publisher, and that's how it should be. But sometimes the publisher steps out into the limelight. The occasion of Signet Books' Fiftieth Anniversary is such a time.

Briefly, Signet Books was born in 1948 as part of the growing world of mass market paperbacks—a form that revolutionized publishing by bringing to the American people low-priced, high-quality books. Although the paperback was met with resistance from traditional hardcover publishers, readers embraced this convenient, easy-to-read format, and today, fifty years later, the mass market book thrives. Signet began as an imprint of the New American Library, known industry-wide as NAL, and published a vast array of titles, some of which have gone on to become enduring American classics. Among its early titles were William

Faulkner's *Sanctuary,* Thomas Wolfe's *Short Stories,* and James T. Farrell's Studs Lonigan books. A mix of commerce and culture, these books and others represented the new wave of how—and who—America read.

One of those early writers who so helped define the Signet list was Mickey Spillane, whose first Mike Hammer mystery, *I, the Jury,* published in 1948, initiated a relationship that continues to this day. Other notable authors from Signet's infancy included Erskine Caldwell, Norman Mailer, Ralph Ellison, James Jones, Truman Capote, Gore Vidal, James Baldwin, William Styron, Flannery O'Connor, and J. D. Salinger.

As the years progressed, Signet's focus shifted, swayed by the changing tide of America and its appetite. A new determination to survive in an increasingly competitive marketplace had Signet searching for more commercial authors, while maintaining its literary list as well. Among those authors being published were Ian Fleming's James Bond thrillers, Boris Pasternak's *Dr. Zhivago,* Irving Wallace's *The Chapman Report,* Joanne Greenberg's *I Never Promised You a Rose Garden,* and John Fowles's *The French Lieutenant's Woman.* But Signet truly defined itself in the seventies as a leader of blockbuster fiction, with Erica Jong's *Fear of Flying,* Erich Segal's *Love Story,* and the publication of a first novel called *Carrie,* by an author named Stephen King.

No overview of Signet's rich history is complete without Stephen King, who since 1972 has gone on to become the world's bestselling author. His more than thirty novels have all been published in Signet paperback, and indeed, to this day, King continues to re-invent not just himself and his fiction, but publishing itself. His novel *The Green Mile,* published in six installments, revived the nineteenth-century concept of the serialized novel.

The tradition of blockbuster novels continued, and Signet's name continued to prosper. Among other widely popular novels to be published by Signet were Robin Cook's *Coma*, Ken Follett's *Eye of the Needle*, Peter Straub's *Koko*, and Jonathan Kellerman's *When the Bough Breaks*. The nineties introduced to the reading public a host of new, fresh talents, and among Signet's notable books were Nancy Taylor Rosenberg's *Mitigating Circumstances*, Jacqueline Mitchard's *The Deep End of the Ocean*, and Terry McMillan's *How Stella Got Her Groove Back*.

Diversity has always defined the Signet name, and in this collection of eighteen stories, written specifically for this occasion, diversity is the name of the game. There are crime stories from Ed McBain and Lawrence Block. Intrigue from Larry Collins and Stephen Frey. Tales of vengeance from Tabitha King, Sharyn McCrumb, Wendy Hornsby, and Joan Hess. Poignant tales that go right to the heart from Nancy Taylor Rosenberg, Eileen Goudge, Linda Lay Shuler, and Joy Fielding. Suspense from Jeffery Deaver. Beautiful prose and human struggle from Lisa Alther, Joyce Carol Oates, and E. L. Doctorow. The richness of poetry from Erica Jong. And a horror tale from Stephen King.

Now as Signet looks back on its rich and varied past, and looks forward to its vital future, we invite readers to delve into these stories and see for themselves the wonderful authors who have graced its list these past fifty years; many continue to do so. We could think of no better way in which to celebrate this milestone anniversary than to give our authors—past and present—a chance to showcase their talents. These eighteen authors share with us their unique vision, their quirky and individual interpretations of the world we live in. We think within these pages there is something for everyone.

So, read these stories, savor them and the brilliant minds

that brought them to fruition. And then, by all means, rush to your nearest bookstore and discover these talented authors again and again.

Enjoy.

—Elaine Koster
President and Publisher
Dutton Signet

—Joseph Pittman
Senior Editor
Dutton Signet
November, 1997

Stormy Weather
by Lisa Alther

Lying facedown on her watermelon beach towel, Jesse tries to decide what to wear to this party by the lake that she doesn't want to go to. But since it's her own fiftieth birthday celebration, she has no choice, short of dropping dead. Still, it strikes her that if you feel like celebrating at fifty, you just don't understand what's happening.

She rolls over on her back and, propped on her elbows, glances down at her no-longer pert breasts. Gravity is winning out over centrifugal force. At fifty maybe you're entitled to accept the laws of nature and abandon the struggle for fitness?

She studies the grass around the pool, scorching in the summer sun. In the late sixties Robert and she dragged Cybele to swimming holes all over Vermont. Naked parents smoked pot along sunstruck creek banks, while embarrassed children with names taken from natural phenomena—Forest, Coyote, Sky, Storm—concealed themselves under layers of towels.

But then Robert went suburban on her, spending their savings on this pool, which has leaked ever since. Several years ago he moved to a condo in town, leaving her to patch and bail this cracked concrete vessel alone. But a love affair with herself was the only variation she hadn't tried, and she is finding solitude soothing after the sweet and savage sex wars of her youth.

Picking up the long-handled pool brush, she begins to sweep the white bottom with long, slow strokes, pretending she's a gondolier on the Grand Canal. As she stirs up clouds of debris, she hears Thor barking in the driveway. Laying down the brush, she tiptoes to the copse of Russian olives that separates the pool area from the white gravel driveway. A car door slams.

Bent over petting Thor is Rachel, wearing an Hawaiian-print bathing suit with leg holes to her waist. She's one of the few women Jesse knows who looks good in that style. Robert is standing beside her in baggy bathing trunks to his knees and an antique Grateful Dead T-shirt. Now that the dust has settled, Jesse is fond of them again, individually and together. But this particular birthday afternoon she prefers to assess the damage of the decades unassisted.

"She's not here," Robert decides.

"Her car's here," says Rachel.

Someone could have stopped by to pick me up, Jesse silently suggests.

"Let's knock," says Robert, starting up the driveway. The laces on his high-tops are untied, and he trips.

"If she's here, she probably doesn't want to be disturbed, or else she'd have come out by now."

Jesse nods in agreement, watching Rachel straighten up. Thor, not ready for her to stop patting, licks her well-tanned calf.

"Let's leave her present by the door." Robert gestures to a package wrapped in gold foil with a wide maroon ribbon, which Rachel is holding.

"Shouldn't we take it to the party?"

"She might want to wear it tonight."

Reaching the back door, Robert rings several times.

Jesse is impressed that he doesn't walk right in. He knows the hiding spot for the key, and he still sometimes regards this house as his, since he and she restored every square inch with hand tools. Jesse recalls sawing a ten-foot two-by-four in half lengthwise, Robert insisting that to use electricity was to support the military-industrial complex that was fueling the war in Vietnam.

"She's not here," he concludes. "Let's take a swim." Grabbing Rachel's hand, he leads her up the slope crowned by the grove of Russian olives where Jesse is standing.

Jesse's heartbeat kicks into high gear, and a hot flash sweeps up her thighs and across her abdomen. What's the polite thing to say when your friends find you naked in the bushes spying on them?

"I'm not sure this is such a good idea," says Rachel, pulling on Robert's hand.

No, it's not, Jesse assures her. Rachel rarely steps on her toes, whereas Robert cripples her several times a month.

"Come on. It's fine. Jesse won't mind. We're all old friends." Robert drags Rachel across the granite ledge, which is etched by glaciers to resemble a giant circulatory system.

They amble past Jesse, no more than ten feet away. She's a statue, a stone nymph, Daphne turning into a laurel tree.

Thor pads along behind, panting from the heat despite his summer crew cut. He stares at Jesse, wagging his tail. Having always believed pets are telepathic, Jesse beams him a message: "If you want supper tonight, keep walking." Thor just stands there, mouth agape, tongue lolling. Jesse frowns and grimaces, trying to look punitive. Sweat from her hot flash is trickling from her armpits down her sides. It tickles but she can't scratch.

Thor follows the merry swimmers, who are now reclining on the watermelon beach towel, backs facing the Russian olives. He collapses in the shade of the barn-board pool house, doleful eyes fixed on Jesse, nostrils twitching.

A quick dip and they'll be on their way, prays Jesse.

"A towel and her robe," muses Robert like the private investigator he's always wished he was. "She must have split in a hurry."

"Who's she seeing now?" asks Rachel.

"Nobody that I know of."

"Oh, that's right. The last time we had dinner she regaled me with the erotics of celibacy. The frisson when your eyes meet those of the postman."

Damn Rachel. She'd pretended to agree that night in the restaurant by the lake that there were pleasures more subtle than sex. As she'd struggled to crack a lobster claw, she'd even suggested that sex was a sublimation of love.

Robert turns his shaggy head to smile at Rachel. Jesse spots his gold earring flashing in the sun. How is a newly appointed judge able to get away with that? Do they still wear long gray wigs? Robert has developed an unfortunate double chin that puffs up like a frog's throat when he gets pompous. The same thing is starting to happen to his belly.

"Sour grapes, if you ask me," says Robert. "Do you think she still resents our being together?"

Jesse is seized with indignation. *She* is the one who left, relieved to stop spending all her free time and money on therapy. Rachel and she, Robert and she, Robert and Rachel, Rachel and her husband, Peter, were all doing couples therapy. The four of them did group therapy. Each did individual therapy. Rachel and she processed the dynamics of their quadrangle at their women's group and in their Multiple Relationship group. Robert and Peter processed it with their men's group. Aging is a bore, but at least the seventies are over.

"Probably," says Rachel. "It must be hard for her to see us so happy together."

In the first place, Jesse replies, I'm confident that each of you will eventually drive the other mad. In the second place . . .

Realizing that she's about to blow her cover, Jesse shifts her outraged gaze to the gnarled branches of the ancient honey locusts at the foot of the hill on which the pool is perched. Her favorite hour of a summer day is underway— late afternoon before the sun begins to set, when its slanting rays lend the fence posts by the cornfield in the valley shadows ten feet long. The mountains on the far horizon are exuding a golden glow. Flecks of violet and coral on the granite outcroppings signal the conflagration soon to come. She hears the plaintive coo of a mourning dove.

The bottoms of Jesse's new shorty pajamas were damp. She'd climbed down from the four-poster bed and trotted across the carpet to the bathroom. Lowering the seat her father had left up, she climbed onto the toilet. Too late, she realized she was still lying in bed, dreaming this journey across the rug.

Time after time she waved the top sheet so it billowed like a sail, trying to dry out her pajamas and the bottom sheet before her mother came in. As her mother changed the sheets she'd put on fresh yesterday, the muscles in her jaws would clench and unclench like fists. Jesse didn't like to make her cross. She worried that her mother might be sick. Sometimes after her father went to his insurance office downtown, her mother put on high heels and perfume and left Jesse with Mrs. Morris next door to go to doctor appointments.

Recognizing the hopelessness of her efforts, Jesse lay perfectly still while the floating sheet settled down over her. It was a blanket of snow, and she was the Little Match Girl, frozen to death.

Coming through the window from the magnolia tree outside, Jesse heard a hollow tune like her father sometimes played on his clarinet on the back porch after supper. Her mother had been the singer with her father's band at nightclubs all over the South. A man from Hollywood took pictures of her and asked her to act in a movie, but she married Jesse's father instead. Sometimes she spread these photos on the kitchen table and studied them.

Once again the strange sound floated through Jesse's window from the magnolia tree. It was a sad song with five notes—low, high, low and long, low, low. Then silence.

Rolling out from under her shroud of snow, Jesse went to the window and looked through the screen into the jungle of waxy leaves and creamy blossoms that filled her room with the same scent as the perfume her mother dabbed at her throat.

The door opened and her mother walked in. Sniffing, she threw back the covers and discovered Jesse's accident. The muscles in her jaws began to pulse. The melody out the window began again.

"Mommy, what's that sound?"

Her mother was poking the wet spot on the bottom sheet. "It's a bird called a morning dove. It's probably calling its mate."

"What's a mate?"

"Its partner. Its husband. Or its wife. I don't know which." With a sigh she began to remove the sheets.

"Where's its mate?"

"I don't know. Apparently the dove doesn't either. That's why it's calling."

After her mother left, Jesse searched the tangled branches for the dove. Since the sound was so ghostly, she

pictured a bird version of Casper the Friendly Ghost—
white, with floating wings and a smiling mouth.

The dove called again. Pursing her lips as her neighbor
Daryl Morris had recently taught her, Jesse whistled the
melody, hoping the dove would think that she was its mate
and fly over to her windowsill. But its next call came from
halfway across the yard, heading for the woods.

". . . it was like walking on eggs," Robert is saying. "I
never knew what was going to bug her next."

"You do realize she had PMS?" says Rachel. "She's less
touchy now that she's nearly through menopause."

Good God, protests Jesse from the bushes. _Robert_ is the
one who's moody, in a perpetual funk that the nuclear arms
race hasn't yet destroyed the world, as he predicted in the
sixties. And _Rachel_ has PMS, erupting over water spots on
glasses from the dishwasher, or the surly attitude of a
supermarket cashier. Rachel learned in her counseling program that it was healthy to express anger and she hasn't
shut up since. Jesse admits, however, that she herself is
more mellow now—because she's free of those two.

Looking down, she discovers that she's standing in a
patch of poison ivy. The shiny green leaves-of-three are
caressing her ankles and lower calves. Venom from leaves
crushed by her feet is seeping between her toes. Rachel
and Robert are engrossed in their analysis of Jesse's personality flaws. Maybe she can sneak through the undergrowth behind her down to the driveway, and escape from
there to the house.

She raises a foot to step backward. Thor snaps to attention in the shade by the pool house. Panting, he struggles
to his feet to come greet her. Jesse returns her foot to its
cushion of oozing leaves and resumes her imitation of

Daphne. With a deep sigh Thor collapses back into the shade.

". . . her fear of intimacy," Rachel is saying.

Intimacy? Intimacy! sputters Jesse. Rachel's test for intimacy involved seeing who could lie in bed the longest on a weekend morning without getting bored. Using that gauge, Rachel was the Intimacy Queen. Never mind that she always jumped up immediately after lovemaking to take a shower and brush her teeth.

Still, Jesse is the one hiding in the bushes while two of her best friends try to visit her. But their notion of intimacy seems to involve bonding with each other by trashing her, which doesn't exactly incline Jesse toward intimacy with either one of them.

"I remember the first time I ever saw her," says Robert. "In the courtyard at Columbia. She looked almost otherworldly, with those cool blue eyes, like ice on the Himalayas. I guess I was challenged by her remoteness. I wanted to bring her back down to earth and roll her around in the mud."

Rachel laughs. "I know what you mean. I remember in our women's group she had this engaging country-girl innocence. When I told the group about sleeping with a woman, she looked like she'd never heard of such a thing. Naturally, it made me want to show her what it was all about. And I must say that she took to it like a horse to oats."

"I think she's afraid of getting too close to people," says Robert. "Her father killed himself. I always worried that it ran in the family, the way musical ability does."

Bingo, thinks Jesse, touched to discover that both understand her better than she has realized.

"He killed himself, yet Jesse always portrays him as this happy-go-lucky rascal."

"I never met the dude, but I've noticed that those bad-boy types are often closet alcoholics. . . ."

Hidden beneath a pile of crisp autumn leaves, head resting on her forearms, Jesse was an Apache warrior being chased by the cavalry. As she lay on the bottom of a pond, breathing through a hollow reed, soldiers in blue uniforms with criss-crossed cartridge belts were ransacking the swamp all around her.

The dust from the dry leaves was sharp in her nostrils, making her want to sneeze, which she knew she mustn't do if she wanted to remain uncaptured. The leaves were tickling her forearms like dancing spiders. Moving just her fingertips, she scratched.

Jesse heard her mother's familiar whistle from the back door—six notes from a song called "Deep Purple," which meant that supper was ready. She burst from the leaf pile, imagining that she was a blue gill leaping from a pond to snag a dragonfly. Dashing across the field, she combed dead leaves from her ponytail with her fingers. Over by his garage door Daryl was yelling, "Ollie, ollie, in free!" But she ignored him, bound for home.

Halfway to the house, Jesse froze behind a bush with thorns and mahogany leaves. She was a fawn hiding from an approaching hunter, concealed by her spotted hide.

For a moment the cicadas in the elm trees ceased their sawing, the grasshoppers paused in mid-jump, and the crickets swallowed their chirrups. The five hollow notes of a dove sounded from a nearby tree.

Jesse looked up quickly, but saw only juicy purple mulberries, hanging from the knotted branches like Jujyfruits you chewed at the movies. Her mother whistled again, her six notes blending with the dove's five.

Jesse pranced through the tall grass toward the back

door, a Tennessee walking horse with weighted hooves, performing in the show of champions. She tossed her muzzle so her arched ponytail swirled.

Reaching the swings, she jumped on and pumped as hard as she could, chains screeching like jungle birds. Worried that she might swing right over the top and around the other side, as Daryl claimed he had once done, she stopped pumping and let the swing die. She was a paratrooper poised in the bay of a fighter bomber, about to drop behind enemy lines. Letting go of the chains, she flew out of her seat, one hand pulling her parachute cord, the other cradling her machine gun. Hitting the ground, she rolled over and over to dodge enemy fire. Then she leapt to her feet and zigzagged to the house, spraying the Nazis with bullets as she ran.

As she hurtled through the back door, safe at last, her mother looked up from the stove. "You're late. Where were you?"

"Out back, playing with Daryl."

"What were you playing?" Her mother glanced down at her grass-stained feet.

Jesse hesitated. She had played so many things. How did you explain this to an adult who seemed to be only one thing all the time? "Magic Circle."

Her father appeared, tie loosened, collar unbuttoned, rolling his starched shirtsleeves to his elbows. "Hey, darling."

"Daddy! You're back!" She hurled herself at him. He swept her up to the ceiling, then settled her on his hip. "Where did you say you went?" she asked, patting his cute, fuzzy bald spot, a nest in the middle of his thick black hair.

"To a convention in Newport News."

"Where's that?"

"In Virginia over on the shore."

"What's a convention?"

"A bunch of morons get together and lie about all the deals they've cut." He glanced at her mother with a crooked smile, squinting in the smoke from the cigarette that dangled from the corner of his mouth.

"Why would they want to do that?"

"You got me, buddy. It's called business."

They sat down at the round wooden table in the corner of the kitchen. Her mother had put some yellow flowers in a glass vase in the middle of the table, and they were using the green cloth napkins. She always tried to make things special when Jesse's father got home from a trip.

"Mommy, I heard that morning dove again. Just now, out in the yard."

"That's nice, dear."

"But why would it sing in the evening?"

Her mother glanced at her. "Why wouldn't it?"

"I thought it was supposed to sing in the morning."

Her mother frowned. Then she smiled. "Oh, I get it. It's not a morning dove, darling, it's a mourning dove. M-O-U-R-N-I-N-G." Remembering that Jesse couldn't spell yet, she said, "It's two different words. One means early in the day. The other means you're sad because someone has died or gone away."

"Why is the dove sad?"

"Maybe it isn't. Maybe it just sounds that way."

"Maybe it's lost its mate," said her father. "They say that if you shoot one, the other calls for it the rest of its life." Raising his dark eyebrows, he looked at her mother.

"Why would someone want to shoot one?" asked Jesse.

"People eat them. They're considered a delicacy."

"I don't think that's very nice."

"Kiddo, sometimes life ain't very nice."

"Isn't," murmured her mother.

"I think life is nice," Jesse said.

"Check in with me again when you're fifty," suggested her father.

After supper they sat on the back porch. Her mother lit a Camel, leaving a ring of scarlet lipstick around one end. Sucking on his reed, her father slipped together the pieces of his clarinet. Jesse stood beside him, watching this transformation of sections of wood into a long black tube that could make sounds like a baby crying for its mother, or water bubbling up from a spring, or a wild cat yowling in the forest. As her father tightened the screws that held the reed to the mouthpiece, Jesse heard the dove calling in the yard.

"Listen!" she ordered her parents. Both paused, while a bat on insect patrol swooped past, silhouetted against the scarlet sky. The dove's five notes echoed from the woods. Holding the clarinet to his lips, her father mimicked the call. They waited, but the dove didn't reply.

Her father began to play, repeating the five notes in different rhythms and keys. Jesse watched her mother's unhappy look change into a soft smile as her father became more and more daring, as when Daryl showed off for Jesse, doing a handstand on his bicycle handlebars, or making his bicycle rear and twist in midair like a stallion.

The song faded into another Jesse had never heard before. Her mother exhaled a stream of smoke that curled to the rafters and drifted out the screen into the night sky. Then she started singing in her deep voice: ". . .Can't go on. Everything I had is gone. Stormy weather. Since my man and I ain't together . . ."

That summer Jesse and Daryl spent their free time sneaking from tree to tree out back, trying to track the dove calls. They rigged traps of string and sticks, baiting them with pieces of Baby Ruth. At Sunday school the deacon showed them a picture of the Holy Ghost, a white bird with outspread wings, flying straight down like an airplane in a nosedive. They decided a mourning dove must look like that. The eerie call from the woods between their houses at dawn and at dusk became a backdrop to their games and chores. But they never saw one.

Jesse realizes that now that she's fifty, she can't check in with her father as he recommended that night so long ago. As Robert pointed out, he's dead.

She hears a discreet meow. Looking down, she discovers her cat Sadie sitting in the poison ivy, jet black against the green, tail wrapped carefully around her front paws, staring up at Jesse through neon gold eyes. Jesse smiles faintly. Sadie narrows her eyes. Jesse blows her a silent kiss. Sadie starts to purr.

Thor lifts his head from his paws. His ears and nostrils quiver. He glances in every direction, long ears swaying. Spotting the cat, he cocks his head.

Before Thor can get up and bound over, something rustles in the undergrowth. Sadie is transformed from a family pet into a serial killer. She crouches. She listens. She creeps forward on flexing paws. Bursting from the bushes like a torpedo, she streaks across the grass to the far side of the pool and, with one leap, vanishes down the hillside, ignoring Robert, who is calling, "Sadie! What's up? Come say hello to the old man!"

Robert returns his attention to Rachel. Her voice is so low and his grin so lascivious that Jesse knows she's saying something dirty. He reaches out and pinches her nipple, stiff beneath her bathing suit.

Please, God, pleads Jesse, don't let them make love. They begin to touch each other in ways she remembers each touching her. Rachel's fingertips stroke Robert's cheek. Robert brushes the hair off Rachel's forehead with the back of his hand. Jesse can almost feel their combined caresses on her own flesh. She nearly hears Rachel's soft down-home accent whispering endearments, reminding her of a faraway time when life had seemed much simpler.

Jesse's stomach clenches just as it did that night they took her to dinner on the lake and confessed that they'd first slept together. She remembers the urge to plant her fork between Robert's eyes and her steak knife in Rachel's throat. This isn't how she had hoped to spend her fiftieth birthday.

Rachel, bless her heart, pushes Robert away.

"What's the matter?"

"Don't be crazy. We can't do this here. What if Jesse comes home?"

"We'll hear the car in the driveway."

"Maybe she's not in a car. Maybe she's gone for a birthday hike. Maybe she's standing on that hill across the valley right now."

"So what if she is? You can't see here from there. I'll make it fast."

Rachel puts her hand on his furry chest to block his advance. "Sweetheart, you know I don't like it fast. It makes me feel like a handy home appliance."

Jesse's blood pressure returns to normal. She congratulates Rachel. Why did Jesse ever let her go? If she had just continued their four-way fray, she and Rachel might have gotten rid of Robert and Peter. Or Robert and Peter might have gotten rid of Rachel and her. Or Robert and Peter might have gone off together. Or . . .

Rachel has dragged Robert to the pool edge. She shoves him in. "Cool yourself off, my love."

God, thinks Jesse, that is one cute, tough woman. Forgetting her earlier enthusiasm for celibacy, she wonders how late is too late to change her mind.

Meanwhile, from the valley into which Sadie has plunged comes the sound of National Guard helicopters. The weekend warriors are moving up the cornfield. Stalks are whipping and lashing beneath their swirling blades. Bursts of Uzi-esque flapping get louder and louder, like an approaching locomotive. Terrific. There's nothing like the peace and quiet of country living.

As the five copters pass above the swimming pool like giant farting June bugs, Robert, who is standing in the shallow end with the whirlwinds scrambling his gray hair, raises both middle fingers above his head and shouts, "Goddam fucking fascist pigs!"

Conveniently forgetting that since he's a judge now, he's a pillar of the Establishment. But Jesse can still glimpse the slender, bearded boy in his red bandana headband whom she first spotted on the steps of the administration building at Columbia, wielding a clawed Chippendale chair leg like a nightstick against advancing security guards.

Jesse and Daryl were standing by the cornfield in the valley below their houses, looking in every direction to make sure no one was watching. They started down a row marked by crossed sticks stuck in the soil. The sun lit their path with wavery yellow ribbons, while the pointed leaves clashed overhead like green swords. They came to a narrow break in the stalks to the right. Turning, they crossed several rows, then headed left up another row, following a route through the maze indicated by sticks, twigs, and rocks. Eventually they arrived at a small clearing in the center of the field.

Removing their knapsacks, they took out two blue chenille bedspreads salvaged from Jesse's attic. She spread
one across the dirt. Daryl suspended the other on stalks
around the perimeter, to form a billowing ceiling. They
were a pioneer couple in the wilderness who supplied all
their needs by their own hands.

Jesse placed their wrapped tuna sandwiches and Cokes
in the shade and made a neat stack of the fabric scraps
from Daryl's mother's sewing room. Daryl disappeared
among the stalks. When he returned, he was carrying three
plump ears of corn, one with blond tassles, one with red,
and the third with dark brown. Jesse, inspecting them,
approved.

Sitting cross-legged, Daryl stripped back and trimmed
the shucks to expose some kernels, which Jesse colored
with Magic Markers to form blue or brown eyes, black
nostrils and red mouths. Using his Swiss army knife, Daryl
drilled holes through the shucks into the ears and inserted
Popsicle stick arms. With bits of ribbon Jesse tied up their
silky hair. Then both worked with scissors, needles, and
thread to cut the scraps of fabric and sew them into outfits
for their daughters.

When they finished, the sun was at an angle overhead.
Sitting on the bedspread, they ate their sandwiches and
drank Cokes. Then they stretched out for a nap, their new
daughters arrayed between them.

"Aren't they beautiful?" murmured Jesse.

"How could they not be with you as their mother?"
replied Daryl, touching her hair.

She smiled. His dark hair was hanging in his eyes. The
boys at school made fun of his curls. But the girls sent him
notes during class and blushed when he spoke to them.

"Do you know how real babies are made?" he asked,

hands behind his head as he gazed up at the billowing blue ceiling, luminous from the summer sun.

"Of course," she said. "Everyone knows that."

"Do you want to try it?"

"I think we're too young."

"We could at least try."

"If it worked, we'd be in big trouble. My parents would never let me marry you. I'm only eleven years old."

"We could just pretend to make one," suggested Daryl. "You're already my wife, aren't you?"

"Yes. But what do you mean—pretend to make one?"

"You do it, but since you don't really want a baby, you don't get one."

"Are you sure that's how it works?"

"Yes, I think so."

"Okay. We can try it."

They did try it there in their pioneer cabin among the cornstalks with their adorable corncob daughters watching. Although they had no idea what they were doing, they liked it. Resting on the chenille bedspread afterward, they heard a mourning dove calling nearby. Daryl jumped up and chased its receding call down the narrow rows, but he didn't manage to see it.

Jesse hears another car coming up the driveway, gravel crunching beneath its tires. The afternoon is beginning to resemble a model-home tour.

The door slams. Thor leaps to his feet and careens past Jesse, barking like a German shepherd in a Nazi film. Robert claims they named him Thor, after the Norse god of thunder, because of this bark. But as Jesse recalls, it was a nickname for Thorazine, which she was considering taking at the time, their quadrangle having reached its pinnacle of complexity.

"Thor!" exclaims Cybele. "How you doing, old boy?"

Thor moans and whimpers. You'd think from his desperation that Jesse has been doing cruel medical experiments on him in Cybele's absence. Thor slept on Cybele's bed for his first several years. Then Cybele left for college and he was exiled to a cushion in the entryway. Jesse is sure he's never forgiven her. No doubt he'll invent a way to expose her in her current predicament.

Thor and Cybele saunter past Jesse, Thor looking back and forth between the two women.

"Hey, Dad. Hey, Rachel," calls Cybele. They climb out of the pool, Rachel giving Robert an I-told-you-so look. Cybele kisses both, avoiding their dripping bodies.

"So where's my short mother?" asks Cybele. The three laugh. Cybele calls Rachel her tall mother and Jesse her short mother.

"No idea," replies Robert. "Her towel and her robe are here, but she seems to have vanished."

"Do you think she's okay?"

Robert picks up on her impulse of panic. "Let's hope so," he says anxiously.

"Relax, you two," says Rachel. "She's probably at the mall buying a new outfit for her party."

As Cybele strips down to her bikini, Jesse inspects the panther etched on her shoulder. Like a Neanderthal cave painter, the tattoo artist has used the jut of Cybele's shoulder blade to emphasize the panther's haunch. As Cybele turns to sit down, the sun glints off the gold hoop in her navel. She's searched high and low for eccentricities with which to outrage her parents. Unfortunately, ex-hippies have seen everything and done most of it. The only thing that really concerns Robert and herself is Cybele's devotion to her job as a stock analyst for Merrill Lynch.

Today Cybele is wearing a studded black leather armband around her bicep, no doubt a statement to her parents that they are pathetic aging practitioners of vanilla sex. Glancing down at her own body, Jesse recalls some of the feats her flesh has performed. Whatever Cybele may prefer to believe, this body has been around the block a few times more than Jesse cares to remember. The creative combinations of appendages and orifices—how have her joints survived the strain?

"Look, honey," says Robert, gesturing to the rings in Cybele's navel and his earlobe. "We match."

"As if," replies Cybele with a grimace that Jesse interprets as meaning, "Dream on, you old goat. You wish your pitiful little hippie hoop was as cool as my really awesome navel piercing."

"So," says Robert, "how's the market this week?"

"Yeah, right," says Cybele. "Like, you really care."

"But I do. I'm starting to think a lot about how to maintain my standard of living when I retire."

"Retire? But, Dad, you've just been appointed judge."

"I know, but I have a lot more years behind me now than I do ahead of me."

"It's Jesse who's supposed to be thinking like that today," says Rachel.

"I guess having someone I met when she was twenty-one turn fifty is sobering for me as well."

"Get over it," suggests Cybele with the insensitivity of the young.

"I was trying to," snaps Robert. "By asking you about the market."

They sit in strained silence.

"I was wondering if you'd take a look at my pension plan and tell me what you think of my investments," says Robert, trying hard.

"Not a problem," says Cybele, accepting his olive

branch. "Have your assistant fax me a list of your holdings on Monday, and I'll be happy to tell you what I think."

"I'd really appreciate it."

Jesse is astonished. There are three possibilities, each equally alarming: Robert is trying to bond with Cybele via the stock market. Robert is putting Cybele on and will laugh about it later with Rachel. Or Robert is having a mid-life crisis. How can he scream at the National Guard one minute, then ask his daughter's advice about Wall Street the next? With relief she realizes that Robert's mental health is now Rachel's problem, not hers.

"I have something to tell you guys," announces Cybele. "I can't wait any longer, so I guess I'll have to tell Mom separately."

Jesse feels the hairs stand up along the back of her neck. Is she pregnant? HIV positive?

"What?" asks Robert, equally alarmed by the solemnity of her tone. Jesse has always adored the seriousness with which he takes his role as Cybele's father, despite everything.

"I know you aren't going to like it, but Karl and I are getting married this fall. By an Episcopal priest."

Robert's mouth drops open. He glances at Rachel.

Good for you, thinks Jesse. You've finally found a way to shock your parents.

"Why?" asks Rachel.

"Because we love each other."

"Fine, but why wreck it by getting married?" asks Robert.

"We're not like you guys. We want to make a commitment before God to live together all our lives in peace and fidelity."

Rachel and Robert look at each other.

"You both got married," says Cybele. "Why shouldn't we?"

"Yes," says Rachel, "but we didn't *stay* married."

"And we certainly weren't peaceful or faithful," adds Robert.

Jesse smiles as she stands there in the poison ivy, tickled by this endless interplay between the generations, each believing itself to be correcting the failings of the previous one.

"I want Karl to be my husband for the rest of our lives."

"Uh, how do you know?" asks Robert, trying to sound respectful.

"Know that I want to be with Karl for the rest of my life?" asks Cybele irritably.

"You're just out of business school. How could you possibly know now what you want for the rest of your life?"

"Dad," says Cybele, rolling her eyes. "Like, you just know, okay?"

"You *think* you know," mutters Robert.

"Whatever," says Cybele.

Jesse was packed up and sent to boarding school at the National Cathedral in Washington, D.C., ostensibly so that she could sing with the Cathedral choir. Her mother informed her that she wasn't going to waste her voice, as her mother had hers. Daryl and she yearned and suffered. Every vacation they were inseparable, vowing to marry as soon as they could. His mother, a widow, couldn't afford to send him to college, so he planned to train in the army for a career.

During Jesse's senior year, her mother divorced her father and married a man who owned a gas station in the next town. When Jesse went home the summer before Juilliard, her father sat on the back porch after work every evening, smoking Camels, drinking Jack Daniel's, and playing plaintive tunes on his clarinet, as though trying to pipe his wife home.

It didn't work. One evening during Jesse's Christmas vacation, he hanged himself from the mulberry tree out back. Jesse found him the next day. His body swayed stiffly in the winter gusts, and his ravaged face was blue.

The following year Jesse's mother was diagnosed with ovarian cancer and died within six months. When Jesse went home for the funeral, she stayed with Daryl's mother. Daryl was flying a helicopter in Vietnam. The afternoon after her mother's service she and Mrs. Morris sat in the den drinking tea.

"Remember when you and Daryl were little?" said Mrs. Morris. "Each day was like a safari. You'd get so excited over the least little thing. Like that bird you chased around the woods all the time."

"Mourning doves. We never did manage to see one."

"I always felt so bad for you, Jesse," said Mrs. Morris, "with your parents running around on each other like that."

Jesse looked at her. "What do you mean?"

Recognizing her slip too late, Mrs. Morris jumped up, grabbed the teapot, and headed for the kitchen.

Jesse pointed at Mrs. Morris's chair. "I don't care for any more tea, thank you, Mrs. Morris. I just want to know what you meant by that."

"Oh, honey, I shouldn't have gone telling tales out of school."

"Please. I need to know."

Mrs. Morris said her mother had been seeing her gas station owner for several years before her divorce, and there had been another man before him. But her father's "conventions" weren't always for business. For the first time

Jesse figured out that her birthday was only six months after her parents' marriage.

Back at Juilliard, Jesse buried herself in work. One night in her carrel at the library, as she read troubadour lyrics for her Early Music course, she came across a chanson by Bernart of Ventadour that ended, "She has taken my heart./She has taken my self./She has taken from me the world,/And then she has eluded me,/Leaving me with only my desire/And my parched heart."

This was what had happened to her father, Jesse realized as she traced with her index finger some graffiti etched into her desktop. Apparently it was the nature of love to bring you great joy, followed by greater suffering. She wanted nothing more to do with it, except as a topic through which to earn her degree.

She wrote her thesis on Bernart of Ventadour, spending a year at the University of Toulouse. She made pilgrimages around the Languedoc to the towns and ruined castles associated with the various troubadours. She took classes in Old Provençal so she could read chansons in the original. She underwent training in the currently accepted modes for singing the lyrics. The best of the troubadours used physical love as a metaphor for spiritual love. If you followed their recipe, you could bypass the earthly variety altogether.

During her year in France Jesse's replies to Daryl's letters from Vietnam became increasingly sporadic. Eventually they stopped altogether. She had no intention of repeating her parents' mistakes. The mulberry tree was not her destination of choice.

Back in New York, applying for a teaching job at Columbia, she met Robert, a Maoist law student with a full beard and a bandana headband. He believed that love, like religion, was an opiate for the people. Having in common

a horror of love, he and Jesse "had sex." They were comrades, roommates, friends, anything but lovers.

One evening after Jesse moved into Robert's apartment
on Riverside Drive in Harlem, she was lying on their bed
scanning a newly discovered score for one of her favorite
chansons, softly singing the notes. Robert was in the living room watching mayhem from Vietnam on the tube.
Right outside the window she heard a mourning dove. The
lonely call echoed down the redbrick canyon formed by
the walls of opposing apartment buildings.

Startled, Jesse padded into the living room.

"What's up?" asked Robert, glancing up from the television. "You look like you've seen a ghost."

"I just heard a mourning dove," Jesse replied. "I never
knew they lived in cities. I used to hear them all the time
back home. But I never managed to see one."

"Jesus," he said. "They're all over the place. Look." He
pulled up the blind, and there on the fire escape perched a
plump brown bird with a breast mottled as though with
food stains.

"You mean, that's it?" Just then the bird's doughy chest
quivered, and it emitted its unearthly call.

"Cousins to pigeons. Rats with wings," Robert announced.

"I prefer how I pictured them in my head."

"That's your whole problem, Jesse. You live too much
in your head." He hated that she wasn't as entranced with
anti-war actions as he. Each new atrocity on the evening
news energized him, whereas all Jesse wanted was to lock
herself up with her troubadours, who passed their days
longing for some disembodied beloved.

One day Robert decided that a way to protest the military-
industrial complex as valid as attacking it was to create an
alternative. He also felt that he and Jesse needed to stop
head tripping and develop subsistence skills like workers

the world over. Since Jesse claimed indifference to her sur-
roundings, they joined the stream of exhausted war protes-
tors from Boston, New York, and Philadelphia who were
moving to Vermont. These nouveau rustics planned to return
to America's pre-industrial promise by raising kohlrabi and
buckwheat. By heating with wood and foreswearing a second car. By plaiting garlic on Sunday nights instead of
watching *Masterpiece Theatre*. They baled each other's hay,
caponized each other's roosters, and ate the placentas at
each other's home births.

To bring in some cash Jesse taught music appreciation
at a local college, and Robert worked for Legal Aid. Eventually Cybele arrived, squalling and irresistible. Jesse soon
realized that, whether she liked it or not, she was now
firmly rooted in the life and loves of the flesh.

This idyll lasted twelve years.

One spring morning Robert woke up, turned to Jesse
and announced, "If the good Lord had meant us to have
gardens, He wouldn't have given us supermarkets."

"She," murmured Jesse, who had recently joined a
consciousness-raising group with nine other women, who
spent most of their time complaining about having to can
and freeze while their men plotted the revolution over bottles of bad wine. One woman, a lanky therapist named
Rachel, had recently confessed to the group that she was
having an affair with a former client named Dinah. She described the satin pillows she put on her bed for Dinah's
visits, and the way she fed Dinah tiny shrimps with her
fingertips, until Dinah could stand it no longer and sucked
Rachel's fingers into her mouth. The women's group was
in a state of collective shock. This was indeed an alternative to canning and freezing. And Jesse was alarmed to feel
something alarmingly close to envy.

* * *

"Hey, Dad, what's this?" asks Cybele, pointing at the gold foil package lying in the shade beside Thor.

Jesse can hear the clanking of a tractor spreading manure in the pasture across the road. Thor's nostrils are twitching. Presumably, he can already smell it. Swarms of seagulls have arrived from the lake and are squawking over worms and insects.

"A present for your mother," says Robert.

"Cool. What is it?"

"A T-shirt."

"A T-shirt?" says Cybele. "For her fiftieth birthday? That's pretty lame, Dad."

"One present among several," he assures her. "Besides, what it says is really neat."

"Neat?" repeats Cybele with a mocking grin.

"Awesome?" asks Robert.

He has always claimed to be the first to use the term *groovy*. Jesse muses that it must be humiliating for him now to be, like, so deeply uncool.

"What does it say?" asks Cybele.

"You'll just have to wait and see."

Jesse watches the gray-green leaves of the Russian olives shimmy in a breeze that is tickling her shoulders. She finally picks up the acrid odor of the manure. Then she realizes that the breeze at her back is a mosquito, which has just bitten her. She can hear it, plump with her own blood, buzzing like a cargo plane around her left ear. She spots another on her right forearm. An entire squadron must have received word that fresh meat is standing helpless in the Russian olives. If she slaps, she'll give herself away. So she grits her teeth and endures the bites. Surely her guests will leave soon? Shouldn't everyone be changing for the party?

She studies the three of them, cross-legged in a circle on

her watermelon beach towel, Thor lying with his head in Cybele's lap. Cybele is kneading his favorite spot, just behind his ears.

Sadie stalks out of the weeds beyond the pool, eyeing the domestic group disdainfully. Even as she walks, she's in transition from the Beast back into Beauty. She rubs the length of her silky black body along Rachel's thigh. Rachel narrows her green eyes, catlike, the way she always does when experiencing a gratuitous frisson.

Jesse studies the tableau. Of all living creatures these are the ones most important to her. All of a sudden, on the afternoon of her fiftieth birthday, with the dog-day sun low in the sky, Jesse realizes that she is a fortunate woman. During her five decades, despite her attempts to evade it, she has given and received more than her share of love. On the balance sheet of her days to date, the pleasure exceeds the pain. Nearly insane from the need to scratch, she feels gratitude well up inside her. She lowers her head in thanks.

"Time to get ready for Jesse's picnic," announces Robert, getting to his feet. Rachel and Cybele follow him from the pool, past Jesse, down to the driveway. Thor noses Cybele's hanging hand. Sadie brings up the rear with a bearing that suggests she has planned to go to the driveway all along, and is not merely trailing along behind these sorry humans and their ridiculous dog.

The cars roll down the driveway. Clawing her bites, Jesse emerges from the Russian olives and notices her present lying forgotten by the pool house. Walking over, she picks it up. She slips off the maroon ribbon and opens the taped flaps. Pulling out a large gold T-shirt, she shakes it open and holds it up. It reads, NIFTY AT FIFTY.

Half a dozen bats swirl down from the pool house loft, where they've been napping all afternoon, upside down along the beams like miniature umbrellas. Bullfrogs by the cattle pond start to croak, viola da gamba tuning up for a twilight sonata. The distant lake gleams like a pool of molten lava. A mourning dove coos from the cornfield.

Jesse slips the T-shirt over her head and arranges it around her chest. She heads for the house to wash the poison ivy juice off her toes, put on some slacks, and grab her car keys. It's time to boogie by the lake shore in the glow from the setting sun.

Headaches and
Bad Dreams
by Lawrence Block

Three days of headaches, three nights of bad dreams. On the third night she woke twice before dawn, her heart racing, the bedding sweat-soaked. The second time she forced herself up and out of bed and into the shower. Before she'd toweled dry the headache had begun, starting at the base of the skull and radiating to the temples.

She took aspirin. She didn't like to take drugs of any sort, and her medicine cabinet contained nothing but a few herbal preparations—echinacea and goldenseal for colds, gingko for memory, and a Chinese herbal tonic, its ingredients a mystery to her, which she ordered by mail from a firm in San Francisco. She took sage, too, because it seemed to her to help center her psychically and make her perceptions more acute, although she couldn't remember having read that it had that property. She grew sage in her garden, picked leaves periodically and dried them in the sun, and drank a cup of sage tea almost every evening.

There were herbs that were supposed to ease headaches, no end of different herbs for the many different kinds of headaches, but she'd never found one that worked. Aspirin, on the other hand, was reliable. It was a drug, and as such it probably had the effect of dulling her psychic abilities, but those abilities were of small value when your head was throbbing like Poe's telltale heart. And aspirin didn't

slam shut the doors of perception, as something strong
might do. Truth to tell, it was the nearest thing to an herb
itself, obtained originally from willow bark. She didn't
know how they made it nowadays, surely there weren't
willow trees enough on the planet to cure the world's
headaches, but still . . .

She heated a cup of spring water, added the juice of half
a lemon. That was her breakfast. She sipped it in the garden, listening to the birds.

She knew what she had to do, but she was afraid.

It was a small house, just two bedrooms, everything on
one floor, with no basement and shallow crawl space for
an attic. She slept in one bedroom and saw clients in the
other. A beaded curtain hung in the doorway of the second
bedroom, and within were all the pictures and talismans
and power objects from which she drew strength. There
were religious pictures and statues, a crucifix, a little
bronze Buddha, African masks, quartz crystals. A pack of
tarot cards shared a small table with a little malachite pyramid and a necklace of bear claws.

A worn oriental rug covered most of the floor, and was
itself in part covered by a smaller rug on which she would
lie when she went into trance. The rest of the time she
would sit in the straight-back armchair. There was a chaise
as well, and that was where the client would sit.

She had only one appointment that day, but it was right
smack in the middle of the day. The client, Claire Warburton, liked to come on her lunch hour. So Sylvia got through
the morning by watching talk shows on television and paging through old magazines, taking more aspirin when the
headache threatened to return. At twelve-thirty she opened
the door for her client.

Claire Warburton was a regular, coming for a reading

once every four or five weeks, upping the frequency of her visits in times of stress. She had a weight problem—that was one of the reasons she liked to come on her lunch hour, so as to spare herself a meal's worth of calories—and she was having a lingering affair with a married man. She had occasional problems at work as well, a conflict with a new supervisor, an awkward situation with a coworker who disapproved of her love affair. There were always topics on which Claire needed counsel, and, assisted by the cards, the crystals, and her own inner resources, Sylvia always found something to tell her.

"Oh, before I forget," Claire said, "you were absolutely right about wheat. I cut it out and I felt the difference almost immediately."

"I thought you would. That came through loud and clear last time."

"I told Dr. Greenleaf. 'I think I may be allergic to wheat,' I said. He rolled his eyes."

"I'll bet he did. I hope you didn't tell him where the thought came from."

"Oh, sure. 'Sylvia Belgrave scanned my reflex centers with a green pyramid and picked up a wheat allergy.' Believe me, I know better than that. I don't know why I bothered to say anything to him in the first place. I suppose I was looking for male approval, but that's nothing new, is it?" They discussed the point, and then she said, "But it's so hard, you know. Staying away from wheat, I mean. It's everywhere."

"Yes."

"Bread, pasta. I wish I could cut it out completely, but I've managed to cut way down, and it helps. Sylvia? Are you all right?"

"A headache. It keeps coming back."

"Really? Well, I hate to say it, but do you think maybe you ought to see a doctor?"

She shook her head. "No," she said. "I know the cause, and I even know the cure. There's something I have to do."

When Sylvia was nineteen years old, she fell in love with a young man named Gordon Sawyer. He had just started dental school, and they had an understanding; after he had qualified as a dentist, they would get married. They were not officially engaged, she did not have a ring, but they had already reached the stage of talking about names for their children.

He drowned on a family canoe trip. A couple of hours after it happened, but long before anybody could get word to her, Sylvia awoke from a nightmare bathed in perspiration. The details of the dream had fled, but she knew it had been awful, and that something terrible had happened to Gordon. She couldn't go back to sleep, and she had been up for hours with an unendurable headache when the doorbell rang and a cousin of Gordon's brought the bad news.

That was her first undeniable psychic experience. Before that she'd had feelings and hunches, twinges of perception that were easy to shrug off or blink away. Once a fortune-teller at a county fair had read her palm and told her she had psychic powers herself, powers she'd be well advised to develop. She and Gordon had laughed about it, and he'd offered to buy her a crystal ball for her birthday.

When Gordon died her life found a new direction. If Gordon had lived she'd have gone on working as a salesgirl until she became a full-time wife and mother. Instead she withdrew into herself and began following the promptings of an inner voice. She could walk into a bookstore and her feet would lead her to some arcane volume that would turn out to be just what she needed to study next. She would sit in her room in her parents' house, staring for hours at a candle flame, or at her own reflection in the mirror. Her parents were worried, but nobody did anything beyond urging her to get out more and meet people. She was upset over Gordon's death, they agreed, and that was understandable, and she would get over it.

"Twenty-five dollars," Claire Warburton said, handing over two tens and a five. "You know, I was reading about this woman in *People* magazine, she reads the cards for either Oprah or Madonna, don't ask me which. And do you know how much she gets for a session?"

"Probably more than twenty-five dollars," Sylvia said.

"They didn't say, but they showed the car she drives around in. It's got an Italian name that sounds like testosterone, and it's fire-engine red, naturally. Of course, that's California. People in this town think you'd have to be crazy to pay twenty-five dollars. I don't see how you get by, Sylvia. I swear I don't."

"There was what my mother left," she said. "And the insurance."

"And a good thing, but it won't last forever. Can't you—"

"What?"

"Well, look into the crystal and try to see the stock market? Or ask your spirit guides for investment advice?"

"It doesn't work that way."

"That's what I knew you'd say," Claire said. "I guess that's what everybody says. You can't use it for your own benefit or it doesn't work."

"That's as it should be," she said. "It's a gift, and the Universe doesn't necessarily give you what you want. But you have to keep it. No exchanges, no refunds."

* * *

She parked across the street from the police station, turned off the engine, and sat in the car for a few moments, gathering herself. Her car was not a red Testarossa but a six-year-old Ford Tempo. It ran well, got good mileage, and took her where she wanted to go. What more could you ask of a car?

Inside, she talked to two uniformed officers before she wound up on the other side of a desk from a balding man with gentle brown eyes that belied his jutting chin. He was a detective, and his name was Norman Jeffcote.

He looked at her card, then looked directly at her. Twenty years had passed since her psychic powers had awakened with her fiancé's death, and she knew that the years had not enhanced her outward appearance. Then she'd been a girl with regular features turned pretty by her vital energy, a petite and slender creature, and now she was a little brown-haired mouse, dumpy and dowdy.

" 'Psychic counseling,' " he read aloud. "What's that exactly, Ms. Belgrave?"

"Sometimes I sense things," she said.

"And you think you can help us with the Sporran kid?"

"That poor little girl," she said.

Melissa Sporran, six years old, only child of divorced parents, had disappeared eight days previously on her way home from school.

"The mother broke down on camera," Detective Jeffcote said, "and I guess it got to people, so much so that it made some of the national newscasts. That kind of coverage pulls people out of the woodwork. I got a woman on the phone from Chicago, telling me she just knows little Melissa's in a cave at the foot of a waterfall. She's alive but in great danger. You're a local woman, Ms. Belgrave. You know any waterfalls within a hundred miles of here?"

"No."

"Neither do I. This woman in Chicago, see, may have been a little fuzzy on the geography, but she was good at making sure I got her name spelled right. But I won't have a problem in your case, will I? Because your name's all written out on your card."

"You're not impressed with psychic phenomena," she said.

"I think you people got a pretty good racket going," he said, "and more power to you if you can find people who want to shell out for whatever it is you're selling. But I've got a murder investigation to run, and I don't appreciate a lot of people with four-leaf clovers and crystal balls."

"Maybe I shouldn't have come," she said.

"Well, that's not for me to say, Ms. Belgrave, but now that you bring it up—"

"No," she said. "I didn't have any choice. Detective, have you heard of Sir Isaac Newton?"

"Sure, but I probably don't know him as well as you do. Not if you're getting messages from him."

"He was the foremost scientific thinker of his time," she said, "and in his later years he became quite devoted to astrology, which you may take as evidence either of his open-mindedness or of encroaching senility, as you prefer."

"I don't see what this has to—"

"A colleague chided him," she said, brooking no interruption, "and made light of his enthusiasm, and do you know what Newton said? 'Sir, I have investigated the subject. You have not. I do not propose to waste my time discussing it with you.' "

He looked at her and she returned his gaze. After a long moment he said, "All right, maybe you and Sir Isaac have a point. You got a hunch about the Sporran kid?"

"Not a hunch," she said, and explained the dreams, the

headaches. "I believe I'm linked to her," she said, "however it works, and I don't begin to understand how it works. I think . . ."

"Yes?"

"I'm afraid I think she's dead."

"Yes," Jeffcote said heavily. "Well, I hate to say it, but you gain in credibility with that one, Ms. Belgrave. We think so, too."

"If I could put my hands on some object she owned, or a garment she wore . . ."

"You and the dogs." She looked at him. "There was a fellow with a pack of bloodhounds, needed something of hers to get the scent. Her mother gave us this little sunsuit, hadn't been laundered since she wore it last. The dogs got the scent good, but they couldn't pick it up anywhere. I think we still have it. You wait here."

He came back with the garment in a plastic bag, drew it out, and wrinkled his nose at it. "Smells of dog now," he said. "Does that ruin it for you?"

"The scent's immaterial," she said. "It shouldn't even matter if it's been laundered. May I?"

"You need anything special, Ms. Belgrave? The lights out, or candles lit, or—"

She shook her head, told him he could stay, motioned for him to sit down. She took the child's sunsuit in her hands and closed her eyes and began to breathe deeply, and almost at once her mind began to fill with images. She saw the girl, saw her face, and recognized it from dreams she thought she had forgotten.

She felt things, too. Fear mostly, and pain, and more fear, and then, at the end, more pain.

"She's dead," she said softly, her eyes still closed. "He strangled her."

"He?"

"I can't see what he looks like. Just impressions." She waved a hand in the air, as if to dispel clouds, then extended her arm and pointed. "That direction," she said.

"You're pointing southeast."

"Out of town," she said. "There's a white church off by itself. Beyond that there's a farm." She could see it from on high, as if she were hovering overhead, like a bird making lazy circles in the sky. "I think it's abandoned. The barn's unpainted and deserted. The house has broken windows."

"There's the Baptist church on Reistertown Road. A plain white building with a little steeple. And out beyond it there's the Petty farm. She moved into town when the old man died."

"It's abandoned," she said, "but the fields don't seem to be overgrown. That's strange, isn't it?"

"Definitely the Petty farm," he said, his voice quickening. "She let the grazing when she moved."

"Is there a silo?"

"Seems to me they kept a dairy herd. There'd have be a silo."

"Look in the silo," she said.

She was studying Detective Jeffcote's palm when the call came. She had already told him he was worried about losing his hair, and that there was nothing he could do about it, that it was inevitable. The inevitability was written in his hand, although she'd sensed it the moment she saw him, just as she had at once sensed his concern. You didn't need to be psychic for that, though. It was immediately evident in the way he'd grown his remaining hair long and combed it to hide the bald spot.

"You should have it cut short," she said. "Very short. A crew cut, in fact."

"I do that," he said, "and everybody'll be able to see how thin it's getting."

"They won't notice," she told him. "The shorter it is, the less attention it draws. Short hair will empower you."

"Wasn't it the other way around with Samson?"

"It will strengthen you," she said. "Inside and out."

"And you can tell all that just looking at my hand?"

She could tell all that just looking at his head, but she only smiled and nodded. Then she noticed an interesting configuration in his palm and told him about it, making some dietary suggestions based on what she saw. She stopped talking when the phone rang, and he reached to answer it.

He listened for a long moment, then covered the mouthpiece with the very palm she'd been reading. "You were right," he said. "In the silo, covered up with old silage. They wouldn't have found her if they hadn't known to look for her. And the smell of the fermented silage masked the smell of the, uh, decomposition."

He put the phone to his ear, listened some more, spoke briefly, covered the mouthpiece again. "Marks on her neck," he said. "Hard to tell if she was strangled, not until there's a full autopsy, but it looks like a strong possibility."

"Teeth," she said suddenly.

"Teeth?"

She frowned, upset with herself. "That's all I can get when I try to see *him*."

"The man who—"

"Took her there, strangled her, killed her. I can't say if he was tall or short, fat or thin, old or young."

"Just that he had teeth."

"I guess that must have been what she noticed. Melissa. She must have been frightened of him because of the teeth."

"Did he bite her? Because if he did—"

"No," she said sharply. "Or I don't know, perhaps he did, but it was the appearance of the teeth that frightened her. He had bad teeth."

"Bad teeth?"

"Crooked, discolored, broken. They must have made a considerable impression on her."

"Jesus," he said, and into the mouthpiece he said, "You still there? What was the name of that son of a bitch, did some handyman work for the kid's mother? Henrich, Heinrich, something like that? Looked like a dentist's worst nightmare? Yeah, well, pick him up again."

He hung up the phone. "We questioned him," he said, "and we let him go. Big, gangly overgrown kid, God made him as ugly as he could and then hit him in the mouth with a shovel. This time I think I'll talk to him myself. Ms. Belgrave? You all right?"

"Just exhausted, all of a sudden," she said. "I haven't been sleeping well these past few nights. And what we just did, it takes a lot out of you."

"I can imagine."

"But I'll be all right," she assured him. And, getting to her feet, she realized she wouldn't be needing any more aspirin. The headache was gone.

The handyman, whose name turned out to be Walter Hendrick, broke down under questioning and admitted the abduction and murder of Melissa Sporran. Sylvia saw his picture on television but turned off the set, unable to look at him. His mouth was closed, you couldn't see his teeth, but even so she couldn't bear the sight of him.

The phone rang, and it was a client she hadn't seen in months, calling to book a session. She made a note in her appointment calendar and went into the kitchen to make a cup of tea. She was finishing the tea and trying to decide if she wanted another when the phone rang again.

It was a new client, a Mrs. Huggins, eager to schedule a reading as soon as possible. Sylvia asked the usual questions and made sure she got the woman's date of birth right. Astrology wasn't her main focus, but it never hurt to have that data in hand before a client's first visit. It made it easier, often, to get a grasp on the personality.

"And who told you about me?" she asked, almost as an afterthought. Business always came through referrals, a satisfied client told a friend or relative or coworker, and she liked to know who was saying good things about her.

"Now, who was it?" the woman wondered. "I've been meaning to call for such a long time, and I can't think who it was that originally told me about you."

She let it go at that. But, hanging up, she realized the woman had just lied to her. That was not exactly unheard of, although it was annoying when they lied about their date of birth, shaving a few years off their age and unwittingly providing her with an erroneous astrological profile in the process. But this woman had found something wholly unique to lie about, and she wondered why.

Within the hour the phone rang again, another old client of whom she'd lost track. "I'll bet you're booked solid," the woman said. "I just hope you can fit me in."

"Are you being ironic?"

"I beg your pardon?"

"Because you know it's a rare day when I see more than two people, and there are days when I don't see anyone at all."

"I don't know how many people you see," the woman said. "I do know that it's always been easy to get an appointment with you at short notice, but I imagine that's all changed now, hasn't it?"

"Why would it . . ."

"Now that you're famous."

Famous.

Of course she wasn't, not really. Someone did call her from Florida, wanting an interview for a national tabloid, and there was a certain amount of attention in the local press, and on area radio stations. But she was a quiet, retiring woman, hardly striking in appearance and decidedly undramatic in her responses. Her personal history was not interesting in and of itself, nor was she inclined to go into it. Her lifestyle was hardly colorful.

Had it been otherwise, she might have caught a wave of publicity and been nationally famous for her statutory fifteen minutes, reading Joey Buttafuoco's palm on *Hard Copy,* sharing herbal weight-loss secrets with Oprah.

Instead she had her picture in the local paper, seated in her garden. (She wouldn't allow them to photograph her in her studio, among the candles and crystals.) And that was enough to get her plenty of attention, not all of which she welcomed. No one actually crept across her lawn to stare in her window, but cars did slow or even stop in front of her house, and one man got out of his car and took pictures.

She got more attention than usual when she left the house, too. People who knew her congratulated her, hoping to hear a little more about the case and the manner in which she'd solved it. Strangers recognized her—on the street, in the supermarket. While their interest was not intrusive, she was uncomfortably aware of it.

But the biggest change, really, was in the number of people who suddenly found themselves in need of her services. She was bothered at first by the thought that they were coming to her for the wrong reason, and she wondered if she should refuse to accommodate such curiosity seekers. She meditated on the question, and the answer that came to her was that she was unequipped to judge the motivation of those who sought her out. How could she tell the real reason that brought some troubled soul to her door? And how could she determine, irrespective of motivation, what help she might be able to provide?

She decided that she ought to see everyone. If she found herself personally uncomfortable with a client's energy, then she wouldn't see that person anymore. That had been her policy all along. But she wouldn't prejudge any of them, wouldn't screen them in advance.

"But it's impossible to fit everyone in," she told Claire Warburton. "I'm just lucky I got a last-minute cancellation, or I wouldn't have been able to schedule you until the end of next week."

"How does it feel to be an overnight success after all these years?"

"Is that what I am? A success? Sometimes I think I liked it better when I was a failure. No, I don't mean that, but no more do I like being booked as heavily as I am, I'll tell you that. The work is exhausting. I'm seeing four people a day, and yesterday I saw five, which I'll never do again. It drains you."

"I can imagine."

"But the gentleman was so persistent, and I thought, well, I do have the time. But by the time the day was over . . ."

"You were exhausted."

"I certainly was. And I hate to book appointments weeks in advance, or to refuse to book them at all. It bothers me to turn anyone away, because how do I know that I'm not turning away someone in genuine need? For years I had less business than I would have preferred, and now I have

too much, and I swear I don't know what to do about it."
She frowned. "And when I meditate on it, I don't get anywhere at all."

"For heaven's sake," Claire said. "You don't need to
look in a crystal for this one. Just look at a balance sheet."

"I beg your pardon?"

"Sylvia," Claire said, "raise your damn rates."

"My rates?"

"'For years you've been seeing a handful of people a
week and charging them twenty-five dollars each, and
wondering why you're poor as a churchmouse. Raise your
rates and you'll increase your income to a decent level—
and you'll keep yourself from being overbooked. The people who really need you will pay the higher price, and the
curiosity seekers will think twice."

"But the people who've been coming to me for years—"

"You can grandfather them in," Claire said. "Confine
the rate increase to new customers. But I wouldn't."

"You wouldn't?"

"No, and I'm costing my own self money by saying this,
but I'll say it anyhow. People appreciate less what costs
them less. That woman in California, drives the red Tos-
teroni? You think she'd treasure that car if somebody sold
it to her for five thousand dollars? You think *People* magazine would print a picture of her standing next to it? Raise
your rates and everybody'll think more of you, and pay
more attention to the advice you give 'em."

"Well," she said, slowly, "I suppose I could go from
twenty-five to thirty-five dollars—"

"Fifty," Claire said firmly. "Not a penny less."

In the end, she had to raise her fee three times. Doubling
it initially had the paradoxical effect of increasing the volume of calls. A second increase, to seventy-five dollars,

was a step in the right direction, slowing the flood of calls; she waited a few months, then took a deep breath and told a caller her price was one hundred dollars a session.

And there it stayed. She booked three appointments a day, five days a week, and pocketed fifteen hundred dollars a week for her efforts. She lost some old clients, including a few who had been coming to her out of habit, the way they went to get their hair done. But it seemed to her that the ones who stayed actually listened more intently to what she saw in the cards or crystal, or channeled while she lay in trance.

"Told you," Claire said. "You get what you pay for."

One afternoon there was a call from Detective Jeffcote. There was a case, she might have heard or read about it, and could she possibly help him with it? She had appointments scheduled, she said, but she could come to the police station as soon as her last client was finished, and—

"No, I'll come to you," he said. "Just tell me when's a good time."

He turned up on the dot. His hair was very short, she noticed, and he seemed more confident and self-possessed than when she'd seen him before. In the living room, he accepted a cup of tea and told her about the girl who'd gone missing, an eleventh-grader named Peggy Mae Turlock. "There hasn't been much publicity," he said, "because kids her age just go off sometimes, but she's an A student and sings in the church choir, and her parents are worried. And I just thought, well . . ."

She reminded him that she'd had three nights of nightmares and headaches when Melissa Sporran disappeared.

"As if the information was trying to get through," he said. "And you haven't had anything like that this time?

Because I brought her sunglasses case, and a baseball jacket they tell me she wore all the time."

"We can try," she said.

She took him into her studio, lit two of the new scented candles, seated him on the chaise and took the chair for herself. She draped Peggy Mae's jacket over her lap and held the green vinyl eyeglass case in both hands. She closed her eyes, breathed slowly and deeply.

After a while she said, "Pieces."

"Pieces?"

"I'm getting these horrible images," she said, "of dismemberment, but I don't know that it has anything to do with the girl. I don't know where it's coming from."

"You picking up any sense of where she might be, or of who might have put her there?"

She slowed her breathing, let herself go deep, deep.

"Down down down," she said.

"How's that, Ms. Belgrave?"

"Something in a well," she said. "An old rusty chain going down into a well, and something down there."

A search of wells all over the county divulged no end of curious debris, including a skeleton that turned out to be that of a large dog. No human remains were found, however, and the search was halted when Peggy Mae came home from Indianapolis. She'd gone there for an abortion, expecting to be back in a day or so, but there had been medical complications. She'd been in the hospital there for a week, never stopping to think that her parents were afraid for her life, or that the police were probing abandoned wells for her dismembered corpse.

Sylvia got a call when the girl turned up. "The important thing is she's all right," he said, "although I wouldn't be surprised if right about now she wishes she was dead.

Point is, you didn't let us down. You were trying to home in on something that wasn't there in the first place, since she was alive and well all along."

"I'm glad she's alive," she said, "but disappointed in myself. All of that business about wells."

"Maybe you were picking up something from fifty years ago," he said. "Who knows how many wells there are, boarded up and forgotten years ago? And who knows what secrets one or two of them might hold?"

"Perhaps you're right."

Perhaps he was. But all the same the few days when the police were looking in old wells was a professional high water mark for her. After the search was called off, after Peggy Mae came home in disgrace, it wasn't quite so hard to get an appointment with Sylvia Belgrave.

Three nights of nightmares and fitful sleep, three days of headaches. And, awake or asleep, a constant parade of hideous images.

It was hard to keep herself from running straight to the police. But she forced herself to wait, to let time take its time. And then on the morning after the third unbearable night she showered away the stale night sweat and put on a skirt and a blouse and a flowered hat. She sat in the garden with a cup of hot water and lemon juice, then rinsed it in the kitchen sink and went to her car.

The car was a Taurus, larger and sleeker and, certainly, newer than her old Tempo, but it did no more and no less than the Tempo had done. It conveyed her from one place to another. This morning it brought her to the police station, and her feet brought her the rest of the way—into the building and through the corridors to Detective Norman Jeffcote's office.

"Ms. Belgrave," he said. "Have a seat, won't you?"

His hair was longer than it had been when he'd come to her house. He hadn't regrown it entirely, hadn't once again taken to combing it over the bald spot, but neither was it as flatteringly short as she'd advised him to keep it.

And there was something unsettling about his energy. Maybe it had been a mistake to come.

She sat down and winced, and he asked her if she was all right. "My head," she said, and pressed her fingertips to her temples.

"You've got a headache?"

"Endless headaches. And bad dreams, and all the rest of it."

"I see."

"I didn't want to come," she said. "I told myself not to intrude, not to be a nuisance. But it's just like the first time, when that girl disappeared."

"Melissa Sporran."

"And now there's a little boy gone missing," she said.

"Eric Ackerman."

"Yes, and his address is no more than half a mile from my house. Maybe that's why all these impressions have been so intense."

"Do you know where he is now, Ms. Belgrave?"

"I don't," she said, "but I do feel connected to him, and I have the strong sense that I might be able to help."

He nodded. "And your hunches usually pay off."

"Not always," she said. "That was confusing the year before last, sending you to look in wells."

"Well, nobody's perfect."

"Surely not."

He leaned forward, clasped his hands. "The Ackerman boy, Ms. Belgrave. You think he's all right?"

"Oh, I wish I could say yes."

"But you can't."

"The nightmares," she said, "and the headaches. If he were all right, the way the Turlock girl was all right—"

"There'd be no dreams."

"That's my fear, yes."

"So you think the boy is . . ."

"Dead," she said.

He looked at her for a long moment before he nodded. "I suppose you'd like some article connected with the boy," he said. "A piece of clothing, say."

"If you had something."

"How's this?" he said, and opened a drawer and brought out a teddy bear, its plush fur badly worn, the stitches showing where it had been ripped and mended. Her heart broke at the sight of it, and she put her hand to her chest.

"We ought to have a record of this," he said, propping a tape recorder on the desktop, pressing a button to start it recording. "So that I don't miss any of the impressions you pick up. Because you can probably imagine how frantic the boy's parents are."

"Yes, of course."

"So do you want to state your name for the record?"

"My name?"

"Yes, for the record."

"My name is Sylvia Belgrave."

"And you're a psychic counselor?"

"Yes."

"And you're here voluntarily."

"Yes, of course."

"Why don't you take the teddy bear, then? And see what you can pick up from it."

She thought she'd braced herself, but she was unprepared for the flood of images that came when she took the little stuffed bear in her hands. They were more vivid than anything she'd experienced before. Perhaps she should have expected as much; the dreams, and the headaches, too, were worse than they'd been after Melissa Sporran's death, worse than years ago, when Gordon Sawyer drowned.

"Smothered," she managed to say. "A pillow or something like it over his face. He was struggling to breathe and . . . and he couldn't."

"And he's dead."

"Yes."

"And would you happen to know where, Ms. Belgrave?"

Her hands tightened on the teddy bear. The muscles in her arms and shoulders went rigid, bracing to keep the images at bay.

"A hole in the ground," she said.

"A hole in the ground?"

"A basement!" Her eyes were closed, her heart pounding. "A house, but they haven't finished building it yet. The outer walls are up but that's all."

"A building site."

"Yes."

"And the body's in the basement."

"Under a pile of rags," she said.

"Under a pile of rags. Any sense of where, Ms. Belgrave? There are a lot of houses under construction. It would help if we knew what part of town to search."

She tried to get her bearings, then realized she didn't need them. Her hand, of its own accord, found the direction and pointed.

"North and west," he said. "Let's see, where's there a house under construction, ideally one they stopped work on? Seems to me there's one just off Radbourne Road about a quarter of a mile past Six Mile Road. You think that might be the house, Ms. Belgrave?"

She opened her eyes. He was reaching across to take the teddy bear from her. She had to will her fingers to open to release it.

"We've got some witnesses," he said, his voice surprisingly gentle. "A teenager mowing a lawn who saw Eric Ackerman getting into a blue Taurus just like the one you've got parked across the street. He even noticed the license plate, but then it's the kind you notice, isn't it? 2ND SITE. Second sight, eh? Perfect for your line of work."

God, her head was throbbing.

"A woman in a passing car saw you carrying the boy to the house. She didn't spot the vanity plate, but she furnished a good description of the car, and of you, Ms. Belgrave. She thought it was odd, you see. The way you were carrying him, as if he was unconscious, or even dead. Was he dead by then?"

"Yes."

"You killed him first thing? Smothered him?"

"With a pillow," she said. "I wanted to do it right away, before he became afraid. And I didn't want him to suffer."

"Real considerate."

"He struggled," she said, "and then he was still. But I didn't realize just how much he suffered. It was over so quickly, you see, that I told myself he didn't really suffer a great deal at all."

"And?"

"And I was wrong," she said. "I found that out in the dreams. And just now, holding the bear . . ."

He was saying something, but she couldn't hear it. She was trembling, and the headache was too much to be borne, and she couldn't follow his words. He brought her a glass of water and she drank it, and that helped a little.

"There were other witnesses, too," he said, "once we

found the body, and knew about the car and the license plate. People who saw your car going to and from the construction site. The chief wanted to have you picked up right away, but I talked him into waiting. I figured you'd come in and tell us all about it yourself."

"And here I am," she heard herself say.

"And here you are. You want to tell me about it from the beginning?"

She told it all simply and directly, how she'd selected the boy, how she got him to come into the car with her, how she'd killed him and dumped the body in the spot she'd selected in advance. How she'd gone home, and washed her hands, and waited through three days and nights of headaches and bad dreams.

"Ever kill anybody before, Ms. Belgrave?"

"No," she said. "No, of course not."

"Ever have anything to do with Eric Ackerman or his parents?"

"No."

"Why, then?"

"Don't you know?"

"Tell me anyway."

"Second sight," she said.

"Second . . ."

"Second sight. Vanity plates. Vanity."

"Vanity?"

"All is vanity," she said, and closed her eyes for a moment. "I never made more than a hundred fifty dollars a week," she said, "and nobody knew me or paid me a moment's attention, but that was all right. And then Melissa Sporran was killed, and I was afraid to come in but I came in anyway. And everything changed."

"You got famous."

"For a little while," she said. "And my phone started ringing, and I raised my rates, and my phone rang even more. And I was able to help people, more people than I'd ever helped before, and they were making use of what I gave them, they were taking it seriously."

"And you bought a new car."

"I bought a new car," she said, "and I bought some other things, and I stopped being famous, and the ones who only came because they were curious stopped coming when they stopped being curious, and old customers came less often because they couldn't afford it, and . . ."

"And business dropped off."

"And I thought, I could help so many more people if, if it happened again."

"If a child died."

"Yes."

"And if you helped."

"Yes. And I waited, you know, for something to happen. And there were crimes, there are always crimes. There were even murders, but there was nothing that gave me the dreams and the headaches."

"So you decided to do it yourself."

"Yes."

"Because you'd be able to help so many more people."

"That's what I told myself," she said. "But I was just fooling myself. I did it because I'm having trouble making the payments on my new car, a car I didn't need in the first place. But I need the car now, and I need the phone ringing, and I need—" She frowned, put her head in her hands. "I need aspirin," she said. "That first time, when I told you about Melissa Sporran, the headache went away. But I've told you everything about Eric Ackerman, more than I ever planned to tell you, and the headache hasn't gone away. It's worse than ever."

He told her it would pass, but she shook her head. She knew it wouldn't, or the bad dreams, either. Some things you just knew.

Baby-sitting Ingrid
by Larry Collins

Her name was Ingrid, Ingrid Ewald. Ingrid had a pair of legs on her that began at ground level and seemed to climb upward forever, the kind of legs you see on the girls who model panty hose in the Sunday *New York Times,* which is not surprising because modeling panty hose is what Ingrid did in Sacherhausen, Germany, before she came to New York to make her fortune with Wilhemina, another lanky German lady who was running the year's hot modeling agency in 1969.

Ingrid's hair was pale blond, so pale it was almost white. She let it hang in a straight line down to her shoulders—not a curl along the way. She had blue-green eyes and a mouth that was, okay, a little oversized maybe, but it came wrapped in a pair of these full lips, the kind that tell you, man, there is going to be a very special treat in store for the guy she focuses on. Her figure? Unbelievable, top of the line. Her body was to your average female's figure what a Mercedes-Benz is to a Ford pickup. With equipment like that, you would have thought Ingrid would make a bundle in the city, right?

Wrong. For some reason the photographers and the ladies with the horn-rimmed glasses at the fashion magazines just didn't take to Ingrid. Teutonic was out of fashion that fall. Ingrid wound up doing what a lot of girls in that situation do—she drifted gently over into the high-class call-girl trade. Three, four, maybe five guys a week at five, ten bills an evening. Not what she'd come to the U.S. to do, but still it paid the rent and who's to know at the IRS?

Well, I've met a few girls in that line of work in my own business, hustling bad guys for the DEA, and one of the things I've noticed is that their personal taste in guys tends to run to scumbags. I'm talking real, first-class scumbags here. It's almost like it's their way of doing a little penance for turning tricks, you know what I mean? "I'll suffer with this slob of mine, and the good Lord will forgive me for what I do Thursday nights."

Anyway, it was thanks to Ingrid's scumbag that we met. He was a guy named Louie J. Serrullo of 1934 Jackson Boulevard over to Queens. Louie ran an Italian bakery, but if you believe he made his living frying up doughnuts, you also believe in the tooth fairy. Louie was, in fact, one of New York City's leading importers of fine heroin. He had some Corsican cousins living over there on the Cannebiere in Marseilles, France, who were his connect. Thanks to the stuff they were moving to Louie, he'd won himself a spot right at the top of our hit parade in the New York office of the DEA.

But he was a slippery bastard, about as easy to nail to the wall as a pile of jello. Finally, in the spring of 1970, we got lucky. The French narcs had caught a Corsican moving six keys from a lab to his stash house. Now, even in France six keys makes for hard time, and hard time, as we say in our business, makes for hard choices. The Corsican made his. He gave up cousin Louie's next load in return for a little indulgence from the French judicial system.

The French bring us into it, and thanks to their information we're able to pick up Louie's mule carrying his load of shit in a brand-new Vuitton suitcase as he's clearing customs at JFK. We tail him on his way to the city. Only, to our surprise, he doesn't take the Van Wyck and go into Queens to Louie's bakery like we expect him to do. He goes into Manhattan by the Midtown Tunnel instead and winds up at Third Avenue and Sixty-first Street, where he hops out of his cab and goes into a high-rise at 234.

I slip out of the first tail car and follow him into the building, gently because we don't want to set any alarm bells ringing in his head. We want to make him putting that suitcase full of shit into Louie's hands.

By the time I get into the lobby, he's already in the elevator with the door closed, but I see he's gone up to the nineteenth floor. Pretty soon we have a half dozen guys, DEA, NYPD, talking to a very cooperative doorman who's telling us all about the occupants of the four apartments on nineteen. 19A is a stockbroker, married, two kids, 19B is a single woman, 19C's a lawyer, also married, no kids, and 19D's three girls working in advertising sharing a flat.

Now, if you're looking for a crook, I'll pick a lawyer anytime, but we decided to hit 19B, the single female, first. Since thanks to our French information we have all the probable cause anybody could want—providing, of course, we've guessed the right flat—we heft the door and guess who's there, his big mouth so wide open you'd think his chin was going to hit the floor? Louie. Even better, the Vuitton suitcase was on the dining room table wide open. There were twenty kilo packs of China white number four heroin inside, which, later down at the lab, would check out at ninety-two percent pure, which is about as pure as the stuff gets. The mule, on the other hand, is nowhere in sight. We open the bedroom door and there, lying on the bed reading *Vogue,* is this beautiful girl. It's Ingrid.

I go back into the dining room, take out my 13A, the

DEA's Miranda card, and read Louie his rights. He's no dope. He opts for the call to his lawyer, who's a whoozie we all know and hate. Ingrid, meantime, is taking in all this leaning against the bedroom door, her face about as pale as that hair of hers, breathing a bit hard.

We cuff Louie and take him out. "Don't tell these fuckers shit!" he screams at her as we shove him through the door. "Wait till you talk to my lawyer."

So now we turn our attention to Ingrid. She, in fact, is pissed off as hell about all this and tells us everything we want to know. Louie told her he has this friend who's going to deliver him a suitcase. Louie says he doesn't want the wife out in Queens to see it, so would she mind him bringing it up here?

No problem, she tells him. She even answers the door when the mule rings, which is what Louie has suggested. She sees the mule hand Louie the suitcase, and as the two of them go into her dining room, she, nice German girl that she is, goes back into the bedroom to watch the TV and read her *Vogue*.

She swears she has no idea there was heroin in that suitcase. She hates people who do that stuff and, sure, she'll come down to the DEA office and swear out a formal deposition recording everything she's told us.

Now, with those kind words of hers, Fraulein Ewald has just become the DEA's case against New York's top heroin importer. We take her up to the boss's suite overlooking the Hudson at the DEA office on West Fifty-seventh Street. He treats her like she was Queen Elizabeth, and we formally take down her statement. She signs it and we're in business. We've got Louie, the dope, and a witness to tie him to the suitcase. Perfect.

The boss now takes the occasion to explain some of the facts of life to Ingrid. Her boyfriend, Louie, is a seriously

bad guy, and her testimony is going to be critical in sending him to federal prison for many, many years to come. In
view of that, it is entirely possible that Louie or some of
his friends might seek to do her grievous bodily harm in
order to prevent her from testifying against him. There-
fore, he wished to offer her the twenty-four-hour protection of his DEA agents. He strongly advised her to accept
his offer although, as he explained, neither she nor anyone
else could be compelled to accept such protection.

Now clearly, that posed a problem for Ingrid. She's not
going to be able to exercise her current professional activities with federal law enforcement officers sitting in her living room. On the other hand, she knows enough about her
Louie to take what the boss was telling her very much to
heart. So, finally, reluctantly, she agrees.

The boss looks at me. "Okay, Kevin," he says, "you're a
single guy. We'll have you baby-sit her nights. O'Brien
can take the day shift."

So the two of us go back to her apartment, and she decides to check out the fridge to see if she can scare us up
something to eat. You think she had some leftover chicken
in there, a bowl of soup, a couple of Stouffer frozen TV
dinners? Forget it. There was Dom Perignon champagne,
that French liver paste they call foie gras, smoked salmon,
caviar. We had a little toast with the liver paste spread on
it, then some scrambled eggs and smoked salmon.

Afterward, we'd settled down to watch TV when the
doorbell rang. Christ, I thought, I can't believe Louie can
work this fast. The bastard probably hasn't even been ar-
raigned yet. Ingrid opens the door while I stand beside it
with my hand on the 9mm. Would you believe who walks
in—one of our leading late-night talk show hosts, stopping
by to say hello after his taping.

Ingrid takes "here's Harry" into the living room to brief

him on her new lifestyle while I have a cup of coffee in the kitchen. After he'd left, we sat down to play gin for a while. Then we started to talk. There was one thing about Ingrid—she was dead honest: honest about herself, honest with herself, honest about other people, about what she wanted out of life. She told me about the modeling, how it hadn't worked out, how, because she couldn't stand the thought of heading back home to Germany a failure, she'd gotten into her current line of work.

I suggested her present life might not be considered all that much of a success back there in Sacherhausen, either. She shrugged. She was dead certain she'd get one of these rich guys she was laying to fall madly in love with her, to marry her. A rich husband, as she pointed out, was considered pretty much of a success story in whatever language you're talking.

I asked her how she could stand being with a creep like Louie. She fixed those pale blue-green eyes of hers on me, a sort of half-mocking, half-challenging glint in them. Louie, she said, had been a terrific lover, and terrific lovers figured big in Ingrid's scheme of things.

Finally, about two o'clock, she got up and yawned. She announced she was going to get ready for bed. I settled down in front of the box watching an old Dick Powell movie, which, I figured, would keep me going until four. Half an hour after she'd left, Ingrid came back in. She was wearing a white silk pajama top that just capped those long, lovely legs of hers, quite a lot of perfume, and not a hell of a lot else. She gave Mr. Powell a scornful regard. Then she gave my nose a playful little tweak with her index finger.

"I guess you'll do okay as a baby-sitter," she giggled, "but how do you think you'll do as a lover?"

Now, the DEA does not have a formal training manual

they pass out to guys on protective-custody assignments. But if they did, you can bet your ass it would say at the top of the first page: "Thou shalt not get involved personally with the person you're supposed to be protecting."

On the other hand, nobody's perfect, most of all a thirty-one-year-old bachelor six inches away from the most beautiful woman he's seen in his life. Ingrid held out her hand. I took it.

That gesture began what was certainly the most extraordinary three weeks of my life, maybe even the best, who's to know? Every night we were together. When we'd cleared all that French liver paste out of the fridge, we ordered in take-out Chinese. Or we'd go to little restaurants she knew, cheap ones to go along with my government salary. We did the flicks. And we made love until I barely had the strength to crawl out of her bed in time for O'Brien's arrival for the day shift.

It was one of those perfect moments, a chunk of time and space carved out of the passage of our lives thanks to Louie Serrullo's troubles. While we were living out our little idyll, he was trying like hell to convince a federal judge to let him out on bail. Finally at his second hearing he got it, three quarters of a million bucks, which he made without batting an eye—more money than I was going to make in twenty-five years in law enforcement.

Obviously, I was nuts about Ingrid. I was also clued in enough to know that this great thing we were living wasn't going to last forever. You had to figure a long-term relation with a GS 12 making 30K a year and living out on Staten Island wasn't going to have too big of a place in any of Ingrid's future plans.

What I hadn't figured on, of course, was how it would end. One day the boss calls me down to the office. Did he know what was going on? Honestly, I don't know. Anyhow, he says to me, "Hey, Kevin, I gotta pull you off that case and ship you down to Philly to run an undercover penetration for the office down there."

I'm a frustrated actor, and I've kind of made a career in the DEA of getting in undercover with the bad guys. I gave Ingrid the news that night. Her reaction was straight-forward. If I was out of there, then she wanted the protective custody withdrawn. I begged her not to do it, the boss begged her not to do it, but there was never any budging Ingid once she'd made up her mind about something. The only compromise she finally agreed to make was to move a German girlfriend into her apartment with her so she wouldn't be alone until I got back from Philly.

The Friday before I left, we went out for a walk along Madison Avenue. It was a windy March day, exactly the kind of day you're supposed to have in March. A sudden gust blew the old man's fedora she loved off her head and into the doorway of a jewelry store. As I was picking it up for her, I spotted something I recognized in the store window, because my mother's family comes from Aleppo in Syria. It was a stone hanging from a gold chain with blue and black circles wrapped around a white center which framed a blue dot. I took Ingrid inside and bought it for her, trying not to think about the dent the $300 price tag was going to make in my bank account. As I was hanging it around her neck, I explained to her that it was a Bedouin good luck charm, a talisman that would keep the evil spirits away from her until I could get back from Philly.

Philly was only supposed to last a couple of weeks, but as those things always seem to do, it dragged on and on. I got back up to the city when I could, and we talked every few days by phone. Anyway, one Saturday night about a month after I'd left, Ingrid tells her girlfriend she's going out to dinner.

The next morning when the girlfriend gets up, Ingrid's bedroom door is shut. Noon comes and still no sign of Ingrid, so the girlfriend decides to go in and see what the matter is. The matter is that Ingrid wasn't there. Her bed hadn't even been slept in.

The next morning when there's still no sign of Ingrid, the girlfriend finally calls the DEA. I get called back from Philly, and we try to figure what's gone down. Had Louie or one of his goons gotten her? Had she skipped, maybe gone back to Germany to escape the heat? The INS runs the airport-departures lists. Nothing. We get the German police to put a wiretap on her mother's line over there in Sacherhausen. Nothing. We run the morgues, the hospitals. Nothing. She's vanished, dropped off the screen.

With her gone, Louie, of course, walks. DEA entrapment, his lawyer says. He'd gone up to the apartment to bang this broad, and the DEA has stuffed the place with heroin to set him up. We couldn't even get a trial date for the bastard before he's back there in Queens frying up his doughnuts. Me, I start using my spare time to run a little surveillance of my own on Louie. Maybe, I figured, he'll take a meet with her, who's to know? He didn't.

The boss gets word of what's going on, so he calls me in one Monday morning. "Hey, Kevin," he says, "this is the DEA, not the Crusades. You want to join a crusade, you go see Billy Graham or one of them guys. In the meantime knock off this shit with Louie unless I order you out to Queens."

Two weeks later, I'm back in his office. "Good news, Kev," he says. "Washington is sending you to Rome as an assistant to our country attaché over there."

I was in Italy five years. By the time I got back Ingrid was a memory. A great memory, maybe the best I was ever going to get, but a memory all the same. They make me a group supervisor in the New York office because of some things that happened in Rome. One morning I'm running a pile of paper when I get a call from a Corrections Department officer over on Riker's Island. "We got a guy here," he tells me, "who wants to see you. Urgent, he says."

So that afternoon I'm out at Riker's. They show me into one of those little gray conference rooms they got there and bring in a guy named Arturo "Big Auggie" Dotti. Mr. Dotti, the correction facility officer guarding him explains, is looking at fifteen to twenty-five for armed robbery and attempted extortion. A sentence like that will make a man think, and Mr. Dotti, it seems, has been doing some serious thinking.

"Look," he says to me, "if I tell you how Louie Serrullo's German broad got done, can we get this down to something like breaking and entering?"

"Yes, Mr. Dotti," I said, "I think we can."

The next day I'm back out there with the guy's attorney and an attorney from the U.S. Attorney's Office for the Southern District. We draw up the deal, use immunity for Dotti for everything he tells us, which means he can't be prosecuted for any of his own crimes he tells us about. He agrees to testify in an open courtroom if we need him to make our case against Serrullo. We in turn agree to go to bat for him in the Manhattan district court if he lives up to his end of the deal. We sign the papers, and Dotti and I go into the next room. I switch on the tape recorder.

"Okay," he says, "to begin with, I'm the guy took the German broad out to dinner that Saturday night."

I swallow a couple of times. "So?"

"I picked her up in front of her place about seven. We go to the Ginger Man, have a couple of drinks, then I take her over to the 21 for dinner, a real nice dinner."

I nodded in grateful appreciation for the attention he'd

showered on her that night. After dinner, he tells me, he suggests they drive over to Jersey to a disco a friend of his owns. They get into his car and head for the West Side Highway. They're going down one of those dark, half-deserted crosstown streets coming up to Tenth Avenue when Louie Serrullo rises up out of the backseat waving a baseball bat he's got in his hands like he's Reggie Jackson doing his Mr. October thing.

"Fucking loud-mouthed whore!" he shouts at Ingrid as he tries to hit a home run with her head.

She slumps down half-conscious in the front seat. Louie tells Dotti to head for the parking area in front of one of those abandoned piers over there. When Dotti stops, Louie finishes the job. This was, remember, a girl that, for whatever incredible reason, had once loved that bastard, a beautiful girl who'd curled that body of hers around his God knows how many times. He batters her face with his Louisville Slugger like it was a melon, not a shred of pity in him. A real gentleman, our Louie. When he'd finished, he and Dotti jammed poor Ingrid's broken body into the trunk and headed for the Lincoln Tunnel.

They'd just gotten into it when, Dotti tells me, they hear a pathetic, muffled little whine coming from the trunk through the backseat.

"Shut up, you dumb broad," Louie laughs. "Whatta you want to do? Wake up the guy in the toll booth?"

They drive out to Secaucus to the edge of one of those huge garbage dumps over there, dig a hole, and stuff Ingrid's body into it.

The next day I had to take Dotti over to the garbage dump with a team from the NYPD's Forensic Sciences Unit. Dotti finds the spot for us, and the forensic guys start to dig. An hour later, under three and a half feet of dirt and garbage, they found what was left of Ingrid Ewald. Foren-

sic made the formal identification forty-eight hours later
from her dental records. I didn't have to wait that long. As
the forensic guys were fitting her remains into one of their
rubber body bags, they found the filth-covered necklace
she'd been wearing the night Louie killed her. We cleaned
it up. It was the blue and white Bedouin good luck talis-
man I'd bought her to ward off the evil eye that windy
afternoon when I was leaving for Philly.

That evening I went out to Louie's bakery with two de-
tectives from the NYPD to bring the bastard in on murder
one. It was one of the most satisfying moments of my career. Even his whoozie lawyer wasn't going to be able to
get Louie off this time.

I convinced the boss to dip into one of those little rat
holes we have at the DEA to buy a plot and a simple headstone to keep what was left of Ingrid out of potter's field. I
figured it was the least we owed her. I decided to bury her
out on Staten Island at Our Lady of the Angels. She would
never have been over there with me in life, but this way, I
figured, I'd be able to keep an eye on her in the years
ahead. Since I didn't know if she was R.C. or Protestant, I
got a couple of pals, a priest and a pastor, to come out and
say a few words over the grave. We just put her name, Ingrid Ewald, her birth date, July 23, 1947, and the day
Louie did her, March 29, 1970, on the stone. It was a sad,
lonely little ceremony, but at least, I told myself as we
started back to the city, we had Louie.

Well, as it turned out, we didn't. About a month later, I
get another call from Riker's Island, where we'd parked
Dotti waiting for his hearing. They'd found him on the
shower room floor that morning wearing an ice pick as a
decoration in his sternum. He was DOA at the hospital.
Without Dotti's testimony the case against Louie fell apart.
The son of a bitch walked on us again.

We didn't hear much about him after that. He got very, very cautious. We kept our eyes on him for two years, but you couldn't even stiff him with a parking ticket, he was so careful. For a while there I used to go out to Our Lady of the Angels fairly regularly to check on Ingrid's grave. But, well, you know how things are. Time goes by. I married a nice Italian girl from the Bronx. Her father had been an agent with the FBI, so she knew what the drill was when you had to live on what the G pays. We did a couple of tours at DEA headquarters in Washington.

By the time I got back to the New York D.O. as the ASAC—assistant special agent in charge—in the summer of 1982, we'd pretty much forgotten about Louie. He was just another file collecting dust in the inactive investigations box. We had other problems on our minds—coke was booming big-time, and the war on drugs was cranking up.

Then early one day in September 1982 one of those Italian Line ships arrives in New York from the Mediterranean. Her last port of call had been Palermo in Sicily, so the Customs guys decide to give her passengers, particularly the ones with cars, a good toss just in case. By the time they get to the last car, a beat-up Honda with New York number plates, the old Italian grandfather and grandmother driving the thing have been waiting to get cleared for two hours. The Customs guy pokes his head into the car, looks at their luggage on the backseat, the cardboard suitcases knotted up with rope, the alabaster Madonnas, whatever, and he gets a pang of conscience. That happens with customs guys. Not often, but it happens.

"Hey," he tells Giuseppe and Maria, "we're sorry about the inconvenience this wait has caused you. If you'll just pull over there to our Customs gas pump, we'll be happy to send you on your way with a full tank of gas."

Now, when cars are loaded onto passenger ships, you

have to drain their gas tanks down to about a gallon so they won't explode if there's a fire on board. Maritime law. Anyway, the Customs guy sticks the nozzle of his pump into their tank and squirts away. Two gallons and suddenly the pump goes "bing-bing." It's full.

"Oh-oh, what have we got here?" he says and calls over the boss.

"Put it on the hoist," the boss orders.

What they have got here is that the Honda's original gas tank has been taken off and a new one soldered on. Inside they find two gallons of U.S. Customs gas and a hundred kilos of heroin.

Customs calls the DEA, which the book says they're supposed to do but usually don't. Why share the evening news with another government agency?

I go over and meet the old folks who are now under armed guard in the Customs shed. She's sobbing her heart out, and he looks like he's about five minutes away from a heart attack. Poor dumb mules, I think. They got into this to get a free trip back to see the old country one last time before they die. I was not, I figured, going to get any of that Mafia hard-guy shit about blood and silence out of them. So I read them their rights and then lay the good news and the bad news on them. The bad news was that for what they were carrying, they were going to be bouncing their grandchildren on their knees maybe once a month for the rest of their lives up in Sing-Sing. The good news was that if they worked with us, we might be able to do something about that. It was a very persuasive argument, and just as I'd figured they would, they saw the light of sweet reason and bought into it.

The Customs guys, meanwhile, have taken out the dope, replaced it with lactose, and soldered the gas tank back into place. We fit a hooter under the left fender. That's one of those bottle-cap–sized transmitters that puts out a radio signal our tail cars can pick up. Makes for easy surveillance.

The old folks get back into their car and do exactly as they were supposed to do. They drive up to an underground parking garage on East Ninety-first, park the car with the keys and the parking check under the driver's seat, and head back home to Rochester—in DEA protective custody.

We put the garage and car under surveillance and wait. Forty-eight hours later, this big black guy in a Knicks warm-up jacket comes in, wanders around the garage like he's forgotten where he's parked his car. Obviously, he's looking for surveillance. When he doesn't make us, he heads straight for the Honda, hops in, and takes off.

We follow him down to the Fifty-ninth Street Bridge, across the river, and into Queens. He heads into a nice middle-class neighborhood, beeps open the garage door of a split-level ranch, drives inside, and beeps the door back down.

About three minutes later, we go in to join him. We are not alone. Standing there with him, rubbing his hands in delight, is the owner of the house, Louie J. Serrullo. A search of the premises turns up another fifty keys of heroin and over two million dollars in cash buried in the garden.

Louie was sentenced to twenty-five years in Dannemora at the Federal Court House on Foley Square the following February by Judge Thomas J. Gerraghty. Not what he would have gotten for murder one, but still not so bad. I went to the courthouse that morning to see him go away. After a guy is sentenced, the marshals take him downstairs to a holding cell, where they prepare him for his trip upstate. I couldn't resist the temptation to go down and watch. After all, Louie was my prisoner. I stood there with a dumb Irish grin on my face while Louie swapped his thousand-dollar threads for prison denim. Then he was manacled to the four guys who were riding up to Dannemora with him.

"Hey, Louie," I said as they marched him out to the van, "you'll learn to love it up there. You better, because it's going to be home for a helluva long time."

"Fuck you," he growled back. "My lawyers'll bust your case to pieces on appeal. I'll be outta there in no time."

Why am I telling you all this so many years later? Because yesterday a guy gives me a copy of the *Albany Times Union.* Louie was out of Dannemora but not on appeal.

"Louis J. Serrullo, 62, of Queens," a piece in the paper said, "died yesterday of congestive heart failure in the infirmary of the Dannemora Federal Penitentiary, where he was serving a 25-year sentence for narcotics trafficking."

I couldn't help it. I let out a delighted yelp that scared my secretary half to death.

So last night after work I went out to Our Lady of the Angels for the first time in years to lay a rose on Ingrid's grave. As I peered down on her headstone, something struck me—her birthdate, July 23, 1947. In just three weeks if she were still alive, Ingrid would have been celebrating her fiftieth birthday. Maybe this was someone up there's idea of a birthday present.

"Hey, Ingrid," I said to the stone or the grass or the wind or whatever, "maybe there is some justice in the world after all."

Wrong Time,
Wrong Place
by Jeffery Deaver

He saw the car five miles down the road, lights swinging left and right as the driver went through the Harrier Pass switchbacks.

Pretty fast for this road, he thought. And found his damp right hand resting on the butt of his revolver.

"Mobile One." The woman's voice clattered from the loudspeaker on top of the Dodge. "Hey, Hal. You there, Hal?"

He reached inside the squad car and snagged the microphone from the dash.

"Go ahead, Hazel."

"Cold out there?"

It was only mid-September but the weather in the Green Mountains could claim lives as early as October, and the wet air tonight was raw as torn metal.

"'Course it's cold. Where's Billy?"

"On Seventeen. 'Bout, lessee, five miles from the interstate. Stopped a drunk and's got him in the car 'cause what else is he gonna do with him? Right? But no sign of the perps."

She said the last word as if she'd been waiting a long time to drop it into a sentence and Runyer guessed this might've been the case. Pequot County had plenty of drunks and disorderlies, a few sickos and, because of the school, cut-ups galore. But real honest-to-God *perpetrators* . . . well, Hal Runyer hadn't had many of them.

"Anything more on the job?" he asked.

"What job?"

"The heist," he said, irritated. "The stickup. The robbery?"

"Oh, yeah. S'why I called. We got a call from *Captain* Jarrett. At Troop G. Known him ten years and he *still* calls himself Captain Jarrett. Anyway, he says the FBI's taking over. Should we be feeling bad about that?"

"No, Hazel. We should be feeling good about that." Runyer watched the lights grow closer. The car was moving damn fast. On the shoulder a time or two but not drunk careless. More *urgent* careless. He reached inside and flicked on the light bar. "Listen. Where's Rudy? He at Irvine, like I told him?"

"Gaithersberg Road and Fifteen. That where you told him?"

"Close enough. When're the feds coming up?"

"Dunno. I can—"

"S'okay. I gotta go, Hazel. Here's a car needs checking."

"Roger, Sheriff." And added a snappy "Over and out." Which Hazel always looked forward to ending transmissions with.

"Yeah, yeah, out."

The wind blew hard and Runyer shivered. Around him were empty shacks and rusting cultivators and the black spikes of a billion trees. This was still supposedly leaf season but the weather'd been mean the past two weeks, and instead of going to vibrant reds and golds the leaves had suddenly turned sick yellow and leapt off the trees. They now lay on the ground like a ragged sou'wester covering the body of a drowned fisherman.

He watched the car lights growing closer through the dank mist, his hand kneading his revolver.

It'd been the biggest robbery in the history of Pequot County.

That evening, just before closing, a Secure Courier truck had pulled up to the back door of the Minuteman Bank & Trust in downtown Andover.

Witnesses said the whole thing couldn't have taken more than ten seconds. The driver and his first assistant opened the truck's door, and the robbers "were just *there,*" Frank Metger, the bank's security guard, said. "I dunno where they were hiding."

He'd gone for his Smith & Wesson but a third robber stepped out of the shadows on the concrete retaining wall behind the strip mall and let loose one shot with his pistol, one of those huge ones with a telescopic sight on it, like the boys were always admiring down at Baxter's Guns but never buying. "Ka-poweee! Hit 'bout an inch from my head," Frank said. "And I went down fast. I'm not the least ashamed to say it. Not that I couldn'ta taken him, I had the old Smittie out and cocked."

The perps jumped into two cars and sped off in opposite directions, taking with them three-quarters of a million dollars.

Not long after which the phone rang in Hal Runyer's split-level. Lisa Lee handed him the cordless, interrupting some important business with his son. Runyer listened to his deputy and realized that the radio-controlled Piper Cub, laid out like a surgical patient in front of them, would have to remain wingless for the rest of the evening, at least.

Now lights like dying suns appeared behind the trees and the approaching car sped through the last curve before the roadblock. The surprised driver skidded the silver Lexus, exhaust simmering, to a stop ten feet from the cruiser.

Two men inside, their eyes following Runyer's with curiosity. The driver seemed amused. They were young. Lean. Buzz cuts under worn baseball caps. Runyer got a faint whiff of beer and thought: Students.

"Hey, Officer," the driver said cheerfully. "Roadblock, huh? Just like the movies."

"That's right. How you fellas doing tonight?"

"Well, truth is we're not finding as many young lovelies as we'd hoped but 'side from that we're doing fine."

"Good," Runyer said and glanced across the seat. "You doing fine too?"

"Yessir," the passenger said. "Top-notch. You bet."

"What exactly's the problem, Officer?"

They seemed like good boys, fun-loving, here in Andover on jock scholarships, armed with Dad's fine car and plenty of pocket money. But one of Runyer's first lessons from his predecessor had been that, even in sleepy Andover, the friendliest-seeming folk often aren't and you've got to be most cautious of the ones leaning hard to be on your side.

The driver kept both his hands on the wheel. His buddy's right hand was just coming up from the crack beside the right-hand door. Putting it away at least—whatever *it* was—instead of picking it up. The bottle probably. But they weren't impaired and Runyer decided to let a DUI check go.

"Where you headed?"

The driver grinned. "Just, you know, out for a drive."

The flashlight strayed into the backseat. No ski masks or black pullovers. No canvas bags chocked with enough money to live on for a hundred years, in Pequot County at least. But what about the trunk?

"There's some bar we heard about," the passenger said. "I don't know. Some action."

"Action?"

The young man swallowed. "Well, we were looking for some action. That's what I meant. You know."

Runyer noticed that with every word his friend said, the driver was getting madder and madder. And he thought: Problem. We got ourselves a problem here. How do I handle it? He didn't know. The bulk of arrests in Andover involved liquor, pot, or cars. Runyer couldn't remember the last time he'd actually handcuffed somebody. He wondered if he could still do it without embarrassing himself or tearing flesh.

"I wonder if I could see your license and registration."

"Well, you know, it's funny," the driver said, the words clipped. Like his mind was somewhere in front of his voice. "Ninety-nine times out of a hundred you got your license with you. That one time you don't, you get stopped."

"You don't." Runyer offered a grin of his own. "How 'bout the vehicle's registration?"

"Sure, Officer."

He searched the glove compartment and door pocket, then found it in the sun visor. The driver glanced at the small card as he passed it out the window.

Runyer read it and looked up. "That's you? Thomas Gibson?"

"Yessir."

The sheriff stared at the slip of DMV cardboard, afraid to take his eyes off it. Reading the name over and over, as if it was a fax about a deceased loved one.

Thomas Gibson . . .

Of 3674 Muller Lane, Portsmouth, Vermont.

The best-known OB-GYN in Pequot County. Who'd delivered Runyer's sister's first not long ago.

Who'd called Hazel exactly thirty minutes before the Minuteman robbery to report his car stolen.

"Fine," Runyer said earnestly. "Good." Wondering why on earth he had.

Pistol out. Stepping back, pointing it from one of the disgusted, sneering faces to the other. Their smiles were gone.

"I'm gonna say some things and you better listen. I want to see all four of those hands at all times. If one of them disappears, I'm shooting whoever it belongs to. If you reach for the gearshift lever, I'm shooting you. I'm going to ask you to get out of the car in a minute and if either of you runs I'm shooting you. We clear on that?"

"Officer, come *on*," the passenger whined.

"Shut up, Earl," the driver barked.

Something flickered in the distance. A flash of light. The driver glanced in his rearview mirror and gave a slight smile. Another car was coming down the road and Hal Runyer knew in his heart it was their partner.

"Driver, hands on the wheel. And you, put 'em on the dash."

"You—"

"Do it!"

"Oh-*kay*," the driver snapped. This was all a huge inconvenience to him.

Earl's shrill voice: "Gare, what're we gonna do?"

"You're going to be quiet is what *you're* going to do," Gare muttered, flexing his long fingers.

The second car had whipped through the switchbacks and was bottoming out of Harrier Pass. The lights vanished as the car went behind a hill. It'd be at the roadblock in three minutes.

"Driver, leave your left hand on the wheel and with your right reach out and open the door." Was this how he should do it? He thought so. But he wished he knew for sure.

Gare sighed and did what he was told. He climbed slowly from the car, keeping his hands extended.

Earl was looking like a spooked bird, eyes flicking sideways in jerky little movements.

Runyer pitched his only pair of cuffs to Gare. "Get those on. Bet you know how."

Light glowed on the near horizon of the highway. Runyer could hear the urgent shush of the tires on the damp asphalt.

Gare glanced toward the light and grinned slightly. He clicked the cuff on one hand.

"Come on, man," Earl said to Runyer. "Can't we work something out? We got plenty of money."

"Oh, shut *up*," Gare barked.

"So. We're adding bribery to all this."

Another flicker of light. The car was growing closer.

Gare tensed and Runyer's pistol lifted slightly. "I want that second cuff on *now*!"

"How 'bout my boy Earl? No bracelets for 'm?"

The approaching car wasn't more than a hundred feet away. "*I* have to put those on, I'll ratchet 'em good and tight and leave 'em that way. You'll wish you'd done it yourself."

Earl opened the passenger door. Something fell to the ground at his feet. No bottle. It was metal.

"Freeze right there."

Earl ducked a little but Runyer brought him up to standing again with the muzzle.

"Look, Officer—" Gare began. The gun swung back his way.

The car rounded the curve.

What do I do? With three of 'em here, what do I *do*? I should call in for help. Should've done that right up front. Hell. And the squad car's thirty feet away.

"Now. I'm not telling you again."

Click, click. The cuffs were on. Runyer led Gare to the front fender. Keeping his pistol aimed at Earl, he eased Gare facedown onto the hood, bent at the waist. His body made a wingless angel in the dew on the glittery silver paint.

"Now you," Runyer said to Earl. "Come here."

The car came around the curve fast and skidded to a stop. The man behind the wheel opened the door and it took Runyer no more than a second to glance at his face and realize he wasn't the partner. But a second was all Gare needed. Fast as falling rock he snapped upright. His cuffed hands slammed into Runyer's head, tearing his ear with the links. He grabbed the sheriff's gun hand.

Earl bent fast at the knees and came up with the gun that had fallen out of the car when he'd opened the door.

Runyer held onto Gare like a college wrestler. The men rolled on the ground, through wet grass, mulchy leaves, oil, deer piss. Struggling to get Gare down and losing—the small man was strong as roots and Runyer had to keep away from the teeth especially.

"Don't *move*," Earl screamed, waving his gun in their direction.

"Officer!" the other driver called.

"Get outa here," Runyer shouted.

The man hesitated only for a moment, then turned to leap back into his car.

Earl ran toward him. "You, stay there! Stay there!"

The gunshot was a short, sharp crack, swallowed by the misty dampness. The man flew backward.

Oh, Lord . . .

Then Gare elbowed the sheriff hard in the gut and won the pistol. He pressed the muzzle against Runyer's throat, cocked the gun.

"No," Runyer whispered.

"Maybe," Gare answered smartly, grinning. He rubbed the muzzle over the sheriff's skin.

"Look what I done, Gare," Earl whispered. "He's dead. His whole head . . . Look."

"Oh, Jesus Christ, quit whining! Put that sack o' shit in the car and get rid of it. Do it!"

Earl gazed down at the limp body of the man he'd just killed. The eyes were open; they caught white moonlight and glowed eerily. Earl looked uneasily at his partner, wiping his palm on his unclean jeans. "Oh, man." Finally he grabbed the body, muscled it into the car.

"Where—?"

"The *bushes*! Drive it into the bushes! Where d'you think?"

As Earl hid the car, Gare turned back to Runyer. He fished the cuff key from his uniform pocket and unlocked them. "Now," he mocked, "we've got some rules. One is, get on your belly." He shoved Runyer onto the cold asphalt.

"Rule two is you give me any crap and you get shot."

"Gare—"

"What? *What?*"

"Tell him it wasn't my fault. I mean, shooting that guy."

"Of *course* it wasn't. It was *his* fault, Earl." He nodded at Runyer. "He shouldn't've stopped us."

"Look, mister," Runyer said, "so far it's just manslaughter. If you—"

Gare sighed, lifted the revolver, and pulled the trigger.

The powder granules hurt most of all, stinging Runyer's face and his right hand, which he'd lifted defensively. He hardly felt the bullet, other than the punch in the stomach and the snap of his rib.

"Oh." Runyer sank down on his elbow. "My." He felt loose inside, unattached.

"I *told* you rule number two. Weren't you listening?"

"Lisa Lee," Runyer whispered. He held his belly. But not too tight. He was afraid to touch the bullet hole.

The cold autumn wind was powerful in the Green Mountains. It carried sounds a long way despite the hilly terrain. They could hear the sirens real clear.

The men looked up at the spiky horizon and saw a carnival of flashing lights.

"Two of 'em," Gare said. "Shit."

"Mebbe three. Could be three."

Gare ran to the squad car, got inside. He shut off the light bar, then started the car over the cliff, stepping out just before it nosed over. It fell with the sound of crushing foliage.

Through a peppery haze Runyer saw Gare lift his head and look up into the hills. There were two faint yellow lights one hundred yards away. Porch lights. They flickered through the branches.

"Up there. Let's go." He nodded at the twin glow through the mist.

Runyer moaned as a wash of pain flowed through him.

Their eyes turned to him. The men looked at each other, then walked toward him.

He wasn't going to plead, he told himself, hearing the skittery boots on the asphalt.

Gare and Earl stood over him, looking down.

"Please," Runyer whispered.

"Get him in the car," Gare said to Earl. "Move."

He drove up the hill real slow, no lights, and that was how he surprised the couple in the cabin.

While Earl hid the Lexus out back, Gare kicked the door

in, fast, pushing Runyer in front of him, poking the gun toward the man and woman, who sat on the couch, drinking wine. She barked a fast scream and the trim, white-haired man turned fast toward the shotgun over the mantel.

Through the haze of his pain Runyer was thinking: No, no. Don't do it.

But Gare cocked the pistol and the man stopped in his tracks at the sound, turned back, hands up high, like in a movie. He was so surprised by the break-in that for a minute he didn't even know he was supposed to be afraid. He squinted at Gare and the sheriff, then glanced at his wife. And you could see his face just cave, like loose shale. "Please," he said, the word rattling from his throat. "Please don't hurt us."

"Just shut up and do like you're told. Nobody'll get hurt."

Runyer lay on the floor, eyes darting around the place. Typical of a lot of the rental cabins around here. A big living room, wood-paneled, filled with mismatched furniture. Two small bedrooms downstairs, a loft upstairs. The walls and floors polyurethaned yellow pine. Glassy-eyed hunting trophies.

Then he found what he was looking for: the phone, on the wall in the kitchen.

But Gare'd been doing his own surveying. Runyer should've guessed that a seasoned perp wasn't going to miss a telephone. He stepped into the kitchen and ripped the unit down.

"Any other phones?" he snapped.

"I . . . No."

"Any *cell* phones?"

A pause. The husband looked mortified.

"Well?" Gare shouted.

"In my pocket," the husband said quickly. "I forgot. My jacket."

"You forgot. Right." Gare smashed the phone under his boot. Then he called, "Get those curtains closed."

The man's wife—*her* white hair was in a French braid, the way Lisa Lee wore it for PTA meetings and church potlucks—hesitated for a moment. She looked at her husband.

"Now!" Gare barked, and she hurried off to draw the thick drapes covering the windows.

"Anybody else in the house?"

"I—" the man began. "We didn't do anything—"

"Is there anybody else . . . in . . . the . . . house?" Gare demanded. Pointing his gun at the husband's sun-wrinkled face.

"No. I swear."

Earl stepped inside. "Hey. They got 'emselves a Lincoln out there. Let's take it and—"

Gare snapped, "We're not going anywhere yet. Keep 'em covered." He stepped to the door, shut off the porch lights. Gazed down the hill. Runyer could see the flashing lights streak past on the highway. The cars—there were two—didn't even slow up. Runyer'd never told Hazel where exactly on the road he'd set up the roadblock. Route 58 was thirty-seven miles long.

Gare closed the door, turned to the couple. The husband had sat down, he was breathing heavily.

"Too much excitement for you, old man?" Gare laughed.

"He has a bad heart," the wife whispered. "Couldn't you just—"

"And *he's* got a bad gut," Gare said, nodding toward Runyer. "So whyn't you shut up, lady, 'fore you catch something too?"

"Listen . . . Gare," Runyer said. "There're troopers out looking for you. We—"

"For *us*?" Earl blurted, panic in his round, peach-fuzzed face.

"Relax," Gare said to him. "He doesn't mean 'us.' Nobody can ID us." He waved the gun at Runyer. "And you, quiet."

The wife sat down next to Runyer and glanced at his wound. "I'm a nurse," she said to Gare. "Let me take a look at him."

"Go on. But don't do anything stupid, lady."

"I just want to help him."

"Hold up there." Gare found some clothesline and tied the husband's hands. His wife's too.

"I can't work on him this way," she protested weakly.

"Then you can't work on him," Gare responded as he rummaged through the breakfront drawers.

In the light, Runyer could see he'd been wrong about them being college kids. He saw bad teeth, scars, callused hands. Their pedigree was all over them: day labor, taverns, construction jobs till they were thrown off the site drunk or thieving, maybe a teenage wife at home—a girl who cringed automatically whenever a man shouted.

"When d'you get shot?" she asked, struggling to open her nurse's kit.

"Twenty minutes ago."

She took his blood pressure, awkwardly with her bound hands. "Not too bad. And"—she examined the entrance wound—"from where you got hit, I'd say the bullet missed the major veins and arteries." She taped a pad over the puncture in his gut.

"But I better get to a hospital pretty soon," Runyer said.

She leveled her blue-gray eyes at him. "That's right."

"How much time do I have?"

The lie died in her throat, and she decided to tell him the truth. "Two hours, three," shooting a prickly injection into his arm. In a few murky seconds the pain was floating out the window, along with the horror of what she'd just told him. He expected the dope would make him groggy and it did a little, but mostly with the pain gone he found he could think straighter.

And what he thought was, once again: What'm I gonna do here? I'm willing, I've still got some strength left. But I don't have a clue. Ten years of law enforcing in Andover doesn't prepare you for this sort of thing.

He looked over the couple as they gazed miserably across the room at their captors. Runyer'd seen plenty of sorrow on his job, pain too. Most of it as a result of car wrecks and domestic violence. But he didn't think he'd ever seen two more sorrowful people than these two. On the table, by the wineglasses, were a few unopened gift packages and a cake. Written on it: "Happy Birthday, Martin." They'd come up here from Boston or Hartford for the celebration and to spend the weekend looking at leaves and hiking. And now this had happened.

"How much of that dope you have left?" he asked, whispering.

She looked his way. "The painkiller? Isn't it working?"

"I don't mean that," he said. "Any chance we could stick him with one of those needles?"

"But he's got a gun," the husband said quickly. "They both do." He reminded Runyer of the young professors from UV, whose gift of smarts didn't quite make up for their paltry self-confidence.

She shook her head and said to Runyer, "Not much. A couple more shots like the one I just gave you. Not enough to knock anybody out."

"Please," the husband gasped suddenly, lifting his tied hands.

"Please what?" Gare whirled around, snapping.

"Just, can't you just take our car and let us be?"

" 'Let us be'?" he growled. "Listen, mister, I didn't *want* to come here. This isn't my fault. If that asshole hadn't stopped us, we'd be long gone by now. And that fellow on the highway'd still be alive."

"What?" the husband whispered.

Runyer answered, "They shot a man who stopped when I was trying to arrest them."

The husband fell silent and stared at the floor. His wife muttered, "My God, my God."

Runyer was looking at her. He saw a long, handsome face whose attractiveness was partly that she didn't pretend to be young. The skin was matte, free of makeup except for a sheen of pink on her lips. She wore a white cashmere sweater and black slacks.

She wiped the sweat from Runyer's forehead with her sleeve and he didn't think he'd ever felt anything so soft as that fuzzy cloth. It reminded him of Pete's baby comforter, a shabby blue thing the boy had carried with him everywhere till the age of five—when balsa wood suddenly took the place of wool and satin as his youthful obsession.

Gare glanced at the birthday cake and presents. "Lookit."

Earl called, "Heh, we're crashing a party, looks like."

"That you, Martin?"

The husband nodded.

Gare asked, "So, Marty, how old?"

"I . . . uh." His voice faded as he grew flustered, staring at the black barrel of the gun.

Gare laughed. "It's not that tough a question."

"I'm fifty," the man finally answered.

"Whoa, that old?" Gare mused. "And you, what's your name?"

"Jude," the wife answered.

"Come on, Jude. We're going to sing 'Happy Birthday' to Marty. Hey, Earl, this'll be a kick."

"Stop it!" she gasped. "Please."

"You better sing too, Sheriff. That's one of the rules."

"You can go straight to hell." Runyer said this before thinking and he fully expected Gare to shoot him again. But the young man was enjoying his game too much to pay the sheriff much mind. He sat down in between the couple and made a show of arranging the cake in front of Martin, who sat with his hands in front of him, nearly paralyzed. He put his arms around the couple. Rubbing the gun over the poor man's cheek, Gare started singing in an eerie, off-pitch voice. "Happy birthday to you . . . Come on, Earl, let's hear you!"

Earl kept a smile on his face but beneath it the fear and distaste were clear. "Gare . . ."

"Sing!" Gare raged. "You too, Goddamn it," he barked at Jude. "Sing! Happy birthday to you . . . happy birthday to you . . ."

Their ragged voices grunted, or whispered, the words to the song. Martin's eyes were closed and Jude's hands quivered in her terror. Runyer watched the piteous spectacle: the gun caressing Martin's face, Jude's glazed expression, Gare's mad smile as he boomed the lyrics, then called for everyone to take it from the top. The sheriff would've traded his house and land to have his pistol back in his hand for ten seconds.

The singing faded, replaced by another sound—sirens again.

Gare was suddenly all business. "Check it out," he commanded Earl, who scurried over to the front window. Gare rose and stepped into the shadows near the door, the gun ready.

Runyer saw clearly that these two weren't really partners at all. Gare was smart—he'd've been the mastermind behind the robbery—and in the end he wouldn't have a lot of patience for people like Earl. And as for *that* boy . . . he kept looking at his friend every half minute, like a puppy. Earl, Runyer decided, was their key to freedom.

"Who are they?" Martin whispered.

"They robbed a bank downtown today. Nearly killed a guard. There's another one too."

"Another one?"

"A partner. He took off in a different car. They do that sometimes. To fool us—'cause we'd be looking for three men together." Runyer didn't add that he knew "they" did this because he saw it on a *Barnaby Jones* rerun, with his son sitting on his lap and popcorn stuttering madly in the microwave.

Runyer closed his eyes and swallowed hard. Man, I'm sweating. Why'm I sweating so much?

Jude wiped his forehead again. She didn't seem like a nurse, not a hospital nurse anyway. With her dangling Indian earrings and her thin figure—from yoga or dancing, he guessed—she reminded him of Lisa Lee's sister. A charmer but the family wacko, into herbs and crystals.

Thinking of his wife, he gave a distant laugh. Jude looked at him with a smile of curiosity.

"I was remembering something. . . . Last week Lisa Lee and I were at this Autumnfest? In Andover?"

"That's your wife? Lisa Lee?"

Runyer nodded. "We were leaving and I couldn't find our truck. I thought, hell, I hope nobody stole it—we've had a bunch of car thefts up here lately. Turned out it wasn't, I just forgot where I parked. But I remember saying to Lisa Lee, 'You know, stealing cars is about the worst we get here in Andover. Makes me feel like I'm just playing at my job. Like I'm not a real cop. Sometimes I wouldn't mind a little more action.' "

Jude laughed softly. Martin didn't. He seemed to be counting his own heartbeats.

"Boy, mistake!" Runyer concluded. "Never ever ask for something you might get. I'd make that a rule of life."

He looked at Jude's hand. She wore a gold ring with a blue stone in it. "That's pretty." He reached up to touch it. Then he realized his finger was bloody and he pulled back. "S'the color of Lisa Lee's eyes. What kind of stone is it?"

"Topaz."

"Thought they were yellow."

"They come in blue too."

The glitchy pain spread a little farther. He gasped. "Oh . . . oh . . ."

Martin looked at him now, wide-eyed. "Please," he called. "This man . . ."

Gare looked up from the cabinet he was ransacking.

"He's hurt bad."

"Of course he's hurt bad. I put a .38 slug through his belly." He grinned. "So, Marty, tell me . . . who're you expecting?"

Martin and Jude looked at each other.

Gare bent from the waist and caressed Martin's face with the muzzle of his gun. "Who . . . are you . . . expecting?"

"Nobody."

"Somebody named Cara, maybe?"

"How—?" Jude began then stopped herself. Gare held up a birthday present. A card said, *Love, Cara.*

Martin couldn't think of anything fast enough. "She's—"

"She's our daughter," Jude said.

"She coming to this party?" Earl asked, jumping playfully over the back of a tartan plaid couch and landing on the cushion.

"No," Martin blurted. "She isn't."

"What's she look like?" Earl asked.

"Just forget her," Martin whined. "Look, what do you want? You want money? I can get you money. Whatever you want, I'll get it for you. I'm well off. . . ."

"Yeah? What do you do, Marty?"

"I have a wholesale business. It makes a lot of money. I can get you—"

"What, write me a check? Let you all take a little drive into town and hit the ATM while Earl and I wait here?"

Edgy, Jude said, "How 'bout if I get you men something to eat?"

"Now, why'd you wanta do a nice Samaritan thing like that?" He was examining the knickknacks on the mantelpiece—a collection of ceramic birds. A spread-wing eagle caught his eye, and he rubbed the detail of the feathers with a finger.

"Because if you're feeling fat and sassy you might be more inclined to let us go." She tried to laugh. The sound fell flat.

Gare shrugged. "I could use some food. Earl, go with her."

Runyer, thinking: The two of them alone in the kitchen. She could talk to Earl, tell him Runyer would testify that the killing was accidental. Tell him to give up Gare before he ended up dead himself or socked away in prison for two lifetimes.

He rolled over so that he was looking into her face. Gare couldn't see him.

"Jude," he whispered. "Listen . . ."

Her eyes flicked down.

"You've got to talk to him. To Earl. Tell him that I'll—"

Gare's hand clamped down hard on Runyer's shoulder and jerked him over onto his back. The pain jabbed him like a dentist's drill.

"What're you saying, Sheriff?"

Sweat dripping into his eyes, Runyer stared at the smooth, round face inches from his.

"You asking her to bring you back a nice little knife or something?" He turned to Jude and set one of her gold earrings swinging with the muzzle of Runyer's own service pistol. "What was he asking you?"

Horrified, Martin opened his mouth but whatever he was going to say was choked off by the sight of a pistol against his wife's head.

"Because," Gare continued, "that'd be breaking rule number two. And we know what happens then." He swung the gun toward Runyer's belly, caressed the bloody front of his uniform.

"I wanted some water is all. Just some water."

"I'll decide what you get and when you get it." Standing up, Gare said to Earl: "Go on. Just be sure and frisk her when you come back." His slick face cracked another of its horrid grins. "Take your time, you want."

"No!" Martin snapped. "You son of a bitch!"

"What'd you say?" Gare spun around, slipped the gun into his belt. Doing that—putting it away, not pointing it—sickened Runyer. It meant violence, not a threat, was coming. "What?" he whispered.

"Don't you dare touch her." At last there was some steel in Martin's voice.

But all this did was notch up Gare's anger.

Circling again, slow, he stared Martin down like a scolded dog.

"Just let me make them some food," she pleaded. "What would you boys like? I'm a good cook. Tell them I'm a good cook, Martin. Tell them."

Gare jerked Martin to his feet. "Now say it. . . . What don't you want me to do?"

"Hurt her."

"Thought you said 'touch her.'"

"I . . . that's what I mean."

"But she might like getting touched." He looked Jude over, her slim figure under the fuzzy white sweater, the close-fitting slacks. "You're an old man, Martin. Bet nothing works quite like it used to, right? I'll bet you've been neglecting her. And she's just coming into her prime. That's what you hear on the talk shows."

"No, just . . . leave her alone."

"Say please."

"Please."

"You say it, but you don't mean it. Maybe if you were on your knees. Get on your knees. Go ahead. Do it."

"Gare," Earl said uneasily.

Martin swallowed and looked from his wife to Runyer. "You go to hell," he shrieked. And lunged for the robber, grabbing him by the collar.

"Whoa, here," Gare said, laughing. He slugged Martin hard in the belly and sent him careening into the wall. He reached out to catch himself, but with his hands tied, he could grip only the drapes. They didn't hold and he fell hard to the floor, knocking the wind out of his lungs. He curled up like a hedgehog as Gare started beating him.

"No!" Jude cried. "His heart . . . Please, don't!"

But Gare lost interest after a half dozen blows. He stood up, flexed his hand. "Now, go make some food like I asked. I want a burger. Or something hot."

She started toward her husband.

"Don't worry about him. I said *food.*"

When Earl came over to take Jude to the kitchen Runyer caught his eye. The young man returned the look, curious for a moment, then lifted Jude to her feet and led her to the kitchen.

Gare glanced at the sheriff but ignored him. He was just a

mote—an expression of Runyer's father-in-law, meaning somebody floating around in the background, inconsequential. No, it was Martin who fascinated him. He pulled a knife out of his pocket and enjoyed watching the man go wide-eyed. Then he chuckled and cut the rope, retying his hands behind his back. "Just so you don't do anything stupid again." Surveying the knots, he said, "So, you're fifty, huh? How 'bout the witch in there?"

"The same. We're the same age."

"That's about how old my mother is. My dad too, he's still alive. I don't remember his birthday. That's funny, isn't it? You'd think I'd remember. You remind me of him sort of. He was kind of a wuss too. No balls."

"Look, son, please . . . I've gotta get to the john. I mean really."

"*Grand*son's more like it," Gare said, grabbing Martin by the hair again, examining the evasive eyes. "Well, grandpa, you really gotta go?"

"I do, yes. See, I'm hyperglycemic . . . borderline diabetic. And—"

"Yadda, yadda, yadda. You wanna piss, just say you wanta piss. Don't explain so damn much. Geez."

Gare dragged him to the bathroom and humiliated Martin further by leaving the door open and staring at the poor man while he did his business.

When they returned he pushed Martin down onto the floor beside Runyer. He smelled the air, the cooking beef. "How's that food coming?" Gare shouted.

"Almost ready," Jude called. The thought of eating nauseated Runyer.

Gare sat down in front of Martin, cross-legged, studied him again, like a bug in a bottle. Finally he mused, "You think a person can live too long?"

"What do you mean?"

"Don't you think there comes a point you're not alive anymore? You're not really living. Just getting by. You might as well just pack it in. Haven't you ever felt that?"

"No."

"You really want to live?" Gare asked, as if he was truly surprised.

"Of course I do," the man answered earnestly. "You think 'cause you're younger and stronger the world's yours. My family and I have a right to live too."

"But live what kind of life?" Gare shot back. "Look at us—a month ago Earl and I did a job near Poughkeepsie and getting away we were driving down the Taconic at a hundred fifteen miles an hour. See, *that* was being totally alive. You ever done that? 'Course not. You're just a goddamn salesman—"

"I'm not a salesman. I own a big—"

Gare wrinkled his face up. "You ever do *anything* crazy? Skydive? Ski?"

"No, but—"

"No, but," he mocked. "How 'bout when you were young? You do anything ballsy then?"

"I guess." He looked at the kitchen as if Jude would testify on his behalf. "I had a souped-up car. I—"

"But then," Gare continued, "you got old, right? You got scared."

"I had a family to support!" Martin snapped back. "I had my business. Employees to take care of. I couldn't afford to screw around like you."

"Pitiful," Gare whispered, shaking his head. "Pitiful."

Runyer lay on his side, bloody, a bullet deep in his body. But it seemed to him that Martin was wounded a lot deeper—by this cold taunting.

"You don't understand," Martin blurted.

"Oh, yeah, I do. I understand perfectly."

Jude and Earl brought the burgers in and she put the dishes on the table. Even across the room Runyer could see her shaking hands.

"Soup's on," she said with fake cheer.

Gare stared at Martin for a moment longer, then went to the table and sat down.

Runyer caught Jude's eye and glanced at Earl, then pantomimed drinking a glass of water. Jude seemed to understand and turned toward the kitchen.

"Where you going, grandma?" Gare snapped.

"To get some water for the sheriff."

"Earl, you do it."

"But—"

"Do it!"

Thank you, Runyer thought. Yes!

Earl fetched the water. As he bent down to set it on the floor, his pistol pointed at Runyer's head, the sheriff whispered quickly, "Let's work out something, Earl. You give him up, and I'll testify for you at trial. About the shooting. That it was an accident. You got my word."

Earl froze, looked at him for a moment. He just about dropped the glass when Gare called, "Earl!"

The young man swiveled around.

"S'getting cold," Gare said. "Come on and eat."

Earl stared at Runyer for a moment, set the glass down, and returned to the table without a word.

Gare put his napkin in his lap carefully, then picked up his utensils with precise gestures. Runyer was surprised at his behavior until he realized he'd seen this before—Gare had learned his manners in reform school.

He and Earl began conversing in whispers.

"Your daughter?" Runyer asked the couple. "She *is* coming here tonight, isn't she?"

Martin's eyes met Jude's. She nodded. And Runyer now understood why Martin was so upset.

"She drove up from Boston this afternoon. She went shopping and was going to meet us tonight for a little party. Stay the weekend."

"When's she due?"

An elaborately carved clock—with a weird grinning face, like the old man in the moon—showed the time. 7:10.

"Ten minutes ago."

The pain stretched luxuriously through Hal Runyer and dripped into his bowels. He gasped and thought of Lisa Lee's aunt, dying of cancer. When they'd talked about the woman—friends, family, and doctors—nobody ever talked about the cancer itself, or about her coming death. They'd talked about pain.

He gasped and closed his eyes. Then risked a look at his belly. The blood had spread in a huge slick. He knew he didn't have much time left. Runyer looked over at the table and once again caught Earl's eye. The man looked away fast, continued to poke at his burger. He nodded as Gare said something to him and went right on nodding.

"What're they talking about?" Martin asked in his nervous lilt.

"Whether or not to kill us," Runyer answered.

Martin lowered his head to his wife's and they huddled, an armless embrace.

Runyer floated away somewhere momentarily—because of the drugs, or the pain, or the despair—and he gazed at the couple as if he were looking down at them from above, saw them with startling clarity. And if maybe they were a little too L.L. Bean for Runyer's taste, if they were spooked as deer at the moment, if they didn't have the inclination, or backbone, to approach life the way Gare thought was important, still they were good people—and brave in their own way. Martin was somebody who'd provided for his family and for the people who worked for him. Jude had raised a child and nursed patients. Which is what real courage was, Runyer reckoned. Not driving fast or sticking up banks. So where their captors felt contempt for these folks, Runyer couldn't. He felt only an overwhelming desire to save them, to salvage what he could of their lives.

The sheriff had pinned his hopes on Earl but it was obvious that wasn't going to work out. So he now eased close to Jude. "Listen. I've been thinking. Your daughter's due here any minute, right?"

Martin nodded.

"Your legs're free. What if you two were to go through that window there? Run down the driveway and hide in the pine trees for her? When she shows up, you all hightail it outa here. You'll probably get a little cut and bruised but that'll be the worst of it."

"How?" Jude asked. "They'd come after us."

"I'll hold 'em off. With that scattergun on the mantel."

"It's not loaded," Martin whispered. "I checked when we got here."

Runyer'd figured. Vermont wasn't NRA territory but people knew guns and nobody'd ever mount a loaded double-barrel within a child's reach.

"But they don't know that."

"Don't!" Martin rasped. "Let's just do what they want."

Jude added, "If you don't shoot them outright they'll figure out the gun's empty."

"Don't think they'd want to take that kind of chance with a ten-gauge goose gun. Besides, they'd figure with me being a cop it'd make sense to give 'em a chance to surrender. 'Put your hands up.' That kind of thing."

Then Jude was smiling kindly. "I know what you're trying

to do," she said. "I appreciate it, Sheriff. But . . . how old're you?"

"Thirty." It had been his birthday too—just last week. He didn't mention this.

"And you're a married man and probably've got kids."

"This's my job," he continued. "I get paid—"

"You don't get paid to sacrifice your life for a couple of stodgy old tourists like us. That's what you'd be doing. And you know it."

"I'm thinking of your daughter too," he said. " 'Sides, if there's any way *I'm* surviving this it's if somebody brings some help. Soon."

Martin said, "You're wrong, Sheriff. I don't think they really want to hurt us. Let's just wait."

"We can't!" Runyer whispered urgently. "Gare's going to kill us."

"How can you be so sure?"

"Because of blame. Weren't you listening to him? He's got this talent for pitching blame like horseshoes. Everything that happens is somebody else's fault. That lets him do whatever he wants. Murder included."

Martin looked at the window Runyer wanted them to leap through. He gazed at it the way a man accustomed to losing foot races looks at a cinder track.

The sheriff said to Jude, "I think it's the only way. I want you to knock that lamp over there. I'll make a run for the shotgun and you two go through the window. It can't be more'n four feet to the ground."

Martin whispered urgently, "But if it doesn't work they'll kill us all, Cara too. If we promise we won't tell anybody, if we *swear* it, they'll probably let us go. I have a feeling."

Jude was Runyer's only hope and he kept his eyes in hers. Finally, she said, "I'll do whatever my husband wants."

Martin asked, "You really think we can make it?"

"That depends," Runyer answered. "How bad do you *want* to make it?"

For an instant Runyer could see Martin was right on the borderline. His eyes grew sharp as he judged the angles, the distance to the window. But then he shook his head slightly.

And so there was nothing to do but go ahead by himself and hope that Jude would rally her husband to make the plunge to safety.

He waited until Gare and Earl were looking at their food, then gripped Martin's shoulder and pulled himself to his feet. "I'm going," he whispered. "Get the hell out that window!"

Ignoring the electric pain that stabbed through him, Runyer moved as quietly as he could toward the gun over the mantel.

Martin's voice scared the hell out of him. "No, don't!" He lurched forward and slammed into the sheriff, who tumbled over on his side in a jolt of agony.

The captors leapt up from the table.

"He was going for the shotgun," Martin cried. "It wasn't us! We told him not to!"

"Martin," Jude spat out in disgust.

"It was *his* idea. . . ." Martin wailed. "We didn't do anything."

And for a moment Runyer found himself agreeing with Gare: the man was truly pitiful.

You've got to be most cautious of the ones leaning hard to be on your side. . . .

Earl dragged them both back into the corner and delivered a kick to Runyer's belly that no amount of morphine would dull. He gasped and rolled up tight.

"Look what you did," Jude cried to her husband.

He just killed us all, the sheriff thought. *That's* what he did.

"I don't want anybody to get hurt."

"Good man, Marty." Gare pulled the scattergun off the wall

and broke it open. "Wouldn'ta done you a lotta good. Stupid of you. Stupid. Tie their feet, Earl."

As the young man cinched their ankles, Gare walked toward the huddling trio and snapped the gun closed. That damn grin of his blossomed again and he drew back with the butt of the gun like a baseball bat. Runyer lowered his head, waiting for the crushing blow.

A loud rap sounded on the door and they heard, "Mom, Dad? Hey, some welcome! What's with the porch lights?"

A tall, attractive woman, mid-twenties, wearing an expensive shearling coat, stepped inside.

"Cara!" Jude cried. "Run!"

But Earl put his hand on her back and shoved her toward them. She barked a panicked scream and flung her arms around her father, buried her head in his chest, sobbing. The girl glanced at Runyer's bloody wound and began to cry harder. "What's going *on*?"

Her mother edged closer and they pressed together.

Gare stepped outside. He returned a moment later. "Nobody else around. She's alone."

"Who are you?" Cara asked.

Gare said nothing. But his eyes told Runyer the whole story: What's coming's our fault. We screwed up their getaway from the bank and a man got killed. Martin reminded Gare of his father and that too set off his anger like a fast-burning fuse. He's innocent; *we've* caused this grief, and that gives him the okay to kill us all.

And damn if he probably isn't going to blame us for him feeling guilty after he does.

"Earl," Gare said. "Come on over here. Stand by me."

"We gonna take her car?"

"No, we're going to take their Lincoln. But there's something we have to do first."

"What?"

"You know."

Earl wiped his hand on his jeans, looked from his buddy back to the people on the floor. He seemed to sense what was coming and glanced at Gare uneasily.

What was he thinking about? What Runyer had told him?

Would he stand up to Gare at the last minute?

"You can do it, Earl," Gare whispered.

Runyer stared into the young man's black eyes. Thinking: Remember what I said, Earl, remember it, remember, remember, *remember.* . . . It's the only way you can save yourself.

"Go on," Gare said.

"I can't," Earl muttered.

His friend's low voice growled, "Listen, Earl, the job tonight went just like we'd planned, right? Piece of cake. And we were heading home, no harm for anybody. It wasn't our fault this happened. We didn't *want* to come here, did we?"

"No."

"They know our names," Gare continued. "They know what we look like."

"Don't do it, Earl," Runyer said. "Don't ruin your life."

"Oh, listen to *him,*" Gare spat out. "*He's* the one tried to shoot us. Marty too—he went for that scattergun. Remember? When we walked in? And don't think that old lady wouldn't shoot us down too, she had the chance."

"Earl!" Runyer called.

The young man's eyes swayed from his friend to Runyer and back again. The gun lowered.

Come on, Runyer thought, come on. . . . *Remember.*

"And know what else he did?" Earl said suddenly, an icy glint in his eyes. "That sheriff there? He said if I turned you in, he'd go easy on me."

"He did that?" Gare, sounding shocked, frowned.

"Whispered it to me when I brought him the water."

"He thought you were a snitch, huh?" Gare said. "That's what he thinks of you—that you'd turn on your buddy."

Earl turned to the sheriff. "You son of a bitch. You thought I'd snitch?"

"Earl, don't—"

"You're first. I do him first, Gare?"

"That's fine by me."

Martin and Jude were silent. Runyer lowered his head.

"No," Cara whispered. "God, no."

Runyer fixed his wife and son in his mind and dropped his head to his chest. Earl stepped closer. Ten feet away. He couldn't miss.

Lisa Lee . . .

Hal Runyer knew he wasn't going to the heaven he promised Petey was "up there," somewhere beyond where the boy's fragile planes flew. No, he was going to black sleep. His breath hissed in and out and he squinted as the tears came.

Picturing his wife, his son, losing himself in the sad euphoria of this final daydream . . .

Then he heard something odd. Like the punch of unexpected thunder. A voice. Martin's, but different. Matter of fact. Calm. He said one word. "Down."

The women dropped to the floor. Cara hit the pine floorboards and hooked Runyer's collar, yanking him prone too. Martin's hands—somehow free—swung around from behind his back, holding a huge pistol. His feet were still tied so he stood tall as he began firing, not even trying to duck. He fired the first shot at Gare but the boy's instincts were honed and he dove to the floor behind a couch in a hair second.

Earl was crouching, staring at his friend.

Martin said to the terrified young man, "Drop it."

But Earl went wide-eyed and lifted the gun, pulling the trigger madly. The slug missed by a yard and before he could fire again, Martin squeezed off another round and a tiny dot appeared in the center of Earl's chest. He stumbled backward with a choked "Gare, oh, look, look." Then collapsed on his side.

With the knife she was holding, Cara sliced through the rope binding Martin's feet and he dropped down behind a table. Runyer realized this was how she'd cut the ropes tying his arms—reaching around his back to hug him. She now cut Jude's hands free too and pulled a second pistol from her waistband, passed it to the older woman.

Fast as snakes, Gare popped up behind the couch and fired. Three, four times. But they were panicked shots and all of them missed. Gare emptied Runyer's pistol and snagged Earl's from his bloody, twitching hand. While Gare peppered the wall with bullets Martin took his time and squeezed off rounds carefully, forcing the captor back into the corner behind a cedar chest.

"Go right," Martin called. Jude rolled toward the kitchen, an elegant maneuver, and made her way around Gare's flank.

"Think you're hot shit?" Gare screamed, scared as a baby.

Martin ignored him, jumped over the low table, and ducked as the spray of bullets from Gare's gun slapped the walls. He rolled behind a large armoire.

"Position," he called to Jude.

"You son of a bitch," Gare snarled. "You're dead! You're both *dead*."

"Position," Jude called.

Martin sized up the room and said, "All right, son. It's over."

"Like hell." Three more shots. A window broke, raining glass onto Cara and Runyer.

"Shoot?" Jude asked.

"Wait." Then he called, "We've got you in a cross-fire,

Gare. And we have more ammo than you do. You can't win. But you can save your life. If you want to."

They heard hard breathing. Gare coughed once and spat.

"Shit. I'm bleeding. My shoulder!"

"You don't want us to come get you, son."

Slowly Gare stood.

"Gun down," Jude barked. "Now. I won't tell you a second time."

The pistol hit the couch. Cara snagged it before it bounced twice and had it unloaded in an instant. She pulled some plastic hogties from her shearling coat pocket and handed them to Martin, who bound Gare's hands.

"How did . . ."

"Just lie down there." Martin and Cara helped him down on his belly. They tied his ankles.

"You're going to kill me," he blubbered. "Just do it! Get it over with! I dissed you, I said all those things. And now you're going to kill me."

Runyer was gazing at the gun in Martin's hand. It was a big pistol, a Colt Python with an eight-inch barrel. With a telescopic sight mounted on the top vents.

Martin went through Gare's pockets, pulled out a box cutter, some papers, a wad of bills. He tossed them on a table. Then he nodded at Jude, and together the couple dragged him into the bedroom. They rested him facedown on the floor, where he cried and moaned.

They returned to the living room and sat down in front of the sheriff. Martin pulled on gloves and began wiping the big Colt.

"You were good," Runyer said to him. "Really good." Deciding that it was a lot harder for a brave man to act like a coward than the other way around. Since they so rarely need to.

"Had to get their guard down," Martin said, meticulous as he removed the fingerprints.

"Had *me* fooled too," Runyer admitted.

"Wished we *could've* kept you fooled too. But . . . well, didn't work out that way."

"No. I guess not. She's not your daughter, is she? Cara?"

"Nope," Martin answered, distracted by his task. "She's our partner. Backup mostly."

"How?" Runyer asked her. "How'd you know?"

"Oh, we have codes," Jude said as if it was obvious.

Martin continued, "When we meet at a safehouse after a job, if there's anyone in the place who shouldn't be there, we leave a sign. Tonight if both the bathroom and kitchen lights were on at the same time Cara'd know something was wrong. She was supposed to pretend she was our daughter. Buy us some time and maybe get a weapon to us. I staged that fight to pull the shade down so she could look in and get an idea about what was going on."

Taking a breath a little deeper than he should've, Runyer gasped at the pain.

Cara said, "I got here ten minutes ago. I saw those two. I could've taken them out then but I didn't know if there was anybody else upstairs or in the basement."

"But you're a nurse," Runyer said to Jude. Trying to disprove these facts encircling him.

"I just know some first aid. Helpful in this line of work."

"But your birthday . . . ?" Runyer began, looking at Martin.

"Oh," he answered, "that's true. It's today. And I *am* fifty."

"You picked a funny way to celebrate."

The man shrugged. "Big cash delivery at a low-security bank. Didn't have much choice. We go where the work is."

The friendliest-seeming folk often aren't . . .

Jude looked over Martin with a cryptic gaze, then said to Cara, "Let's get the car packed up."

The women vanished.

. . . and you've got to be most cautious of the ones leaning hard to be on your side.

When they were alone Martin said, "What you were going to do . . . with the ten-gauge . . . Appreciate it. But it wouldn't've worked. They'd've killed us on the spot."

Runyer nodded at Earl's body. "Stealing the Lexus . . . *that's* what they meant by the job tonight. Not the bank."

"I guess so." Martin turned toward the sheriff, who was gazing at the pistol in his hand. Man, it looked big. Bigger than any weapon Runyer'd ever seen. "So," he said.

"So," Runyer echoed. "Say, one thing I noticed."

"What's that?"

"You've been pretty free telling me who you are and what you did and all. Just wondering, d'I just jump outa a frying pan?"

"That depends," said Martin.

Jack Applebee, president of Minuteman Savings, had wanted to give the hero a nice watch, bestowed at an official ceremony. Juice and cake and Ritz crackers. Paper streamers. Folks in Andover just love their official get-togethers.

But Runyer wasn't in the mood. Besides, Sheriff's Department regulations won't let officers accept rewards. So Applebee settled for a handshake at Runyer's hospital bedside, surrounded by Lisa Lee, Pete, a half dozen friends and family, and a Pequot County *Democrat* reporter.

The banker talked about gratitude and courage, and also managed to work in a few words about the new Minuteman branch at Elm and Seventeenth and, naturally, the grand opening home-equity loan special. The old guy was in a great mood, and why not? Of the $687,000 stolen, nearly half was recovered. More than he'd ever expected to see again. Gare's and Earl's partner made off with the rest of it. The federal agents and Vermont troopers couldn't figure out how he slipped through the roadblocks—they were plentiful and well manned. But clearly the robbers were pros and would've had escape routes worked out ahead of time.

Defendant Garrett Allen Penbothe adamantly denied that they'd even stuck up the bank in the first place and so he wasn't about to offer any information about the elusive third partner. He and Earl, he claimed, had bussed up to Andover that afternoon to steal a car, which they'd done a half dozen other times over the past month. And he came up with a version of the robbery so far-fetched that even the *Democrat,* which'll print anything shy of alien visitations, decided not to include it in their articles about the trial.

The prosecution witnesses—a businessman and his family whose rental cabin Gare and Earl tried to hide in—confirmed Runyer's story about the shoot-out and offered generous words about the sheriff's courage, and marksmanship, in a tense situation.

Gare's defense lawyer tried to argue that the young man was the real victim of these events. "My client and his friend just happened to be in the wrong place at the wrong time."

But prosecutor Harv Witlock latched on to the phrase for his own and used it liberally during his summation, saying excuse me but wasn't it Sheriff Runyer and the murdered passerby who'd had the bad luck here? A question that took the jury all of thirty-two minutes to answer. Gare is presently a long-term guest at a piney resort near the Canadian border known as the Tohana Men's Colony.

Hal Runyer elected to take sick leave for the first time in his decade of wearing the sheriff's badge. And after that fortnight he took another batch of time: vacation, which he'd also earned plenty of. Not that he had much choice about going back to work. Mentally, he was a mess. He couldn't sleep for more than an hour without waking in a torrid sweat. And he was plenty skittish when he was awake too. Noises especially would send him bouncing off the walls. His wound took forever to heal and he could barely move on damp days.

So he spent his time puttering around the house, learning to cook, helping Lisa Lee with her realtor paperwork, shaving wing struts with a razor knife and painting fuselages. Petey had the classiest RC model plane in the county that fall.

A month after the robbery Runyer woke up early one frosty Tuesday and called the mayor at home. He quit the force. No explanations given or asked for. And when he hung up the phone he felt great. That night he took his family out to dinner and while they ate Houlihan's prime rib special he told them the news. He tried to gauge his wife's reaction and didn't have a clue.

It was a week later that a small package, no return address, was delivered to the house. Runyer started to open it, then noticed it was addressed only to Lisa Lee and he passed it over to her. She opened it with mixed suspicion and anticipation and gave a brief gasp. The black velvet box held a gold ring set with a big blue topaz. No name of a store, nothing other than a card that said, "For Lisa Lee."

Runyer was a generous man but his gifts leaned more toward the practical or, at best, decorative. A luxury like this was quite a jolt for her. She threw her lengthy arms around his neck. "But we can't afford it, honey."

Gazing at the anonymous note, piecing things together, he said, "No, it's okay. It's a thank-you present."

"From who?"

"Those people in the cabin."

"The ones you saved after the bank robbery? The couple and their daughter?"

"The wife . . . she had one of these rings and I told her it re-minded me of your eyes. I guess she remembered that."

"It must've cost a fortune," Lisa Lee said, dazzled by the stone.

"He runs some kind of business. Bet he got it wholesale."

"We'll have to send them a nice note."

"I'll take care of that," he said. If he sounded evasive, she didn't seem to notice.

Life's a funny thing, Runyer found himself thinking as he stood in that hot kitchen with his wife in his arms. Sometimes every soul in the world but you seems to know what's what and is more than happy to tell you so. And most of the time you go along with them. But if you live long enough—maybe thirty years, maybe fifty—you get to the point when you're just not willing to hand off certain choices anymore. The im-portant ones anyway. You do what you think's best and go on about your business.

"Which finger should I wear it on?" Lisa Lee asked.

"Well, let's see where it looks right." Runyer took his wife's hand and gratefully endured the hug despite the loving pain she inflicted on his torn belly.

The next day Hal Runyer climbed the stairs to the Sheriff's Department office, moving a little slower than he had before the shooting.

"Well, look who it is," Hazel said, eyeing his starched khakis. "You didn't *call.* We heard you were quitting."

"Naw, just a mix-up. I straightened it out with the mayor last night."

He snagged the report log from the desk in her cubicle and asked, "What's going on 'round town?"

"Not too much. Pretty quiet morning."

Runyer lifted aside a stack of files from his chair and sat at his desk. He started to read.

Untitled
by E. L. Doctorow

We were one boxcar of a long train of boxcars of the packed standing and swaying, living and dying and stiffened dead. Each car was the standard carriage for freight, nine point six meters in length, four meters wide, with a battened roof slightly saddled for runoff, a bolted steel chassis with four flanged Krupp Steelwork wheels set at European track gauge, and coupling mechanisms front and back. A common sight, absurdly homely top-heavy things, their wooden sides painted rust or olive green, weathered links of them waiting in every train yard of the continent, or creaking and rattling through the countryside, through villages at three in the morning under a cold moon, shuddering, banging away in the sweeps of wind coming off the wide valleys, these commonest transports for the businesses of nations arousing the lean, visibly ribbed dogs of the villages to run alongside and yelp and leap into the air and snap their jaws at the stench in their nostrils.

I was squeezed tight against the sealed door, inhaling the historic odors in the wood of hay, of hide, and with my lips pressed to a thin plane of slatted air of the ordinary indifferent earth outside.

The plane of air was heated by light, cooled by the darkness, and so I was able to count off the days and nights. I detected the first light of dawn by the changing sensation on my tongue. I could occasionally hear something as well, such as the lowing of a cow at dusk, distant and almost indistinct amidst the moans and prayers of the people around me.

Since the catastrophe was ours alone, it did not impinge on the traditional practices of railroad transport. Periodically the train was shunted to a side track and left to sit there hour after hour, deaf to all our importunings and cries of despair, or it would creep forward, but then drift backward to stop in the silence of the impassive night, only to be suddenly on its way, rasping and shuddering through the switches, back on track, where it would clump along like some dumb and dogged beast of the *mitteleuropean* peasantry.

After the first or second day I began to gnaw on the slot in the siding through which I breathed the outside air, or as I thought, the wide expanse, as far as the horizon, beyond it, infinitely extending, of destinies not of this train. I had not any purpose in mind, it merely seemed reasonable to mouth the hard wood hour after hour without stopping, except of course when I passed out and slept. When I was fortunate enough to have an actual splinter come away in my mouth I chewed it for food. For water I had one night the wind-driven rain, which felt like cold needles on the tip of my tongue. As I worked away, I found myself listening to the clacking wheels, applying rhythms to them, making up songs in my head to go with the rhythms: but somehow these songs were in my mother's voice, or my father's, and the voices were really more in the nature of evanescent images of my mother and father, and the evanescent images more like fleeting sensations of their beings, momentary apperception of their moral natures, which caused me to call out, as if they could be brought to resolution in the persons of my whole real mother and father. For my trouble I found myself returned to the mindless incessant clacking of the train wheels. I reasoned then that if I could gnaw an opening large enough to climb through, they would be happy to greet me, these flanged wheels that would flip me along one to the other, and end my life sharply and cleanly.

But then someone directly at my back, a girl who had wept and wept the first day, so that my shirt was wet by her tears, but had since then only whimpered in a high pitch almost like a cat, and, among the shifting stiffened bodies had come to hold her arms around my waist, with her cheek pressed between my shoulder blades—this girl, with no warning sound, ceased to live, and the train rocketing around a curve, her legs sank under her, and her arms slid over my hips and down around my knees so that I was pulled by her weight down a few inches to where I found myself looking through the slot through which I had breathed the air not of the train.

A blur, brush, a woods so close to the railroad embankment that leaves slapped against the siding, a dense woods so thick as to create shadows dark as night. Then suddenly, a falling away of this darkness, and a broad sunlit vista of a green field with a house and barn in the distance. "A farm!" I called. I was momentarily, insanely, joyful. "Now a road. A horse and wagon." And so I broadcast the news of the world to those who would listen. Birch trees. A brook. Women and children culling potatoes. A stationmaster lighting his pipe.

Among the people in my car whom I had seen climbing into it before me were several from my neighborhood. When I sensed from the smell of soot and the appearance of a track yard that the journey was coming to its terminus, it seemed to me important to recall who they were: Mr. and Mrs. Moses Barbanel and their son, Joseph, who was a year ahead of me in school, the twin old maid sisters Chana and Deborah Diamond, the postman Mr. Lichtenstein, the principal of the lower school Dr. Jack Hornfeld and his wife and three children, my friend Nicoli, who shared with me his German-language cowboy novels, and the blond girl Sarah Levin with her pretty mother, Miriam, who taught piano, and who had told my mother that Sarah had an eye for me, a bit of news that I heard with feigned indifference. They were not visible to me now, these people I had known all my life. They might be here with me but they were of the past. Even had I been able to turn and look behind me, what of them would I have recognized, at this time of their degradation, when, like myself, they had been sundered from their names, when their beings were undone, when whatever they had been was in process of industrial transfiguration, when all together we were no more than a suspension of disjunctive torments of the living dying and stiffened dead of this boxcar?

Then those who were still living their dying fell, tumbled, dropped to the ground, and staggered to their feet, even as the stiffened dead in the boxcars behind them were slammed into animation by the pressure hoses . . . to be clubbed along on their numb-legged stumbling, shot if they fell, drilled in the engineered language of expectorated shrapnel . . . until the Germanic sense of order was satisfied and we were penned inside the wire, and stood there while they joked or yawned and finally got down to business, a man in civilian clothes, a slouch hat with the brim turned down and a belted coat of gray wool, and well-shined black shoes, a thin, sallow-faced man with a

recessive chin, sitting on a wood chair in the yard, indo-
lently crossing his legs and leaning forward to rest on one
elbow while pointing with his cigarette some of us one
way some of us the other way, I in the instant of his attention remanded to labor, at a trot in a company of males to a
disrobing shed, and there given to cover my nakedness
with the striped pajamas stained with dry sweat and
smelling of death, and then to queue up for the dispensary
for the almost considerate tattooing of my numbers on the
skin of the inner forearm above the wrist at a ceramicized
metal table the astonishing color of white, and then in the
chill black dawn to stand in ranks in the yard and be given
to contemplate those who had been enslaved to their
shame to the state of beasts, and shouted and driven naked
past us one way, then later seen pressed on to another station farther away, and then seen with difficulty in the bleak
gray light going off again a greater distance away, receding in some urgency, their spectacles having been carefully
lifted from them, and their valises and knapsacks loaded
on wagons, and their dropped clothes carefully stacked,
and the billows of black smoke later attesting to the ex-
plicable wartime industry behind our inexplicable destinies, I deduced that there is no God though there is a
Hell, and that if not today then tomorrow I would be with
those pushed and crowded into the cement-walled chambers, and at the moment of understanding I had arrived
at the termination point, hear the iron doors clang shut, and
the bolts sent home, a shout from the outside carrying into
the air-tight darkness the deadly instruction, leaving me to
scream in the screams from the sealed blackness as the
first hisses of the gas from the shower heads abrades the
eyes, and slithers down the throat and clamps its fangs into
the lungs, a heart-bursting suffocation perceived as a few
minutes of the usual day's work, no more than the sound

of the machinery to the ears of the efficient guards shaking their heads in some disgust at the tenacity of these Jews still kicking, trying to tear the claws from their throats, the spasming energies of their sucked heaving lung-shredded breaths a sound like the files drawn across metal, the grindings of a metal shop . . . until finally the last heart having burst mid-cry the valve is shut and the bolts are pulled back and the doors swung open, and the silent dead, piled in poses of clawing comically inelegant desperation, are removed and flattened even if the bones have to be broken, stacked neatly twenty to a sledge, and taken to the next station, where others receive them and shear off the hair and bundle and sack the hair, and knock the teeth out of the heads and pull the rings off fingers or sometimes cut off the ring fingers, still others flense the skin of the younger hairless ones, lift sheets of skin from the back and buttocks and thighs, in all diligent industry disassembling these stiffened dead into salvageable by-products, and the mutilated remains then slid from long-handled pallets into the furnaces, where they flare, blacken, wheeze, sing, explode, and crumble to ash, which others, later, sift for the overlooked unburnable appointments like miners panning for gold, and the billows of black smoke that darkened the sky have settled over the nearby village where the muttering hausfraus have learned to dry their wash indoors and peevish elders grumble in their daily *spaziergangen* that the grease-blackened cobblestones make walking hazardous . . .

By order: A manifest of property collections in accord with the directive of the Reichsleiter by which the Institute for the Exploration of the Jewish Question is to establish a museum for the acquisition, inventory and exhibition of items of Judaic historic or anthropological interest such as archives and libraries, religious artifacts, productions of folk art, and all personal property of intrinsic value.

The crating and despatch via military transport of all such property is simultaneous with the removal of the Jewish source populations from each of the 153 cities, townships and villages of the Protectorate (Directives 1051, 1052). This assures the accurate attribution of inventory according to region and province, heretofore a particularly complex undertaking given the increasing volume, on a daily basis, of received materials.

Numbers of each item are not supplied, being provisional: Torah (Pentateuch) parchment scrolls handwritten, Torah scroll mantles silk, Torah scroll mantles velvet, Torah scroll vestments hammered and engraved silver, Torah scroll crowns engraved chased silver with semi-precious stones, Torah scroll valances silk, Torah scroll valances silk velvet, Torah text pointers silver, Torah text pointers wood, Torah text pointers silver or wood in the shape of small hands with index finger extended, Torah finials engraved silver, Torah finials gilt leaf, Torah binders silk, Torah binders linen, Torah curtains silk, Torah curtains silk velvet, Torah curtains velvet, prayer shawls silk, prayer shawls linen, prayer shawls silk gold-embroidered, prayer shawls silk silver-embroidered, prayer books daily, prayer books holiday, books midrash (theology), candelabra silver, candelabra brass, mezuzot (door amulets) carved wood, mezuzot leather, Hanukkah (holiday) lamps silver, Hanukkah lamps pewter, Hanukkah lamps brass, dreidlach (children's spinning tops) wood, dreidlach cast lead, keys synagogue, "eternal" lights pewter, "eternal" lights brass, readers' desks oak, readers' desks pine, lecterns oak, lecterns pine, combs burial society, ewers burial society, shroud cloths burial society, uniforms burial society, banners trade guild, flags trade guild, synagogue ark lions rampant carved wood, synagogue ark lions rampant carved wood painted, alms boxes wood, alms boxes copper, alms boxes silver-plated, skull caps velvet, skull caps silk, wedding rings gold, engagement rings silver and diamond, ceremonial wedding dishes silver, ceremonial tankards silver, salvers silver, place settings china, place settings silver, serving bowls, cups, saucers crockery, cooking pots iron, cooking pots enameled, kettles iron, skillets iron, cutlery steel, tools carpentry, implements farm, portraits men oil on canvas, portraits women oil on canvas, portraits children oil on canvas, hand-colored photographs bride and groom, hand-colored photographs children, hand-colored photographs family groups, country scenes oil on canvas, country scenes watercolor on paper, cameras, typewriters, book sets uniform binding, books individual, books reference, books art, sheet music bound, sheet music unbound, music instruments stringed, music instruments woodwind, music instruments brass, music instruments percussion, surgical instruments steel, surgical instruments chrome steel, music records, record players mechanical, record players electric, radios console, radios table, rugs, furniture upholstered, furniture wood, furniture wood and cane, bedsteads wood, bedsteads brass, mattresses horsehair, quilts, duvets, pillows down, pillows cotton, washbasins ceramic, washbasins pewter, evening clothes men, evening clothes women, coats men, coats women, suits men, dresses women, wallets leather, purses leather, purses beaded, school uniforms boys, school uniforms girls, combs, cosmetics, hairpins, barrettes, shoes women, notions women, pipes, cigarette cases, cigar cutters, shoes men, shoes children, binoculars, opera glasses, eyeglasses, watches wrist, watches pocket, hearing trumpets, inkstands, pens nibbed, pens fountain, stationery plain, stationery embossed, walking sticks wood, walking sticks wood and silver, chess men ivory, chess men wood, pull toys children, dolls children, board games children, wagons children, snow sleds children, books children, paint sets children, pencil boxes with pencils children.

Mother's Day
by Joy Fielding

Susan Lichtman is sitting in the crowded reception area of the orthodontist's office. She is waiting for her daughter, Nicki, to arrive, even though Nicki's last words out the door this morning were to forget it, she had no intention of letting anyone put braces on her teeth, and that no one could make her. Not even her mother. *Especially* not her mother, Susan thinks now, the emphasis hers.

She checks her watch. Almost four o'clock. Still a few minutes before Nicki's scheduled appointment. Even if she does show up, Susan recognizes, she'll be late. Nicki is always late, unlike her mother, who is always early. Susan smiles at the receptionist, who doesn't seem to notice. The unfamiliar young woman, whose tight mass of angry black curls mimics the pinched expression on her face, is busy on the phone. What happened to the regular receptionist? Susan wonders, recalling that woman's placid blond exterior, the calm, somehow reassuring set of her nondescript features.

"What happened to Judy?" she hears herself ask. The room stills. Eyes peek out from behind old magazines. Everyone waits.

The receptionist puts down the phone. "She left," she says. A slight shuffling of feet, then silence returns. Clearly the young woman will say no more. Eyes drift back to old magazines.

Susan feels a twinge of anger, perhaps even a slight stab of betrayal. She wishes that Judy had given some advance warning of her departure. She finds it disconcerting the way people just suddenly disappear from your life. She doesn't like it.

Like that poor woman she's been reading about in the morning papers, the one who called her daughters to tell them she was on her way home from work, only to vanish without a trace. Weeks now, and not a word, not a clue what happened to her, although police suspect foul play. Just . . . gone.

She stares toward the reception room door, willing it to open and Nicki to walk through. But Nicki has been remarkably resistant to her mother's will of late, and the door stays firmly closed. Are all fifteen-year-old girls so stubborn? So argumentative? So headstrong? So reason-proof? What happened to the little girl whose love for her mother was once so all-encompassing, whose every glance was filled with sweet and total admiration? Now whenever Nicki deigns to look her way, it is through eyes heavy-lidded with disgust, as if she is overwhelmed that this woman so out of touch with reality, this archaic, irrelevant holdover from the dark ages, could actually be her *mother*. Surely someone, somewhere, has made a terrible mistake.

The mistakes are all hers, Susan acknowledges silently. She's the one who is either too lenient or too strict, too inquisitive or too disinterested, too old-fashioned or too trendy, too much or too little. Too angry. Too protective. Too moody. Too intense. Too tired. Whatever she can be, she's too much of it, except for the one thing all the books say mothers should be—consistent. Unless consistently inconsistent counts for something, she thinks hopefully.

Not like her own mother.

Susan's eyes automatically brim with tears, as they do every time she thinks of the mother she lost to cancer just months after Nicki was born. So beautiful. So patient. So instinctively correct in everything she said and did. What would she think of the mother her daughter had become? What advice would she give her? How would she have handled the increasingly challenging young woman her infant grandchild had grown into?

As if on cue, the door to the reception area opens and Nicki sweeps through. Nicki always sweeps. She moves as if there is a camera following her, recording her every gesture, her eyes on guarded alert for the camera's telltale red light that signals she is "on." Susan watches in awe of her daughter's total self-absorption as Nicki removes her jacket and hangs it up, fluffs her long brown hair in the small mirror next to the coat rack, then retrieves a magazine from the coffee table in the middle of the room. She has yet to acknowledge her mother's presence.

"Hi, sweet thing," Susan whispers as Nicki occupies the seat beside her.

She hears a grunt, close-mouthed, barely audible. Maybe "Hi," maybe not. Nicki stares straight ahead, then without warning flicks her hair away from her shoulders, absently whipping it across the side of her mother's cheek.

"Ow! Watch that," her mother says, a touch too loud.

Nicki's entire body tenses, her soft features hardening into a sullen mask. Not here two minutes, Susan thinks, and I've already managed to offend her. She wonders only briefly why it's her daughter who's angry when she's the one who's been hurt.

"How was your day?" Susan asks.

"Fine."

"Anything interesting happen?"

"No."

"Did you get your math test back?"

"No."

Susan envisions herself a lonely scavenger pecking at barren rocks, searching for nourishment. "So," she ventures, undeterred, "nothing interesting to tell me?"

"I'm not getting braces."

Serves her right for asking, Susan thinks, the smile freezing on her face. "Well, why don't we wait until you've had a chance to talk to the dentist . . . ?"

"I'm not getting braces. They're ugly. They'll hurt. I'll look ridiculous. End of discussion."

"Some discussion."

Nicki opens her magazine and pretends to be reading. It is Susan's turn to stare straight ahead. The discussion is over. She has been dismissed.

Was she ever this dismissive of her own mother? Could she possibly have treated her with such casual disdain? And how had her mother reacted when faced with such rudeness? How had she handled her difficult daughter? What had she said to her? What would she say to her now?

Susan closes her eyes, sees her mother. Smells her. Longs to rush into her arms. She was a tall woman with the classical features of Greta Garbo and the wicked glint of Lucille Ball. Her hair, always her crowning glory, regularly changed from brown to blond to red and back to blond, from long to short, from style to style, depending on her frame of mind. No matter what she did to it, it always looked terrific. Once a week she visited the hairdresser, and, miraculously, it stayed exactly as it had been set until her next appointment, unlike Susan's hair, which often looks as if it has been styled in a Cuisinart.

She was a naturally slim woman who didn't believe in diets, and ate whatever she pleased. Occasionally she ex-

ercised with Jack LaLanne in front of her TV. Susan remembers watching transfixed one morning as her mother
stood naked in front of her full-length bedroom mirror,
snarling at her stomach. "I hate you," she said, grasping
the stubborn bulge of flesh. "Go away. I hate you."

"Your stomach's fine," Susan had protested from the
sidelines, unable to understand her mother's dismay. She
was married and a mother, wasn't she? What difference
did it make that she had a stomach? Who cared? Who
would ever look? She was *old,* for heaven's sake. Almost
fifty. What she was so upset about?

Her mother would have been younger then than Susan is
now, she realizes, unconsciously patting her own stomach,
kept in check by a strict low-fat diet and a library of Jane
Fonda videocassettes. In many ways her body is remarkably similar to her mother's. It is only her temperament
that is different. Why couldn't she have inherited her
mother's calm, her wisdom? Susan twists in the narrow
seat, unable to find a comfortable position. Why is it that
her mother always knew the right thing to say? Why is it
that she never does?

Susan opens her eyes and looks over at her daughter,
who is dressed all in black. Nicki is seemingly engrossed
in an article about Cher's latest tattoos. Susan thinks she
should be grateful that Nicki hasn't expressed a similar inclination, or come home from school with her nose pierced
or her head shaved. Or drunk. Or stoned. Or pregnant.

"What?" Nicki asks without even turning her head.

"What?" Susan repeats dully, feeling guilty, as if Nicki
has somehow reached inside her brain.

"You're staring at me."

Susan tries to think of something clever to say, something
that will bring a smile to Nicki's mouth, a conspiratorial

twinkle to her eyes, but nothing comes and she lapses into silence.

In fact, there have been no problems at all about drinking or drugs or boys. Nicki doesn't even date yet, undoubtedly a source of consternation to Nicki but one of great relief to her mother. At almost six feet tall, Nicki's height is a mystery to the entire family, and no doubt a sufficient deterrent to most would-be suitors. ("Do you realize that most boys my age are short and ugly?" she once complained when Susan picked her up after a school dance. "It doesn't get much better," Susan commiserated. "They get fat and bald.") And they'd laughed together, something they rarely seemed to do these days.

In the distance Susan hears her own mother laugh. She sees herself at nine years old, running home from school with pigtails flying to regale her mother with her first dirty joke. ("And the thunder rolled over the mountains, and the little boy ran in the cave," Susan hears the child recite triumphantly, still able to recall the punch line though not what preceded it.) And then, tears of laughter streaming down her mother's cheeks, they'd settled in, side by side, as they did every lunchtime, for half an hour of *Search for Tomorrow* and *Guiding Light*.

Her friends all envied her. "Your mother's so different," they invariably said. "There was no one like your mother," they commented after her death.

Why was she different? What had made her so special?

That she never asked for help with the dishes? That she never nagged about homework? That she didn't believe in setting curfews? That she rarely lost her temper, almost never yelled? Was it as simple, and as superficial, as that?

The woman was hardly Pollyanna, although she occasionally embarrassed Susan with her almost juvenile sense of enthusiasm and ribald sense of humor. She was certainly not Betty Crocker. She hated housework, cooking even more; she once made a chicken pie and forgot to put in the chicken.

Perhaps it was because her mother was so comfortable with herself that it was so comfortable being with her. Her honesty was never mean-spirited. When she was angry, everyone knew it. But no one feared it. She didn't play games, play coy, play dirty. She never took advantage of her age, her height, her power. Just because her daughter was small, she never made her feel that way. And as Susan matured, her mother continued to treat her with unfailing respect and support. She never tried to be her daughter's best friend, but only, always, her mother. And because her mother trusted her, she learned to trust herself.

When did she lose that? Susan wonders now. When had that part of her wandered off and disappeared?

"Nicki Lichtman?"

Nicki and Susan Lichtman turn as one toward the voice. A cross-eyed young woman in a starched white uniform over faded blue jeans stares vaguely in their direction, a clipboard in her hands.

"Nicki Lichtman?" she repeats, checking the name against her list.

"Here," Nicki replies, her hand rising into the air before she self-consciously returns it to her side.

The cross-eyed young woman swivels on her heels out of the reception area, clearly expecting Nicki to follow. Nicki doesn't move.

"I'm gonna look ugly," she whispers, desperation clinging to each word.

Susan reaches out to stroke her daughter's hair. "I guess it doesn't help much to know that your mother thinks you're beautiful, no matter what."

Nicki permits herself a sad smile. Then she pushes herself out of her chair and walks toward the inner office, her shoulders thrust back in proud defiance, as if she is about to face down a firing squad.

It's so hard being young, Susan thinks, recalling how awkward she herself had been at fifteen, how serious, how fragile. Is it possible she actually has a daughter that age? It doesn't seem fair. She isn't prepared for this change in her status. It's all happened too fast.

She remembers the day she found out she was pregnant, how thrilled she'd been, how she couldn't wait to share the news with her mother. And yet the instant she heard her mother's hello, she knew her news would have to wait.

"What's wrong?" she asked, holding her breath.

For a few seconds her mother said nothing, then, "The doctor called. The X rays show the cancer has spread."

The air turned cold around her. "What does that mean?" Susan asked, seeing her breath suspended before her, hearing her voice hollow, like an empty tin can.

It meant her mother was dying.

It meant that the cancer that had first manifested itself four years earlier as a lump in her left breast, then spread the following year to several lymph nodes in her neck, had now reached its ugly tentacles into her lungs and spine. It meant that it was only a question of time. Maybe a year. Maybe not.

It meant she was becoming a mother just as she was losing her own.

She called her mother back that night, told her the news, listened to her laugh and cry with joy, heard her promise that she would be all right. And for a few months it looked as if the radiation was keeping the cancer at bay; her mother even felt well enough to try a few weeks in Florida. "I actually went bicycle riding today," she reported happily one evening, and Susan had patted her growing stomach reassuringly. Her mother would be all right.

And then the call that said her mother had collapsed while walking on the beach, the flight back home, the news that the cancer had spread to her brain. A new round of treatments. "I'll lose my hair," her mother said, the only time throughout her ordeal that Susan saw her cry. Her beautiful hair, Susan thought. Her beautiful mother.

"I love you," Susan said.

"I love you, sweet thing," her mother said. "I'll be all right. I promise."

She said the same thing just days before she died, the infant Nicki lying propped in her arms. "She's so beautiful," she said. "Even more beautiful than *my* babies." The ultimate compliment. Susan had never loved her more. And when she died, Susan understood that she had lost her cheering section, that she would never be happy in quite the same way again.

But wasn't it supposed to get easier with time? Weren't fifteen years long enough to dull at least part of the pain? Why does she feel as lost now as she did then? Why can't she be half the mother that her mother was? Why does she always fall so short of the mark? Why can't she ever measure up?

Susan thinks again of the woman who recently disappeared and the three frightened and confused daughters she left behind. How lost they must feel, how lonely, how abandoned. How helpless. How betrayed.

They are the ones, after all, who were supposed to leave. Isn't part of their job as children to grow up and leave home? To spread their wings and fly away? Isn't that what daughters are supposed to do? And aren't mothers supposed to watch from the sidelines, shouting words of encouragement as they take flight, silently praying that their daughters land safely, trusting that they've taught them how? As her own mother had done. As she was trying to do now.

Susan becomes aware of movement beside her. She watches as Nicki emerges from the inner office. She holds her breath. "Nicki?" she begins tentatively. "How'd it go, sweet thing?"

Nicki's mouth opens in a wide, frozen grimace. Susan sees a flash of white teeth, nothing more, before Nicki's mouth clamps shut.

"What happened?" Susan asks, approaching cautiously. "Didn't he put them on?" Was her fifteen-year-old daughter such an intimidating force that she had managed to persuade the orthodontist not to go ahead with the scheduled braces?

"They're white!" Nicki laughs happily, reopening her mouth just long enough for her mother to have a peek at the row of porcelain braces that stretch across her top row of teeth. "I can't believe you didn't notice them!"

"I didn't," Susan admits, laughing now as well.

"Let me see again," Nicki says, sweeping toward the small mirror on the wall, tossing her long brown hair away from her face.

Mirror, mirror, on the wall, Susan recites silently, watching her daughter as she examines her mouth from a variety of angles. How beautiful she is. How grown-up she is becoming. How ready to burst free of her cocoon, to take flight. To soar.

Susan draws in a deep breath, her eyes once again filling with tears. Her daughter is going away from her, she understands in that moment. And her mother is never coming back.

"Have we missed *The Young and the Restless*?" Nicki asks.

Susan checks her watch, takes a surreptitious swipe at

her tears. "If we hurry, we can still catch the last twenty minutes."

They start for the door. Suddenly Nicki stops. "You really think I look all right?"

"I think you look lovely."

"You're not just saying that because you're my mother?"

"I'm not just saying it because I'm your mother."

Nicki smiles, then pulls open the door and sweeps through.

"Hey, wait for me," Susan calls after her. But if Nicki hears her, she makes no such acknowledgment. She is already halfway down the corridor, her hair swinging carelessly from side to side, her eyes on the alert for the red light of the camera.

Paranoia
by Stephen Frey

Scene 1

"**Y**our horoscope says you should be *extremely* cautious today. I don't think walking out onto Wall Street is a good idea. There's a huge crowd. You'll be terribly exposed to an assassination attempt."

Senator-elect John Ashworth leaned down. At six five he was more than a foot taller than his wife, and because of the difference in height had not heard her words over the din of trading on the New York Stock Exchange. "What, Emmy?"

Emily Ashworth glanced suspiciously at the Secret Service agents leading them slowly through the controlled chaos on the exchange floor, then motioned for her husband to put his ear to her lips. "My psychic says we need to be very careful for the next few days. She feels we're in danger and that we should stay away from crowds. I don't think we ought to walk down Wall Street as your aides have planned."

Ashworth smiled and shook his head. Emmy had been so worried about an attack lately, her distress stemming from a dream she claimed to have had a week ago in which both of them were shot to death by a lone gunman as they made their way through an unruly mob. But she was always having those kinds of dreams. Always paying pitiful attention to psychics, palm readers, and horoscopes. "Are you kidding me, Emmy? There are probably fifty thousand voters outside, all waiting to get a glimpse of me." Ashworth paused. "This whole day has been perfectly scripted." He gestured around the huge trading room to make his point. "It's been a wonderful P.R. opportunity with all the cameras and pictures of me with senior Exchange and Federal Reserve officials. And we're going to finish it by showing everyone that I'm a man of the people," he said gregariously. "That I'm strong and not afraid to wade into a crowd and shake a few hands." Ashworth held his wife's frail arm tightly. "Everything will be fine, Emmy. Don't worry."

Emily's heart rate accelerated slightly, and she felt an eerie tingling sensation in her fingertips. She was far from convinced everything would be fine but said nothing more.

As they walked from the massive trading floor and into the Exchange's Wall Street lobby, Emily suddenly pried her arm free of Ashworth's grip and moved to a large painting depicting a busy nineteenth-century day on New York City's waterfront. She stood before the painting for several moments, then, moving her hand in a clockwise direction, beginning at the upper left of the canvas, touched each corner of the frame twice. The ritual finished, she darted self-consciously back to her husband and clasped his large arm with both of her tiny hands.

The Secret Service agent in charge of security rolled his eyes behind the sunglasses he had just donned. Emily Ashworth. What a piece of work. Obsessive-compulsive and superstitious beyond comprehension. Being Senator Ashworth's head of security wasn't going to be an easy tour of duty.

As the group moved out onto Wall Street, a great cheer arose from the assembled masses lining the streets and hanging out of skyscraper windows. John Ashworth had

been a hugely popular two-term governor of New York before being swept down to Washington on a populist tide.
As Ashworth hesitated on the steps of the Exchange for a
moment, waving warmly to fifty thousand of his closest
friends, Emily's heart began to pound frantically.

"This is not right," she murmured into the arm of his
gray wool suit jacket, shaking her head vigorously. "Not
right at all."

Bruce Shelby leaned over her shoulder from his position
behind the couple. "Look happy, Mrs. Ashworth," he
growled through clenched teeth. "You must look happy. It's
critical. Many of these people are watching you, not the
senator." Shelby was already referring to Ashworth as senator even though he wouldn't be officially sworn in to office
for several weeks.

Emily gave Shelby a quick, cold stare. He had been Ashworth's chief of staff for what seemed like forever. She had
tried many times over the years to have him relieved of his
responsibilities, but to no avail. "I'll be fine." She turned
back around and lifted her arm hesitantly, finally forcing
herself to wave the hand that now seemed so far away from
her body.

Senator-elect Ashworth descended the steps and began
walking east, toward Federal Hall, where he would deliver
a short address. The crowd, confined to the sidewalk
on the north side of Wall Street—a surprisingly narrow
thoroughfare—cheered and screamed from behind blue
sawhorse barricades and a thin line of city police officers.
Ashworth smiled broadly, enjoying the attention.

Suddenly he spotted a young Hispanic girl being pushed
roughly against the barricades by an unexpected surge of
the crowd. He sensed the photo opportunity and immediately threw caution to the wind, dropping Emily's arm and

bolting through the ring of Secret Service agents to the young girl's aid.

For Emily the pace of action turned to slow motion. She watched in horror as her husband moved sluggishly across the asphalt, pulled several people in the throng away from the young girl, and lifted her over the barricade to safety. Admirers smiled and reached out to touch him. Suddenly Emily seemed able to distinctly follow the actions of the individuals near him, as if her vision had become a collection of separate lenses, each focused on a single person in the crowd.

And then she saw him through one of the lenses. A young man dressed in dark pants, a suede jacket and a Yankees baseball cap, the brim pulled far down over his eyes. He was reaching into a large pocket of his jacket, fumbling for something. She recognized him immediately. This was the man in her dream. The one who had been sent to kill them. Suddenly everything raced back to real time.

Emily ran screaming toward her husband, pointing at the young thug as he dug furiously into his pocket. Secret Service men tore after her, and policemen instinctively drew weapons at the sound of commotion as the scene turned chaotic. The sight of guns drawn instantly threw the crowd into panic. Some people dropped to their knees and covered their faces with arms and hands. Some poured over the barricades toward the thin blue line. Still others sprinted away wildly, knocking over the weak in their attempt to escape.

In the confusion Emily lost sight of the assassin for a split second, then spotted him once more. He was pointing his weapon at her husband. "There!" she screamed. "The one in the cap. With the gun. Get him!"

Instantly, four events transpired in distinct but rapid succession. Emily heard the sharp crack of gunfire. She saw the young man cartwheel backward as if he'd been hit by a truck. She and Ashworth were forced roughly into the backseat of a limousine that had screeched up to the scene from out of nowhere. And then they were hurled against the backseat—several Secret Service men literally on top of them—as the huge black car sped away amidst screams from the crowd.

Scene 2

The Ashworths, originally from upstate New York, owned homes in Buffalo, Albany, and Washington, D.C., but maintained no residence in New York City. When they visited Gotham, they typically sojourned in the nine-room Fifth Avenue penthouse apartment of oil baron and close friend Roger Van Stern. But tonight they were staying at the Plaza Hotel. Ashworth's itinerary had originally called for him to travel to Washington after the now aborted address from the Federal Building steps. However, because of the unfortunate Wall Street incident, he had decided to remain in the city and, Stern being unavailable on such short notice, the staff had hastily arranged for the Plaza suite.

The senator-elect slumped down in a large wing chair in the living room of the suite, staring silently out the window into cold December darkness. Emily sat beside him in an identical chair a few feet away, staring at her hands clasped tightly in her lap. Her knuckles were whiter than the early winter snow dusting Central Park just outside the window.

Emily rose from the chair, moved to the bedroom, then to its large walk-in closet, where she made certain the ten pairs of shoes she had brought with her were arranged perfectly—highest heels to the far left, then ordered by descending heel height all the way to her flats on the far right. She leaned down to straighten a loafer that was violating the perfect symmetry of the line, then returned to the living room after picking up her astrology guide from the nightstand.

As Emily retook the seat next to her husband, the suite door opened and Bruce Shelby entered the room. He moved directly to the senator-elect without acknowledging Emily, bent down, and began whispering in Ashworth's ear. Ashworth nodded several times dejectedly, then brought his hands to his face and shook his head. Shelby straightened up, gave Emily an odious glance, turned around, and exited the luxurious room.

For several minutes Ashworth rubbed his eyes, then finally allowed his hands to drop to his lap and gazed at his wife. "Emmy," his voice was barely audible, "we need to talk."

"What is it?" The astrology guide dropped from her hand to the carpeted floor, but she barely noticed.

Ashworth inhaled heavily. "The police shot the young man you identified this afternoon down on Wall Street." He stressed the word *identified* as if he wanted to use another verb but hadn't out of decorum. "A rookie officer discharged his weapon."

Emily nodded several times. "The officer should be commended for acting so quickly. You could have been killed, John." She let out a long sigh. "I don't know what I'd do without you, sweetheart."

"Emily!" Ashworth's tone turned quickly unpleasant as he abandoned the pet name by which he typically addressed her.

"What?" she asked meekly.

"The young man was killed." The senator's voice was hushed.

"Oh, no." Tears welled in Emily's eyes. "That's awful. But you have to remember, he meant to kill you. It sounds so terrible to say, John, but better him than you."

"He was unarmed." Ashworth slammed his palm down on the chair arm, stood, and stalked to the window. "The gun you thought you saw was nothing more than a high-tech camera. He was a photographer for the *New York Times*."

She hesitated. "No, there was a gun. I saw it."

"You saw a camera!" Ashworth screamed, no longer able to control his anger. "A young man is dead because of your inane, irrational paranoia." He passed both hands through his distinguished gray hair. "You need help, Emmy. The drinking has gone out of control again. For all I know, you were drunk this afternoon."

She rose from the chair and moved to him, placing her dainty fingers on his back. "John, I wasn't—"

"There's nothing you can say, Emmy." Ashworth turned to face his wife, gripping both her upper arms firmly with his large hands. He stared down at her. "You need help. You and I both know it." He glanced at the door. "So does Bruce."

"He doesn't know anything," she hissed.

"We need to focus on damage control right now." Ashworth ignored Emily's obvious hatred of Shelby. "Tomorrow morning the papers will be screaming about your performance. About how you had a man killed because you panicked. And they'll start digging. They'll find out about your therapy four years ago. About how you almost tried to commit suicide."

"It wasn't suic—"

"Silence!" Ashworth held up his hand.

Dutifully she shut her mouth. Her husband would not accept the fact that the near drowning in their pool had been nothing more than an accident. It was too easy to use the incident as a manifestation of alcoholism. Too easy to use the incident against her to his advantage. And she knew her husband was a master at using others' mistakes to his advantage.

"Emmy, you must begin taking responsibility for your actions," he said ominously. "And you must realize I have to do what is best for my political career. I'm going to make full disclosure."

"What does that mean?" she whispered, suddenly petrified.

"It means I'm going to tell the press about your problem. It means you have to go back to Richmond for therapy."

"No, John, please." Tears instantly began streaming down her pale cheeks.

"There is no alternative, Emmy. Shelby and I have already made the decision. If we don't take this action immediately, the press and my political enemies will rip me to shreds. They'll say the whole affair was my fault. They'll attack my ability to lead. You know, if I can't even control my wife, how can I control anyone else? By sending you back to Richmond immediately, we address your problem and I avoid blame." He said the last few words to himself.

"Please don't make me go back," she pleaded.

"It's already arranged. You leave tonight so that my spin on today's awful event has instant credibility tomorrow morning when I face the press."

Emily began to object once more but saw in Ashworth's face that any further entreaty would be pointless. Quickly she turned and raced back to the bedroom's walk-in closet. She had a terrible feeling one of her shoes was out of place again.

Scene 3

"Ladies and gentlemen, the president of the United States of America!"

To thunderous bipartisan applause Richard Jamison

entered the House chamber from the rear of the room. Every few feet he paused to shake another hand as he slowly made his way toward the podium to deliver the first state of the union address of his second term.

Finally he reached the dais and faced the full complement of senators, representatives, Supreme Court justices, cabinet members, and invited guests. For a full eight minutes he stood before the throng, basking in the bright lights and admiration of a nation as the applause continued unabated. And each time he motioned for quiet, the cheering intensified and another broad smile brightened his face.

As Jamison stood before the country, absolutely confident of his place in history now that the second election was over, he allowed himself the privilege of acknowledging the power he wielded as president. Before him was arguably the most important gathering in the world. The most influential lawmakers, judges, civic leaders, and captains of industry on the face of the earth—all assembled in one room. The state of the union address was a truly awesome event, and *he* was the focal point. Of everyone in the chamber, he was the most powerful. A shiver raced up Jamison's spine as he suddenly realized how much he would miss this when the second term was over four years from now.

Senator John Ashworth enthusiastically joined in the applause from his seat at the back of the chamber—the area from which all freshman members watched their first state of the union in person. He smiled as President Jamison once more motioned for quiet and was again met with a raucous reply. Ashworth had led a political life for many years now and was not easily impressed or driven to sincere emotion, but the awesome agglomeration of power—and the realization that he was part of it—was intoxicating, and he indulged himself by uncharacteristically throwing both fists in the air and cheering at the top of his lungs along with the other freshman legislators.

Scene 4

"I just want to tell you again, Emily, I think we made great progress in the last six weeks." Angela Holt guided her Jaguar off Interstate 64 and onto the Richmond airport exit ramp. "I know you didn't want to come to the hospital again"—Angela reached across the seat and patted Emily's knee gently as the car glided to a stop at the bottom of the ramp—"but now you can see it was all worthwhile."

Emily smiled tightly but said nothing as she stared through the windshield into the icy February night. Six weeks at the Dole Clinic for Alcohol and Drug Rehabilitation had done nothing except cause her to question even more seriously her own sanity. But somehow Emily had convinced her husband, the doctors, and Angela—her personal therapist—that she had improved. So, on the proviso that she return for another six weeks in April, they were allowing her a furlough.

"You are flying to New York tonight, right?" Angela gunned the car out onto the airport road.

"Yes," Emily replied quietly. "I'm meeting an old roommate from Smith College there. We're going to spend a few days in the city, then travel through Europe. I should enjoy myself immensely." She exaggerated the sincerity in her tone, knowing Angela was listening for it. Emily was well aware that Angela and her husband had arranged this long European vacation to keep her away from Washington and out of harm's way.

"It should be wonderful," Angela commented.

"Oh, yes. I can't wait to see London in February," Emily

said contemptuously. She cursed herself, but the tone and the words had slipped out involuntarily.

Angela glanced at Emily and raised an eyebrow. She had heard the sarcasm. "What airline are you flying?" Her voice bore sudden suspicion.

"Northeast Express."

"Uh-huh." For a moment Angela considered returning Emily to the hospital. However, that would interrupt all the arrangements, and Senator Ashworth might be upset.

The Jaguar pulled smoothly to a stop in front of the Northeast Express counter, and the two women stepped out of the car. Angela opened the trunk, and two red caps quickly unloaded Emily's baggage and wheeled it away.

"Well, good luck." Angela, a tall, angular woman, smiled down at Emily. "We'll see you in a few months."

"Okay." Emily gave her therapist a quick reassuring hug, then turned and moved briskly into the terminal, scarf pulled up over her head.

Angela watched the senator's wife disappear into the terminal, suddenly uncertain any progress had been made in the last six weeks. But there was nothing she could do now. Ashworth wanted Emily in Europe. Angela shrugged her shoulders, pulled the fur coat tightly around her, got back in the car, and drove away.

Emily noticed the man immediately. He was swarthy with jet black hair streaked by gray, a dark five o'clock shadow, and an olive complexion. As he stood waiting in the ticket line, he shifted nervously from foot to foot, glancing constantly about. At one point during the wait Emily came very close to the man as the line snaked back and forth, and she noticed that he seemed to be perspiring profusely despite the chill pervading the terminal. But the dark man produced a picture identification at the counter and was issued a boarding pass. Emily watched closely as he hurried off toward the lavatory.

"Ticket, please." The thin, balding man behind the counter smiled at her.

Emily produced the ticket, still watching the dark man move away.

"Mrs. Jones, could I see a picture identification?"

Emily handed the forged driver's license to the attendant. Senate spouses were not afforded Secret Service protection, so the service made available a full "alternative ID package" that Emily had been only too happy to accept. She also took their advice on staying out of first-class so as not to attract attention. One could never be too careful in these times, they had warned at a training session only days after the election, and she wholeheartedly agreed.

"Has anyone you don't know asked you to carry a package for them onto the plane?"

Emily shook her head.

"Very good, Mrs. Jones. Here is your driver's license back and your boarding pass. The flight to LaGuardia will be leaving from gate twelve tonight. Have a pleasant flight."

Emily nodded, stuffed the license and boarding pass into her purse, and hurried away toward the gate.

Only one X-ray machine was operating, and the line seemed unusually long. As a large woman attempted for the third time to pass through without setting off the alarm, Emily groaned and turned around. The dark man stood immediately behind her, his cold black eyes gazing directly into hers. Involuntarily she brought a hand to her mouth and looked away. God, perspiration was pouring from his forehead, and he appeared to be under intense stress, as if he was terribly worried about something or hadn't slept in days. He must be sick, or perhaps strung out on drugs. In any case he shouldn't be getting on a plane. Couldn't airport security see that?

Emily passed quickly through the metal detector without incident, but hesitated as she reached to pick up her purse just now inching through the X-ray machine on the black conveyor belt. She snuck a quick glance at the dark man as he took a deep breath before walking through the metal detector, then moved through it, careful not to make eye contact with the security guard. Instantly the alarm began beeping loudly. The man shook his head, then emptied his pockets of change and passed through the detector a second time. This time he did not trip the alarm.

Emily snatched her purse from the conveyor belt and walked quickly away toward gate twelve, hoping desperately that the dark man would not be on her flight to LaGuardia. There was something wrong about him. Something more than just the perspiration and strung-out appearance. She couldn't put her finger on it, but somehow he permeated evil. For a moment she considered calling her psychic, then remembered the woman was on vacation.

Smoke filled Emily's lungs, and she held it inside longer than normal. It was her first cigarette in six weeks—they were forbidden at the clinic—and it was heaven. Finally she exhaled, then took another long drag from the Marlboro as she scoured the gate's waiting area. But he was nowhere in sight. Slowly she began to relax. She closed her eyes and leaned back. Everything would be fine. After all, what were the odds he would be on her flight?

As Emily opened her eyes again, the dark man walked past her and sat down three seats away. A strong scent of body odor wafted to her nostrils, and her upper lip curled. He was going to be on her flight. There were no other imminent departures at any nearby gates.

The burning cigarette shook wildly in Emily's fingers as

she tried to plot a course of action. She could miss the flight and take the first plane out tomorrow morning. But then her friend waiting at LaGuardia would call Angela and her husband, and they would all decide that missing the plane signaled a lack of improvement—that she was still suffering from rampant paranoia—and they would force her back to the hospital immediately. That was clear. She would stay out of the hospital at any cost. Even if it meant getting on the plane with the dark man.

Emily stole another quick glance at the man. He was still perspiring, and his hands trembled as he held a book open in front of him. She focused on the pages and realized the words were written in a foreign language—not one she recognized immediately. Emily was fluent in French, Italian, and German—a result of her advantaged prep school upbringing—and she realized instantly that the writing was not European. She looked again. Arabic, wasn't it? Oh, God. She sucked on the cigarette as if she would pull the tobacco through the filter. Of course. He was a terrorist. The realization surged through her, and her mouth ran dry.

"We will now begin boarding flight 1210 bound for New York's LaGuardia Airport." A stewardess made the announcement from behind a small podium near the jetway's entrance. "First-class passengers, Gold Club members, and anyone needing extra time are welcome to board at this time. Everyone else please wait until I have called your row number."

Emily's eyes were riveted to the dark man. At the sound of the stewardess's voice he had stuffed his book back into a knapsack. She shook her head and felt tears spilling from her eyes. She was going down in a massive fireball. The horrible image was crystal clear.

"Rows fifteen and higher may now board."

The dark man stood. Emily looked quickly down at her seat assignment—16D. God help me, please.

She buried her face in her hands, then took a deep breath. She was paranoid. They were right. There was no reason to be afraid. He was just another passenger on another flight to New York City. Not a man with Middle Eastern connections who meant to blow the plane to small fragments in midair.

Emily allowed herself one more look at his eyes. The pupils were so large and black and cold. Like a shark's eyes. She recoiled. Sharks were such horrid creatures. She had never entered the ocean because of them. They were blood-lust creatures. Vicious predators, just like this man. She turned away and tried to take a last drag from the cigarette, but it fell from her shaking fingers and tumbled to the floor. She stamped it out with her heel, then reached for the plastic cup on the seat beside her and in one swallow finished what remained of the scotch and water she had purchased at the airport bar.

A fat man moving toward his seat in the back of the plane grazed Emily's shoulder as she sat rigidly in her aisle seat, staring down at the purse in her lap. It took some people so damn long to get to their seats. God, she wanted this flight to be over, and these inconsiderate morons were taking forever to board.

"Excuse me."

Emily did not bother looking up. She recognized the voice without ever having heard it before. It was fate. That was the only explanation. Dutifully she swung her knees to the side, allowing him access to the window seat.

Before moving past her the dark man reached up to stow his knapsack in the overhead bin. As he did, his leather jacket swung slightly open.

Emily's eyes opened wide in horror. In the moment the

jacket parted she had seen the shoulder holster and the gun nestled within. Perhaps it had been hidden for him in a lavatory past the metal detector. Perhaps it was plastic and hadn't tripped the detector on his second pass through. Of course. That was why he had been perspiring so badly. He was packing a weapon. Her heart beat furiously now and her breath became short. She had to tell someone.

The dark man pushed past her knees—his jeans scraping against her stockings—then sank into his seat. His body odor misted down on her again, and she turned her head instinctively. "Steward," she called, raising her hand.

The young man nodded, finished helping another passenger with a bag, then moved toward Emily, smiling. "What can I do for you, ma'am?"

She swallowed as she stared into his youthful eyes, wondering what to do. If she said something and she was wrong—if the dark man wasn't really carrying a weapon— word of the incident would make its way back to her husband and there would be hell to pay, perhaps even another beating.

"Ma'am?"

"Can I get something to drink?" she asked quickly. "A scotch and water would be wonderful."

The steward shook his head, still smiling. "I'm sorry. Only first-class passengers are allowed a pre-takeoff drink."

Emily grabbed his arm. "Please."

"I really can't." He patted her hand and moved away.

She stole a quick glance at the dark man. He was no longer perspiring. She shut her eyes tightly.

Eleven minutes into the flight, the plane passed over Fredericksburg, a small city located halfway between Richmond and Washington. There, as it reached an altitude of exactly twenty thousand feet above sea level, the altimeter sent an electric pulse to the detonator and a small bomb exploded inside the cargo bay of the Boeing 737, blowing a tiny hole in the side of the fuselage. A tiny hole big enough to bring the plane down if it remained aloft too long.

Emily's eyes opened for the first time since the plane had left the ground. She had felt the gentle jolt, as if they had suddenly hit a pocket of unfriendly air. She glanced quickly at the steward, but he seemed unconcerned as he served drinks.

The terrorist smiled as he too felt the jolt. The bomb had exploded exactly as planned. Only fifty miles away the United States president was in the middle of his state of the union address. In attendance were both houses of Congress, the Supreme Court, the cabinet, and many other VIPs. It was the most inviting target he and his rogue group could possibly imagine. When the flight was done, he would be dead, but so would most of America's leaders. It was a sacrifice worth making. He would be immortalized by his comrades for this act of ultimate bravery.

"Ladies and gentlemen, this is the captain." The voice was dead calm, reflecting no agitation. "We've developed a tiny little problem up here in the cockpit."

Emily swallowed and her fingers curled around the ends of the armrests. Suddenly she had a very bad feeling.

"It's nothing to worry about," the captain continued, trying hard to reassure his passengers. "Some of our instruments are giving us strange readings. The plane is fine. It continues to operate normally, but as a precaution we're going to land at National Airport in Washington."

A collective groan arose from the passengers.

"Not to worry, we'll get you to New York just as soon as possible. I'll be back to you in a few minutes with more details."

The young steward passed Emily on his way to the back

of the plane. She grabbed his arm and he leaned down. "What is it, ma'am?" he asked.

"Does this have anything to do with the jolt I felt a few minutes ago?" she whispered.

The steward shook his head. "What jolt?"

It was a stupid question, she realized. He wouldn't admit to anything even if he knew. "Why are we going to National?"

"What do you mean?" He seemed sincerely puzzled at the inquiry.

"It's after ten at night. National closes no later than nine for noise reasons."

"I believe that's true, but I don't understand why you are concerned."

"If there's nothing really wrong, we should divert out west to Dulles or east to Baltimore–Washington International. The problem must be worse than the captain is letting on if we have to get down so fast."

The steward took her hand. "Everything is fine. Just stay calm, okay?"

Emily didn't respond for a few moments. The dark man seated next to her had a gun. Somehow she knew he was connected to the jolt. She knew it with all of her soul. She had to tell the steward. She had to save herself. Finally she nodded and the steward moved away. John was down there, so close, attending to his first state of the union address. At least he wouldn't be able to blame this on her.

"You really think it was a bomb?" The first officer eased the plane into a gentle turn to west, setting up their approach to National Airport.

"Yes," the captain answered tersely. "I know it was. Fortunately, it didn't take us down, but the structural damage might be severe. We could still break up if the damage was bad enough. We've got to get this thing on the ground as quickly as possible. Make your turns wide and gentle. We want as little pressure on the plane as possible."

The first officer inhaled deeply and nodded. He had never heard fear in the captain's voice despite flying through violent weather with him several times. But he heard it now.

Emily did not take her eyes from the dark man. He was leaning forward, one hand on the seat in front of him, the other on the armrest, his eyes constantly in motion, constantly glancing about. He was obviously agitated, obviously bearing some terrible secret. And then she looked down at the unoccupied seat between them. Lying there was a copy of the *Washington Post* the dark man had been reading. Circled in black magic marker was a story concerning the president's state of the union address. Her gaze rose slowly back to the dark man's face. He was staring back at her now. A slight, almost indistinguishable smile turned the corners of his evil mouth. Or was it simply her imagination?

Slowly he reached down, picked up the paper, and stuffed it into the seat pocket.

Emily's mouth hung open for a moment as she turned and sat back in the seat. Was that it? Was he going to take over the plane and fly it into the Capitol during the president's speech? Or was it simply paranoia?

The terrorist took several short breaths to sedate his nerves, furtively glancing at his nemesis as he performed the calming exercise. The act would have to occur quickly and smoothly. First, he would neutralize the cockpit so the captain and first officer could not alert ground control as to what was transpiring. Then he would do the same to the cabin to take out his nemesis and any other would-be hero. But he would need a diversion. He turned to the window. Through the clear plastic he identified the dark ribbon twisting through the lights of suburban Washington below them as the Potomac—a landmark the pilot would follow straight to the runway constructed on the shores of the famous river. The plane was close. It was almost time.

Emily's pulse pounded so loudly in her ears she could barely hear the jet engines screaming just outside. The plane had been diverted to National Airport so this man could fly it straight into the Capitol and kill or maim those attending the state of the union. Her psychic had told her so many times to heed her intuition. Ashworth had told her so many times to ignore it. If she said nothing, he might die. But then so many *innocent* people would die as well.

She hated him, she now realized, with every fiber of her being. For his willingness to sacrifice her for his career. For his wanton neglect over the years. For his physical abuse. She wanted him to die. She grabbed her hair with both hands and pulled hard, inflicting sharp pain. But then all of the others would die too.

The dark man stood up, hunched forward beneath the overhead bins.

Emily saw his move instantly.

"I need to go to the bathroom," he growled at her. "Get out of my way."

Her heart suddenly felt as if it would explode in her chest. This was it. She knew it beyond a shadow of a doubt. "They made an announcement." The sides of her throat grabbed at the words. "They said not to leave our seats until we landed."

The man moved toward her. "I said, get out of my way."

Emily swallowed. It was now or never. A young photographer lay dead because she had been certain he was carrying a weapon, certain he was trying to kill her husband. Would this be another grave mistake?

The dark man forced his jeans against her knees.

She stared up into the black eyes.

"Move," he hissed.

"He's got a gun!" Emily pointed at the dark man as she screamed the words over and over.

The cabin turned instantly to chaos as the steward and three passengers grabbed for the dark man. People cowered behind seats or tumbled over them as the struggle ensued. Finally the heroes wrestled the dark man to the aisle and took the gun from the shoulder holster.

"Get off me, get the hell off me," he yelled like a wildman. "I'm FBI. I'm FBI!"

The heros relented, and the agent was able to struggle to a sitting position. But it was too late. The terrorist had already taken full advantage of the diversion. During the struggle he had moved smoothly up the aisle, jimmied open the cockpit door, opened the canister of deadly gas, thrown it inside, and shut the door. It had taken him less than four seconds to perform the maneuver, and the two aviators were already dead.

"It's him you want." The agent pointed at the terrorist now donning his gas mask just outside the closed cockpit door. "I've been following him for days."

Suddenly the plane banked to the left, throwing passengers and luggage into the aisle. But the terrorist had anticipated the movement, knowing the pilots were dead. He braced himself against the lavatory door, pulled a second canister from his bag, opened it, threw it into the aisle, and disappeared into the cockpit.

The gas reached Emily's nostrils almost immediately. Her brain recognized it as foreign and instinctively did not allow her to breathe. But it didn't matter. The toxic vapors entered through the pores of her skin, and she felt herself drifting off. If only she had heeded her intuition and stayed in Richmond. If only.

Seconds later everyone in the cabin was dead.

The terrorist unstrapped the pilot, pulled him out of the seat, and slipped behind the controls. "May day, May day," he yelled into the radio. "This is Northeast Express bound for LaGuardia."

"National tower. What's the problem, Northeast Express?" The voice at the other end was strained.

"I am not the original pilot of this flight. I'm an off-duty Northeast pilot. Both pilot and first officer are unconscious. I'm going to bring this thing down the best I can."

"Thank God you're there," the tower voice screamed. "We're with you all the way."

The terrorist smiled. He was the only one left alive on the plane, and no one on the ground knew. There would be no jets scrambled to shoot him down. No antiaircraft fire from the White House roof. Just clear sailing to the Capitol.

Scene 5

The fifteen-year-old boy sat in his Bronx bedroom admiring the sleek 9mm pistol. In the commotion on Wall Street he had pulled it from the outstretched hand of the man in the Yankee hat who lay prone on the sidewalk after being clipped by the police bullet. The boy grinned. No one had seen him slip the gun in his pocket and melt into the crowd. The headlines had all screamed about the man who was shot being unarmed, but the boy knew the truth. However, the gun had already come in handy—he had shot two rival gang members with it—and he wasn't about to tell anyone what he knew.

"God help us!"

The boy heard his father's voice and hurried out into the

sparsely furnished living room. A huge orange fireball covered the television screen.

"What is it, Dad?"

The father shook his head. "An airliner just crashed into the Capitol. The president is dead."

The Price of Tea
in China
by Eileen Goudge

"Gardenias have always made me think of your father."
The fan-back wicker chair in which my mother is sitting creaks delicately as she leans toward the stone planter at her feet to caress an ivory petal between her thumb and forefinger. Its scent is released into the summer afternoon, sweet and somehow tangible, even a bit fussy, reminiscent of lace-edged hankies and rustling taffeta. "Can't you just picture it, Lydia . . . a bowl of gardenias on every table?"

I want to say that too many gardenias, even in the ballroom of the Wentworth Hotel—where three months from now our family and friends will gather to celebrate my parents' golden wedding anniversary—might be cloying, not to mention monotonous. But a knowing smile is already rearranging the intricate lines and creases that over the years have made of Mother's once flawless face a faded Renaissance fresco with patches of pentimento peeking through.

In the large Spanish–style house she and my father have shared for thirty-five of their nearly fifty years of marriage, a black-and-white Hollywood–style studio portrait of my mother as a wet-lipped ingenue, circa 1940, hangs framed on the stucco wall over the fireplace. Other than that, you would never guess what pride she once took in her beauty. No face lift or eye tuck for Margaret Pierce; at seventy-four, she would no sooner go under the knife for the sake of appearing five or six years younger than buy a dress simply because it was marked down. The same goes for reinforced undergarments, costly moisturizers holding out the promise of eternal youth, and hair rinses the various burnished hues of expensive luggage. "I'd rather look ancient," she'd sniff, "than pathetic."

Mother is a prime specimen of what most women claim to want even while desperately doing everything within their grasp to prevent it: growing old gracefully. Only traces remain of the ashy-lidded glamour queen over the fireplace that made a mockery of my own crabbed, self-conscious crawl toward womanhood. Her weathered beauty has taken on a kind of monolithic status more akin to Mount Rushmore than Rita Hayworth.

Those qualities of grace and apparent sincerity, however, only deepen the puzzle that is my mother, who can still make my eyes water, as when I'm stripping paint from an old set of dresser drawers, with her stubborn resistance to anything resembling the truth.

Like this business of my father and the gardenias. I know what she's going to say before she says it. I also know it will be almost entirely fiction.

"When Daddy and I were dating back in college," Mother recalls in a faintly singsong voice that rises and falls like her looping signature, which is as lovely as it is illegible, "both times he took me to his fraternity's big spring dance, he brought me a gardenia corsage. Not orchid. Much too showy for his taste. And orchids have no scent." She smiles. "Isn't that just like Daddy?"

I happen to agree, but for reasons entirely apart from my mother's. So I bite the inside of my lip to keep from sniping, *It's only because gardenias are cheaper.* Mother, you see, subscribes to a peculiar value system. Not satisfied with merely enduring my father's inveterate stinginess, she

actually *glorifies* it. An otherwise budget-conscious trip to
Europe is made thrilling and picturesque by a succession of
"cozy" side-street *pensiones* that their less adventurous
(and more unstinting) contemporaries would turn their
noses up at in favor of the Savoy and George V. And thanks
to my mother's sewing skills, her I. Magnin charge card remains tucked away in her wallet, virginal as the bride who
fifty years ago stitched her own wedding dress. My parents
hardly ever go out to dinner, either, though they can well
afford it. Mother, you see, among her many accomplishments, also happens to be an excellent cook.

"I guess a few gardenias here and there wouldn't hurt," I
mutter. There's no point in arguing with my mother, since
she's always right, and never less than watertight in her
opinions, even when appearing to solicit yours. "Have you
spoken to Dad about it?"

"Your father's leaving all the arrangements to me," she
replies with an indulgent little shake of her softly waving
silver hair, as if to say, *You know how hopeless men are at
this sort of thing.* Her smile deepens into something just
shy of serene. Only at the corners of her mouth, where the
patented smile I associate with my father has grown trem-
bly and threadbare, do I catch just a glimmer of yearning—
that of a neglected wife who has worked so hard at
spin-doctoring her husband's image in the eyes of her
friends, and, yes, even her children, she has no energy left
to devote to her own needs.

What I know is that my father, though retired from the
accounting firm he founded and made a success of, is too
caught up in other business to give more than a cursory nod
to anything like this. Business having to do with Mrs. Conrad three doors down. Dating back to when I first spotted
the two of them in what my sister and I as teenagers would

have called a "heavy clinch," I'd say the affair with Bernadette Conrad has been going on close to eight years. But, of
course, I would no more reveal this poisonous secret than
plunge a dagger in my mother's heart. So I merely nod and
offer up a wan smile, feeling slightly sick to my stomach,
like someone nursing a chronic ulcer.

"I'd be happy to give you a hand," I volunteer, feeling
vaguely guilty for reasons I can't quite pinpoint. "I'm taking
the whole month of August off, so if you need anything . . ."
I let the sentence trail off in a way that suggests I have all
kinds of free time, which truly isn't the case. Though I'm
not teaching this summer, I've finally begun writing the article for which I've been gathering research over the past
three years: on the love-hate relationship between Ernest
Hemingway and F. Scott Fitzgerald as manifested in *A
Moveable Feast*.

Not that I'd mind helping with party arrangements. It
just seems so hypocritical—a celebration, not of my parents' mutual devotion, but of one woman's triumph over
reality.

"There's all kinds of time . . . I've only just started
putting together the guest list." With a graceful wave of her
mottled hand, Mother rises from her chair to drift along the
patio's raised brick border, where she plucks at a row of unruly dwarf astors like a seamstress fussing with an uneven
hem. "There are the relatives, of course . . . except Uncle
Dick and Aunt Penny, they'll be in Vermont. And all our
friends. Emil and Joyce. Arthur and Gert. That nice couple
we met in Crete last year, you remember the Hathaways?
Oh, and I've decided to ask the Conrads."

I let this seemingly innocent remark hang in the air,
holding my breath for a count of two, as when my mother
sprays under the eaves for the black widows that nest there.
Mother and Mrs. Conrad haven't spoken in four years.

With my master's in English literature, and ten years of cramming classics down the throats of college freshmen more interested in having sex and surfing the Internet, the brightest response I can come up with is, "Oh?"

Mother cocks her head upward as the sun's brightness is momentarily dimmed by a nearly transparent cloud smudged across the sky like a thumb print on a windowpane. "It's easier than having to go into some long, drawn-out explanation when people ask," she sighs. "Well, *you* know."

In actual fact, I don't. To my knowledge, Mother has never given any sort of explanation as to why she no longer speaks to the woman she once counted among her closest friends. I vaguely remember hearing about a borrowed vase that was never returned . . . and something about Mrs. Conrad repeatedly insisting on them all going where *she* wanted that time my parents and the Conrads traveled to Italy together. In other words, nothing that should have amounted to more than a minor squabble.

"Your father was against it at first," Mother continues, her mouth pursing as if about to spit out something sourtasting. "I'll tell you something, even in the old days he never cared much for Bernadette. That woman is . . . well, bossy doesn't begin to cover it. But I convinced him it would be for the best."

I watch my mother as she putters about, awed by the staggering breadth of her self-deception. She yanks at a weed, pinches a leaf, looking every bit the magnificent wreck in the floppy straw hat she's clapped on her head to guard against the sun, and her gauzy cotton dress that floats at her freckled calves as she moves about the garden fiercely prodded into bloom by her throughout the long growing season that consists of spring, summer, fall, and a good part of the winter in the San Fernando Valley. It's the middle of July, and the tea roses that form bowers at either end of the lawn are still crazed with blooms. Hyacinth and honeysuckle and scarlet bougainvillea have made a painter's palette of the high board fence. And the tubs of gardenias that form fragrant islands alongside the path . . . well, their collective scent is enough to smother a newborn.

Suddenly, it's all more than I can bear. I mutter something about having to pick up a book at the library, promising to stop by some time in the next couple of weeks to see if there's anything she needs help with.

I hug her as I'm leaving, a bit too hard perhaps. I can feel the outline of her bones beneath flesh that has loosened its once firm grip, and skin the texture of old, expensive pigskin gloves. Without warning I blurt, "I love you, Mom."

"Well, of course you do," she replies, directing a fond, if somewhat befuddled smile at me, her errant daughter, who is forever insistent on things making sense. As I'm letting myself out through the back gate, she calls over her shoulder, "Oh, and Lydia? Your sister asked to borrow the big tablecloth for a dinner party she's having . . . it's in the bottom drawer of the dining room buffet. Would you mind dropping it off on your way home?"

I know what she really wants: for me to make up with Torey, who I've been avoiding ever since we argued over what my sister calls my "cavalier attitude" toward our mother. Mother has a sideways mode of communicating that makes a crossword puzzle out of every conversation. Even gifts come loaded with more double meaning than letter bombs. Like last year for my forty-fourth birthday, when she sent me that framed snapshot from the family archives of my brother pulling my sister and me in Torey's brand-new Flexi-Flyer. (I believe I was six at the time.) Mother had gone to some trouble. She'd had a five-by-seven print made of the negative, and attached to it was a card on which she'd written in her frail, sloping hand, "Remember what fun you girls had! Poor David had blisters from pulling you around in that thing."

I propped the photo by my bed—on the nightstand that had until just recently served as rest stop for my husband's Swiss army watch, braided leather key ring, inhaler, and pocket change, before Steve pulled up stakes and moved on to greener pastures in the form of his allergist's twenty-six-year-old receptionist—thinking, *how nice*. Mother, for once, had stopped to consider what a tough time I was having. Clearly, she wanted to remind me that if nothing else I would always have my family. Mother and Dad, Torey and David, *they* would never desert me as Steve had.

But as it turned out, that wasn't it at all. When I called to say thank you, my sister picked up the phone instead, informing me, sotto voce, that Mother was upset over my having begged off dinner several Sundays in a row. The photo was meant as a reminder that I had a family, all right. A family I had neglected. A family that was not suffering their fool of a daughter gladly. For after all (Torey was quick to remind me), had I listened to Mother way back when, I wouldn't have married that no-good Steve to begin with.

Now, as I make my way down the path that slips like a cool, shady creek alongside the house I grew up in, the house in which I learned to read between lines well before I could recite my ABC's, I'm looking forward to my parents' anniversary celebration with about as much enthusiasm as I would the inaugural ball of a banana republic dictator.

For the next month or so, whenever Mother calls, I have a ready, mostly truthful excuse for not popping over—computer meltdown, my cat needing to be taken to the vet, a desperate rush to get my fall classes scheduled. It's nearly September by the time I make the twenty-minute drive from Pasadena to help with the anniversary gala. By now the RSVP's are all in, the seating arrangements plotted, Maggie Pierce–style, on corkboard, with colored pins and construction paper cutouts marked with the guests' names. The orchestra has been hired, and the hotel's special events coordinator has long since collected the deposit check reluctantly written by my father. Nineteen floral arrangements prominently featuring gardenias have been ordered, one for each table.

Torey and I are meeting at our parents' house to put together a collage of family photos that will be mounted on poster board and displayed on an easel at the entrance to the ballroom. I agreed to this weeks ago, yet somehow I can't help feeling I've been set up. More to the point, as if I've sold out, handed over my freedom in exchange for a seat in the dictator's high council.

By the time I arrive, it's apparent that Torey has been at it for hours. Wearing a pair of oversize navy shorts, she's settled cross-legged on the living room sofa, sorting through a shoebox of photos, and I can't help thinking she looks a lot less like my sister than a detective sifting through evidence for clues as to how she and I could possibly be related. Torey inherited my father's green eyes and reddish-blond hair, while I have the dark looks of our mother, minus her elegance. My sister is younger than I by two years, but people often mistake her for being the oldest. It's all the weight she packed on with the twins; her "baby fat," she calls it, which she keeps swearing she'll take off. I don't know. The boys are ten, and the only thing wearing thin are Torey's excuses.

She holds up a black-and-white snapshot curling at the corners. "Hey, Lyd, check this out. Remember the time we all went to the zoo, when we were feeding the seals and Daddy wouldn't give us any more quarters for seal food? Look, there you are sulking."

"How do you know I'm sulking?" The skinny dark kid in the photo looks to me as if she's screwing her face up against the sun.

"You were *always* sulking in those days." She's careful to strike a teasing tone, but buried in it is a note that suggests my sulking days are far from over. Maybe she has a point, but only where she's concerned.

Mother sails in just then, grazing my cheek with a dry brushstroke of a kiss from her lipstick-free lips. "What are you two girls up to?" she chimes in a merry, mock-scolding voice, as if Torey and I, like the children in the snapshots spread over the coffee table and floor and sofa cushions, had stopped growing at the ages of eight and ten.

Torey dips into a pile that's sloping into the depression formed by her heavy bottom on the nubby sofa cushion, and holds up another, smaller photo. "Look, Mom, here's one of you and Dad with the Conrads. Do you still have those earrings? I would kill for those earrings. The other day I saw a pair just like it in an antique shop in Westwood Village."

I feel the blood drain from my face. Torey doesn't know about Dad and Mrs. Conrad. I never told her what I saw that day in front of Zuppa di Pesce—Dad kissing plump, bottle-blond Mrs. Conrad in a way that wasn't exactly neighborly. Not out of any desire to protect him, but because my sister wouldn't have believed me. She would have said I was imagining things, or that I was only making it up out of spite because I was still mad at Dad for missing my wedding.

Mother shrugs and begins tidying the already spotless room, which is comfy without being stuffy, a blend of beiges and off-whites brightened by splashes of vivid color. "Those? Who knows. I must have given them away at some point," she answers distractedly.

"But you save *everything,*" Torey objects, shoveling up a fistful of photos. "Look at all these, for goodness' sake."

"I save what counts." Mother straightens, turning to beam at us. To her credit, she's never openly favored Torey over me, though I'm sure the temptation must have been overwhelming at times.

My sister's eyes narrow as she takes another look at the Conrads and the Pierces in their evening duds, tanned arms draped about each other's shoulders in a slap-happy fashion that suggests one of the block parties the Conrads were always throwing. New Year's Eve? Or the Christmas Mr. Conrad got drunk and backed his car onto our lawn?

"So, Mom, are they really coming?" Torey knows the answer, she's just fishing for details.

"It's been long enough," Mother answers cryptically, her tone making it clear there will be no further discussion of the subject.

Torey isn't getting the hint, though. "Whatever happened with you and them, anyway? It's like they suddenly disappeared off the planet." I notice the rope-soled espadrilles on the carpet in front of her are splayed at the sides where her feet have spread. It's the little things that at odd times make me feel sorry for my sister, like her pretending the heat is the reason she's stopped wearing regular shoes.

"I have no quarrel with Gene." Mother's body tightens as if an invisible wing nut between her shoulder blades has been given a hard clockwise twist.

"What about *her*? Mrs. Conrad?" my sister persists.

"What about her?" Mother becomes suddenly absorbed in rearranging a vase of snapdragons on the mantel, while the youthful studio portrait on the wall above seems to regard her with heavy-lidded irony.

"I thought you two weren't speaking." Am I only imagining the sly look winking at the edges of Torey's innocent-seeming curiosity?

"We aren't."

"Is this your way of making up?"

"I should say not!" Mother shoots a look at us, clearly outraged at the suggestion.

"Well, honestly, I don't see the point of inviting her, then. Lydia might just as well ask Steve, for that matter."

I don't at all like the turn this conversation is taking. "I would appreciate very much your leaving Steve out of this, please," I respond with majestic disdain.

"What *I* would like to know," says Mother, enunciating each word as she swivels slowly to face us with a glint in her eyes that inspires in me a little shiver of hope that this time, amen Jesus, we are finally getting somewhere, "is what any of this has to do with the price of tea in China?"

That's when I recognize the glint for what it is: fool's gold. For years she's been using that expression as an escape hatch whenever the subject at hand comes too close to hitting a nerve. Such as: *What does that idiot boy's rudeness have to do with the price of tea in China? Look at the bright side, Lydia. There are plenty more where he came from.* Or (on the phone with Aunt Sarah): *I heard you the first time, and it's pointless even to discuss it. What does Joe going to San Francisco without me have to do with the price of tea in China?*

My sister finally gets the hint and shuts up. A minute later, she hoists herself from the sofa and heads into the kitchen, her bare soles slapping against the Mexican tiles our mother laid herself with the help of only their Filipino handyman. "Any of that chicken left over from last night?" she calls.

"Oodles. Your dad never made it home for dinner." Mother waves the gnarled hand of a Grimm's fairy-tale witch, dusted with gold pollen. But a witch who could easily be a queen under a sorcerer's evil spell. "He was out late with his golf buddies."

Golf buddies? Now, that is rich. With Steve it was always a business deal being wrapped up over dinner. Looking back, what's so amazing to me is that I never questioned him. Not once. Maybe I didn't want to know. Maybe ignorance is indeed bliss. Maybe I would have been better off like my mother, who is truly clueless except for some dogged instinct that keeps telling her something is wrong without telling her what it is.

Except I don't really believe I'd be better off not knowing. Even on those nights when I miss Steve so much I find myself switching on the TV at two in the morning just to keep from crying into my pillow, I know I'm better off this way. Ignorance isn't bliss. It's just another word for stupid.

What can my father possibly see in Bernadette Conrad? I wonder. My mother is graceful and pure of form; she wears her age like an heirloom. Mrs. Conrad is built like Torey, big-breasted and thick around the waist. She dyes her hair. She laughs too loud at parties. She smokes. Both her children, a boy and a girl I used to play with when we were little, grew up to be as pedestrian as their mother.

There is no justice in the world, I've decided, when a man frequently mistaken for Clint Eastwood, who, by the way, professes to adore his wife, can conduct a torrid eight-year affair with a chubby, Modern Maturity–set Gidget who wears orange nail polish and collects Fiestaware.

As the big event draws near, I find myself growing more and more apprehensive. Suppose this anniversary celebration is, in a cosmic sense, merely the vehicle for some darker purpose, at which point my father's secret will come spilling out into the open like a ruptured piñata. Even while I'm cringing at the idea, there's something almost laughable about the picture that forms in my mind: my parents' doddering friends and relatives gathering about in horror to watch my father and Mr. Conrad take turns at rearranging each other's bridgework.

Arriving at the Wentworth Hotel on the long-awaited night, I am relieved at not immediately finding the Conrads among the swarm of familiar faces. What strikes me at once is how absolutely lovely it all is. My mother has outdone herself; even the gardenias tucked into the shallow bowls of flowers on each table bring to the occasion a richly annotated touch. Candles, hundreds of candles, flicker all around us, imbuing the space with a sense of Arthurian drama, and lending a liquid sheen to the taffeta skirts Mother herself stitched for every table. Overhead, leafy boughs strung with ropes of faux pearls form a swagged canopy that makes me feel as if I'm in an enchanted garden. I half expect a flock of doves to burst from the greenery . . . but that would not have been Mother's style. She has an uncanny sense for when enough is enough.

She's chosen the sit-down menu with equal care— delicate tufts of lobster on plump pillows of pâté brise, pheasant consommé, roast loin of lamb daringly glazed in Chinese plum sauce, fresh berry tarts with green apple sorbet for dessert. Even Uncle Herbert, who spent most of his career as a civil engineer living abroad in colonial luxury, is impressed. Hard of hearing now, he leans across the table halfway through dinner and shouts that he hasn't eaten so well since the shah of Iran had him over for breakfast.

My brother, David, seated beside me at a round table for six, not only basks in the reflected glow, he radiates it back. Though I can't help noticing he's hardly touched his food, and is already on his fourth triple scotch. David is the kind of drunk who tends to slip between the cracks at functions like this; while around him, others might grow boisterous, he tends to sink further and further into himself. Middle-aged, with a receding hairline and ruddy jowls fixed in an expression of generic good cheer, not to mention his habit of nodding beatifically in response to even the most innocuous remarks, he has begun to remind me, disturbingly, of the Jack-in-the-Box clown.

Though we almost never discuss personal matters with one another, David once confided in me that the reason he never married was because he could never find a woman as tolerant as our mother. The truth is, Mother doesn't even know she's being tolerant with him. From her point of view, David is a wonderful son who likes having a good time at parties, and who only occasionally forgets her birthday.

After coffee and plates of teensy fluted cookies, the orchestra begins to play. Torey and her husband get up to dance. My sister is wearing her bridal gown, shortened to knee length and let out a few inches; her husband, Kurt, looking awkward in his tuxedo, offers her his arm while at the same time absently patting his cummerbund in search of the beeper he normally wears on his belt, a nervous habit of his. He makes me glad I never needed surgery at the hospital where Kurt is chief of anesthesiology. With his deep-set eyes and habit of blinking rapidly when he talks, my brother-in-law has always struck me as more than a little unstable. He and Torey have been together for eighteen years, and the worst thing my sister ever confessed, late one night after too many black Russians, was that if she ever had to go under the knife, she wouldn't trust Kurt either.

Mother and Dad are the first to reach the floor. The orchestra is playing "As Time Goes By," a song they danced to at their wedding half a century ago. They move in seamless unison, with a grace and rhythm that can't be taught, both of them slender, silver-haired, as perfectly matched as a pair of sterling candlesticks.

A lump forms in my throat, refusing to go down. Like a seasoned magician's act, the illusion is so convincing that for a moment I almost buy it: the fairy tale of their undying love, of husband and wife inextricably bound by trust and devotion. Suddenly, the reality my mother has woven for herself out of gossamer and moonbeams seems more solid than the lonely apartment I come home to every day, and the tinny voices that greet me from my answering machine. I look away, as if from a too-bright light, dabbing one eye with the corner of a napkin. Traitorously, the thought of Steve comes sneaking in. I miss him. Whatever he's done or is doing, goddamn it, I miss him.

"Get a load of that, will you?" murmurs David thickly in my ear. Following his gaze, I catch sight of portly Gene Conrad with his wife in tow, making straight for my parents. My breath bottles up in my throat. What is the man up to? It's the first time all night I've spotted either of the Conrads, but Mr. Conrad doesn't look as if he's about to erupt in violence. He's smiling. He . . . he's tapping Dad's shoulder, cutting in to take my mother's elbow with a stagey flourish.

"Do you think he knows?" I whisper to David as our former neighbor whirls Mother out of our father's orbit.

"Hell, yes. But he won't make a scene." Years ago, in one of my weaker moments, I confided to David about Dad and Mrs. Conrad. "The poor guy wouldn't dare."

"Why not? Dad is sleeping with his wife, for God's sake," I hiss.

David hoists his nearly empty glass. "Oh, I can think of a few reasons." His large head bobs sagely, only this time it's not because he's gone AWOL behind that glazed smile of his. There is pain in his eyes, the same blunted, lambent pain I once saw in those of a caged chimpanzee in the university's medical research laboratory. My brother knows what he's talking about.

All at once I'm remembering the blustery authority with which Mr. Conrad commandeered the wet bar in their living room. The dispatch with which he could whip up a bloody Mary at nine-thirty in the morning. And at the cocktail parties the Conrads frequently threw, the stance he would adopt at the bar, one heel hooked over the lowest rung of the stool on which he sat perched, while the other foot remained planted on the floor, ready to propel him forward to refresh a guest's drink . . . thus providing an excuse to refresh his own.

David is right; Gene Conrad will not be sharpening any axes tonight. Even from this distance I can see the well-worn look of apology on his aging stockbroker's face as he leads my mother in a stiff-gaited waltz that is painful to watch.

At the other end of the dance floor, Dad, ever the gentleman, is dancing with Mrs. Conrad. She is wearing a dress that makes her look like an easy chair upholstered in brocade satin, her peach-blond hair swept up to reveal a pair of rhinestone-studded earrings the size of coasters. Her eyes remain carefully averted from my father's . . . maybe too carefully. Are others noticing the studied gingerliness with which he holds her? Or am I just being paranoid?

I am struck anew by the absurdity of it all. What could he want with that cow? It couldn't be just the sex; Dad and Mother still share a bed, and she's made it clear to us on more than one occasion that it's not just out of habit.

I realize halfway through the waltz number that I'm still holding my breath. The danger is far from past, I think. There could still be a scene. I see Mrs. Conrad tripping a little in her high heels, trying to keep up with Dad's long-legged steps. Suppose, unable to contain her long pent-up feelings for him, she bursts into tears? Oh, God. All the years of intrigue, of guilt, of dropping her eyes as she and my mother silently wheeled their shopping carts past one another in Safeway. Worse, what if she's conniving to snag Dad? This could be her big chance to force things to a head.

Someone jostles my elbow. I turn to find Torey, flushed and breathless, wriggling back into her chair at our table. As my gaze is inexorably pulled back to the dance floor, I hear her remark casually under her breath, "Relax. Mom wouldn't see it for what it was if she happened to walk in on them in bed."

"You . . ." Shocked, I turn to confront my sister.

Torey shrugs. "I've known for years. Sometimes, like the other day, I test her . . . just to make sure. She never bites."

I let out my breath in a huge sigh. "Even if we said something, she wouldn't believe it."

That's when it hits me: there will be no scene, no grand denouement to this Feydeau farce. *We* are the ruptured piñata at this party celebrating my parents' golden anniversary, Torey, David, and I. Whatever the gene that enables my mother to spin her illusions, none of us has inherited it. Instead, we are forced to see only what is real, however ugly or painful that may be. Each in our own way, I think, has struggled to master the craft at which my mother is so supremely skilled. And in small, varied ways we've succeeded. David, afloat in his boozy twilight, and Torey with her small pretensions and coquettish vanities. Me, nursing my heartbreak and clinging to the memory of a husband who made a fool of me long before he abandoned me.

Watching my mother as she whirls back into the safety of my father's arms with hardly a break in her step—the Conrads falling away like a background dissolve in a film—I realize that I've kept my mouth shut all these years not for her sake so much as my own. My silence was the cost of admission to Mother's secret garden, and I, unlike Eve, having plucked from the tree of knowledge, was not about to share the apple with her. Being forced out of the garden would be worse than anything I could imagine. Or so I believed.

Now I'm not so sure. I think the price of tea in China might be more than I can afford.

The remainder of the evening goes exactly as I imagined it would. The expansive champagne toasts. The tide of love and well-wishes on which my parents are borne out into the night, where a full moon beams down like a papal blessing. The discreet black Town Car idling at the curb that will whisk them off to the airport, to their weekend at the seashore. Surprising us all, Dad had offered to take her to Hawaii for their second honeymoon; it was Mother who suggested the more sedate and accessible Balboa Island, where, she teases as she's stepping into the limo's backseat, you can get the same sunburn without spending a fortune.

Torey, David, and I wave goodbye from the curb. What's the point in telling her that Hawaii really is better? She wouldn't believe it. Besides, she's right about one thing: you can have fun anywhere.

It's all in how you look at it.

Six Shades of Black
by Joan Hess

In the beginning, as we were inclined to say when we were innocent children who demanded physical proof, who lived in a venue in which bushes didn't burn, the Holocaust never happened, and June Cleaver made meatloaf once a week, I believed there was only one shade of black. Black was black. A color easily and succinctly defined: the absence of light. I was enamored of the definition. I might not have been able to understand the essential nature of blue or yellow or red, but I understood black. Hadn't I found it in the sky at night and at the bottom of the river before dawn?

There's no way to gloss over the decade in which we, as an entire generation, were rudely nudged awake, and then inundated thereafter with the racial issues, the societal nuances, the reasons for all the unpleasantness that took place while I was at college. At that time there were no gradations of inequality, and we refused to concede any injustices we could define. Giddy with fervor, I participated in a demonstration or two, chanting, waving a sign, shrieking at the "pigs" to cart us away to the nearest dungeon where we could actually meet some dignified person of color and clasp our hands in solidarity.

The pigs didn't, possibly because we were armed with navy skirts and madras blazers, loafers, the right brand of socks, and whatever battle armor necessary to insure us that a parent would provide bail and make the charges vanish like a wisp of steam out of a teapot.

And the charges did vanish, of course. We waved the most outrageous signs, and the administration sighed. We screamed, we marched, we seized the buildings, and the administration sighed more plaintively and conducted a parental fund-raiser. We demanded publicity for those victims of discrimination, those outcasts, those swept under the carpet by the injustices of academia. And they sighed, did academia—as long as our parents paid the hefty tuition fees.

The day came, predating graduation, when it began to sink in—with or without lectures from our fathers—that perhaps we ought to reanalyze our perceptions, that we might reconsider the wisdom of marrying a nice boy with the right connections, a solid country club membership, a guaranteed wedding announcement in the *Times* (New York, not London).

In order to accomplish this, I donned panty hose and took a job with an advertising agency. They might not have hired me if my father hadn't promised to keep his gazillion-dollar account there, but I will argue to my dying day that they felt no actual pressure to hire me. I was imaginative, wasn't I? Didn't I suggest we market the Kitty Witty account with the slogan, "If it's good enough for you, it's okay for your cat"?

A slogan to die for, if I say so myself.

Frankly, I was good. A lot of my slogans may not have been aired that year, but the aging sexist pigs who were running the agency didn't always get it. The potbellied pig selling bacon may not have worked as well as I'd hoped, but I masterminded the memorable ad of the vermicelli on the fan. Innovative? I think so—and so did my father.

It was going well, for the most part, with me tossing out ideas and mostly getting tossed around like a turnip, when I met Brad.

Trumpets and fanfare? Why not? I still wonder. I was at a party, nothing that would warrant the gossip column, when I met Brad. Brad was perfect. I'd hoped, looking back, to find something else to say about him—that he was chic, daring, rebellious, a rebel with a cause, a toll booth operator on the yellow brick road. Alas, Brad was what he should have been.

He'd graduated that year from Harvard, not at the top of his class but respectably midway down. No law school was screaming for him, but neither was one squirming at the idea. Although initially we merely shacked up together (did I clarify that this was the seventies?), we agreed to put my career on hold in order to trundle him through law school.

So off we went to the Midwest to an alien milieu which neither of us ever understood. Brad was teaching a few undergraduate classes comprised of ninnies and asses, as he said, and I found a job at a factory. I won't burden you with the unsavory details, but the job involved the retrieval of internal organs of a lesser species. One summer we married. We did so to please my parents as much as anything, but Brad had suggested it and I was too tired to resist.

I sound as if this was a marriage without love, without commitment, without any sort of gratification. This was not so. I loved Brad, and he loved me. We spent what time we could together. When I discovered I was pregnant, Brad showed up on the line with an armful of roses and tickets to Aruba. A month later we wined and dined, walking the beaches and making up silly stories about our nonexistent children. The moonlight was a blessing on our child to be.

Brad was there for me when labor began, too. He'd attended all the Lamaze classes, perhaps more enthusiastically than I, and squeezed my hand every minute of the ordeal. He was committed to our child, and not, I think, in some sort of obscurely chauvinistic way. Brad wanted a child. He was obsessed with the concept of breeding a clone; he wanted to be a gentle, loving parent. His eyes literally watered at the idea of the PTA, scouts, soccer, piano lessons, and baseball. He knew the drill, as did I.

My parents determined that I was no longer to work, but this was not a problem. Brad graduated and found a job at a decent East Coast law firm. I joined the appropriate groups, volunteered what time I could, and had a second child. Having had a son and a daughter, Brad pointed out that we'd perfected reproduction and could retire with grace and style. He never had much of a sense of humor, so this may have been his finest line. Humor was not his strength.

But I sound as if I'm being critical, don't I? Brad was the husband all the other women sighed over, the one who coached soccer, cochaired the school Halloween carnival, served on the city council, and dedicated himself to the neighborhood crime watch. He mowed when no one else mowed. He raked and slaved over the greenspace surrounding the neighborhood pool, because, as he well knew, no one else would. A mere two years after we moved into the development, he was elected greenspace chairperson. It was a matter of months before he became chairperson of the property owners' association.

I was not deemed Lady Chairperson, but that would have been silly, wouldn't it? I was pregnant once again, and hardly able to handle politics as I strolled Braddie and Chelsea down the hill and around the pool. One would have thought a neighborhood fraught with stockbrokers and bankers might have produced a subculture of wives who stayed at home, but these stockbrokers and bankers were as likely to be women as men. Even when I encountered a potential friend, I found her as likely to whip out a cell phone as a disposable diaper.

At this point you think I'm ready to lapse into angst. Yes, I had a degree in marketing, as well as wealthy parents buying bonds so my children could attend any college on the East Coast that had adequate ivy. My in-laws were perfectly lovely. Not what I'd grown up with, mind you, but pleasant and willing to go home after no more than three or four days of cooing at their grandchildren.

Brad often worked late, but that's what junior members of the firm do. In my free time, which was defined by the moments when I could find a fifteen-year-old to baby-sit, I was busy with the obvious obligatories. Society does not function without committees, from the school library fundraiser to the art center annual gala. One dresses. One sacrifices. One must.

I suggested to Brad that three children had covered all bases, and then one. He agreed and discreetly endured a procedure that removed the burden of birth control from me. When I suggested we share a bottle of champagne to celebrate, it struck me that he was a tad surly, but I held my tongue.

Perhaps I should have clutched my tongue between my fingers and howled. A nice noise, don't you think? Primitive, evocative, haunting—all those wonderful literary descriptions of human anguish. The reality was that I was simply pissed, which is not a word that my parents or my sister (a psychotherapist) would condone. They, however, were all busily going about their business, while I pushed the damn stroller up and down the hillsides as if I were attempting to qualify for the Indianapolis 500. Ladies, start your strollers.

Motherhood had its charm, and I knew my contributions to the school and community were invaluable. My mailing lists were the envy of every organization in town. I was wooed by book and garden clubs. I rose to a position of prominence in the Junior League. But it was difficult not to wonder if I was missing something during that time.

Heavens no, I told myself on more than one or two or three occasions. I had every woman's true dream—not the silly fifties fantasy that I'd be wearing an apron and pulling out the pot roast when hubby came home, or the sixties fantasy that I'd be arriving home from the grueling day as CEO of some major corporation just as hubby pulled out that same pot roast. Or the seventies fantasy, for that matter, although this one was harder to define. Two oven mitts on the pan, two tired but delirious parents celebrating because, "She said her first word in French today."

I shouldn't be saying all this, should I? I've been warned to be discreet, and I do understand that word. Brad did, too. He and Alisha were very discreet that first year. Two associates at the law firm, working late, having meals at odd hours, finding reasons to stay in the city in order to be at work at the crack of dawn. As if the firm cracked a whip, I used to joke when he called to explain. "Crackle, snap, pop," he'd say, laughing. I was still laughing then.

Should I be laughing now?

Don't think for a moment that I disliked Alisha. There was nothing to dislike, despite a certain vapidity and a studied vagueness when it came to popular fiction and the newest discourse about raising one's children in what seemed to be an increasing swell of decadence and perversion. Brad was no more aware than she, despite my articulate analysis of the ever present dangers at the day-care center where I left the children.

Alisha was single. My friends and I did all we could to come up with appropriate suitors for her, not so much out of charitability as out of a sense of obligation. She needed a husband and all the security that came with the vows. What could be more fulfilling than to stand on the sidelines of a cold, wet soccer field a mere hour after dawn, cheering a child more often than not running the wrong direction, while one sipped coffee from a thermos and fretted about the school board's latest disastrous decision? This was reality, not some glamorized sit-com. This is what we deserved.

Did I say deserved?

Then I shall step back and regroup, as we used to say in the agency, and take a take from the consumer's point of view. How does one take a take? How does one ever sort out the ambiguous aspirations of the early seventies, when we were torn between June Cleaver and Modesty Blaise? To be or not to be—and be or not be what?

Brad and I joined the country club so that the children would blossom in the right milieu. I took up golf, chaired the junior tennis tournaments for four years in a row, and ran for the school board. Brad worked late, but he was in a position to gain partnership, and we were already sinking under the private school tuition. We discussed the possibility of my returning to work at the agency, but we both agreed this was impossible. At the peak, and this was only last spring, the children as a collective unit of transportation had eight music lessons a week, as well as fourteen practices (soccer overlapped with T-ball and basketball) and the various year-end recitals (piano, ballet, gymnastics, and, I seem to think, a program glorifying the sixth graders' graduation to junior high).

Brad missed many of these memorable moments, but always with cause. He worked very hard, as he was fond of reminding me, so that the children could enjoy the house, the pool, the Volvo, and all the various lessons and activities that enriched their lives and enhanced their self-esteem. I was able to attend the teacher conferences, after all. How many parents does it take to coo over a carefully colored map of the Balkan peninsula?

Thus far I've been describing paradise, but I must admit there were fleeting moments of dissatisfaction. One night Brad failed to warn me that he was staying in the city, and I was obliged at the last moment to find a baby-sitter so I could attend the school board meeting. A month later, he canceled our "second honeymoon" to Aruba because of a major in-house audit of billing records. Nothing was uncovered, of course, but I was somewhat disappointed that I'd missed ten days of beaches, gaudy drinks, and passionate sex in a bungalow beneath the palm trees. Brad was very stressed those days, however, and I sympathized. After all, we were married and had promised to love, honor, and obey till death us did part.

Which we did, for the most part. We never talked when Alisha was found killed in her pricy Manhattan apartment, shot in the chest and left to bleed to death all over that luscious Persian carpet. The police were ever so amazed that someone had a key to the building and slipped past the doorman without raising concern. Someone, I suppose, who looked as if she belonged there. A designer dress and understated mink might have done the trick, especially for someone with a key taken from a desk drawer.

Many demands are tolerable these days. Teachers want parental supervision regarding the current week's spelling list, and I have no problem with that. Piano teachers feel entitled to require an hour a day of practice, and soccer coaches act as if the universe might cease to exist if a single practice is missed. And so it might.

But when one's husband, who has never put a sock in a dirty laundry hamper, much less taken one out of a dryer, announces that his socks are mismatched because there are six shades of black . . . and furthermore, he will leave a pile of socks on the living room floor until the situation is corrected . . .

It's unfortunate that he will be present when the burglar breaks into our house on the one night that our children are staying with my parents and I'm at a school board meeting. A local-access television station will confirm my presence should proof be required. One does meet the most unsavory people if one tries, particularly if one has a checkbook and a certain amount of free time while children are deposited at various activities. All I can do is take comfort in knowing his socks will match at his funeral. I may be a bumbling incompetent, as Brad has told me time and again, but I know I can get the socks right for this significant occasion. Brad will soon be able to ascertain how many shades there are of eternity.

Most likely there are more than six.

The Naked Giant
by Wendy Hornsby

Where California Highway One passes through Big Sur, the roadway is nothing more than a two-lane shelf cut across the face of a vertical cliff that rises straight up from the Pacific. The terrain is stark and magnificent, and treacherous. There is little margin for error on the highway. And there is no escape route once the commitment has been made.

Three times a year between the summer after my twelfth birthday and the winter before my eighteenth, I rode this natural roller coaster with my father. Christmas, Easter, and summer vacations, Dad sprung me from Saint Agnes's Preparatory School for Young Ladies in Carmel-by-the-Sea, and drove me south through Big Sur to Los Angeles. Even then, before there was a freeway through the inland valley, Big Sur was the long way around.

I drove the highway by myself for the first time many years after those trips with my dad. Little seemed changed. Every rainy season, chunks of the road slide into the sea hundreds of feet below. The road department bridges the gaps or cuts deeper into the cliff face, making the trip a bit more harrowing every season; the sensation is something like heading blind into the abyss. But after thirty-two winters I still knew what I would find around every turning.

I slowed going into the curves, and punched the accelerator coming out, the way my dad taught me, letting the sideways thrust of gravity determine how fast was too fast. Pushing my husband Richard's new Mercedes to the very edge of control.

Coming out of Ragged Point, at the windingest part of the trip where the road also descends precipitously, I miscalculated the last hairpin and veered into the path of a Toyota van: sleeping bags and a tent tied to the roof, six sets of scared eyes staring at me through the windows. I yanked the wheel to the right, over-corrected. My tires—Richard's tires—ground into the shoulder, spitting gravel over the side into nothingness.

I was twenty-four inches from the edge when I stopped the car.

The jagged ridge of the Santa Lucia Range turns to the east at that point, and the terrain that lay ahead was a dramatic change from the wild Sur: rolling foothills covered with short grass, grazing cattle in the shade of live oak trees, now and then a farm building at the base of the hills. Atop a high peak in the distance, Hearst's Castle rose from a gray mist.

"The giant's castle," my father would always say when we reached that point. Always. "And there's the giant, fat and lazy as ever, sleeping the day away under his blanket. But tonight, before the moon rises, he'll wake up and he'll be powerfully hungry. 'Little girls,' he'll bellow. 'Bring me little girls with long black ponytails for my supper.' " Then, of course, Dad would flip up my long ponytail and make disgusting ogre noises.

Later, when I was too old for Dad's stories, I continued to see the giant lying beside the road. I can still see him.

The round, smooth contours of California's coastal hills give the giant his human shape. His velvet blanket is the short scrub grass that burns to a soft gold during the long, dry summer.

The summer I was twelve, I made the trip alone with my father for the first time. He drove a three-year-old Chrysler New Yorker. With my dad, it was always a Chrysler, but that New Yorker was a marvel: two-tone, desert pink on top, charcoal gray on the bottom, with a slash of pink along the tail fins. Eight feet of tail fins behind us. A trunk big enough to sleep a family of four.

We were a family of only three. And, shortly, not even that.

My mother hated the car, and let it be known that she wanted a new one. "Tail fins are passé, old hat, out. I'm embarrassed to be seen in that old bus."

Dad, stubborn in the face of change-for-change's sake, held out. A wonder of a car, he said, 435-cubic-inch-hemi-head engine purring under the hood. He couldn't replace the car because Chrysler didn't build them like that any-more. Perfect aerodynamics, heavy body, low center of gravity, took the curves of Highway One like a dream. Like a dream.

Dad and I came out of Ragged Point onto the straight-away, driving between the ocean and the rows of rolling coastal hills, making up the usual stories about the giant and his castle. I pretended to be bored by the stories, end-less variations on the giant's adventures we had made up on every trip for as long as I could remember. The only dif-ference that time was, for the first time, my mother wasn't with us.

I pretended to be bored by the old stories, but I wasn't. And Dad knew I wasn't. And I knew he knew. That was part of the game between us that summer.

"Ach!" He pointed to cows grazing on a grassy hillside. "The old boy has fleas in his bed like a dog."

Dad laughed in a wicked way when I said that a stand of live oak was curly hair on the giant's chest.

"Chest hair?" He was having way too much fun at my expense. "What happened to his blanket?"

I couldn't answer. I was at a particular age. The mere idea that the giant might have body hair, attractive body hair, was way too much to think about.

We drove on in silence, or relative silence. My dad whistled the melody of "Red Sails in the Sunset" and I whistled harmony, trilling the high notes the way he had taught me. I watched the landscape roll past my window at seventy miles an hour, the hills a liquid blur of gold.

I knew that if we stopped the car and went for a walk, the ground cover would be brittle, full of stickers like nasty little foxtails that hook into your socks and work their way into your shoes and won't come out. But through the window the grass looked smooth, translucent, delicate like the fuzz on a fresh peach held up to the sun. Or like the corner of my jaw where, in the sideview mirror, I could see downy hair in the sunlight. I put my hand against the warm window, and tried to imagine how the curve of the giant's blanket would feel. Everything I touched was deliciously smooth and warm.

The scene outside was so vast and so beautiful that my eyes could not take it all in. The scope of all that loveliness seemed to move into my chest, pressing tight like the elastic of the new bra my mother had forced upon me for the first time that very week. I knew the bra was punishment for knowing grown-up things.

My dad was still whistling. He had progressed to "Ode to Joy," and lost me after the first refrain. I listened to him, his true pitch, his elegant phrasing, while I made up my own story about the giant. This story I kept to myself because it was private, and it was scary.

The giant was no longer the grizzled ogre my dad always conjured up. The giant wasn't ugly at all anymore. And he certainly wasn't fat-bellied.

My giant was tall and slender and beautiful. His shoulder was broad, the tallest hill. The hill tapered into a valley, forming a lithe waist, then a mound rose to form his narrow hip. Rolls of land were the muscles of his long thighs.

I wanted to get the proportions just right, so I glanced down at my own skinny, sun-tanned thighs.

My eyes must have been dazzled, filled by the endless gold flying past. Because when I glanced down, my leg appeared to me to be exactly the color of the grass, and had the same downy texture. When I looked out again at the giant's thigh, I realized that he was lying there without any blanket at all.

"He *is* naked," I whispered.

"Who is?" Dad craned his neck, looking, I supposed, for a tramp.

"Never mind." I hunkered down in the seat and crossed my arms over the stiff peaks formed by the hated bra. When I looked up again, the giant's leg had segued into the next series of naked shoulder, waist, then hip and thighs, followed by another and another, naked giants stretching to the horizon.

Dad tugged my ponytail. "You okay?"

"I guess."

"Then be useful. I'm ready for 'Beautiful Dreamer.' You can do the melody this time if you'll sing loud enough."

I sang with him, my hand on my bare thigh, the skin hot from the sun coming through the side window, as we passed the endless naked giants lining the highway.

Somewhere near San Luis Obispo, the song ran out. For

a few moments there was no sound except the hum of the car's big motor.

"Rainey?" Dad's voice was so soft, so strange, that I sat up to see what he saw outside, expecting a red-tailed hawk in the sky—always a source for reverence. Only the same old red barn in the crook made by two round hills was out there.

"I have to pee," I said as I leaned back again, vaguely disappointed. "How much longer?"

"Can you hold it till Buellton?"

I said, "I guess."

"Rainey?"

"What?" Without much interest I looked out again. "What do you see?"

"Listen to me." He reached across the seat and took my hand. "You're an old girl now, Rainey. You understand what makes the world go 'round."

I eyed him with suspicion. Compliments about maturity, in my experience, usually meant I was going to be hit with something I wasn't ready for. They had already told me I was going to boarding school in the fall. If there was anything worse, I didn't want to hear it.

When he took a deep breath, building courage, I said, "Oh, look. A bald eagle."

"Bald eagles are extinct."

I slouched down, glared out the window. The giant was gone: farms and fields were all around us, the barren peaks of the mountains now far off to the left.

"You know, Rainey, things between your mom and me haven't been all hunky-dory lately."

I knew what was coming, but I did nothing to help him out. I had walked in on the truth.

"Mom and I think it would be best for all of us if Mom and I take a little breather from each other. My job keeps me down in L.A. so much, we thought I might as well get a place in the city." His voice caught. "Just for a while."

"How long?" I demanded. Dad hated to make people unhappy. I knew he would let the truth out way too slowly.

That little while he mentioned was going to stretch into forever, one week at a time, or one month at a time, and he would never come right out and say in so many words what the situation really was.

He used a lot of words to avoid saying what I needed to know. "We're going to have this week, Rainey, just you and me in my new place. We'll have one helluva vacation, put our own mark on the map of the city. Then right away, after this week, school starts. You'll be so busy at Saint Agnes's, getting used to a new school, you won't have time to think about your old mom and dad. Before you know it, it's Christmas. Your mother says you can spend Christmas with me. And then Easter. Turn around twice and it's summer. My new place is on the beach. Best place in the whole damn world for a kid to spend the summer."

"Hold on." I wouldn't look at him. "So, the only time I'll spend with Mom is Easter?"

"No, Rainey. You'll be with me for Easter, too."

"If I spend Christmas, Easter, and summer with you, when do I stay with Mom?"

He took too long answering for me to trust what he finally said. "Weekends, when she can manage it, she'll come down to Carmel to visit you."

"But when will I go see her? When will I go home?"

"Home is in L.A. now." His smile was too big, too phony. "See, kiddo, Mom's going through something right now, and, well, her schedule isn't as set as mine is. When she wants to see you, she'll come to you."

"This is why I'm being sent to boarding school, isn't it? You're getting a divorce."

He sighed. Some unpleasant things are so obvious there's no point trying to deny them.

I had not said a single word to anyone about what I knew. But Mom knew I knew, so I had to be shipped out.

My best friend and I had spent the month of July that year at a camp in the Sierra Nevada. I had worried about my mother being alone all that time, because my father was down south working the entire month. I was delighted when there was some horrible bacteria found in the mountain water the camp used, and we were all sent home a couple of days early. Somehow, my mother didn't get the message. She wasn't at the airport to meet me.

When my friend's parents dropped me off at my house, the morning newspaper was still on the driveway, meaning Mom wasn't up yet. As I walked in, I plotted a grand surprise entrance. I was too big to throw myself onto her bed the way I used to. I thought about getting out my clarinet and blowing reveille. I went to my parents' room.

Standing in the doorway, I could see my mother's outline recumbent under a soft, cream-colored blanket. Under the blanket next to her, there was a second set of mounds, tangled with her like an intersecting range of hills: a long, slender, broad-shouldered form.

The summer I turned twelve, I was too young to be the by-product of a broken marriage. The summer I turned fifty, I was too old.

My husband, Richard, was away on business the week before my birthday. He traveled often. When he was away, when he was home, for that matter, he was always considerate, always careful to reassure me that what happened to my parents would never happen to us. For my part, I made myself trust him.

Two days before my birthday, Richard called me to talk about the party he had planned to mark the end of my first half century, payback for the five years of old-age jokes and teasing I had meted out ever since he passed that particular milestone. He said it would be a roast, but I knew that he had actually planned something quite elegant. I had overheard him talking on the telephone one day a week earlier, ordering champagne and flowers. I heard him say candlelight and satin sheets.

Richard and I lived in a town house in San Francisco, and used the beach cottage in Carmel I had inherited from my mother for weekending: a small, romantic place she had bought so that we could have weekends together when I was at school. I overheard Richard order wine and flowers to be delivered to the beach house.

How sweet he was, I thought, to plan a romantic weekend. We'd had a rocky year. To use my dad's expression, things hadn't been all hunky-dory. Here was evidence that we had crossed the rough patch.

Richard would be tired after his business trip. I wanted to surprise him by driving down to Carmel ahead, have the house aired out and the bed made before he arrived. To chill the wine.

But the wine was chilled long before I arrived.

After Ragged Point, the highway drops onto a narrow coastal plain and runs along the ocean at very nearly the surf line. During winter storms, especially when the storms coincide with the annual high tide, waves sometimes break over the highway. Motorists have been swept right out to sea.

I pulled into a turnout at San Simeon and walked down to the water, carrying a bottle of Richard's champagne. Across the road, the remnants of William Randolph Hearst's zebra herd grazed among ordinary cattle. The cows were oblivious to their exotic colleagues, but drivers now and then, seeing what cannot be there, will run right up the back of the car in front of them. Or stop dead.

There was a small sandy beach, and beyond it tide pools like gnarled fingers of black rock extended many yards out into the surf. At the far edge of the tide pools, rafts of sea otters snacked on clams and crabs, floating on their backs in a kelp bed.

I sat on the sand and drank Richard's wine and watched the otters. About halfway through the bottle I began to sing, first "Red Sails in the Sunset," then "Beautiful Dreamer." There was no one to sing harmony, and I began to feel pathetic, sitting alone on the beach.

In all the years I had lived among the California hills, it had never occurred to me that the figure recumbent under the golden blanket of grass could be a woman. A giant woman. An insurmountable, endless young woman. Naked shoulders and narrow waist and round hips, long thighs, stretching to the horizon.

I did some quick arithmetic. When I had walked in and found my mother in bed beside Dr. Jacks, she was thirty-two. Dr. Jacks was fifty-three. Two years younger than Richard was now.

In the soft yellow morning light in my parents' bedroom, when Dr. Jacks pushed the blanket aside, he did not seem old to me. He was beautiful in a way I had never expected a man to be. My dad was handsome, but he was my dad: a big, hairy plaything. Dr. Jacks was like a marble god. All of a sudden my perception of the world changed radically. A lot of mysteries began to make sense.

Later, when Mom admitted to the fact of Dr. Jacks, sometimes he would come with her on weekend visits to Saint Agnes's. In full sunlight, lying on the beach in his little French swim trunks, he didn't look quite so wonderful to me as he had that first morning. His skin was old, and his abdomen wasn't only flat, it was caved in, and the bulge in the front of his trunks looked weird. But that first summer he was, to my mind, both handsome and fearsome.

Mrs. Jacks was the same age as her husband, give or take a couple of years. As were Richard and I. And the young thing making bumps under the satin sheets in my Carmel cottage? I hadn't stayed long enough to ask her age. There didn't seem much point in doing so.

Dr. Jacks and my mother lasted only a few years. After a while she started bringing someone new when she came to visit me on weekends. I believe it was during the second man, but maybe it was during the third, that she bought the beach house near my school in Carmel. If she had to drive down regularly, she said, she might as well be comfortable. Comfort and appearances vied for preeminence.

Dad would have appreciated the way Richard's new Mercedes handled. A fine car on a curve. Treacherous for the bank account, but a good car for the road.

Richard and I had argued over buying the car. I thought we should pay off his last one before buying a new one. It seemed to me perfectly reasonable that a person should hang on to a luxury car as long as the engine ran beautifully and the body was in reasonable condition. I guess that, like my father, I misunderstood what it was that made new better.

The last trip I took with my father through Big Sur was the June I graduated from Saint Agnes's. Dad was unusually quiet all the way down the coast. We sang, as always, but he didn't have much to say. By that year he had gone through two more Chryslers. Not one of them gave him a fraction of the pleasure the old charcoal and desert rose New Yorker had, but he remained faithful to the maker.

There had been in turn a green one and a white one, and finally a coffee brown one. The last Chrysler was wide and boxy, too long in the wheelbase to hold the road, and it was incredibly ugly. Didn't corner worth a damn. The engine was so tricked out with pollution-control devices that it had no acceleration. Felt like a turtle, Dad said as the big car rocked and swayed through curves. Worst of all, it was no fun to drive.

I had one last, hot summer in Los Angeles. Years before, we had moved from the beach to a house built on stilts overhanging Coldwater Canyon. I never liked the isolation in the canyon, though my father seemed to crave it. I looked for any excuse to stay away.

That summer after high school, I avoided Dad, the way young people headed out into the world avoid their parents. Dad and I rarely saw each other. I had a job as lifeguard at the local kiddie pool, and that kept me away from home all day. Evenings I spent with a boyfriend, a surfer I dumped the night before I flew east for college. If my father was unhappy during those months, I did not bother to notice.

Over the years after the divorce there was a steady erosion of Dad's high spirits. I attributed his growing quietude to his age, the pressures of business, the smog that filled his canyon nearly every afternoon, the emptiness of his house when I wasn't there, the noise when I was. I never worried about him.

I got the call from my mother about halfway through my first college semester. Dad had driven his newest Chrysler, the coffee brown one, up the coast highway to Big Sur. Just north of Lucia—guest cabins and a diner were the town—where the highway is three hundred feet above the ocean, his car left the road.

"Miscalculated a curve," Mom said. "He always drove too damn fast."

I had driven that road with Dad enough times that I

knew she was wrong. The only curve in his entire life he ever miscalculated was my mother.

Divers retrieved Dad's body from the ocean floor, but they couldn't bring up the car. They were, however, able to answer one question for me: there hadn't been a blow-out. A flat tire was the only variable I had wondered about.

I poured the flat remains of Richard's champagne into the tide pools and carried the empty bottle with me back to the Mercedes. The big birthday party was tomorrow. I needed to tell my children not to come, that the party was off. Richard had the car's cell phone with him at the cottage: how easy he made it for me to reach him anywhere, anytime he was out of town, no bother with hotel desk clerks. I headed back north, looking for a telephone.

A busload of tourists was just unloading at the general store at San Simeon. I didn't want to wade through a lot of people to use the public phone. I didn't want strangers to see me if I started to cry. Instead, I drove on to Lucia.

All the way up, I imagined my father making his last trip alone in that car that he resented. I tried to sing "Ode to Joy," imitating Dad's phrasing, but gave it up. I never could sing as well as he did.

Lucia is nothing more than a turnout with a few parking places on the ocean side of the highway. An old log-cabin restaurant hangs out over the water there. Below the restaurant a narrow wooden stairway courses down the face of the cliff, branching off to a dozen or so tiny guest cottages. The cottages have few amenities, but the view of the water three hundred feet straight down is incomparable.

The lot in front of the restaurant was full, so I drove on to the first turnout and parked there, though the space was narrow and the side of the car was too close to the highway. I decided to trust the skill of drivers coming around the bend because, more than anything at that moment, I needed coffee from the restaurant before I spoke with my son and daughter. Wine had left me light-headed, had made it impossible to push away the picture of Richard rising naked from the bed. My bed. Once, my mother's bed.

At the exact spot where my father went over the side, the guardrail was missing. Someone had hit it, or had gone right through it, but who could say when? The broken edges of the metal rail were rusty, a tribute to the sorry shape of the state's highway budget.

I walked to the edge and looked down. Then I picked up a boulder and threw it out as far away from the bluff as I could. It seemed to hang on the air, and then, silently, dropped against the rocks sticking out of the ocean far below and disappeared.

If a car drops into the sea and no one is there to hear it, does it make a noise?

My children and their spouses had booked flights into San Francisco the following morning. I called my daughter in Seattle and my son in Denver and left messages on their machines. "Don't bother to come. I've decided not to turn fifty after all. The party is off. I'll call you when I get home."

I was glad no one was at either home to ask the requisite questions. What could I say to the kids? I shouldn't have argued with Richard about a new car? I shouldn't have let myself become last year's model? With my family history should I have seen it coming?

A car pulled out of the restaurant lot and left an open space. I went back for the Mercedes, relieved to have a safer place to park. What would I say to Richard if someone sideswiped his investment?

I started Richard's Mercedes, felt the power of its big engine rumbling under the hood. I waited for a car, then a motorcycle, to pass, and then eased onto the highway. I

can't say exactly what happened next. I was thinking about
the many times Dad and I had stopped in Lucia for hot co-
coa or cold lemonade, depending on the school holiday.
I remembered when we stopped the day he drove me
to Saint Agnes's after our first summer vacation in Los
Angeles.

Dad had almost cried when it was time to get back into
the car for the last leg of the trip: he was moving me in
to boarding school and continuing on to remove the last of
his things from the house he had shared with my mother.

Dr. Jacks had already taken over Dad's dresser and
closet, and Dad's half of the cream-colored blanket on the
bed. The reason I was not allowed to go to that house on
weekends to stay with my mother was the adulterous presence of Dr. Jacks within her walls.

As I turned the Mercedes onto the highway, Richard's
empty champagne bottle rolled from under the seat and
bumped my ankle. Maybe that little nudge was the trigger.
It occurred to me that if the bottle had rolled under the
brake pedal, say, or under my foot, it could have made me
lose control of the car. I could have slipped over the edge,
just the way my father had.

When that empty bottle rolled against my leg, all cold
and hard, for just a bare instant I thought about what might
happen if I drove into the silence beyond the broken
guardrail. No one would know what happened to me, any
more than we ever knew what happened to Dad.

Maybe the divers who went down for me would come
up with the empty bottle, giving people a wrong idea. A
somewhat wrong idea, at any rate.

And Richard? I couldn't trust him to say, "I ripped
Rainey's heart out of her chest by sleeping with another
woman, incidentally a younger woman, on the very eve of

a treacherous birthday. *Mea culpa. Mea culpa. Mea maxima culpa.*"

I knew Richard would let me take the long plunge all by myself. With that realization, at last I was furious with him. If I went over the edge, I wanted everyone to know exactly why. But why should I be the one to go over the edge?

The road ahead rose slightly and then, going into the curve, descended. If the wheels of Richard's Mercedes were set straight—what wonderful steering the Mercedes had—and were headed against the angle of the banked road, and if the champagne bottle was wedged against the accelerator when the car was popped into drive, the car's low center of gravity and perfect alignment would keep it on a true course as it came off the rise. The car should go straight across the curve, over the narrow gravel shoulder, right between the rusted edges of the broken guardrail, and over the edge, motor still humming as it dove straight off into nothing.

At a window table in the Lucia restaurant, I had two cups of coffee and a turkey sandwich. While the waitress, a cheerful woman who loved a healthy appetite, prepared for me a slice of homemade apple pie à la mode, I went to the telephone beside the front counter and called Richard's cell phone. How long had it been since I allowed myself to eat a piece of pie à la mode?

"Jesus, Rainey, honey. What can I say? I'm so sorry. She's nothing to me. Nothing. I can't explain. It was something that just happened."

"Something that just happened?" I thought about the phone calls he'd made, all the preparations for the tryst: candles and wine, flowers and satin sheets. "Just happened the way a car wreck just happens?"

"Where are you, Rainey? Come home. We have to talk."

"Actions speak louder than . . ."

"Are you all right?"

"I'm fine, all things considered. Tomorrow is my birthday and I'll be older than dirt. And I'll be alone." I returned the waitress's wave when she set my pie at my place. "I've called the children and told them not to come tomorrow. I'll leave all the others to you. I can't imagine what you'll say to everyone."

"I'll just say you're under the weather."

"In that case, I'll make the calls."

The waitress whispered to me as she swept by, "That pie's real hot. Don't let the ice cream all melt if you want the good of it."

"Rainey, honey."

"Richard, don't call anyone. I've decided that I want to go ahead with the party. Please don't think you have to come. In fact, don't come. I'll make your excuses."

"I can't blame you for being upset."

"I'm not upset," I said. "At least, not anymore. I have to go now. My dessert is ready. I have just enough time to finish it before the car rental people from San Luis Obispo get here to pick me up."

"Car rental? Where the hell is my car?"

"Exactly," I said. "Where the hell is your car?"

I ate as much of the pie as I wanted. When I was finished, I waited out in front of the restaurant for the car rental people to come and fetch me. All the way down the highway to San Luis Obispo, the young driver and I shared stories about the giant who slept under the gold velvet blanket. When I told him the giant was naked, the kid already knew.

"So," I asked him, "can you sing harmony?"

"Sure," he said. "If you don't sing too loud."

Songs in the Key of *I*
one essay and a dozen new poems by erica jong

Yeats' Glade and Basho's Bee:
The Impossibility of Doing Without Poetry

People think they can do without poetry. And they can.
At least until they fall in love, lose a friend, lose a
child, or a parent, or lose their way in the dark woods of
life. People think they can live without poetry. And they
can. At least until they become fatally ill, have a baby, or
fall desperately, madly, in love.

> I care not for heaven and I fear not hell
>> If I have but the kisses of his proud, young mouth . . .

wrote Moireen Fox in a poem called "The Faery Lover."
And it is hard to imagine a better conjuring of that cliché
"madly in love." Instead of a dead metaphor, we have
a living image—an image with color, speed, defiance.
We have the love, the mad yearning for the lover, and we
also have the feelings the love evokes—all in two lines.
We know that it is a love not only to die for, but to go to
hell for. And we know that the speaker—whoever she may
be—is a furious, passionate person, someone who throws
caution to the winds. We know more about her from two
lines than we know about many people with whom we

have conversed for hours because we know not only her thoughts but her feelings. We know the tone of her voice: incautious, passionate, proud. We know that she is free and ready to pay the price for freedom. We know this woman's character in just two lines.

Only poetry can do that. Only poetry gives us language packed with feeling and personality. Which is why there are times in life when only poetry will do. Interestingly enough, they are the times when we feel most vulnerable, most human.

"The blood jet is poetry," said Sylvia Plath, "there is no stopping it." And that is another example of why only poetry will do at certain times. "Blood" tells us: essential, necessary for life, spillable. "Jet" tells us: moves fast, moves under pressure, once turned on not so easy to turn off. The language of poetry is heightened, emotional, imagistic, condensed. It concentrates meaning as perfume oil concentrates flowers.

I said we need poetry most at those moments when life astounds us with losses or gains. We need it most when we are most hurt, most happy, most downcast, most jubilant. Poetry is the language we speak in times of greatest need. And the fact that it is an endangered species in our culture tells us that we are in deep trouble. We treat our poets as outcasts, lunatics, starvelings. We give least respect to those who give us the most.

Our public attitude toward poetry and poets shows that spiritual needs count for little in America. We may take care of the outer being, but we allow the inner being to languish. The skin, not the soul has all our care—despite lip service to the contrary. And many of us are dying for want of care for the soul. The poet is the caretaker of the soul; in many civilizations, the poet's contribution is central.

Poetry need not consist only of images. It can be declarative utterance packed with meaning. When Yeats directs to have these words inscribed on his tower ("Inscription at Thoor Ballylee"),

> And may these characters remain
> When all is ruin once again

he is giving us a sense of time's carelessness. He is evoking the mutability of all earthly things. Shakespeare is obsessed with time and the changes it brings.

"Devouring time, blunt thou the lion's paws," is also an image imbedded in a command. It is as if, for the moment, the poet assumes God's perspective rather than the human vantage point.

And why shouldn't the poet have God's perspective—if only temporarily? As Anne Sexton once said to me: "We are all writing God's poem." The individual identity of the poet hardly matters. What matters is that the blood jet of poetry continues to spurt.

The blood jet is endangered in our culture not only because we do not respect our poets (poets can survive neglect if they are true poets: think of Emily Dickinson), but because we are destroying not only solitude but the ability to *enjoy* solitude. Try to find a place without media, traffic sounds, music, advertisements. You have to be a billionaire to escape the overstimulation of selling that is ubiquitous in our cities, suburbs, airplanes, airports, cars, and trains. Solitude has started to feel strange to us. We walk into the house and immediately turn on the TV for company. The sounds of silence seem peculiar. But poetry, like all creative work, is *triggered* only by solitude. When Yeats described the "bee-loud glade," in "The Lake Isle of Innisfree," you knew he had listened to bees, not traffic. Only the poet knows how loud the bees are in the bee-loud glade. Only the poet refrains from walking through the meadow with a boom box. Constant audio and video input drown our own output. The "wild mind" (as poet Natalie Goldberg calls the poetry-creating place in our brains) needs space to dream and quiet to retrieve images. We have nearly lost that space. Perhaps we have willfully abolished it. But frenzied consumption of material things cannot do for us what poetry can.

Where does the poet go to find necessary solitude? And where does the reader of poetry find the space to *read or to hear*? The truth is, both writing and reading are endangered in our own world. But the need for poetry is such a basic human need that it adapts itself to new circumstances. When so-called mainstream publishers stop publishing poetry and ignore the needs of young people for poets of their own generation, those young people turn to poetry slams and coffeehouse readings. Or to rap music. When the book world turns its back, poetry springs up in the world of music. An oral medium, it returns to its root: the tongue.

Which brings us to poets reading and poetry as a medium for both ear and eye.

I fell in love with poetry as a teenager by hearing poets read. I went to readings at the Poetry Center of the 92nd Street Y in New York. And I listened to the great recordings of Dylan Thomas, T. S. Eliot, Robert Frost, Edna St. Vincent Millay. Poetry is given life by the voice because it is, basically, a transcription of breath—and of the silences between breath. When a poet reads, the creative process is recapitulated. We almost hear the muse whispering in the poet's ear.

Our age is rich in poetry recordings and poetry readings, so perhaps the poetic impulse will survive all our neglect.

One thing is sure: Poetry cannot be killed. We do it for love, not money. We do it for the sake of our souls, not our bodies. Arts practiced without ulterior motive may be the most durable arts of all. Their medium of exchange is love—and love's helplessness against time.

Poetry preserves the living moment and our lust to inhabit it fully. As the seventeenth-century poet Basho says:

> Having sucked deep
> In a sweet peony
> A bee creeps
> Out of its hairy recesses

Is all poetry about lust? Sometimes it seems so. Lust is the opposite of death. And since we know that death will gobble us in the end, we lust for lust. We suck on words as Basho's bee sucks on honey. The sweet peony makes us hungry where most she satisfies.

Beauty Bare

for Angelo Bucarelli and Nina von Furstenberg

"Euclid alone has looked on beauty bare."
> —Edna St. Vincent Millay

*"Helen being chosen found life flat and dull
and later had much trouble from a fool."*
> —William Butler Yeats

> We are not in Troy
> but still a man
> with three daughters
> may have much trouble

from fools
and a woman who bears
three daughters is heroine
in my book
even though
I am not Homer—
and even though Homer
had little use for heroines.

Nina, Angelo,
this new beauty
you have made—
this beauty bare—
affirms life
in the midst of death—
affirms your *Vita Nuova*
(and somehow also mine).

The middle of three daughters,
the joker in the pack,
the meat in the sandwich,
I know the gravity
of what you've done
(and so does Palma).

For what fairytale King and Queen
does not have
three daughters?
And what are daughters for
but to drag their parents
kicking and screaming
out of fairyland?

But here comes Helena
with her fierce desire to live,
her fists beating
against the golden skies of Rome,
her tender feet kicking the air
until it eddies about her,
altering everything.

Suddenly Cosima becomes
the eldest of three Graces
painted by Botticelli,
Springtime's summoner,
the ring-leader of muses.

And Palma becomes herself
only more so—in the middle,
winning her place with wit.
(Sometimes the one
whose place is *least* assured
strives hardest to be heard).

What will the world be like
when these three do their dance?
May we be there
to witness it!

A glow of Eden suffuses
your three blond beauties.
Oh, may they return us to
the Golden Age—
Cosima, Palma, Helena—
may they dance us back
on their thirty pink toes
to the garden we left
so long ago.

Creation Myth, with Figs

> Italians know
> how to call a fig
> a fig: *fica*.

Mandolin-shaped fruit,
round
as the belly
after love,
feminine as slippery seeds
(amber as twilight
or livid green as Spring)
and bearing large leaves
to clothe
our splendid nakedness.

I believe it was
not an apple but a fig
Lucifer gave Eve
knowing she would find
a fellow-feeling
in this female fruit

and knowing also
that Adam could not but
lose himself
in the fig's fertile heart
whatever the price—

God's wrath, expulsion,
angry angels
pointing with swords
to a theoretical world
of woe.

One bite into
a ripe fig
is worth galaxies
beyond
the innocence of Eden,
Adam must have felt.

And as for Eve,
how could she not know
that Spring would come yearly
to redeem our fall?

And what a Fall
producing
fruit of the earth's cornucopia—
zucchini's striped green penises,
ridged golden wombs of pumpkins,
tomatoes bursting with red flesh,
melons pink as babies' bottoms,
the aroma of that ripeness
which is all.

The maternal goddesses
have not yet
deserted us.
Ceres, Persephone,
Flora still dance
three by three
for the brush
of Botticelli.

Even here on earth
Adam and Eve are born
again and again

with their terrible
progeny.

Surely
we will also be born again
out of the belly
of eternity's
great fig.

Splayed among seeds,
bursting with juice,
we will colonize
new planets,
glowing distant fruits
we have not yet tasted.

May the goddesses bless
that exploration
and give us
descendants
worthy of our visions
(which are theirs),
our slippery seeds
of love.

Poem for a Fax Cover Sheet

Hating cameras, Plato said:
look how everything grays
with duplication, blurs
at the edges. The Parthenon:
a postcard! & who are
those clowns loitering in
the (kodacolor) agora?
Negatives of negatives?

For Grace in the Hospital

The pink parasols
of the weeping cherry
remind me to give thanks
for another Spring—
so unexpected, unearned,
pure gift

we were never promised,
always given.

And you, my friend,
caught between
letting go
and not letting go—
your body a shipwreck,
your soul a sail
hungering
for its big wind—
what shall I tell you?
That I need you here?
Selfish!
That you mothered
me and my words
into flowering
with your abundance,
your Ceres-given gift
to make the earth flower,
your amazing grace?

Grace, Grace, Grace,
what you have given me
can only be passed on
like mother's milk.
It is not intended
to be kept.

Weeping cherry
whipped by the wind,
I hold you flowering
in my heart.

Please stay.

I Dreamed That the Sea

I dreamed that the sea
had begun to swallow the land
and my old redwood hot-tub
was full of dying shellfish—
crayfish missing claws, clams putrid
with death, opulent aphrodisiacal oysters.

You said: "The sea has washed up
unanswered questions."

But I live on a high rockledge
miles above sea level.
If the sea reaches me here,
it will reach us all
and things submerged for eons
will die gasping in their exoskeletons.

In my dream, I am building
an ark for these creatures—
and for myself—
though perhaps we are all past saving
even though we have such dreams.

Ode Against Grief

for Gerri Karetsky

Sometimes we are asked
to carry
more than we can bear,
and the weight
is so heavy
that it seems easier
to lie under the earth
than to stride upon it,
easier to stretch out
in a damp grave
than to stand up
and salute the sun.

The past
is a block of granite
suspended over your head
by a thin, gold wire
or a grand piano
floating up
to a ninth-story window
carrying all the chords
it has ever played,
or a portmanteau falling
from the old wire rack

of a long-distance train—
the Trans-Siberian Express
possibly—
or the rusty red train
that hoots
from Beijing
to Hong Kong,
carrying all the dreams
of the world's
most populous nation.

But the past
is only the past.
It takes
your present
to keep it alive.

The present is bright copper,
untarnished silver
slippery as moonbeams;
it is burnished gold.

It sings:

I am all the riches
you will ever have.
Afternoons in bed,
fresh raspberries
and cloudberries,
clear water
from a confluence
of mountain streams . . .

Catch me if you can!
Grab me!
I am a kiss, a caress,
a slice of yellow lemon,
a crystal tumbler of mineral water
studded with bubbles . . .
Drink me, Alice!

The chemistry
of the present
is volatile—
you must leap
into its test-tube

with both bare feet
or it will turn
to base metal
and come back to earth.

There is time
enough for that.
Meanwhile, dance
on the bubbles
in your glass
as you were meant to.

Even a goddess cannot
grieve if she wants to create
new life.
And you partake of her force
if only you *know* it.
You keep life going
only by
being alive!

Poplars in Provence

Round
undulating
avenue of leaves,
each one a banner waving,
a light reflecting
our dying star.

Between two poplar trees,
there is an inverted poplar—
almost a negative—
made of provençal sky blue.

The branches ascend
as if in prayer.
The green tremulo
of leaves
stipples the sky
as paillettes
on a chiffon dress
catch the kleig lights,

dazzling themselves
in man-made mirrors.

Self-regarding poplars
in love with your leaves,
your light, your undulance,
I stand beneath you
studying to become
some green future thing.
A poplar tree
would do.

Risotto

The integrity
of sun and water,
the single grain of rice,
fused in a starchy cup
to be filled up
with the essences
of our lives,
the rich brown broth
infused with saffron,
garlanded by
tidbits of porcini,
more precious
than platinum
or gold.

I stand here
endlessly stirring
the ingredients of our lives,
watching the rice expand
lose its translucency,
and become
a palimpsest
of fused flavors.

Oh leftover life
in the sizzling skillet!
Stir, stir, stir
until you have concocted
that ecstatic paste,
harbinger of heaven,

manna of Milano—
risotto!

Sentient

for Lisa Alther

Awake at four
with the old brain beating
its fast tattoo—
I *want,* I want—
I think of love,
of the hot scramble
of limbs in darkness;

of the mind
pulsing its secrets
in metaphor;
of synapses firing
need, longing, love;
of the body
with its midnight hungers;

of the mind
caught between dream and waking,
wondering what it is,
self-creating always;

of god,
whatever *she* is
asking the questions:
Who are you anyway?
and *How did you get here?*
and *What is the distance
between two stars?
Between two brain cells?
Between two lovers?*

Here in the rosy
pink-ringed dark
where all the birds—
sentient in their own way
as we—
are on the verge

of wakefulness
and song.

Sleep

I love to go to sleep,
when bed takes me like a lover
wrapping my limbs in
cool linen, soothing
the fretfulness
of day glaring like
the Cyclops' eye
in a forehead
of furrows . . .

But I wake
always reluctantly, brushing
the dreamcrumbs
from my lids,
walking sideways underwater
like a crab,
spilling coffee,
knocking the mug
to the floor
where it shatters
in a muddy river
to my continuo of
"Shit, shit, shit!"

What if death
is only a forgetting
to wake in the morning,
a dream that goes on
into other corridors,
other chambers
draped with other silks,
libraries of unwritten books
whose kaleidoscopic pages
can be read
only by the pineal eye,
music that can be heard only
by the seventh sense
or the eighth or ninth,
until we possess

an infinity of senses—
none of them
dependent on flesh?

What if our love of sleep
is only a foretaste
of the bliss that awaits us
when we do not have to wake again?

What frightens us so
about falling?
To drop the body and fly
should be as natural
as drifting into a dream—
but we are insomniacs
tossing on soaked sheets,
hanging on
to our intricate pain—
while God with her sweet
Mona Lisa smile
sings lullabyes
the ears of the living
cannot hear.

Waiting for Angels

Like Sappho,
my mind
is divided
between tribute
to angels
and dark hosannahs
to demons.

I sit shiva
for the dead world—

where the bride's
hair is cut
to undo
her power

(everywhere but
in her home),

where a glass is crushed
to denote permanence,

where books
are looked forward to
like love letters.

where a Rabbi,
Priest, or Shaman
may be asked
for definitions
of good and evil.

And we may debate
all night
of angels
dancing
on the heads
of silver pins.

No more.
All gone.

We celebrate our own
Black Masses in bed

or on the blood-strewn streets.

We believe in no higher law,
no higher power,
no representative on earth
of the divine dialogue,
no one who speaks—
or even whispers—
the truth.

And so we wait
for angels,
hoping that these messengers—
half-god, half-human—
will fill the vacuum
of our hearts.

Never have so many
waited for so few!
Never has hope

had so few feathers
to fly upon!

In the dark air
of Armageddon
we hear the beating
of iridescent black reptilian wings.

Angels? Demons?
How little we care
as long
as *someone*
comes!

When Jew Kills Jew

(in memory of Itzak Rabin)

What does it mean
when Jew kills Jew,
when the old enmity
of Cain and Abel,
Judas and Jesus,
erupts again
in the city
of sepulchre and wall,
of women keening
for the loss of sons—
as Mary did,
and Eve before her?

When Jewish sons
forge prayershawls into swords,
are drunk with the fumes
of gunpowder,
does God
flood Noah again,
unmake the dove,
the rainbow,
the parting of the Red Sea,
the deliverance from Egypt,
smash the Tablets
and cancel
the covenant itself?

What shall we do
without Commandments
emblazoned in living rock,
without prophets trembling
on Sinai?

Without the law,
without our brothers,
what is a Jew
but a convert
hiding from
the light?

When Jews adopt Jihad,
the Inquisition reigns
and Hitler becomes
the new Messiah.

Then God sends us
impotent angels
who can only sing
falsetto
and are deaf
to the music
of eternity.

All this has happened
many times before.

The Diaspora's singing instruments—
auto-da-fé, poetry, prayer—
go mute.

And there is no difference
between walking
into the ovens of your enemy
and killing your own brother.

When Jew kills Jew,
God vanishes again
for another long sabbatical.

Firing thunderbolts with Zeus and Thor,
raping Europa for a lark,
playing amid the Bacchae
and drunken fauns,
God has no time for the people
he so carelessly created.

We walk out of the garden
barefoot, with uncovered heads.

God is not dead
but missing,
and we are destined to wander again
for more millennia
than there are stars.

L.T.'s Theory of Pets
by Stephen King

My friend L.T. hardly ever talks about how his wife disappeared, or how she's probably dead, just another victim of the Axe Man, but he likes to tell the story of how she walked out on him. He does it with just the right roll of the eyes, as if to say, "She fooled me, boys—right, good, and proper!" He'll sometimes tell the story to a bunch of men sitting on one of the loading docks behind the plant and eating their lunches, him eating his lunch, too, the one he fixed for himself—no Lulubelle back at home to do it for him these days. They usually laugh when he tells the story, which always ends with L.T.'s Theory of Pets. Hell, *I* usually laugh. It's a funny story, even if you *do* know how it turned out. Not that any of us do, not completely.

"I punched out at four, just like usual," L.T. will say, "then went down to Deb's Den for a couple of beers, just like most days. Had a game of pinball, then went home. That was where things stopped being just like usual. When a person gets up in the morning, he doesn't have the slightest idea how much may have changed in his life by the time he lays his head down again that night. 'Ye know not the day or the hour,' the Bible says. I believe that particular verse is about dying, but it fits everything else, boys. Everything else in this world. You just never know when you're going to bust a fiddle-string.

"When I turn into the driveway I see the garage door's open and the little Subaru she brought to the marriage is gone, but that doesn't strike me as immediately peculiar. She was always driving off someplace—to a yard sale or someplace—and leaving the goddam garage door open. I'd tell her, 'Lulu, if you keep doing that long enough, some-one'll eventually take advantage of it. Come in and take a rake or a bag of peat moss or maybe even the power mower. Hell, even a Seventh Day Adventist fresh out of college and doing his merit badge rounds will steal if you put enough temptation in his way, and that's the worst kind of person to tempt, because they feel it more than the rest of us.' Anyway, she'd always say, 'I'll do better, L.T., try, anyway, I really will, honey.' And she *did* do better, just backslid from time to time like any ordinary sinner.

"I park off to the side so she'll be able to get her car in when she comes back from wherever, but I close the garage door. Then I go in by way of the kitchen. I check the mailbox, but it's empty, the mail inside on the counter, so she must have left after eleven, because he don't come until at least then. The mailman, I mean.

"Well, Lucy's right there by the door, crying in that way Siamese have—I like that cry, think it's sort of cute, but Lulu always hated it, maybe because it sounds like a baby's cry and she didn't want anything to do with babies. 'What would I want with a rugmonkey?' she'd say.

"Lucy being at the door wasn't anything out of the ordi-nary, either. That cat loved my ass. Still does. She's two years old now. We got her at the start of the last year we were married. Right around. Seems impossible to believe Lulu's been gone a year, and we were only together three to start with. But Lulubelle was the type to make an impression on you. Lulubelle had what I have to call star quality. You know who she always reminded me of? Lucille Ball. Now that I think of it, I guess that's why I named the cat Lucy, although I don't remember thinking it at the time. It might have been what you'd call a subconscious association. She'd come into a room—Lulubelle, I mean, not the cat—and just light it up somehow. A person like that, when they're gone you can hardly believe it, and you keep expecting them to come back.

"Meanwhile, there's the cat. Her name was Lucy to start with, but Lulubelle hated the way she acted so much that she started calling her Screwlucy, and it kind of stuck. Lucy wasn't nuts, though, she only wanted to be loved. Wanted to be loved more than any other pet I ever had in my life, and I've had quite a few.

"Anyway, I come in the house and pick up the cat and pet her a little and she climbs up onto my shoulder and sits there, purring and talking her Siamese talk. I check the mail on the counter, put the bills in the basket, then go over to the fridge to get Lucy something to eat. I always keep a working can of cat food in there, with a piece of tinfoil over the top. Saves having Lucy get excited and digging her claws into my shoulder when she hears the can opener. Cats are smart, you know. Much smarter than dogs. They're different in other ways, too. It might be that the biggest division in the world isn't men and women but folks who like cats and folks who like dogs. Did any of you porkpackers ever think of that?

"Lulu bitched like hell about having an open can of cat food in the fridge, even one with a piece of foil over the top, said it made everything in there taste like old tuna, but I wouldn't give in on that one. On most stuff I did it her way, but that cat food business was one of the few places

where I really stood up for my rights. It didn't have anything to do with the cat food, anyway. It had to do with the
cat. She just didn't like Lucy, that was all. Lucy was her
cat, but she didn't like it.

"Anyway, I go over to the fridge, and I see there's a note
on it, stuck there with one of the vegetable magnets. It's
from Lulubelle. Best as I can remember, it goes like this:

"'Dear L.T.—I am leaving you, honey. Unless you
come home early, I will be long gone by the time you get
this note. I don't think you will get home early, you have
never got home early in all the time we have been married,
but at least I know you'll get this almost as soon as you get
in the door, because the first thing you always do when
you get home isn't to come see me and say, "Hi sweet girl
I'm home" and give me a kiss but go to the fridge and get
whatever's left of the last nasty can of Calo you put in
there and feed Screwlucy. So at least I know you won't just
go upstairs and get shocked when you see my Elvis Last
Supper picture is gone and my half of the closet is mostly
empty and think we had a burglar who likes ladies' dresses
(unlike some who only care about what is under them).

"'I get irritated with you sometimes, honey, but I still
think you're sweet and kind and nice, you will always be
my little maple duff and sugar dumpling, no matter where
our paths may lead. It's just that I have decided I was never
cut out to be a Spam-packer's wife. I don't mean that in
any conceited way, either. I even called the Psychic Hot-
line last week as I struggled with this decision, lying
awake night after night (and listening to you snore, boy, I
don't mean to hurt your feelings but have you ever got a
snore on *you*), and I was given this message: "A broken
spoon may become a fork." I didn't understand that at first,
but I didn't give up on it. I am not smart like some people
(or like some people *think* they are smart), but I *work* at

things. The best mill grinds slow but exceedingly fine, my
mother used to say, and I ground away at this like a pepper
mill in a Chinese restaurant, thinking late at night while
you snored and no doubt dreamed of how many pork-
snouts you could get in a can of Spam. And it came to me
that saying about how a broken spoon can become a fork is
a beautiful thing to behold. Because a fork has tines. And
those tines may have to separate, like you and me must
now have to separate, but still they have the same handle.
So do we. We are both human beings, L.T., capable of loving and respecting one another. Look at all the fights we
had about Frank and Screwlucy, and still we mostly managed to get along. Yet the time has now come for me to
seek my fortune along different lines from yours, and to
poke into the great roast of life with a different point from
yours. Besides, I miss my mother.' "

(I can't say for sure if all this stuff was really in the note
L.T. found on his fridge; it doesn't seem entirely likely, I
must admit, but the men listening to his story would be
rolling in the aisles by this point—or around on the loading dock, at least—and it did *sound* like Lulubelle, that I
can testify to.)

" 'Please do not try to follow me, L.T., and although I'll
be at my mother's and I know you have that number, I
would appreciate you not calling but waiting for me to call
you. In time I will, but in the meanwhile I have a lot of
thinking to do, and although I have gotten on a fair way
with it, I'm not "out of the fog" yet. I suppose I will be
asking you for a divorce eventually, and think it is only fair
to tell you so. I have never been one to hold out false hope,
believing it better to "tell the truth and smoke out the
devil." Please remember that what I do I do in love, not in
hatred and resentment. And please remember what was

told to me and what I now tell to you: a broken spoon may be a fork in disguise. All my love, Lulubelle Simms.' "

L.T. would pause there, letting them digest the fact that she had gone back to her maiden name, and giving his eyes a few of those patented L.T. DeWitt rolls. Then he'd tell them the P.S. she'd tacked on the note.

" 'I have taken Frank with me and left Screwlucy for you. I thought this would probably be the way you'd want it. Love, Lulu.' "

If the DeWitt family was a fork, Screwlucy and Frank were the other two tines on it. If there wasn't a fork (and speaking for myself, I've always felt marriage was more like a knife—the dangerous kind with two sharp edges), Screwlucy and Frank could still be said to sum up everything that went wrong in the marriage of L.T. and Lulubelle. Because, think of it—although Lulubelle bought Frank for L.T. (first wedding anniversary) and L.T. bought Lucy, soon to be Screwlucy, for Lulubelle (second wedding anniversary), they each wound up with the other one's pets when Lulu walked out on the marriage.

"She got me that dog because I liked the one on *Frasier*," L.T. would say. "That kind of dog's a terrier, but I don't remember now what they call that kind. A Jack something. Jack Sprat? Jack Robinson? Jack Shit? You know how a thing like that gets on the tip of your tongue?"

Somebody would tell him that Frasier's dog was a Jack Russell terrier and L.T. would nod emphatically.

"That's right!" he'd exclaim. "Sure! Exactly! That's what Frank was, all right, a Jack Russell terrier. But you want to know the cold hard truth? An hour from now, that will have slipped away from me again—it'll be there in my brain, but like something behind a rock. An hour from now, I'll be going to myself, '*What* did that guy say Frank was? A Jack Handle terrier? A Jack Rabbit terrier? That's

close, I know that's close . . .' And so on. Why? I think because I just hated that little fuck so much. That barking rat.
That fur-covered shit machine. I hated it from the first time
I laid eyes on it. There. It's out and I'm glad. And do you
know what? Frank felt the same about me. It was hate at
first sight.

"You know how some men train their dog to bring them
their slippers? Frank wouldn't bring me my slippers, but
he'd *puke* in them. Yes. The first time he did it, I stuck my
right foot right into it. It was like sticking your foot into
warm tapioca with extra big lumps in it. Although I didn't
see him, my theory is that he waited outside the bedroom
door until he saw me coming—fucking *lurked* outside the
bedroom door—then went in, unloaded in my right slipper,
then hid under the bed to watch the fun. I deduce that on
the basis of how it was still warm. Fucking dog. Man's
best friend, my ass. I wanted to take it to the pound after
that, had the leash out and everything, but Lulu threw an
absolute shit fit. You would have thought she'd come into
the kitchen and caught me trying to give the dog a drain-
cleaner enema.

" 'If you take Frank to the pound, you might as well take
me to the pound,' she says, starting to cry. 'That's all you
think of him, and that's all you think of me. Honey, all we
are to you is nuisances you'd like to be rid of. That's the
cold hard truth.' I mean, oh my bleeding piles, on and on.

" 'He puked in my slipper,' I says.

" 'The dog puked in his slipper so off with his head,' she
says. 'Oh, sugarpie, if only you could *hear* yourself!'

" 'Hey,' I say, 'you try sticking *your* bare foot into a slipper filled with dog puke and see how *you* like it.' Getting
mad by then, you know.

"Except getting mad at Lulu never did any good. Most
times, if you had the king, she had the ace. If you had the

ace, she had a trump. Also, the woman would fucking *escalate*. If something happened and I got irritated, she'd get pissed. If I got pissed, she'd get mad. If I got mad, she'd go fucking Red Alert Defcon 1 and empty the missile silos. I'm talking scorched fucking earth. Mostly it wasn't worth it. Except almost every time we'd get into a fight, I'd forget that.

"She goes, 'Oh dear. Maple duff stuck his wittle footie in a wittle spit-up.' I tried to get in there, tell her that wasn't right, spit-up is like drool, spit-up doesn't have these big fucking *chunks* in it, but she won't let me get a word out. By then she's over in the passing lane and cruising, all pumped up and ready to teach school.

"'Let me tell you something, honey,' she goes, 'a little drool in your slipper is very minor stuff. You men slay me. Try being a woman sometimes, okay? Try always being the one that ends up laying with the small of your back in that come-spot, or the one that goes to the toilet in the middle of the night and the guy's left the goddam ring up and you splash your can right down into this cold water. Little midnight skindiving. The toilet probably hasn't been flushed, either, men think the Urine Fairy comes by around two a.m. and takes care of that, and there you are, sitting crack-deep in piss, and all at once you realize your *feet're* in it, too, you're paddling around in Lemon Squirt because, although guys think they're dead-eye Dick with that thing, most can't shoot for shit, drunk or sober they gotta wash the goddam floor all around the toilet before they can even start the main event. All my life I've been living with this, honey— a father, four brothers, one ex-husband, plus a few roommates that are none of your business at this late date—and you're ready to send poor Frank off to the gas factory because just one time he happened to reflux a little drool into your slipper.'

" 'My *fur-lined* slipper,' I tell her, but it's just a little shot back over my shoulder. One thing about living with Lulu, and maybe to my credit, I always knew when I was beat. When I lost, it was fucking decisive. One thing I certainly wasn't going to tell her even though I knew it for a fact was that the dog puked in my slipper on purpose, the same way that he peed on my underwear on purpose if I forgot to put it in the hamper before I went off to work. She could leave her bras and pants scattered around from hell to Harvard—and did—but if I left so much as a pair of athletic socks in the corner, I'd come home and find that fucking Jack Shit terrier had given it a lemonade shower. But tell her that? She would have been booking me time with a psychiatrist. She would have been doing that *even though she knew it was true.* Because then she might have had to take the stuff I was saying seriously, and she didn't want to. She loved Frank, you see, and Frank loved her. They were like Romeo and Juliet or Rocky and Adrian.

"Frank would come to her chair while we were watching TV, lie down on the floor beside her, and put his muzzle on her shoe. Just lie there like that all night, looking up at her, all soulful and loving, and with his butt pointed in my direction so if he should have to blow a little gas, I'd get the full benefit of it. He loved her and she loved him. Why? Christ knows. Love's a mystery to everyone except the poets, I guess, and nobody sane can understand a thing they write about it. I don't think most of them can understand it themselves on the rare occasions when they wake up and smell the coffee.

"But Lulubelle never gave me that dog so she could have it, let's get that one thing straight. I know that some people do stuff like that—a guy'll give his wife a trip to Miami because he wants to go there, or a wife'll give her husband a NordicTrack because she thinks he ought to do something about his gut—but this wasn't that kind of deal. We were crazy in love with each other at the beginning; I know I was with her, and I'd stake my life she was with me. No, she bought that dog for me because I always laughed so hard at the one on *Frasier*. She wanted to make me happy, that's all. She didn't know Frank was going to take a shine to her, or her to him, no more than she knew the dog was going to dislike me so much that throwing up in one of my slippers or chewing the bottoms of the curtains on my side of the bed would be the high point of his day."

L.T. would look around at the grinning men, not grinning himself, but he'd give his eyes that knowing, long-suffering roll, and they'd laugh again, in anticipation. Me too, likely as not, in spite of what I knew about the Axe Man.

"I haven't ever been hated before," he'd say, "not by man or beast, and it unsettled me a lot. It unsettled me *big-time*. I tried to make friends with Frank—first for my sake, then for the sake of her that gave him to me—but it didn't work. For all I know, he might've tried to make friends with me . . . with a dog, who can tell? If he did, it didn't work for him, either. Since then I've read—in 'Dear Abby,' I think it was—that a pet is just about the worst present you can give a person, and I agree. I mean, even if you like the animal and the animal likes you, think about what that kind of gift says. 'Say, darling, I'm giving you this wonderful present, it's a machine that eats at one end and shits out the other, it's going to run for fifteen years, give or take, merry fucking Christmas.' But that's the kind of thing you only think about *after,* more often than not. You know what I mean?

"I think we did try to do our best, Frank and I. After all, even though we hated each other's guts, we both loved Lulubelle. That's why, I think, that although he'd sometimes growl at me if I sat down next to her on the couch during *Murphy Brown* or a movie or something, he never actually bit. Still, it used to drive me crazy. Just the fucking *nerve* of it, that little bag of hair and eyes daring to growl at me.

"'Listen to him,' I'd say, 'he's growling at me.'

"She'd stroke his head the way she hardly ever stroked mine, unless she'd had a few, and say it was really just a dog's version of purring. That he was just happy to be with us, having a quiet evening at home. I'll tell you something, though, I never tried patting him when she wasn't around. I'd feed him sometimes, and I never gave him a kick (although I was tempted a few times, I'd be a liar if I said different), but I never tried patting him. I think he would have snapped at me, and then we would have gotten into it. Like two guys living with the same pretty girl, almost. *Menage à trois* is what they call it in the Penthouse *Forum*. Both of us love her and she loves both of us, but as time goes by, I start realizing that the scales are tipping and she's starting to love Frank a little more than me. Maybe because Frank never talks back and never pukes in *her* slippers and with Frank the goddam toilet ring is never an issue, because he goes outside. Unless, that is, I forget and leave a pair of my shorts in the corner or under the bed."

At this point L.T. would likely finish off the iced coffee in his thermos, crack his knuckles, or both. It was his way of saying the first act was over and Act Two was about to commence.

"So then one day, a Saturday, Lulu and I are out to the mall. Just walking around, like people do. You know. And we go by Pet Notions, up by J.C. Penney, and there's a whole crowd of people in front of the display window. 'Oh, let's see,' Lulu says, so we go over and work our way to the front.

"It's a fake tree with bare branches and fake grass—

Astroturf—all around it. And there are these Siamese kit-
tens, half a dozen of them chasing each other around,
climbing the tree, batting each other's ears.

"'Oh ain' dey jus' da key-youtes *ones*!' Lulu says. 'Oh
ain't dey jus' the key-youtest wittle *babies*! Look, honey,
look!'

"'I'm lookin','' I says, and what I'm thinking is that I
just found what I wanted to get Lulu for our anniversary.
And that was a relief. I wanted it to be something extra
special, something that would really bowl her over, because things had been quite a bit short of great between us
during the last year. I thought about Frank, but I wasn't too
worried about him; cats and dogs always fight in the car-
toons, but in real life they usually get along, that's been my
experience. They usually get along better than people do.
Especially when it's cold outside.

"To make a long story just a little bit shorter, I bought
one of them and gave it to her on our anniversary. Got it a
velvet collar, and tucked a little card under it. 'HELLO, I am
LUCY!' the card said. 'I come with love from L.T.! Happy
second anniversary!'

"You probably know what I'm going to tell you now,
don't you? Sure. It was just like goddam Frank the terrier
all over again, only in reverse. At first I was as happy as a
pig in shit with Frank, and Lulubelle was as happy as a pig
in shit with Lucy at first. Held her up over her head, talking that baby-talk to her, 'Oh yookit *you,* oh yookit my
wittle pwecious, she so *key-yout*,' and so on and so on . . .
until Lucy let out a yowl and batted at the end of Lulubelle's nose. With her claws out, too. Then she ran away
and hid under the kitchen table. Lulu laughed it off, like it
was the funniest thing she'd ever had happen to her, and as
key-yout as anything else a little kitten might do, but I
could see she was miffed.

"Right then Frank came in. He'd been sleeping up in our room—at the foot of her side of the bed—but Lulu'd let out a little shriek when the kitten batted her nose, so he came down to see what the fuss was about.

"He spotted Lucy under the table right away and walked toward her, sniffing the linoleum where she'd been.

"'Stop them, honey, stop them, L.T., they're going to get into it,' Lulubelle says. 'Frank'll kill her.'

"'Just let them alone a minute,' I says. 'See what happens.'

"Lucy humped up her back the way cats do, but stood her ground and watched him come. Lulu started forward, wanting to get in between them in spite of what I'd said (listening up wasn't exactly one of Lulu's strong points), but I took her wrist and held her back. It's best to let them work it out between them, if you can. Always best. It's quicker.

"Well, Frank got to the edge of the table, poked his nose under, and started this low rumbling way back in his throat. 'Let me go, L.T. I got to get her,' Lulubelle says, 'Frank's growling at her.'

"'No, he's not,' I say, 'he's just purring. I recognize it from all the times he's purred at me.'

"She gave me a look that would just about have boiled water, but didn't say anything. The only times in the three years we were married that I got the last word, it was always about Frank and Screwlucy. Strange but true. Any other subject, Lulu could talk rings around me. But when it came to the pets, it seemed she was always fresh out of comebacks. Used to drive her crazy.

"Frank poked his head under the table a little farther, and Lucy batted his nose the way she'd batted Lulubelle's—only when she batted Frank, she did it without popping her claws. I had an idea Frank would go for her, but he didn't. He just kind of whoofed and turned away. Not scared, more like he's thinking, 'Oh, okay, so that's what *that's* about.' Went back into the living room and laid down in front of the TV.

"And that was all the confrontation there ever was between them. They divvied up the territory pretty much the way that Lulu and I divvied it up that last year we spent together, when things were getting bad; the bedroom belonged to Frank and Lulu, the kitchen belonged to me and Lucy—only by Christmas, Lulubelle was calling her Screwlucy—and the living room was neutral territory. The four of us spent a lot of evenings there that last year, Screwlucy on my lap, Frank with his muzzle on Lulu's shoe, us humans on the couch, Lulubelle reading a book and me watching *Wheel of Fortune* or *Life-styles of the Rich and Famous,* which Lulubelle always called *Lifestyles of the Rich and Topless.*

"The cat wouldn't have a thing to do with her, not from day one. Frank, every now and then you could get the idea Frank was at least *trying* to get along with me. His nature would always get the better of him in the end and he'd chew up one of my sneakers or take another leak on my underwear, but every now and then it did seem like he was putting forth an effort. Lap my hand, maybe give me a grin. Usually if I had a plate of something he wanted a bite of.

"Cats are different, though. A cat won't curry favor even if it's in their best interests to do so. A cat can't be a hypocrite. If more preachers were like cats, this would be a religious country again. If a cat likes you, you know. If she doesn't, you know that, too. Screwlucy never liked Lulu, not one whit, and she made it clear from the start. If I was getting ready to feed her, Lucy'd rub around my legs, purring, while I spooned it up and dumped it in her dish. If Lulu fed her, Lucy'd sit all the way across the kitchen, in front of the fridge, watching her. And wouldn't go to the dish until Lulu had cleared off. It drove Lulu crazy. 'That cat thinks she's the Queen of Sheba,' she'd say. By then she'd given up the baby-talk. Given up picking Lucy up, too. If she did, she'd get her wrist scratched, more often than not.

"Now, I tried to pretend I liked Frank and Lulu tried to pretend she liked Lucy, but Lulu gave up pretending a lot sooner than I did. I guess maybe neither one of them, the cat or the woman, could stand being a hypocrite. I don't think Lucy was the only reason Lulu left—hell, I know it wasn't—but I'm sure Lucy helped Lulubelle make her final decision. Pets can live a long time, you know. So the present I got her for our second was really the straw that broke the camel's back. Tell *that* to 'Dear Abby'!

"The cat's talking was maybe the worst, as far as Lulu was concerned. She couldn't stand it. One night Lulubelle says to me, 'If that cat doesn't stop yowling, L.T., I think I'm going to hit it with an encyclopedia.'

" 'That's not yowling,' I said, 'that's chatting.'

" 'Well,' Lulu says, 'I wish it would stop chatting.'

"And right about then, Lucy jumped up into my lap and she did shut up. She always did, except for a little low purring, way back in her throat. Purring that really *was* purring. I scratched her between her ears like she likes, and I happened to look up. Lulu turned her eyes back down on her book, but before she did, what I saw was real hate. Not for me. For Screwlucy. Throw an encyclopedia at it? She looked like she'd like to stick the cat between *two* encyclopedias and just kind of clap it to death.

"Sometimes Lulu would come into the kitchen and catch the cat up on the table and swat it off. I asked her once if she'd ever seen me swat Frank off the bed that way—he'd get up on it, you know, always on her side, and leave these nasty tangles of white hair. When I said that, Lulu gave me a kind of grin. Her teeth were showing, anyway. 'If you ever tried, you'd find yourself a finger or three shy, most likely,' she says.

"Sometimes Lucy really *was* Screwlucy. Cats are moody, and sometimes they get manic; anyone who's ever had one will tell you that. Their eyes get big and kind of glary, their tails bush out, they go racing around the house; sometimes they'll rear right up on their back legs and prance, boxing at the air, like they're fighting with something they can see but human beings can't. Lucy got into a mood like that one night when she was about a year old—couldn't have been more than three weeks from the day when I come home and found Lulubelle gone.

"Anyway, Lucy came pelting in from the kitchen, did a kind of racing slide on the wood floor, jumped over Frank, and went skittering up the living room drapes, paw over paw. Left some pretty good holes in them, with threads hanging down. Then she just perched at the top on the rod, staring around the room with her blue eyes all big and wild and the tip of her tail snapping back and forth.

"Frank only jumped a little and then put his muzzle back on Lulubelle's shoe, but the cat scared the hell out of Lulubelle, who was deep in her book, and when she looked up at the cat, I could see that outright hate in her eyes again.

"'All right,' she said, 'that's enough. Everybody out of the goddam pool. We're going to find a good home for that little blue-eyed bitch, and if we're not smart enough to find a home for a purebred Siamese, we're going to take her to the animal shelter. I've had enough.'

"'What do you mean?' I ask her.

"'Are you blind?' she asks. 'Look what she did to my *drapes*! They're full of holes!'

" 'You want to see drapes with holes in them,' I say, 'why don't you go upstairs and look at the ones on my side of the bed. The bottoms are all ragged. Because *he* chews them.'

" 'That's different,' she says, glaring at me. 'That's different and you know it.'

"Well, I wasn't going to let that lie. No way I was going to let that one lie. 'The only reason you think it's different is because you like the dog you gave me and you don't like the cat I gave you,' I says. 'But I'll tell you one thing, Mrs. DeWitt: you take the cat to the animal shelter for clawing the living room drapes on Tuesday, I guarantee you I'll take the dog to the animal shelter for chewing the bedroom drapes on Wednesday. You got that?'

"She looked at me and started to cry. She threw her book at me and called me a bastard. A *mean* bastard. I tried to grab hold of her, make her stay long enough for me to at least *try* to make up—if there was a way to make up without backing down, which I didn't mean to do that time—but she pulled her arm out of my hand and ran out of the room. Frank ran out after her. They went upstairs and the bedroom door slammed.

"I gave her half an hour or so to cool off, then I went upstairs myself. The bedroom door was still shut, and when I started to open it, I was pushing against Frank. I could move him, but it was slow work with him sliding across the floor, and also noisy work. He was growling. And I mean *growling*, my friends; that was no fucking *purr*. If I'd gone in there, I believe he would have tried his solemn best to bite my manhood off. I slept on the couch that night. First time.

"A month later, give or take, she was gone."

If L.T. had timed his story right (most times he did; practice makes perfect), the bell signaling back to work at the W.S. Hepperton Processed Meats Plant of Ames, Iowa, would ring just about then, sparing him any questions from the new men (the old hands knew . . . and knew better than to ask) about whether or not L.T. and Lulubelle had reconciled, or if he knew where she was today, or—the all-time sixty-four-thousand-dollar question—if she and Frank were still together. There's nothing like the back-to-work bell to close off life's more embarrassing questions.

"Well," L.T. would say, putting away his thermos and then standing up and giving a stretch, "it has all led me to create what I call L.T. DeWitt's Theory of Pets."

They'd look at him expectantly, just as I had the first time I heard him use that grand phrase, but they would always end up feeling let down, just as I always had; a story that good deserved a better punchline, but L.T.'s never changed.

"If your dog and cat are getting along better than you and your wife," he'd say, "you better expect to come home some night and find a Dear John note on your refrigerator door."

He told that story a lot, as I've said, and one night when he came to my house for dinner, he told it for my wife and my wife's sister. My wife had invited Holly, who had been divorced almost two years, so the boys and the girls would balance up. I'm sure that's all it was, because Roslyn never liked L.T. DeWitt. Most people do, most people take to him like hands take to warm water, but Roslyn has never been most people. She didn't like the story of the note on the fridge and the pets, either—I could tell she didn't, although she chuckled in the right places. Holly . . . shit, I don't know. I've never been able to tell what that girl's thinking. Mostly just sits there with her hands in her lap, smiling like Mona Lisa. It was my fault that time, though, and I admit it. L.T. didn't want to tell it, but I kind of egged him on because it was so quiet around the dinner table, just the click of silverware and the clink of glasses, and I could almost feel my wife disliking L.T. It seemed to be coming off her in waves. And if L.T. had been able to feel that little Jack Russell terrier disliking him, he would probably be able to feel my wife doing the same. That's what I figured, anyhow.

So he told it, mostly to please me, I suppose, and he rolled his eyeballs in all the right places, as if saying "Gosh, she fooled me right and proper, didn't she?" and my wife chuckled here and there—they sounded as phony to me as Monopoly money looks—and Holly smiled her little Mona Lisa smile with her eyes downcast. Otherwise the dinner went off all right, and when it was over L.T. told Roslyn that he thanked her for "a sportin-fine meal" (whatever that is) and she told him to come any time, she and I liked to see his face in the place. That was a lie on her part, but I doubt there was ever a dinner party in this history of the world where a few lies weren't told. So it went off all right, at least until I was driving him home. L.T. started to talk about how it would be a year Lulubelle had been gone in just another week or so, their fourth anniversary, which is flowers if you're old-fashioned and electrical appliances if you're newfangled. Then he said as how Lulubelle's mother—at whose house Lulubelle had never shown up—was going to put up a marker with Lulubelle's name on it at the local cemetery. "Mrs. Simms says we have to consider her as one dead," L.T. said, and then he began to bawl. I was so shocked I nearly ran off the goddam road.

He cried so hard that when I was done being shocked, I began to be afraid all that pent-up grief might kill him with a stroke or a burst blood vessel or something. He rocked back and forth in the seat and slammed his open hands down on the dashboard. It was like there was a twister loose inside him. Finally I pulled over to the side of the road and began patting his shoulder. I could feel the heat of his skin right through his shirt, so hot it was baking.

"Come on, L.T.," I said. "That's enough."

"I just miss her," he said in a voice so thick with tears I could barely understand what he was saying. "Just so goddam *much*. I come home and there's no one but the cat, crying and crying, and pretty soon I'm crying, too, both of us crying while I fill up her dish with that goddam muck she eats."

He turned his flushed, streaming face full on me. Looking back into it was almost more than I could take, but I *did* take it; felt I *had* to take it. Who had gotten him telling the story about Lucy and Frank and the note on the refrigerator that night, after all? It hadn't been Mike Wallace or Dan Rather, that was for sure. So I looked back at him. I didn't quite dare hug him, in case that twister should somehow jump from him to me, but I kept patting his arm.

"I think she's alive somewhere, that's what I think," he said. His voice was still thick and wavery, but there was a kind of pitiful weak defiance in it as well. He wasn't telling me what he believed, but what he wished he could believe. I'm pretty sure of that.

"Well," I said, "you can believe that. No law against it, is there? And it isn't as if they found her *body*, or anything."

"I like to think of her out there in Nevada singing in some little casino hotel," he said. "Not in Vegas or Reno, she couldn't make it in one of the big towns, but in Winnemucca or Ely I'm pretty sure she could get by. Some place like that. She just saw a Singer Wanted sign and give up her idea of going home to her mother. Hell, the two of them never got on worth a shit anyway, that's what Lu used to say. And she *could* sing, you know. I don't know if you ever heard her, but she could. I don't guess she was great, but she was good. The first time I saw her, she was singing in the lounge of the Marriott Hotel. In Columbus, Ohio, that was. Or, another possibility . . ."

He hesitated, then went on in a lower voice.

"Prostitution is legal out there in Nevada, you know. Not in all the counties, but in most of them. She could be working one of them Green Lantern trailers or the Mustang Ranch. Lots of women have got a streak of whore in them. Lu had one. I don't mean she stepped around on me, or *slept* around on me, so I can't say how I know, but I do. She . . . yes, she could be in one of those places."

He stopped, eyes distant, maybe imagining Lulubelle on a bed in the back room of a Nevada trailer whorehouse, Lulubelle wearing nothing but stockings, washing off some unknown cowboy's stiff cock while from the other room came the sound of Steve Earle and the Dukes singing "Six Days on the Road" or a TV playing *Hollywood Squares*. Lulubelle whoring but not dead, the car by the side of the road—the little Subaru she had brought to the marriage—meaning nothing. The way an animal's look, so seemingly attentive, usually means nothing.

"I can believe that if I want," he said, swiping his swollen eyes with the insides of his wrists.

"Sure," I said. "You bet, L.T." Wondering what the grinning men who listened to his story while they ate their lunches would make of this L.T., this shaking man with his pale cheeks and red eyes and hot skin.

"Hell," he said, "I *do* believe that." He hesitated, then said it again: "I *do* believe that."

When I got back, Roslyn was in bed with a book in her hand and the covers pulled up to her breasts. Holly had gone home while I was driving L.T. back to his house. Roslyn was in a bad mood, and I found out why soon enough. The woman behind the Mona Lisa smile had been quite taken with my friend. Smitten by him, maybe. And my wife most definitely did not approve.

"How did he lose his license?" she asked, and before I could answer: "Drinking, wasn't it?"

"Drinking, yes. OUI." I sat down on my side of the bed and slipped off my shoes. "But that was nearly six months ago, and if he keeps his nose clean another two months, he gets it back. I think he will. He goes to AA, you know."

My wife grunted, clearly not impressed. I took off my shirt, sniffed the armpits, hung it back in the closet. I'd only worn it an hour or two, just for dinner.

"You know," my wife said, "I think it's a wonder the police didn't look a little more closely at *him* after his wife disappeared."

"They asked him some questions," I said, "but only to get as much information as they could. There was never any question of him doing it, Ros. They were never suspicious of him."

"Oh, you're so sure."

"As a matter of fact, I am. I know some stuff. Lulubelle called her mother from a hotel in eastern Colorado the day she left, and called her again from Salt Lake City the next day. She was fine then. Those were both weekdays, and L.T. was at the plant. He was at the plant the day they found her car parked off that ranch road near Caliente as well. Unless he can magically transport himself from place to place in the blink of an eye, he didn't kill her. Besides, he wouldn't. He loved her."

She grunted. It's this hateful sound of skepticism she makes sometimes. After almost thirty years of marriage, that sound still makes me want to turn on her and yell at her to stop it, to shit or get off the pot, either say what she means or keep quiet. This time I thought about telling her how L.T. had cried; how it had been like there was a cyclone inside of him, tearing loose everything that wasn't nailed down. I thought about it, but I didn't. Women don't trust tears from men. They may say different, but down deep they don't trust tears from men.

"Maybe you ought to call the police yourself," I said. "Offer them a little of your expert help. Point out the stuff they missed, just like Angela Lansbury on *Murder, She Wrote*."

I swung my legs into bed. She turned off the light. We lay there in darkness. When she spoke again, her tone was gentler.

"I don't like him. That's all. I don't, and I never have."

"Yeah," I said. "I guess that's clear."

"And I didn't like the way he looked at Holly."

Which meant, as I found out eventually, that she hadn't liked the way Holly looked at *him*. When she wasn't looking down at her plate, that is.

"I'd prefer you didn't ask him back to dinner," she said.

I kept quiet. It was late. I was tired. It had been a hard day, a harder evening, and I was tired. The last thing I wanted was to have an argument with my wife when I was tired and she was worried. That's the sort of argument where one of you ends up spending the night on the couch. And the only way to stop an argument like that is to be quiet. In a marriage, words are like rain. And the land of a marriage is filled with dry washes and arroyos that can become raging rivers in almost the wink of an eye. The therapists believe in talk, but most of them are either divorced or queer. It's silence that is a marriage's best friend.

Silence.

After a while, my best friend rolled over on her side,

away from me and into the place where she goes when she finally gives up the day. I lay awake a little while longer, thinking of a dusty little car, perhaps once white, parked nose-down in the ditch beside a ranch road out in the Nevada desert not too far from Caliente. The driver's side door standing open, the rearview mirror torn off its post and lying on the floor, the front seat sodden with blood and tracked over by the animals that had come in to investigate, perhaps to sample.

There was a man—they assumed he was a man, it almost always is—who had butchered five women out in that part of the world, five in three years, mostly during the time L.T. had been living with Lulubelle. Four of the women were transients. He would get them to stop somehow, then pull them out of their cars, rape them, dismember them with an axe, leave them a rise or two away for the buzzards and crows and weasels. The fifth one was an elderly rancher's wife. The police call this killer the Axe Man. As I write this, the Axe Man has not been captured. Nor has he killed again; if Cynthia Lulubelle Simms De-Witt was the Axe Man's sixth victim, she was also his last, at least so far. There is still some question, however, as to whether or not she *was* his sixth victim. If not in most minds, that question exists in the part of L.T.'s mind which is still allowed to hope.

The blood on the seat wasn't human blood, you see; it didn't take the Nevada State Forensics Unit five hours to determine that. The ranch hand who found Lulubelle's Subaru saw a cloud of circling birds half a mile away, and when he reached them, he found not a dismembered woman but a dismembered dog. Little was left but bones and teeth; the predators and scavengers had had their day, and there's not much meat on a Jack Russell terrier to begin

with. The Axe Man most definitely got Frank; Lulubelle's
fate is probable, but far from certain.

Perhaps, I thought, she *is* alive. Singing "Tie a Yellow
Ribbon" at The Jailhouse in Ely or "Take a Message to Mi-
chael" at The Rose of Santa Fe in Hawthorne. Backed up
by a three-piece combo. Old men trying to look young in
red vests and black string ties. Or maybe she's blowing
GM cowboys in Austin or Wendover—bending forward
until her breasts press flat on her thighs beneath a calendar
showing tulips in Holland; gripping set after set of flabby
buttocks in her hands and thinking about what to watch on
TV that night, when her shift is done. Perhaps she just
pulled over to the side of the road and walked away. People do that. I know it, and probably you do, too. Sometimes people just say fuck it and walk away. Maybe she
left Frank behind, thinking someone would come along
and give him a good home, only it was the Axe Man who
came along, and . . .

But no. I met Lulubelle, and for the life of me I can't see
her leaving a dog to most likely roast to death or starve to
death in the barrens. Especially not a dog she loved the
way she loved Frank. No, L.T. hadn't been exaggerating
about that; I saw them together, and I know.

She could still be alive somewhere. Technically speaking, at least, L.T.'s right about that. Just because I can't
think of a scenario that would lead from that car with the
door hanging open and the rearview mirror lying on the
floor and the dog lying dead and crow-picked two rises
away, just because I can't think of a scenario that would
lead from that place near Caliente to some other place
where Lulubelle Simms sings or sews or blows truckers,
safe and unknown, well, that doesn't mean that no such
scenario exists. As I told L.T., it isn't as if they found her
body; they just found her *car,* and the remains of the dog a

little way from the car. Lulubelle herself could be anywhere. You can see that.

I couldn't sleep and I felt thirsty. I got out of bed, went into the bathroom, and took the toothbrushes out of the glass we keep by the sink. I filled the glass with water. Then I sat down on the closed lid of the toilet and drank the water and thought about the sound that Siamese cats make, that weird crying, how it must sound good if you love them, how it must sound like coming home.

Djinn & Tonic
by *Tabitha King*

Once upon a time—well, it was last Tuesday, or *next* Tuesday—a Tuesday, certainly a Tuesday. Certainly it could not have been a *Monday*, what with long postal holidays and if not, everything backed up from the weekend, and it could not have been Friday, *try* ringing anybody at work on a Friday afternoon, just try. And a Thursday would be out of the question, please let's not discuss it. A Wednesday would be ridiculous, *look* how it's spelled, *that knot of extra letters in the middle*. So it *was* a Tuesday . . .

A couple was walking on a beach. A man and a woman, barefoot. A middle-aged couple, a bit saggy, a bit chubby, a bit bored, more than a bit married. Walking on a beach, the woman with her sandals in her hand, the man with his shoes—he did not own a pair of sandals, as he was not truly shoe-minded, frequently buying shoes that did not fit him very well and forcing his feet into them or slopping about in them, and developing corns and calluses and blisters. He was just as likely to go for a very long walk in the very expensive thin-soled dress Bally pumps she bought him when she was feeling guilty about what she spent on shoes as he was to attend a wedding in a pair of high-top Converse sneakers. Naturally, his naked feet were not very attractive. This is telling, but he neglected his toenails, too, and they were shockingly long and jagged, and made his wife quite cross.

The woman's toenails were properly trimmed, though not polished, as it was a little effort to reach them just to trim. Her heels were rather cracked and she had some hair on her big toes, too. But otherwise, Heidi Kravitz considered her feet to be, if not attractive, at least not *un*attractive, or nasty. And she quite liked shoes, and quite understood Mrs. Marcos' enthusiasm for buying the same shoe in different colors. She knew, of course, that some people regarded shoes fetishistically, but they were exactly the sort of people who did not care if a shoe was comfortable. And she did. Heidi might *buy* a shoe for its style, but she wouldn't wear it if it were uncomfortable. She would just enjoy owning such a shoe, admiring it, as she selected a comfortable pair. People who thought of shoes as vaginas— men, of course, men who thought of shoes as vaginas, well, all she could say was they were powerfully confused. It was her opinion that the male of the species had vaginas on the brain, which made an unfortunate image, but there was no arguing that men, at least heterosexual men, had terrible trouble distinguishing any number of things from a vagina. It wasn't just Dr. Freud's baleful influence, as it had gone on for ages before him. She was quite relieved to be female, even with the curse and pregnancy and children and getting paid seventy cents on the dollar, and the flushes she was having these days despite the fact she was *too young* for the Change. At least she could tell a vagina from a shoe. And would be happy to inform Dr. Freud that she had never mistaken a cigar for a penis. She suspected he had only said sometimes a cigar is just a cigar because he smoked the nasty things, and didn't want anybody getting the idea he needed a penis substitute in his mouth, and of course the nasty things killed him—the cigars—not that he would still be alive if he had sucked some penises instead.

Scott and Heidi Kravitz had been married since a Tuesday twenty years previous, and were on vacation. They had decided to do it cheaply, in day trips from home. They had picked strawberries on Saturday and had lobster at a shack that evening, and on Sunday they had taken a boat tour to see the whales and had spaghetti at an Italian place. On Monday it had rained torrentially and they had played Scrabble and lazed about reading the newspapers left over from Sunday, and for supper they had grilled steak and a nice red Italian wine (di Montalcino) and ate alfresco, appropriately, on their own back porch, and watched lightning in the sky. The weather had cleared in the morning, so they packed a picnic and headed back to the coast, which was only thirty miles away from home. The picnic cooler was still in the trunk of their sedan, along with a pair of folding lawn chairs, an umbrella, some towels, a bag with sunblock and bathing suits and fat paperback novels (Stephen King for him, John Grisham for her). The invigoration of the ocean air immediately inspired Heidi to shed her sandals and set off down the beach. Scott had to stop and take off his shoes and roll up the legs of his Dockers, which she had bought him. He did not like them as much as his Levi's, but she had been blunt about how he looked from the rear in his jeans these days.

When she stopped abruptly at the waterline to stare out at the ocean, and let the water wash over her feet, he caught up with her. She always liked to stand at the very edge of the water and let the water suck the sand out from her feet, even though it made her lurch and grab his arm for balance. It also always made her smile, and he did like it when she smiled, even if it was usually over something silly.

She was cat-like, he had long ago concluded, quite pleased at his poetic perspicacity, and he enjoyed observing her cat-like habits, her self-absorption and sensuality. He considered it to be feminine and naturally her femininity made him feel masculine, even when it was irritating, as it frequently was. She was never, for instance, satisfied with how he loaded the dishwasher, when he thought it ought to be admirable that he was doing it at all. She had a knack for disappearing in department stores. And she had so many shoes that she would never in this life actually know for sure what it was to walk in her own shoes, all of them, let alone someone else's. For goddamn sure he had seen shoes in her closet that he had never seen on her feet.

They slogged down the beach together, Heidi being sensual and savoring the grains of sand rolling under her feet, and the tug of the ocean breeze and the smell of it, and the sound of the water sucking in and out, and Scott thinking the ocean smelled like a vagina and the water had that pull, and digging his toes into the wet sand was like fingering a vagina. And he tripped, and grabbed his wife, who staggered at the unexpected weight thrown on her.

"Fuck," he exclaimed, sitting down abruptly to examine his toe. He had broken his big toenail on whatever it was.

Heidi sank into a crouch over the object that had tripped him and brushed away the sand with the fastidiousness of an archaeologist uncovering an incisor of the missing link. She showed him her find: It was a curious vessel, a brass pot shaped rather like a large and flaccid womb and with a red rubber stopper in its poorly made neck. It was somewhat scummy with having been submersed, and a straggle of seaweed bearded the rubber stopper.

"Looks like a brass twat," the man observed.

"Don't be silly," his wife said tartly.

An inveterate sniffer, she raised it cautiously to her nose. She grimaced; it smelled distinctly of clams. Holding it to her ear, she shook it gently. There was no slosh of liquid contents, or rattle of dry, or shift of weight. It seemed to be empty. She held it in both hands, studying it, and then tried to pull out the stopper. It was quite stuck.

Scott left off tugging the curl of torn nail on his big toe, and scuttled to her side. "Here, let me," he said, and took hold of it, but she held on, shaking her head, telling him, "No, I can do it," and he gave a yank and she yanked back and fell over from her crouch and he fell over from his, and the pot fell between them. They sat up, glaring at each other, and then noticed, simultaneously, that the pot was on its side, the stopper dislodged. A vapor seemed to be seeping from the open neck, a vapor that thickened and twined and twisted and braided and wavered in the sea air over the pot and Heidi and Scott, kneeling on the sand. The vapor—which had a very pleasant odor, rather like bergamot, with a touch of honey and lemon—solidified into a man-shape, a pear-shaped man, in baggy silk pajama pants over which his rolls of tummy bulged beneath an open silk vest. His head was turbanned and he wore slippers with turned-up toes. He grinned a very fine grin that displayed truly marvelous teeth, teeth that an oyster might envy, if oysters know envy, which in this fallen creation may sadly be the case. In one ear he wore a large gold ring, and his fingers were all be-ringed, and his fat arms were braceletted above the elbow in multiple bands of heavily chased gold.

"Oh my gawd!" Heidi said.

"No, no, dear lady," the apparition soothed, "I beg you, no such blasphemous declarations."

"A djinn," said Scott. "Heidi, it's a djinn."

And the Djinn nodded his head politely at Heidi, confirming this, and then at Scott.

"Education is a wonderful thing," the Djinn observed. "It is rare of late that I am not recognized." He laughed heartily, and clapped his hands. "You surely know, as you knew me, that I must grant you wishes three."

The Kravitzes looked at each other. Heidi's hands went to her breast. Scott stared at her, his eyes wet and his mouth loose with panic. She turned her gaze slowly back to the Djinn. She cleared her throat. And said slowly to the Djinn, "May we consult, my husband and I?"

The Djinn frowned thoughtfully and crossed his arms and nodded, briskly, but affirmatively. He glanced at his wrist, where a Rolex appeared at once, the new Visible-Only-When-You-Need-to-See-It, Special-to-the-Djinn-Trade model. Gold links and diamond chips glinted in a dazzling disk in the sun, to allow the Djinn to note the time. Man and Wife conferred frantically in whispers. Suddenly there was a loud bong, as of a striker hitting a—gong, what else, and the Rolex disappeared from the Djinn's wrist. The Djinn's smile focused politely on Woman and Husband.

It was Scott's turn to clear his throat—they had been married long enough to take turns in such matters. "That's three wishes apiece, right?"

The Djinn rolled his eyes, grinned mirthlessly and chuckled without warmth. "A little education is a dangerous thing," he said. "I see you do not understand the rules."

His hands spread and in his broad square palms, several shades lighter than the backs of his hands, a large, heavy book, ornately bound in leather and stamped in gold appeared, open, the sea breeze riffling its fine vellum pages. The couple squinted at it. Words appeared on the page as if directly from the tip of a calligrapher's brush, a very impressive effect as you can no doubt imagine.

USERS MANUAL
RULE THE FIRST:
WISHES THREE UNTO THEE.
NO LESS NO MORE.
NO FOUR. FORGET IT.
DO NOT EVEN THINK ABOUT IT.

The Kravitzes sat back upon their haunches.

"We have more wants than three," Heidi blurted.

Scott covered his eyes.

The Djinn wrinkled his nose and sniffed at the air.

"Wants are not wishes, wishes are not wants—what is it, people, you cannot tell the diff'?" demanded the Djinn. "As my old mother used to say, clams are not fishes and kisses are not scrams. Speak the word *wish* and for *three* times, your wish will be, and after that, ta ta to Thee."

Mouth pursing, the Djinn clapped his hands soundly, and the shock wave knocked the Kravitzes flat onto the sand, wherein they buried their faces while covering their ears with their hands. There was a great rumble, like laughter, or perhaps a very loud Bronx cheer, and when the couple dared to lift their heads, the Djinn was gone.

The water had crept up and the curious vessel bobbed in it, the water drawing it swiftly away. Scott scrambled after it, but the water increased its speed, the curious vessel seeming to skitter on invisible feet, and a wave like a fat foam-be-ringed hand reached out and snatched it away from his grasping hands.

Scott trudged back to Heidi, and held out his hand. She took it and he pulled her to her bare and sandy feet.

"You would ask for more," he said crossly.

"You couldn't even stop it floating away," she retorted, brushing sand from the fanny of her shorts.

There was definitely a quarrel brewing.

"I wish," he began, and she clapped her hand over his

mouth so quickly that he was almost unbalanced right off his feet and had to grab at her.

"Don't," Heidi shrieked, "whatever you do, don't use that word!"

A Rolex watch appeared in the air between them, rotating gently to allow both of them to see it. "Well?" inquired the Djinn's disembodied voice.

"We have to talk about this!" cried Heidi as Scott peeled her hand off his mouth.

"I wish I was a billionaire!" shouted Scott.

With the sound of the bong, the Rolex vanished. The Kravitzes looked about frantically, but no bundles of bills appeared, nor did coins rain down from the blue skies.

Scott's shoulders slumped eloquently, with that special eloquence, in fact, that only shoulders have. "Just as I figured. Bullshit. Unadulterated bullshit." He began to trudge back down the beach the way they had come.

Heidi stamped her feet. "Goddamn it, Scottie, you just charged ahead and didn't let me have any input!"

"Stuff it, Heidi," Scott said, much to her surprise, but he was a sorely disappointed man.

Tears sprang to her eyes, for there was a tone in his voice he rarely used and that was enormously hurtful to her. Heidi gathered her sandals, dropped in all the excitement. She noticed his shoes but straightened her shoulders and left them. If he bothered himself to come back for them, they would be good and wet.

She trotted after him. "Goddamn it, I wish he was dead," she muttered.

Ahead of her, Scott suddenly clutched his chest, and she heard the echoing sound of a bong.

There was a moment, as she looked at her late husband in his coffin, that Heidi thought about using the last wish to bring him back, but she restrained herself.

She had discovered while looking for a pair of shoes for the undertaker that the shoeboxes in his closet were filled with checkbooks on dozens of accounts in banks around the world, and that her husband had died a billionaire. Making her a very wealthy widow, and she still had her youth. After all, it was *she who had found the bottle on the beach.*

When she wasn't shopping, she spent most of her time thinking about what to do with the third wish. She could wish herself beautiful, and then she would be wealthy and beautiful but still forty-two. She could wish for a perfect body, which wasn't exactly the same as beautiful—look at Stallone and Schwarzenegger. And who wanted to have a great body and a wrinkled face? She could wish herself twenty again, and she expected that even as ordinary as she had been at twenty, she would have a lot more fun as an ordinary twenty with a ton of money. But then she would have to give up her kids and she did not really want to erase them, or at least not all three of them (Scottie Jr. had been transformed into an instant pest over the M-O-N-E-Y). And now that Scott was dead, she couldn't have them all over again. Too bad he had never banked any sperm. No, that die was cast.

She could wish herself powerful, which she already was, to some degree. People were really sitting up and taking notice of her now, but that was just because of what she could buy. But she did not have a clue how one used money to do anything else but buy things.

She could wish herself famous, and her money was also already doing that to an extent, but it wasn't really famous for her own accomplishments. She did not want to be president—her current hairstyle on the Internet, the whole world discussing her weight and the size of her fanny, and what she was spending on clothes and shoes, and how they looked on her and, of course, politics, all those self-important old men making laws to benefit lobbyists. Nor did she want to be pope—all those self-important old men muttering Latin, that hat, though Rome might be okay if she could have up-to-date plumbing, and the Italians had shoes *down,* but then there was the celibacy—no thank you.

Sprawled on the newly purchased gorgeous antique Persian rug on her bedroom floor in a nest of wrapping tissue and surrounded by beautiful expensive shoes, she made a list: Beauty, Great Body, Youth, Fame, Power. What else was there to want? She congratulated herself on her sense of moderation. Now the trick would be to discover a way to get all of those things in one wish. But she couldn't think of it just then, so she went shopping.

Three hours later, she was just exhausted. She slumped into a chair in the café in Borders and just sat, staring at her decaf latte, her bundles and bags around her feet. Which were sore. She slipped off her shoes. Ferragamo. Black with a touch of horn, a nice two-inch heel. It wasn't the shoes; she had done a lot of shopping lately and her feet were talking back to her.

"I wish," Heidi muttered, her thoughts on how nice it would be not to have sore feet, but she stopped herself in time, horrified that she had nearly thrown away the third wish, wishing for feet that didn't hurt.

But she had said it aloud, and sure enough, there was the Djinn's Rolex hanging in front of her in midair. She glanced around, but nobody seemed to notice, so presumably it wasn't visible to them.

"I didn't mean it," she whispered.

"Ho-ho," the Djinn's voice said sardonically. "Too bad."

It occurred to her she had no idea how much time she actually had to complete the wish. Her memory of the Manual was there had not been a time limit, but then she and Scott had only been shown the first rule. For an instant she was distracted, missing Scott, whom she could always beat at Scrabble. She decided to ignore the crystal face with its parade of diamonds and swiftly circling hands. She wiggled her toes. If only she could wiggle her toes and solve everything. And she realized that was exactly the answer.

"I wish," she said teasingly, drawing it out, "I had a pair of magic shoes."

The Rolex wavered. "Hmmmn," the voice of the Djinn hummed, like an open telephone line. "Please," the Djinn finally said sulkily, "could one be more specific? Orlando? Ervin Johnson?" and then, whining, "*What?*"

A little thought and then she said, "*Magical* shoes."

A bong so loud it seemed to shake the floor sounded in her ears, and she clapped her hands over them and clenched her eyes shut against the noise. It rumbled on like the Djinn's own laugh, shaking the whole building, and she fell out of her chair.

Several people who had seemed to be oblivious to her exchange with the Djinn jumped up from their chairs at other tables in the café to help her up. In something of a daze she thanked them, and sank back into her chair. Only then did she notice that her Ferragamos had disappeared and her feet were now clad in Ruby Slippers. They were not exactly like the ones from *The Wizard of Oz* but they were very similar, as if they were the same label. The heel was higher and blockier and the sole thicker, in next season's style. They sparkled and gleamed and felt, she thought, quite heavenly. Most remarkably, her feet no longer ached at all.

After admiring them for several moments, she gathered her purchases and set off for her limo. As she walked, she wondered if her step really had become lighter, or if it was the shoes. And then she frowned. She had no idea how the shoes—how the shoes—*operated*.

Dorothy had clicked her Ruby Slippers twice, and wished to go home. And had woken up in Kansas, with Aunt Em and Uncle Ugly, or whoever the old fart was. After that, the only thing Heidi could remember about the Ruby Slippers was that they had been sold at auction sometime or other. The prop slippers.

It was confusing, the movie and reality, and of course the movie was *part* of reality, a fantasy that really existed on film and in print. Heidi started to feel a migraine coming on. Her migraines were always preceded by a peculiar kind of aura—the odor of fried clams.

With no idea how many wishes the shoes empowered, she had to fight wishing the migraine away. The horrifying thought that maybe all they would do for her is take her *home,* or possibly to *Kansas,* struck her, igniting the migraine full force. Home, from whence she had fled at eighteen, was a mill town in New Hampshire. The air there had looked like a yellow fog and tasted like sulfur. Until she bought the mansion after her husband bought the farm, home had been a ranch house in Olde Haddock, New Jersey. At the time it had been pleasant enough, but it was no mansion. She had definitely outgrown New Jersey ranch houses. She had never been to Kansas and had no desire to go. They probably had real ranch houses there. Teeth gritted, she flung herself into the limo.

"Home," she moaned to the driver.

"Yes, ma'am," he said, glancing at her suffering face in the rearview mirror. Knowing she was a recent widow, he assumed she must be overcome with a sudden upwelling of grief.

At home in the mansion, she had the maid, Simone, draw her a bath, while she endured her migraine on the dull gold shot-silk coverlet of her beautiful round bed. She was so wracked, she simply fell on it, and writhed about moaning until the maid told her the bath was ready. Simone helped her from the bed and into the bathroom and then had to assist her with her buttons. At last Heidi was down to her panties, panty hose, and the Ruby Slippers. She lifted one foot wearily as Simone knelt at her side, prepared to remove the shoe while providing support for her. The maid tugged at the shoe. It did not move. Simone tugged harder.

"Your feet must be swollen up, Miz Kravitz," said Simone, "no wonder your head aching."

The shoe did not come off. Heidi dragged the bench from the vanity table under her bottom and sat down, to give better purchase. But the shoe would not be removed, nor would the other.

"Never mind," Heidi told Simone, "I'll get them off myself."

"Whatever."

Heidi waved her out. Simone backed out reluctantly since she was curious about the slippers. She could swear her hands were still tingling from them.

"Goddamn it," Heidi cried as her own efforts proved useless.

The odd thing was that her feet were not swollen. The shoes appeared to be a perfect fit. Her toes wiggled in them very comfortably. Her feet were not even hot, though usually all day in panty hose would make them sweat.

Plumping herself down on the edge of the spa, she gingerly lowered her feet into the foamy water. Hastily she squiggled backward, lifting them out, and toweled the shoes dry. Still the Ruby Slippers sparkled and gleamed and appeared to be quite undamaged. Her panty hose was wet around the ankle, though. Yuk.

All day traipsing around in search of shoes, the migraine, the struggle to remove the Ruby Slippers, and she felt the way she used to feel back in high school after a night of shlepping fried clams at Austin's Clam Shack. Four years of paranoia that she stank of fried clams, no matter how much she shampooed her hair and doused herself with perfume. She was not relieved by her friends' jokes about Heidi of the Clam Necks. In local parlance, clam necks were erect nipples. She had not eaten clams since she was a freshman in high school.

The hell with it, she concluded. Concluding the hell with it had gotten her pregnant, it could be said, and married to Scott. Never mind her parents and their bickering, it was Austin's Clam Shack that had made Heidi who she was. A woman so humiliated and depressed by the ghosts of the vapors of deep fat fryers in which clams had met their fate that she was prone to migraines and wont to jump off metaphoric cliffs.

"Let the good times roll," she muttered, and lowered herself into the spa until the freesia-scented foam was up to her clavicle. She raised a leg, and the shoe on her foot remained as beautiful as ever, the water beading on it like little diamonds. So she had a nice soak, considering the wet underwear clinging to her. When she climbed out of the spa, the panties and panty hose were running water, of course, and she tried to towel them dry. It was an ineffective process to say the least.

"There should be a manual," Heidi said aloud.

She could wish for one. But it would waste a wish and she did not know how many she had. She hoped for a minimum of three, but perhaps it would only be one. Bingo.

"I wish for all my wishes to come true," she declared, and remembering what Glinda and Dorothy had both done, she clicked the heels of the slippers together with great brio.

Nothing happened.

She took a deep breath. "I wish my panties and panty hose were gone."

And they were. She was buck naked, except for the magical slippers.

"I wish I was a size six."

And she was.

"Thirty-six C."

And she was.

Rapidly she ran through a list of physical attributes, eliminating the softness under her chin, the bags under her eyes, the sagging of fanny and boobs and belly, the stretch marks, making herself a natural blonde with hazel eyes with perfect vision with perfect teeth. She wished herself seventeen, with a courtesan's skills, if courtesans really had any. Later, she promised herself, she would wish herself Kevin Bacon to try them out on.

She wished herself witty, brilliant, musical, with perfect pitch and a soprano voice that would cause an archangel to despair and slink off to the netherworld. She wished herself artistic, with an incredible eye for what the art market would be in ten and twenty years, yet flawless taste of her own. She wished her children all the things she had wished for herself, less ten percent. She wished her parents would stop bickering. She wished Austin's Clam Shack to burn down and all species of clams to become inedible to human beings. She wished for wisdom.

At that point her feet began to feel a little warm, and when she looked down, she saw the Ruby Slippers were now a dull ashen gray, like barbecue coals. And they no longer fit her feet, but slopped about them like runover bed slippers. They were used up, she realized, and stepped out of them. Yet she had asked for all her wishes to come true.

She had many more wishes to wish. World peace, a cure for cancer. To live forever.

And then it occurred to her. Everything she had yet to wish would come true. Peace would come to the planet when it was an ash, whirling in space, after the sun novaed. Cancer would be cured, and something worse would kill people. She would one day wish she could die, and it was better if she did; life must be renewed and not lived forever by one organism. Her DNA would go on through her children and grandchildren—she had forgotten to wish for grandchildren! Oh, well—in any case her DNA would be transformed into another form of matter.

She looked into the mirror and saw that the size-six body was not her, but only an approximation of a strung-out boy with implanted boobs, the ideal of a decadent fashion industry. She realized that what she had wished for her children would take away their own free will, and their own random luck, the very process of the life she had given them. She had no right. And it came to her that her parents bickering was only the style of their marriage and they both enjoyed the engagement.

If she had talent, musical or artistic or any other kind, she should find it in herself and do the work of developing it for it to be any good. That was innate in anything worthwhile. It was the process that made the artist.

And some people, she thought, quite a few people, really enjoyed eating clams—and some birds and beasties too—and she had no right to take that small sustaining pleasure from them.

"Aw, shit," she muttered. She stepped out of the slippers and watched sadly as they withered completely to ash. The ash whirled suddenly into miniature twin dust devils and was gone.

Suddenly she was lonely. "I wish Scott was here," she

said, "I'd like to tell him I'm sorry. I wish I could take it all back."

But there was only a long silence.

She took her robe from the hook where Simone had hung it and shrugged into it. She found her terry cloth bath slippers with her monogram in teal.

"I'm going to have to live with this," she said aloud. "Aren't I?"

She stood very still and listened intently and after a moment thought she heard the humming of an open telephone line, meaningless as the sound of the sea in a conch shell.

here or When
by Ed McBain

He knows he's done something terribly wrong, but he can't remember where or when or what it was. It torments him day and night, this inability to remember it all clearly. He has the certain knowledge that he will never make peace with whatever it was until he knows exactly what happened. But there are only broken shards of what he believes to be memory, teasing rather than satisfying.

There is a bar. Neon sputters into the darkness of the night. ART'S TAVERN. A blond girl in a red dress comes out of the bar, staggering slightly on very high-heeled shoes.

In the beginning, this is all he can remember.

He is afraid to mention any of this to Phyllis because she might think he's going crazy. She probably considers him a bit strange, anyway, the way he's always sitting at the computer, talking to people far away on the Internet. He tries to explain that this is his hobby, a form of relaxation from a job that's enormously stressful.

"A security guard?" Phyllis says. "That's stressful? When's the last time you broke up a big bank robbery, Fred?"

And laughs.

Sometimes when she laughs at him, he feels like . . .

Well.

The manager at the bank is a woman named Helen

Cartwright. She is about Fred's age, thirty-eight, thirty-nine, but of course she's a person in a position of prominence, and she doesn't have to be nice or even courteous to someone who's a mere security guard. Before the shooting, when Fred was a detective first grade, he would have commanded respect from someone like Miss Cartwright. Someone like Miss Cartwright might even have feared him back then when he was working out of Robbery Division. But that was before the shooting, of course.

He sometimes thinks this is only a dream, this terrible thing he believes he's done. Nothing but a bad dream. A nightmare. And yet bits and pieces of it come back to him while he's awake, at unexpected times, so how can it be a dream?

He'll be walking down the street when suddenly he'll see the sputtering neon sign spelling out ART'S TAVERN. And it will disappear in a minute. Or sometimes at the bank, standing just inside the big stainless steel doors, wearing the gray uniform with the square shield, hands behind his back, smiling at people as they come in, sometimes in a brilliant flash of light, he'll see the blond girl coming out of the bar. Or late at night, sitting at his computer, she'll suddenly appear on the screen, walking out of the bar again.

It is a steamy summer night, her red dress is gossamer and clingy. The high-heeled shoes are red, to match the dress. She wears her blond hair short. She is perhaps nineteen or twenty, a tall, angular girl who appears awkward in the tight dress and high-heeled shoes, as if she's playing dress-up in her mother's clothes.

Swaying, she opens her bag and takes a package of cigarettes from it. She puts one between her lips, begins searching the bag for a match. In the bar behind her, someone begins playing a piano, and a sad, wistful, nostalgic song floods the night. She can't find a match, he hears her sigh of exasperation. She snaps the bag shut, takes the cigarette from her mouth, looks up, sees him all at once, smiles, and begins walking toward him, the cigarette in her hand.

And then she is gone from the screen.

So he knows it's not a dream. Not if he can see her while he's awake. No, he's sure this is something that really happened. Something quite terrible.

But when? Or where?

Phyllis always kids him about breaking up bank robberies, ha ha ha, but that was actually how he'd got shot. In movies and on TV, your average squadroom detective is always running around with a gun in his hand, chasing the bad guys, but this rarely happens in real life. In reality, most squadroom investigations don't end in gunplay. Unless you're a Rob Cop. If you're working out of Robbery Division, you'll nine times out of ten catch a robbery-in-progress squeal, which means the perp is still inside the liquor store or the bank or somebody's house. This was what happened with Fred.

He was riding shotgun with his partner, Louis, when they caught the 10-30, a robbery in progress at 1140 Third Avenue, Bankers Trust building on the corner of Third and Meade. Louis hit the hammer, and they went screaming toward the bank, getting there just as two guys in ski masks came barreling out, spilling money from canvas bags and waving AK-47's. The first burst killed Louis on the spot. The second burst shattered four of Fred's ribs, pierced his left lung, and sent him to the hospital leaking blood from everywhere. He was in a coma for seventy-two hours. Both perps got away.

Now he is a security guard.

And Helen Cartwright keeps telling him to put a glossier shine on his black shoes.

"You wouldn't happen to have a light, would you?" the blonde asks.

Her voice is somewhat slurred. She is smiling now, the hand with the cigarette held close to her mouth in anticipation. He no longer smokes, not since the shooting, but he still carries a lighter, and he takes this from his jacket pocket now and thumbs it into flame. The girl leans into it, head bent, blond hair dangling. She lets out a stream of smoke that is carried away swiftly on a mild summer wind.

"Thanks," she says. "I'm Suzie."

He also still carries a gun.

If this really happened . . .

And of course it really happened.

. . . then there is a place in this city called Art's Tavern. And if there *is* such a place, then a detective—well, a *former* detective—should be able to find it. But he checks the directories for every section of the city, white pages and yellow pages both, and he can't find a listing for any bar with that name, in big neon capital letters or any *other* kind of letter.

So where *did* this happen?

If it happened.

It happened.

In the police department, they believe that a cop who gets shot is a cop who doesn't know his job. If he's doing his job right, he doesn't get shot. That is the way the department thinks.

Never mind that the two sons of bitches came barreling out of that bank at almost the same instant Louis and Fred got out of the car; never mind that the surprise was total, two bank robbers looking at a max of twenty-five in prison, they don't hesitate, they just squeeze triggers and the automatic weapons do the rest.

Doctors were actually inside Fred's chest, massaging his heart, working to save his life.

In the coma there were flashes of blinding light, an electrical storm in his head.

Phyllis's sister Mame says something like that can affect a man for the rest of his life.

Now he sees pictures of a young blond girl coming out of a bar on a steamy summer night.

At the bank, he is bored to death most of the time. He was once part of a twelve-man team that responded to holdups all over the city, came in after the fact, too, investigating robberies past, trying to work out whodunit. Detective First Grade Frederick Sloane Prescott, the Sloane after his mother's maiden name, twice decorated for bravery. Gets cold-cocked stepping out of a car by a pair of kids wearing ski masks. He guessed they were kids. Who the hell else would walk into a bank at high noon in broad daylight? Crazy bastards.

They think you can't cut it anymore.

Also, they're afraid to work with you.

You get shot once, they think you'll get shot again. Shit, look what happened to your partner. Louis dead on the sidewalk, you in the hospital bleeding, who the hell wants *you* for a partner?

You tell the police psychologist you want to go back to work. You're okay now. You feel fine. He tells you he doesn't think that's such a good idea. What'll happen if you come up against the same situation again? Another hood in a ski mask waving an AK-47?

Take another job.

Quit the force.

Is what the police psychologist recommends.

He sometimes gets mad as hell over what happened.

He sometimes feels like shooting someone.

The gun he still packs is a Colt .45 caliber automatic. He has a carry permit for it, which he got because he was once such a sterling member of the police department, and also because he is now a security officer, a bank guard, a square-shield bank *dick*.

He sometimes gets so angry.

Phyllis pisses him off even more than Helen Cartwright does. Phyllis works for the telephone company, and she is trained to be rude to people, but he is, after all, her husband, and she doesn't have to carry her work habits home with her.

"Are you going to sit there talking to phantoms all night long?" she asks.

She is referring to the Internet, of course, the people he talks to on the computer. But at first he thinks she has somehow learned about the blond girl coming out of Art's Tavern, asking him for a light—but the bar doesn't exist. He looked it up, he knows there is no such bar in this city. And if the bar doesn't exist, then how can the girl exist? Suzie.

"Thanks. I'm Suzie."

"I'm Fred."

"Nice to meet you, Fred."

Voice still slurred. Dragging on the cigarette. Wind carrying away the smoke, flattening the thin dress against her thighs. Wobbly on the high-heeled shoes. "Oops," she says as she steps off the curb, *tries* to step off the curb, and grabs his arm for support. "Wee bit much to drink in there," she says, and winks at him conspiratorially, and tosses her head, her hair, toward the bar. She is really quite beautiful. She reminds him a lot of Phyllis when she was this age, the blue eyes and high cheekbones, the full, pouting mouth and the spatter of freckles across the bridge of her nose. Well, not the blond hair. Phyllis's hair is dark. So is Helen Cartwright's, come to think of it.

He wonders why all the women who annoy him have dark hair.

The other two guards at the bank are in their sixties, retired men with time on their hands. He is here at the bank to face his demons. He could have taken any other kind of security job. He is, after all, a man with sixteen years' experience in police work. That counts for something in security work. The experience. They always ask you why you left the force, though. Young man like you. Why'd you leave the force? You either have to lie or tell them you got shot. Some of them back off at once. Well, Mr. Prescott, thanks for coming in, we'll let you know. *Detective* Prescott, he feels like telling them. Detective First *Grade* Prescott. But he wants the job.

The job at First Federal is perfect for him. It even resembles Bankers Trust on Third and Meade, where he got shot. Same big steel doors. Same marble floors. He is not hoping anyone will come in to rob the bank. But he is there to stop anyone who tries. There is a gun in a holster on his hip. Not his personal gun, the .45 for which he has a carry permit. This one is a Police Positive Special.

He prefers his own weapon.

* * *

In the dream . . .

He knows it isn't a dream.

In the memory, then . . .

But he's not sure it's a memory, either.

Whatever the hell it is, then, Suzie asks him if he'd mind walking her home. She lives about ten blocks from here, she tells him, and this isn't a particularly terrific neighborhood, but she *would* like some fresh air before she walks in drunk on her mother watching a late-night movie.

"Well, not *drunk,* Ted," she says, "but certainly a little . . ."

"Fred," he says.

"Fred," she says, and nods. "Is what I said, didn't I?"

"You said Ted."

"Was what I meant. Fred. So will you walk me home, Fred?"

"Sure," he says, "why not?"

What am I doing here? he wonders, and is suddenly glad he's strapped. If he wasn't carrying the .45, he might be concerned in a shitty neighborhood like this one. But there *is* no such neighborhood because there's no such place as Art's Tavern. Besides, he's been in worse neighborhoods, so why is he suddenly so frightened?

He is frightened because he know what is going to happen.

Now it is only a matter of where and when.

It has been a hot, steamy August, and today is no different from any of the others. At the bank, he swelters in the gray uniform and white shirt with its constricting starched collar and black silk tie. When he was a detective, he favored open-throated shirts and loose-fitting sports jackets or sweaters. He used to carry the piece in a holster clipped to his belt on the right-hand side, same as he does now.

Here at the bank, there is a big, wide belt at his waist, with the .38 hanging there in a black holster with a flap on it.

Helen Cartwright comes over to him and whispers, "Keep an eye on the guy with Mr. Hastings."

Mr. Hastings is an assistant manager. The guy sitting with him is a portly gentleman in his late fifties. If he is a bank robber, Fred will eat the man's brown leather briefcase. But he keeps a dutiful, watchful eye on him, just as instructed, until the man gets up, shakes hands with Hastings, and waddles out of the bank.

Helen Cartwright comes over to him a moment later.

"Good work, Prescott," she says, and claps her hand on his shoulder.

"Thank you, Miss Cartwright," he says, and is pleased when she gives him a smile and an appreciative nod. And then, quite suddenly, he is ashamed of himself for having curried her favor and savored her praise.

Detective First Grade Fred Prescott would have told her to go straight to hell.

"So what do you do for a living?" Suzie asks him.

The streets are deserted at this hour of the night, one-fifteen by a big clock in the window of a gated jewelry store they pass. What is he doing in this neighborhood at this time of night with this young girl who is beginning to sober up as they walk?

"I'm a police detective," he says.

"Really?"

"Robbery Division," he says, and nods.

"That must be exciting."

"Sometimes," he says. "Usually it's just a lot of legwork and paperwork."

"Oh, sure, I'll bet," she says.

"Really," he says.

The street ahead seems unusually still.

All at once he *does* feel like a cop again, his senses alert, gauging the area ahead where he notices that the street lamp has been shattered, and that a fair portion of sidewalk is in complete darkness. An alley joins the black stretch of pavement, gaping even blacker on its left. There is a sudden faint sound in the alleyway. A cat?

"Did you hear something just then?" Suzie whispers.

He says nothing.

Places his left hand on her arm, quieting her. Throws back the flap of his jacket to liberate the butt of the .45. Puts his hand on it. Curls his fingers around the walnut stock. Feels the spring-assisted release easing the pistol out of the holster.

His hand is wet with sweat.

He realizes too late that this is a classic mousetrap ambush. The smashed street lamp, the darkened sidewalk and alley were merely the bait, the squeaking little mouse attracting attention ahead while the predatory cat creeps up from behind.

But the pair drop from a fire escape instead, winged marauders wearing black from head to toe, black T-shirts and black jeans, black sneakers, their hands and faces the only show of white in the otherwise blackness of clothing and night. At the same moment the two who'd decoyed them rush out of the alley ahead, similarly dressed, so that Fred and the girl are flanked front and back. It is going to be Bankers Trust all over again, total surprise, and then the abrupt, shocking explosion of gunfire, and Louis falling soundlessly to the pavement, and his own chest erupting in searing pain, oh Jesus, it is the same thing all over again.

But he sees no guns, only the faint glint of metal on the soot black night. Knives, then, it is to be knives, more frightening somehow unless you've been shot and know the difference. All four armed with knives and closing in with the speed of practice and repetition, these are not amateurs. This quartet believes it owns the night.

Suzie screams. She has seen the knives.

The two who'd dropped from overhead are the closest, and so he takes them out first. Slams Suzie back against the side of the brick building with a swipe of his left arm, and still turning, still in motion, brings up the gun hand and fires as he whirls on them, two in the chest for the one on the right, a single shot to the shoulder for the one on the left, dropping them both just as they are about to spring forward, surprising them as completely as he and Louis had been surprised back then on the day of the Bankers Trust heist.

Suzie is still screaming.

There are yet two more of them, and he whirls on them calmly now, adrenaline pumping, the gun coming up and around, stopping them dead in their tracks because now they realize exactly what is happening. The mousetrap isn't working, two of their number are down, and there is a man standing in the middle of the sidewalk with a gun in his fist and a deadly calm look on his face and in his eyes. It is the calmness that frightens them. They turn to run, wanting no part of it, but they are the ones who started this, they are the ones who played into his fear and his anger, and he is not about to let them end this on their own terms.

"You!" he yells and shoots the first one twice in the chest as he is turning to run. "Here!" he yells at the second one, shooting him once in the back because he has already turned away, shooting him in the back again as he begins to fall forward, and yet again when he is lying still on his face on the sidewalk. He walks over to the other two. One of them is lying dead in a pool of his own blood. The other one, the one he shot in the shoulder, is still alive, lying on his back directly under the fire escape. He is just a boy, Fred sees now, no more than sixteen or seventeen. He levels the gun at him. Pulls the trigger. The hammer falls on an empty chamber.

Calmly, he ejects the spent clip, takes a fresh one from his jacket pocket, slams it home into the handle of the piece. "No, please don't," the boy says, looking up into the barrel of the gun, and Fred says, "Oh, please *don't*?" And fires directly into his mouth.

The blackness of the night closes around them like a fist.

He is beginning to find Helen Cartwright attractive. Perhaps it is because she praised him so highly for his acute surveillance of the fat guy with the brown briefcase. Perhaps it is because at home things aren't going too well between him and Phyllis. He can remember when they used to make love three, four times a week. But that was before the Bankers Trust holdup. That was before he'd got shot. Seventy-two hours in coma. *Something like that can affect a man for the rest of his life.* Phyllis's sister Mame speaking. The oracle of Cutler Heights, where she lives with her wimp accountant husband, Harold. Mame has dark hair, too, and a tongue as sharp as her sister's.

The only blonde he knows is the one he saved from the punks.

And she doesn't exist.

This can't be the terrible thing he thinks he's done, shooting the four punks. He's shot punks before and they never came back to haunt him, so he knows he wouldn't be this upset if what happened—whenever it happened, wherever it happened—was merely whacking four would-be muggers or rapists or both. Good riddance to bad rubbish, as his mother used to say.

Besides, if there's no place in this city called Art's Tavern, then there's no blonde named Suzie and no punks oozing blood on the sidewalk.

None of it ever happened.

None of it.

During the summer months the bank is closed on Saturdays. On Friday afternoon they shut the doors at three, but nobody leaves till five, six o'clock at night because they have to do their tallies and close out the books, or whatever it is that keeps them bustling around while Fred and the other guards stay there to protect them and the money until the armored car comes to pick it up.

At ten minutes past six on this last Friday in August, Fred is standing on the sidewalk waiting for Helen Cartwright to set the alarm and leave by the side entrance. It is a hot and sultry evening. The armored car has come and gone, and everyone has left for the weekend except Helen Cartwright, whose footfalls he now hears on the narrow walk leading to the sidewalk where he stands waiting.

She is surprised to see him.

"Fred!" she says. "You startled me."

"Sorry," he says, "I didn't mean to . . . Helen." He hesitates again. Then he says, "I was wondering if I could buy you a drink."

She looks up into his face.

"You've got to be kidding," she says, and turns on her heel and leaves him standing there on the sidewalk with his face flushing red in embarrassment that turns to rage when he hears her quiet laughter on the sultry air.

* * *

"I never saw anything like that in my *life*!" Suzie says. She is craning her head over her shoulder, looking back excitely at the bodies strewn all over the sidewalk. He is trying to rush her away from the scene because it has occurred to him that he is no longer a police officer and he has just slain four young men, boys, whatever. Punks. In self-defense, yes. But that would be for a jury to decide, and he doesn't feel like affording any twelve men, or women, or whoever, that singular opportunity. What he wants to do is get the hell away from here fast, get the girl home, wherever she lives, and then disappear into the night again.

She's cold sober now—all the action back there seems to have snapped her out of her mild intoxication. So she doesn't have to worry about smelling like a distillery when she walks in on her mother. Oh, no, she can breeze right in now and ask what movie Mom's watching, and then maybe casually mention . . .

Well, no, she wouldn't do that.

Would she?

Guess what, Mom? This nice man I met outside Art's Tavern just killed four kids who were trying to rape me. No, really, Mom, I'm serious. This very brave man pulled out a gun and . . .

No, she wouldn't.

"Listen," he says. "About what happened . . ."

And suddenly she throws her arms around his neck and kisses him.

The argument with Phyllis starts at about a quarter to eleven, and as usual it is about sex. She always gets ready for bed as if she's a hooker in a porn flick, short, filmy baby doll nightgown with no panties, high-heeled shoes, parading around the bedroom while she brushes out her hair; fifty strokes every night before retiring was what her mother taught her two darling daughters, Phyllis and Mame. Stroking the long, dark hair while she marches around the bedroom in the high heels, wiggling and jiggling, seemingly unaware that he's lying on the bed in just his pajama bottoms, watching her.

She still gets him excited, he has to admit that.

He has to admit, too, that if Helen Cartwright had accepted his offer to have a drink with him, he'd have tried to get her in bed, that was the whole idea of it. After all, she was the one who'd encouraged him . . .

Good work, Prescott.

Clapping her hand on his shoulder. Physical contact, right?

Thank you, Miss Cartwright.

A smile. An appreciative nod. Did he imagine a backward glance as her high heels clicked her away on the bank's marble floors?

Teases him along, gets him to dare calling her *Helen* instead of Miss Cartwright, and then shoots him down when he extends a gentlemanly invitation to share an after-hours drink.

Are you kidding?

Laughing at him.

"You going to brush your hair all night long?" he asks.

"Thirty-seven, thirty-eight, thirty-nine," she says out loud, to let him know she's counting strokes, and please don't bother her.

"Well, are you?"

"Forty, forty-one, will you please shut *up*?"

"Why don't you come over here?" he says.

"Forty-two, forty-three . . ."

"All right, after fifty," he says.

She counts the next seven strokes silently. He is counting them with her, silently. At last she walks back to her dressing table, puts down the brush, and is heading for the bathroom when he says, "Come here, Phyllis."

"Why?" she says, turning to him. Hands on her hips now. Bunched gown riding higher on her thighs. A glimpse of her.

"I want you, Phyll," he says.

"I'm about to get my period," she says, and walks into the bathroom and closes the door.

He wants to say, So what, it didn't used to matter years ago whether you had your period or you didn't. Before Bankers Trust, none of that mattered. I'm still the same man, Phyll, what difference does it make you're about to get your period or you're not? I want to make *love* to you, Phyll, why are you closing the door on me?

He wants to say all this, but instead he gets out of bed and dresses silently. He lifts the .45 from the dresser top, checks the clip. Full. He takes an extra clip from the middle dresser drawer, slips it into his jacket pocket.

Phyllis is still in there behind the closed door when he lets himself out of the bedroom and out of the house.

"That's to thank you for what you did," Suzie says. "I never saw anything so brave in my life." She kisses him again, breaks away, laughs. "There," she says. And kisses him again. And again laughs. "There."

He pulls her into him.

"Hey!" she says, and laughs again.

He pulls her closer, tries to kiss her again. She turns her head away. "No," she says. "Come on," he says. "No, damn it," she says, "get *away* from me!" and suddenly she is out of his grasp and running, *trying* to run. He reaches for her, "Hey, come on, Suzie," grabs the back of her dress near the collar, yanks it, feels it tearing away in his hands. She turns toward him, breasts exposed where the dress has fallen away, blue eyes blazing, hands coming up, fingers curling into claws.

"What the hell's *wrong* with you?" she shouts.

And comes at him, both hands going for his eyes. He feels her nails raking his face, feels searing pain where they slash him, feels embarrassed and ashamed and bewildered all at once. She kissed him, didn't she? Is he wrong about that? Didn't she kiss him? Three times? Didn't she say she'd never seen anything so brave in her life?

He remembers Helen Cartwright asking him if he's kidding, laughing at him, Phyllis asking when he last broke up a big bank robbery, laughing at him, and now Suzie's words echo inside his head, What the hell's *wrong* with you? and all at once the gun is in his hand, wrong with you, and he is firing at her, wrong with you, firing at her, wrong with you, firing, firing, firing.

He drops the gun only after the clip is empty.

Suzie lies still and broken on the pavement near the wheel of the car. Her blood runs into the gutter.

Now he knows what terrible thing he's done.

It is a steamy summer night.

As he lurches away from his house, he can see the bathroom window still lighted upstairs, can visualize Phyllis brushing her teeth in there. He lurches blindly into the night, wondering if Mame was right, wondering if something like the shooting at Bankers Trust *can* affect a man for the rest of his life. Is that why he keeps thinking he's done something terrible when he knows he's done nothing at all, knows that none of it ever happened, Suzie, the four punks, the bar that doesn't exist, none of it is real.

He is in a strange neighborhood now.

He doesn't know where he is, can't remember when he left the house or how far he's come. He hears piano music in the distance, and then the music stops and he turns a corner and sees . . .

There is a bar.

Neon sputters into the darkness of the night.

ART'S TAVERN

But . . .

It wasn't in any of the phone directories.

So how . . . ?

He squints up at the sign, sees that the neon is sputtering only because there's something wrong with the initial letter. Yes, he can see its outline now. Yes, the letter is a B. *Bart's* Tavern.

A blond girl in a red dress comes out of the bar, staggering slightly on very high-heeled shoes. Swaying, she opens her bag and takes a package of cigarettes from it. She can't find a match; he hears her sigh of exasperation. The piano starts again. She sees him all at once, smiles, and begins walking toward him, the cigarette in her hand.

His blood runs cold when she says, "You wouldn't happen to have a light, would you?"

An Autumn Migration
by Sharyn McCrumb

The ghost of my father-in-law arrived today, smiling vaguely as he always does (or did), taking no notice of me. He acted for all the world as if I were the ghost instead of him. Not even a nod of greeting or a funny remark about the weather, which was about all the conversation we'd ever managed when he was alive. I'm not very good at conversing with people. Stephen says that I have no small talk. I listened a lot, though.

With my father-in-law I became an audience of one to his endless supply of anecdotes, and I think he enjoyed having someone pay attention to him. He used to tell funny stories about his days in the Big One, by which he meant World War II, and he could always find a way to laugh at a rained-out ball game or a broken washing machine. This did not seem to endear him to his energetic wife and son, especially since his inability to hold a job made ball games and washing machines hard to come by, but his affability had made him a comforting in-law for the nervous and awkward bride that I had been. We were never really close, but we enjoyed each other's company.

Later I sometimes shared Stephen's exasperation for the smiling, tipsy ne'er-do-well who could never seem to hold on to a paycheck or a driver's license, but in truth I would have forgiven him a great deal more than poverty and drunkenness for giving me a few moments of ease in those early days when I had felt on trial before Stephen and his exacting mother, for whom nothing was ever clean enough.

I didn't hear the front door open and close—or perhaps it didn't.

When he arrived, I was alone, of course, in that long emptiness of the suburban afternoon. I told myself that I was waiting for Stephen to come home, but I was careful not to ask myself why. Certainly I was not expecting any visitors that day—or any other day—and my father-in-law was as far from my thoughts as he had ever been in life.

I had been dusting the coffee table, a favorite pastime of mine, because you can make your hand do lazy arcs across a smooth wooden surface while thinking of absolutely nothing, and if you happen to be holding a damp polishing rag in your hand at the time, it counts as actual work. When I looked up from my shining circles, I saw my father-in-law clumping soundlessly up the stairs in his baggy brown suit and his old scuffed wingtips. He was probably wearing a worn silk tie loosened at his throat. He looked just as I remembered him: a portly old gentleman with sparse gray hair and a ruddy face. I even fancied that I caught the scent of Jack Daniel's and stale tobacco as he sailed past. He was carrying the battered leather suitcase that used to sit in the hall closet at his house. I wonder where he is going, and why he needs luggage to get there.

He did not even glance around to see if anyone was watching him before he went upstairs. Perhaps he was looking for Stephen, but Stephen is never home at this hour of the day. For most of the year I scarcely see him in daylight. He works very hard, unlike his dad (or perhaps because of him), and he doesn't talk to me much these days. He is impatient with my depression, although he always asks if I am taking my medicine, and he is careful to remind me of doctor's appointments. But I know that secretly he thinks that I could snap out of it if I wanted to. An aerobics class or a new hairdo would do wonders for me, he suggests now and then, trying to sound casual about it. He thinks that depression is a luxury reserved for housewives whose husbands have adequate incomes. Perhaps he is right. Perhaps those who are forced to go out and face the world with such a mental shroud about them throw themselves in front of trains or run their cars into trees rather than endure the tedium of another dark day. I have thought of such things myself, but it would take too much effort to leave the house.

I always promise to cheer up, as Stephen puts it, and that ends the discussion. Then when he leaves for the office, I crawl back into bed and sleep as long as I can. Sometimes I play endless games of solitaire on Stephen's home computer, watching the electronic cards flash by and scarcely caring if the suits fit together or not. I do not watch much television. Seeing those noisy strangers on the screen making such a fuss over a new car or a better detergent always makes me feel sadder and even more out of step with the world. I would rather sleep.

I am tired all the time. I manage to get the washing done every day or so, and by four o'clock I can usually muster enough energy to cook a pork chop or perhaps some spaghetti, so that Stephen won't get annoyed with me, and ask me what it is I do all day. I push the emptiness around the polished surfaces of the coffee table with a polishing rag. It takes up most of my time. There is so much emptiness. I force myself to eat the dinner, so that he won't lecture me about the importance of nutrition to emotional health. Stephen is an architect, but he thinks that being my husband entitles him to express medical opinions about the

state of my mind and body. It is practically the only interest he takes in either anymore.

He is not so observant about the state of the house. He
never looks under the beds, or notices how long the cleaning supplies last. With only the two of us, there isn't much
housekeeping to do. He has offered to hire a maid, but I
cannot bear the thought of having someone around all the
time. I do enough housework to get by and to stave off the
dreaded cleaning woman, and he does not complain. I am
so tired.

My father-in-law was still upstairs. At least, he hadn't
reappeared. I could not be bothered to go and look for him.
I sat down in Stephen's leather chair, running the polishing rag through my fingers like a silk scarf.

"Stephen isn't home!" I called out, in case that made any
difference to my visitor. Apparently it didn't. Shouldn't a
ghost know who is home and who isn't without having to
make a room-to-room search? Surely—ten months dead—
he was sober?

I wondered if I ought to call my mother-in-law in Wis-
consin to tell her that he is here. He died last November.
She'll be glad to know where he is. She had wanted to go
to Florida for the coming winter, but she said she didn't
like to go and have a good time, with her poor husband
alone in his urn. They had been married fifty years to the
month when he passed away, and they had never been
apart in all that time. He had always talked about taking
her somewhere for their fiftieth anniversary, but by then he
was too ill and too broke to manage. They spent their anniversary in his hospital room, drinking apple juice out of
paper cups. Now his widow talks wistfully of Florida, and
Stephen has offered to pay for the trip, but she said that she
hates to travel alone after all those years of togetherness.
Why shouldn't she, though? He is.

I wonder why he has decided to call on us. It seems like a very unlikely choice on his part. I can imagine him haunting Wrigley Field, or a Dublin pub, or perhaps some tropical island in the South Pacific, or a Norwegian fishing village. We gave him a subscription to *National Geographic* every year for Christmas so that he could dream about all those far-off lands that he always claimed he wanted to visit, if his health would stand it. You'd think he would make good use of his afterlife to make up for lost time. But, no—after all those years of carefully paging through glorious photographs of exotic places, he turns up here, two states from home, uninvited. Surely if he could make it to Iowa, he could reach Peru. What does he want here? His pre-mortem communication with us consisted of a few cheery monologues on the extension phone when Stephen's mother phoned for her monthly chat. Why the interest in us now? He cannot be haunting us out of malevolence. In life, he never seemed to mind about anything— no empty bottle or underachieving racehorse could darken his mood for long. Not the sort of person you'd expect to stay bound to the earth, when presumably he could be in some heavenly Hialeah, watching Secretariat race against Man o' War and Whirlaway in the fifth—*with* a fifth. How could he pass up such a hereafter to haunt a brick colonial tract house in Woodland Hills, Iowa? He never came to visit us. Stephen said the old man wouldn't be caught dead here. Apparently he was wrong about that.

He can't be angry at us. We went to the funeral; we took a wreath to the crematorium. I even wrote the thank-you notes so that Stephen's mother could concentrate on her bereavement. Stephen packed his clothes in cardboard boxes and took them to Goodwill, and he took the whiskey bottles in the top of the closet to the recycling place. We ordered the deluxe bronze urn to put his ashes in, and we even paid extra to have his name engraved on a little plaque on the front. And now here he is, swooping down on us like a migrating heron, dropping in for an unannounced rest stop on his way south—or wherever it is that he is going.

If I called my mother-in-law and asked her if the brown leather suitcase was there in her hall closet, I wonder what she would say. Perhaps it is a ghost, too. After all, it is leather.

In the end I sat in the recliner in the living room and took a nap. We can resolve this when Stephen gets home, I thought. It is, after all, *his* father.

Stephen finally arrived home at eight tonight, moaning about the heat of Indian summer, and the tempers of his co-workers. I watched him go upstairs with a feeling approaching clinical interest. What will he say when he meets his father on the landing? Should I have warned him? I could have told him that a relative dropped in for an unexpected visit. He would scowl, of course, but then he might have said, "Who?" and I could have said, "Someone from your side of the family," and thus we could have eased on to the subject of his late father, and I could have broken the news to him gently. But I was too tired to plan conversational gambits, and Stephen's attention span for discussions with me is many minutes shorter than such a talk would have required, so I merely smiled and gave him a little wave as he pulled his tie away from his collar and hurried upstairs. Then I waited—I'm not sure what for. A shout perhaps, or even a scream of terror or astonishment. Certainly I expected Stephen to reappear very quickly, and to descend the stairs much faster than he went up. But several minutes passed in silence, and when I crept close to the banister, I could hear drawers opening and closing in the bedroom. Stephen changing his clothes, as he did first thing every evening. I made myself climb the stairs to see if the apparition was gone. If so, I won't mention it to Stephen, I thought. He would only think that my seeing ghosts is another symptom of my disorder. *Not* seeing the ghost may be a symptom of his.

I stood in the doorway, smiling vaguely, as if I had come upstairs to ask him something but had forgotten what. Stephen was sitting in the lounge chair beside the window, putting on his running shoes. He looked up at me, and when I didn't say anything, he shrugged and went back to tying the laces. His father was sitting on the edge of the bed, watching this performance with interest.

"Stephen, look at the bed," I said.

He frowned a little and glanced at the bed, probably wondering what sort of response I was expecting. Was I propositioning him? Did I want new furniture? Was there a mouse on the pillow? He gave the question careful consideration. "The bed looks fine," he said at last. "I'm glad you made the bed, dear. It makes the room look tidy. Thank you."

Stephen was looking straight at his father. He could not miss him, and yet all he saw was a blue-flowered bedspread and four matching throw pillows.

My father-in-law looked at me and shrugged, as if to say that Stephen's lack of perception was not *his* fault: he was certainly visible, plain as day, and if Stephen could not or would not detect his presence, there wasn't much that either of us could do about it. I could have said, "Stephen, your dead father is sitting on the bed," but that would have gotten us nowhere. In fact, saying that would have been worse than ignoring the matter, because Stephen would have insisted on analyzing my medication to see if I was taking anything that might cause delusions, and this would distract me from considering the real problem at hand: What is my father-in-law doing here, and what does he want me to do about it?

Upon reflection I was not surprised that Stephen failed to see this apparition. Stephen never saw rainbows when I pointed them out through the car windshield as he was driving. Finally I stopped pointing them out, and then one day I stopped seeing them, too. He is completely unable to tell whether people are happy or sad by looking at them. And he insists that he never has dreams, nightmares or otherwise. Of course he would not notice anything so unconventional as a ghost. It is beneath the threshold of his rationality. As he is not likely to take my word for it, I have abandoned the idea of telling him about his father's visit. Some people do not qualify to be haunted.

We ate a hastily prepared meal of soup and salad (in the excitement I had forgotten to cook dinner). I asked Stephen a question about a project at work, and he answered so volubly that I knew he was talking to himself, and had forgotten I was there. It was a very restful dinner. No awkward silences while one of us tried to think of something to say.

When we went upstairs afterward, my father-in-law was nowhere to be seen. I wandered from room to room, on the pretext of shutting windows and making sure that the lights were off. I peeked into closets and behind doors, but he was not in evidence. I did not think that this absence was permanent, however. I suspect that he is on some astral plane, biding his time until Stephen has left the house again. Perhaps even ghosts find it awkward to communicate with Stephen.

I had thought about the problem all through dinner, which I barely touched, and I puzzled over it later in bed. While Stephen read *Architectural Digest,* I scanned the room beyond the pool of light from the reading lamp to see if one of the shadows was grinning back at me, but no one was there. Later, when Stephen's breathing evened out into the monotone of sleep, I lay awake wondering about the visit. He must be here for a reason, I thought. Since I am the only one who has noticed him, I suppose it is my problem.

He has been here for five days now. He does not speak to me. Perhaps he can't. I see him here and there around the house, and sometimes we exchange looks or smiles, so I know he is aware of my presence, but he makes no sound. He does not seem distressed, as if he were anxious to communicate some urgent information to me about a lost bank account, or a cache of gold coins buried in the backyard. He does not seem to want any messages of love or regret taken to his wife or conveyed to Stephen. (I think if my father-in-law ever had any gold coins, he would have cashed them in for Jack Daniel's long ago. I have more money in my savings account from my grandmother's legacy than he probably left to his family after a lifetime of desultory jobs. Messages for his loved ones? My father-in-law was a gentle and pleasant man, but I do not think his love for wife or son was the sort that would extend beyond the grave. They have certainly recovered from the loss of him, and I have no reason to suspect that the feeling is not mutual.) He is just . . . here.

I am no longer shy about his presence in the house. He is a courteous ghost. He never materializes in the bathroom, or sneaks up behind me when I am dusting. I find, though, that I am less inclined to sleep late, and I spend less time polishing the furniture. Even with uninvited guests there is the obligation to play hostess, I suppose. I tried turning the television on to the news channel, because I thought that the ghost might be interested in what is going on in the world—an idle curiosity in familiar things, the way one might subscribe to a hometown newspaper after one has moved away—but he only glanced at the screen and drifted away again, so I gave it up. Perhaps the news is no longer interesting when nothing is a matter of life or death to the viewer. I didn't find it very interesting myself, though. I wonder what that means.

Today when Stephen came home I had fixed beef stroganoff, and he grudgingly said that I seemed to be snapping out of it. I wish I could say the same for him. He is as monotonous as ever. I found myself thinking that I had more to say to the ghost than I did to my husband.

I wonder where he keeps the piano. In the attic? The broom closet under the stairs? Sometimes when I am downstairs with the polishing cloth, I can hear sounds floating down the stairs, the tinkly lilt of a barroom piano: Scott Joplin tunes. I polish to the rhythm of a ragtime piano, and I wonder what he is trying to tell me. It has been a week now, and I find myself talking aloud to the ghost as I work. I still call him the ghost. He had a first name in life, of course, but I never used it. I called him "Umm," the way one does with in-laws. I still thought of him as "Umm," and I made an occasional remark to him while I vacuumed the dust bunnies under the bed, and dusted the tops of the bookshelves, because who knows where a ghost goes when he's not in sight? It took a couple of days to get the house back into decent order, and then I began to wonder what else I could do. He was still there; he must be in need of something. Or perhaps he couldn't think of anywhere else to go.

The next time I cleaned the living room, I considered turning to ESPN, on the off chance that a horse race might be broadcast. He always did love a good horse race, but I

decided that I have to watch enough sports as it is during
football season with Stephen around. I certainly wasn't
going to defer to the wishes of a dead man. Something
else, then.

I switched to the Discovery Channel, and we watched a
nice program about castles in the Alps. He seemed to enjoy
the travel documentary much more than he had the news
channel. He floated just behind the sofa and watched the
screen intently. After a few minutes I put down my dust
cloth and joined him, and we marveled in the splendors of
Neunschwanstein and Linderhof for nearly a quarter of an
hour, until at the end of a long commercial I looked over
and found that I was alone. Overdecorated castles can fas-
cinate one for just so long, I decided, but I had thoroughly
enjoyed the tour, thinking how horrified Stephen would be
by the glorification of nineteenth-century crimes against
architecture. Still, his father had seemed to enjoy it. I felt I
was on the right track.

After that I kept the television tuned to travel documen-
taries for as much of the day as I could. I noticed that my
father-in-law's ghost had no particular fascination with
Europe, and only a fleeting interest in Africa and the Middle East. I was about to give up the project and try the
Shopping Network when the programmers turned their attention to Polynesia. For the ghostly viewer the Pacific
islands were another matter altogether.

A program on Hawaii brought him closer to the television than he had ventured before, and he actually sat
through two commercials before fading away. A few days
later, when Samoa was featured, he hovered just above the
sofa cushions and gazed enraptured at the palm trees and
outriggers with a smile that no longer looked vague. Easter
Island was the clincher. Not only did he watch it in its
entirety, he even stayed through the credits, apparently

reading the names of the crew and filmmakers as they rolled up the screen.

I had watched all these programs as well, and quite enjoyed the imaginary holidays they provided. Still, after hours of looking at the shining sands and turquoise sea of the South Pacific, my own living room looked dingy and worn. This did not inspire me to further cleaning efforts, however. My reaction was more along the lines of "What's the use?" No matter what I did to our sensible tweed sofa and the fashionable cherry colonial reproduction tables, it would still be dankest, brownest, latest autumn within these walls, and I was beginning to long for summer.

"It's a pity that we are dead and stuck here," I remarked aloud to the visitor. Something in his smile made me realize what I'd said. "I mean that *you're* stuck here," I amended.

On Monday, the daily documentary featured the irrigation system of the Netherlands, but neither my father-in-law nor I was ready to come back from the tropical paradises of the South Pacific. We sat there in gloomy silence for a few minutes, politely studying placid canals and bobbing fields of tulips, but neither of us could muster any enthusiasm for the subject. I clicked off the set just as he was beginning to fade out. "I'll go to the library," I said to the dimming apparition. "Perhaps I can borrow a video of the Pacific Islands—or at least a travel guide."

Stephen occasionally sent me to the library to research something for him, but I had never actually checked anything out for my own use. I suppose Mrs. Nagata, the librarian, was a bit surprised to see me walk past architecture and into the travel section. Or perhaps she was surprised to see me in jeans with my hair in a ponytail. In my haste I had not bothered to change into the costume I thought of as Suburban Respectable. Half an hour later, I had managed to find two coffee table books on the Pacific Islands, a video documentary about Tahiti, and the old Disney film of *Treasure Island* that I remembered from childhood. As an afterthought I picked up a guidebook to Polynesia as well.

When I entered the house again, I could hear the strains of "Bali Hai" being played on a honky tonk piano. I wondered if that was a hint. Surely Bali Hai would be featured in one of the books I had selected. Where was it, anyhow? And had my father-in-law been there before? I tried to remember his stories about World War II, but exotic islands did not play a part in any tale that I recalled. "He's simply getting into the spirit of the thing," I said. Realizing my pun, I laughed out loud.

"What's so funny?"

Stephen was home. I nearly dropped the books. He was lounging on the sofa, watching the sports network. "The air conditioning was broken at the office, so I came home," he told me without taking his eyes off the flickering screen. "I was surprised to find you gone. I thought you moped around here all day."

"I went to the library," I mumbled.

"Oh?" He raised his eyebrows in that maddening way of his. "Whatever for? I didn't send you."

I felt like a child caught playing hookey. "I just went," I said.

I edged closer to the screen, careful not to block his view, and held out my armload of books and videos. "I just thought I'd do some reading."

A commercial came on just then, and he turned his attention to me, or rather to the materials from the library. He flipped through the stack of books, inspected the videos, and set them down on the sofa beside him. "The South Pacific," he said, sounding amused.

"Yes," I said. "Isn't it beautiful?"

"If you like heat and insects."

"I thought we might go there someday."

Stephen turned back to the television. "Paul Gauguin went to Tahiti. He was a painter."

"Yes."

"Went to Tahiti, got leprosy there and died," said Stephen, with evident satisfaction that Gauguin's lapse of judgment had been so amply rewarded. Before I could reply, the commercial ended, and Stephen went back to the game, dismissing the subject of Polynesia from his thoughts entirely.

I left the room, unnoticed by Stephen, who was absorbed in the television and completely oblivious to my existence. Before I left, though, I took the pile of books, which he had discarded on the sofa beside him.

I was sitting on the bed, leafing through color pictures of beaches at sunset and lush island waterfalls, when my father-in-law materialized beside me and began peering at the pages with a look similar to Stephen's "television face." Once when I turned a page too quickly, he reached for the book and then drew back, as if he suddenly remembered that he could no longer hold objects for himself.

"It's beautiful, isn't it?" I sighed. "I wish I could see it for real."

The ghost nodded sadly. He tried to touch the page, but his fingers became transparent and passed through the photo.

"Just go!" I said. "Do it! I'm tied here. Stephen refuses to go anywhere. I'm too depressed to go to the mall, much less to another country. But you! *You're* not a prisoner. I wish *I* were a ghost. If I were, I certainly wouldn't be haunting a tract house in Iowa. I'd do whatever I wanted.

I'd be free! I'd go to Tahiti—or Easter Island—or wherever I wanted!"

The ghost shook his head, and immediately I felt sorry for my outburst. Apparently there were rules to the afterlife, and I had no idea what his limitations were. I shouldn't have reproached him for things I don't understand, I thought.

"I'm sorry," I said. "I just wish we weren't trapped here." My eyes filled with tears. One of them plopped onto the waterfall picture and slid down the rocks, as if to join the cascading image.

I looked up to see my father-in-law's ghost smiling and shaking his head. He looked very much like Stephen for just that instant: his expression was the one Stephen always has when I've said something foolish. I thought over what I had said. *I wish we weren't trapped here.*

Why was I trapped here?

I had Grandmother's legacy in the savings account. It had grown to nearly twelve thousand dollars, because in my depression I couldn't be bothered to go out and actually buy anything. I had a suitcase, and enough summer clothes to see me through a few months in the tropics. And—most important—I had no emotional ties to keep me in Woodlands Hills. I felt that I had already been haunting Stephen for the last few years of our married life. It was time I left, and when I went, his memory would never haunt me.

I opened the closet and reached for the canvas suitcase on the top shelf. As I was pulling it down, I heard a thump at the back of the closet, and I stood on tiptoe to see what had been knocked over. It was a large bronze vase. I had to stand on a chair to reach it. When I pulled it out of a tangle of coat hangers, I saw the brass plate on the front bearing a name and two dates. My father-in-law!

I left the suitcase on the floor and ran downstairs.

"Stephen!" I said. "Did you know that your father's ashes are in the bedroom closet?"

"Shhh! They're kicking the extra point."

I waited an eternity for a commercial and asked again, keeping my voice casual.

"Dad? Sure. I took them after the funeral. I thought it would upset Mother too much to leave them on the mantel, where she'd have to see them all the time. I figured I'd wait for the anniversary of his death—next month, isn't it?—and then scatter him under the rose bushes out back. Bone meal. Great compost, huh?"

"Great," I murmured.

As I fled back upstairs I heard him call out, "Thanks for reminding me!"

It took me twenty minutes to clean out the fireplace in the den, and another half hour to pack. Ten minutes to locate my passport and the passbook to my savings account. Five minutes to transfer the contents of the urn to a plastic cosmetics bag in my suitcase, and to replace them with the fireplace ashes. I didn't think I'd need my coat, but I put it on anyway, as a gesture of finality. My father-in-law was wearing his.

We stood for a moment in the foyer, staring at the back of Stephen's head, haloed in the light of the television. I picked up my suitcase and flung open the door. "I'm going out!" I called.

"Yeah—okay," said Stephen.

"I may be some time."

Color Blind
by *Joyce Carol Oates*

Esmé Pick, a sand-colored Caucasian woman, was attracted to her downstairs neighbor Morse Kendrick not because he was a black man and she was a liberal Democrat, nor even because he was tall, handsome, trimly muscular, with a deep-gravelly laugh, but because, at their first meeting, in the foyer of her apartment house the day after he'd moved in, he'd smiled happily at her and said, "Hello! You're my new neighbor? Upstairs?" This came at a time when Esmé's heart was broken; no one had smiled at her, in the sense of doing so by choice, happily, in perhaps a week. Taken by surprise, Esmé blinked at the handsome stranger. For a moment she was disoriented: wasn't *he* the new tenant, hadn't *she* been living here for six years? But she liked the man's forwardness, his pushy-manly confidence. She liked his playfulness that inspired her own, like one child nudging another in the ribs. Esmé peered at the white card in the slot of the mailbox for apartment 1C saying, " 'Morse Kendrick,' is it?—I'm Esmé Pick." The tall black man bared big glistening teeth in a smile and laughed, as if Esmé had said something witty—was he laughing at her? with her? did he guess they were destined to be friends?—and Esmé found herself laughing with him.

They shook hands. More accurately, "Morse Kendrick"

seized Esmé Pick's hand and shook it, exuberantly. So
there suddenly was her slender hand in his big pawlike
hand, her skin startlingly anemic beside his, like a sea
creature bereft of its protective shell. There was the unexpected warmth and strength of a stranger's handshake, re-
verberating up her spine. Immediately they were at ease
together, like old, friendly acquaintances. Esmé Pick was a
tall, lank woman with doubtful eyes, blond, though lack-
ing, as she thought, a blonde's soul; she had been given,
since adolescence, to morose exaggeration; but how quick
to brighten at a friendly word, an unsolicited smile! She
believed that she disliked most people on principle, judg-
ing them shallow, superficial, and vain, but those she liked
she often liked too much, and too eagerly. Still, Esmé was
certain she had not fallen in love with Morse Kendrick at
their first meeting. It must have been at least three meetings, three conversations. At least.

    She would have said that she had numerous black ac-
quaintances and, at the Art Institute, a black colleague; yet,
she had no black friends and never had. Though the color
of Morse Kendrick's skin was not an issue here.

    By chance—it *was* chance—Esmé saw the man often
that summer. At the 7-Eleven store at odd late hours, or on
the street. In the foyer of their apartment house. The building had only nine tenants and a single staircase, and if
Esmé's timing was right, she passed by 1C when the door
happened to be open; if not, she might knock in her bright
cheery way (invented for this purpose) and say *Hello! How
are you? how was your week?*—and Morse might invite
her inside for a beer, or maybe she'd invite him upstairs to
her place for dinner—Esmé was an improvisational cook,
fired by enthusiasm and anxiety in equal measure; throwing things together out of her virtually empty refrigerator,
opening select cans, emptying jars into a casserole dish,

mixing the ingredients with pasta, rice, or couscous, one of her specialties, all the while talking brightly, wittily. It was all very casual, of course. *Just friends, we're just friends* ran through Esmé's mind like a ticker tape. And it *was* chance, certainly—they never planned any of these meetings, these evenings at Esmé's dining room table, or, trays on their knees, on her bathtub-sized balcony overlooking a weedy rose garden. They told hilarious anecdotes about their respective jobs—Morse bartended at a popular rowdy café downtown; Esmé was assistant curator of the city's Art Institute, which was in desperate need of funds. Most of their conversation was light, meant to amuse, but Esmé came to notice how, at some point, Morse would introduce the expression *white folks*—as in *white folks' logic* or *white folks' lifestyle*—in a teasing, winking way. He'd mentioned casually that he'd been born in Brooklyn, in "Bed-Stuy" as he called it; he was a man "who knew his roots" but was "not political." Esmé wondered what he was getting at, if there was some codified, intimate message here. And that deep gravelly laugh like the sound of an expensive car's motor turning over—what did that mean? Maybe, in Morse Kendrick's eyes, Esmé Pick was an honorary *non*-white? Maybe, drinking beer, eating her food, served by her eager hands, Morse Kendrick forgave her her skin?

Once she objected, "Look, Morse, there isn't any category of 'white folks' if you are one."

Not missing a beat, like a TV comedian with an audience far vaster than just Esmé Pick, Morse Kendrick said, grinning, "And if you *aren't,* man?"

Esmé was not her name, exactly. Her real name was Margot—Margot Ripley Pick!—a sound you might make hurriedly ridding your mouth of some foul substance. At the age of fourteen she'd read J. D. Salinger's short story "For Esmé, With Love and Squalor," and it had made a strong impression on her. There were names that were romantic, magical. Names to inspire luck. Esmé was one of them, so why should she not be Esmé instead of dull, chill Margot? Her family had never acknowledged Esmé, still called her Margot, which was a good enough reason for avoiding them. Her friends all called her Esmé, perhaps to humor her. Morse Kendrick was one who knew her solely as Esmé—he rolled the name, the melodic-exotic sound, on his tongue, seemed virtually to be tasting it. "Delicious name, 'Esmé,'" he'd said. "Is it French?—Spanish?" Esmé blushed and said, "Oh, yes, either."

Esmé Pick was thirty-two years old but thought of herself as a *girl*: she looked much younger than her age, undiscovered, *untilled*. An argument might be advanced that she was a *virgin*, poetically speaking. (Her *heart* had never once been penetrated.) For the past twenty years she'd been absurdly unlucky in love. One of her great missed romances had been with her art history dissertation adviser at Yale, a leonine-headed "distinguished" elder; Esmé had been his devoted research assistant, supplying the crucial information for his much acclaimed study of American Modernism, and when the book was awarded a coveted scholarly prize, it was Esmé who insisted upon celebrating by taking him to dinner at the Ship's Inn, an expensive and "historic" inn in New London. This was surely to have been a night of love, idyllic and abandoned. But the Ship's Inn contained several dining rooms strung out along dim, winding corridors, and Esmé searched for her lover-to-be in one room after another, as he searched for her; by the time they found each other, it was 9:35 and the Inn's kitchen had closed. Another time Esmé was to have had a tryst at the Parker Meridien in New York but at the last minute this lover-to-be, like her adviser a married man, was obliged to bring his seven-year-old asthmatic son with him, for reasons never entirely clear except it spelled the end of that romance, abruptly. Another time, meeting a man for dinner in Philadelphia, Esmé had broken out in lurid red hives after eating a paella; this lover-to-be had had to take her to a hospital emergency room for a shot of cortisone. And so forth.

"Sometimes I think," Esmé complained to her friend Veronica, "that I'm accursed with rotten luck."

"Why would you ever think that, Esmé?" Veronica said.

Esmé had few friends, but Veronica, twice-divorced, glamorous in a despoiled way, dated back to fourth grade in East Adams Elementary School, East Adams, New York, a suburb of Buffalo. How depressing, Esmé thought, to have a friend so *old,* who knows you so *well.* As if you hadn't found anyone better in all those years.

The building in which Esmé Pick and Morse Kendrick rented apartments was a converted Victorian monstrosity on the edge of the university district. It was overpriced, undermaintained, very likely a fire trap. The kind of residence in which you know your fellow tenants all too intimately yet not well. Esmé had long ago divided these men and women into X and O groups, like blood. The X's with whom she might have wished to be friends had no time for her; the O's, who seemed to wish to be friends with her, *she* had no time for. Until there came Morse Kendrick, who was both blood types. That is, he seemed to wish to be her friend, to a degree; and she certainly wanted to be his. She'd even asked him, in a playful semi-drunken mood one evening, what his blood type was. Morse looked thoughtful and said, "Y'know, I don't know. You looking for a blood donor or something?" It was a friendly enough question, but Esmé laughed awkwardly and said, "Well, you never know!" This was meant to be one of her witty rejoinders, made as she carelessly brushed wings of her *burnished-gold* hair back from her face, but somehow it failed to strike sparks.

Just friends, we're just friends rattling through her head like a children's TV commercial.

His skin the deep rich hue of eggplant. That smooth purplish-dark sheen. A look of interior heat, light. How warm to the touch! Esmé had read that African-American skin is just slightly thicker than Caucasian skin, the capillaries not so close to the surface; such skin doesn't scratch, bleed, bruise so easily. Those eyes deep-set and intelligent, good-humored. Except when the teasing came close to taunting. *White folks. White folks. White folks.*

Esmé told herself that her interest in Morse Kendrick was not because the man was black, but because he was Morse Kendrick, who happened to be black. If Morse were white, a sand-colored version of himself, Esmé was sure she would have liked him just as much.

At the Luna Café, two men of indeterminate age came to Esmé's and Veronica's table offering to buy them drinks. "No, thank you," Esmé said in surprise, as if this were an unexpected Halloween trick-or-treat. The men retreated without another word, their forced smiles in instant reverse. Veronica objected, "They didn't look too bad. It was only *drinks*." Esmé said, "They looked like entry-level computer salesmen. They looked thumbed through. And they're the wrong color." Esmé began to laugh, and lowered her forehead onto the edge of the glitter-encrusted formica table. She had been drinking only chardonnay, and that sparingly. She and her friend from fourth grade were witchily good-looking this Friday evening, *Cosmopolitan* cover girls with their nakedness clothed, or almost. They were sitting in a fern-choked alcove of the crowded Luna Café at the other end of which, behind the bar, tall assured dark-skinned Morse Kendrick was serving customers. He was oblivious of Esmé and her friend; Esmé, who was not spying on him, had not approached him, even to make her way to the women's room, and would not. She had wished only to point him out to Veronica, and so she had. Rock music issued from all sides in an endless brain-damaged tape—golden-oldies of the Stones, raucous as a field of crows.

"Do you like bartending at the Luna Café?" Esmé asked Morse casually. "Is that going to be your *life*?" It was almost an impertinence. Esmé's pulse leaped at her daring. But Morse just laughed and said, "You got some better suggestion?" in such an ironic tone that the subject had to be dropped. Esmé wanted to protest *But, Morse, you're too special.* She wanted to tease, *Don't you want to be a credit to your race?*

In terms of *life,* a sobering subject, Esmé Pick was not altogether satisfied with her own. Maybe it had yet to begin? Maybe her position at the Art Institute could be classified as a sort of extended interim job? She had a Ph.D. in American art history from Yale and she had some talent for art—*promising!* had been uttered frequently in her presence when she was a schoolgirl—and of course she loved great art, or had once; so how had it happened, aged thirty-two, that she spent most of her waking hours typing into a word processor and filling out forms, some of them ten pages long, requesting money from the State Council on the Arts, the National Endowment on the Arts, the Mellon

Foundation, and every other foundation in the *Grant Applicant's Handbook*? Each year Esmé Pick processed hundreds of pages in a quest for funds; if one-tenth of the applications came through, it was considered a good year. You would not think such dignified institutions as art museums competed with one another like boys trying out for a high school football team, but you would be wrong. The art institute of this particular city suffered from its modest attendance, a shrinking endowment, the propinquity of the old Opera House, shut down for the past decade; it was housed in a glum Greek Revival building that pressed on Esmé's temples like a headache, and its major holdings were gifts of local philanthropists—an entire wing of Dürer woodcuts of lepers and the maimed, a somber portrait of General and Mrs. George Washington by an unknown "primitive" artist of the colonial era, a badly cracked portrait of an obese Dutch burgher "attributed" to Rembrandt. The institute's most popular holding was a sleek oil canvas measuring six feet by nine of deliquescent figs and a melting bicycle ridden by a pink mammalian nude, by Salvador Dali.

Esmé complained to Morse, who'd visited the institute only once and thought the Dali was "cool"—"a barrel of laughs"—that she'd come to realize there were two categories of "art" in America: the serious and the rest. The serious arts had to be funded by continuous begging; otherwise they would disappear overnight, like the woolly mammoth, the saber-toothed tiger, those sad clunky upright birds—dodos. Survival of the fittest. How to adjust to a shifting environment. Culture was no different than nature, wasn't that depressing to realize? Morse pointed out that extinct species didn't disappear overnight, exactly. They had plenty of warning, if they could read the signs. "The popular arts survive because people enjoy them,"

Morse said. "It's not like it's good or evil." "That's what's depressing," Esmé said. "People enjoy trash." Morse, who had favored Eddie Murphy in his prime, Richard Pryor, early Clint Eastwood, said, "What's the big deal? Just ways of spending time, isn't it? White-folks' 'highbrow' culture, everybody else's 'trash'—who's kidding who?" He was angry, but he was laughing; Esmé was angry, too, but couldn't bring herself to laugh. She said, excited, "What do you mean, Morse, by that idiotic expression 'white folks'! You're always saying it—'white folks'! With no provocation! I've heard of racists of all nations, all colors of skin, and so have you. Just look at Africa—" Morse widened his eyes and reared back in mock-alarm, "Uh-*oh*! White folks is color blind when it suits 'em, I guess." He was speaking in a thick syrupy up-from-Georgia accent. Esmé said, tears stinging her eyes, "That's crude. That's crude, and that's cruel. *I hate you.*" For the past forty minutes Esmé had been shamelessly dawdling in Morse's doorway, talking and laughing and waiting for him to invite her inside for a beer, toying with the idea of inviting him to have dinner with her that evening, except she feared being turned down—it was past six p.m. of a Saturday, and she had the idea Morse was going out. Now she stomped upstairs in a fury, and Morse called after her, apologetic, in his normal voice, but still laughing, "Esmé, hey? What's wrong? Can't you take a joke?"

If Morse went out that evening, Esmé wasn't home to be a witness. She had her own life, and she had her own pride, and if she'd been slightly infatuated with him, it was over now. *The man is a racist, he doesn't like me at all,* she thought. On Monday evening when she returned home from work she found, slipped into her mailbox, with no stamp, one of the Art Institute's glossy postcards of the lurid pink nude riding her melting bicycle. Morse had scribbled, *I'm sorry! Forgive me? Yr. friend Morse.*

Veronica called, and remarked that Morse Kendrick was certainly an attractive man, but he wasn't very *black*, more like *café au lait.* "If you're going to go for it, girl, why not go all the way?" Her voice sounded distant, as if she were calling from a mountain peak. Esmé was shocked. "Damn it, Veronica, that isn't funny. That's a racist remark!" Veronica said, "It was meant to be just *girl talk.* You know— one girl to another, and no guys listening in." Esmé said, "You sound like you have a buzz on, where are you?" She realized she hadn't seen her friend in weeks, since the Luna Café. Veronica said, "Jackson Hole, Wyoming." Esmé said, "What?" Veronica said, "I'm here with Perry." Esmé said, "Who?" Veronica said, "The taller of the two, you remember, in the Luna Café? He isn't a salesman, he owns the store. He's *sweet.*" "Wait," Esmé said, "—you're in Jackson Hole, Wyoming, with a man you don't know?" "*I* know him," Veronica said coolly. "*You* don't."

Kitty-corner from the Luna Café was the Green Isle Food Co-Op, where health foods, natural grains, fermenting yogurt cultures, and numerous varieties of tofus were sold. There were fat-free sugar-free salt-free tasteless date bars, there were bins of organic vegetables in strange twisted shapes, like Goya faces. There was a pervading smell of holistic vigor. That summer Esmé had become a steady customer at the Green Isle; not because of Morse Kendrick, who worked across the street, but because she thought it time for her to become seriously health-conscious. She had already given up smoking and she was cutting back on her drinking and she took fewer codeine tablets though she had three current prescriptions from three doctors and obtained these pills legally. And there was the possibility, this had happened once or twice, of running into Morse on the street. And if she didn't run into him she might step inside the café just to say hello. And if Morse wasn't tending bar at the time, Esmé would sigh with relief, and order a club soda with lime, or a single glass of chardonnay, with which to take a single codeine tablet. She was susceptible to migraines, the slightest stress brought it on. A sudden thrumming of her temples *What will I do? what will I do? I love him so.*

Esmé didn't know: was Morse Kendrick a figure of mystery, or had she, with typical exaggeration, invested mystery in him? Sometimes, passing by the door of 1C, she heard voices, laughter—was Morse having a party? Why didn't he invite her? She watched out the window of her darkened living room as, in the early hours of the morning, unnamed friends of Morse's drove away—were they black? white? And there were occasional nights, of which she was painfully aware, when a friend, female, did not leave. (Was this the glamorous light-skinned black woman Esmé had once seen Morse strolling with on the river embankment, arms around each other's waist? Or was there more than one woman friend? Out of pride, Esmé refused to watch from her window in the morning.) Morse frequently stayed away overnight himself, Esmé knew the signs—the unopened mailbox stuffed with flyers, his darkened windows, absolute silence outside the door of 1C. At such times, impulsively, Esmé might dial his number, just to hear his voice that sounded so at ease, so confident, warmly anticipatory of good news. *Hel-lo! Sorry I can't come to the phone right now! But if you'll leave your name and number, at the sound of the beep, I'll get back to you as soon as I can!*

Esmé rolled her eyes and whispered into the phone, "I wwove you, dwadammit!" And slammed down the receiver choked with laughter, eyes spilling tears of laughter, a junior high schoolgirl playing a prank on her crush.

When Morse did return, of course Esmé was careful not to give the slightest sign of knowing he'd been away. Sometimes she was in too much of a hurry even to speak with him, merely waving and smiling breezily as he called after her, "Hey Esmé? How's it going?" "Busy!" Esmé cried, big smile like a woman in a musical comedy. "Crazy!"

I have a life too, you bastard. A life of mystery.

Fall came, abruptly wet, windy, and cold, and of course it was flu season, and passing Morse's door Esmé heard him coughing, and *if he gets ill, I can nurse him*! She invented little daydream narratives about Morse Kendrick and Esmé Pick, sometimes even at her word processor at the Art Institute, so, typing out a grant application for Mellon Foundation she found herself typing: *His skin was heated, feverish, he shivered when her fingers touched his bare chest* and had to erase it, reluctantly. Even in her apartment preparing dinner for herself, her door ajar so she could hear when, or if, Morse came home, she told herself her little stories, which were harmless, romantic rather than erotic, not at all sexy, or at least not yet, like those "nice" comic strips in which, in the final frame, things turned out well; everyone was smiling, no one was humiliated.

Morse Kendrick never caught the flu. Esmé was sick as a dog for three days. Morse brought her yogurt, tofu, date bars, and carrot juice from the Green Isle Co-Op; he made her weak rose hip tea; he checked in on her once or twice a day, like a bossy older brother. But he wasn't crucially worried about her, she could see. He wasn't concocting, in his daydreams, fantasy narratives about her. (In fact, during this flu week Esmé learned the name of the glamorous light-skinned black woman: *Mariana*. A name just as romantic as *Esmé*.) Esmé had the idea that, if she died, Morse would be *sad,* he'd *feel sorry,* go around saying he *missed her,* but that would be about it.

Morse Kendrick had moved into Esmé's apartment house in June, and it wasn't until late October that she learned certain salient facts about him. Such as: though he behaved, and looked, at least Esmé's age, he was only twenty-nine years old. (This came out when he happened to mention his birthday to Esmé—"Some folks are treating me this evening. Sky's the limit!") Such as: he had a bachelor's degree from Hiram College in Ohio. (This came out when Esmé ran into Morse at the dumpster behind the apartment house, and out of a stack of newspapers and magazines in his arms the *Hiram College Alumni Bulletin* went flying in the wind and Esmé ran to retrieve it. She tried not to show her surprise, and curiosity, and Morse took the magazine from her with a shrug, saying, "I went on scholarship, it's a great place.") The most astonishing fact about her friend, in Esmé's eyes, was that, far from being just a bartender at the Luna Café, he was enrolled in the Ph.D. program in economics at the university! Esmé learned this purely by chance, in Morse's kitchen one afternoon where he'd invited her for a beer, and she discovered books on a counter with such titles as *Econometric Theory, Research Methods in Demography, Game Theory.* She felt as if the floor had tilted beneath her. She felt cheated, hurt, humbled. "You didn't tell me! You never gave a hint. You're a Ph.D. candidate in economics and *you never gave a hint*!" Morse's defense was a vague shrug, a face crinkled into a severe frown. "Look, I'm not a hundred percent sure I'm going to stay in the program," he said, not meeting Esmé's accusing eyes. "There's folks in my family don't know what I'm doing. *I* don't know what I'm doing. I could drop out tomorrow. I could get *kicked out*." Esmé said, "Oh, of course. No doubt you'll get *kicked out* by *white folks*." Morse shrugged, cocked his head but still didn't meet Esmé's eyes. "If anybody's gonna kick me out, man, it'd be *white folks*. Yeah!" But his joking was lame, hollow. Esmé didn't laugh.

After that incident she decided that she couldn't trust Morse. He didn't lie to her exactly, but his omissions of fact constituted lies. You can't be friends with someone who cheats you of crucial facts about himself, there's nothing *there*.

He wanted me to think he's a dumb, uneducated "nigger"—is that it? But why?

Not long afterward, Veronica called. When she asked about Morse Kendrick, not by name but as *that good-looking black bartender,* Esmé said quickly, "Oh, that's all over." Veronica said, "All *over*? So *soon*? Did it actually *begin*?" "Never mind what, or when," Esmé said, annoyed. "It's over." There was a pause. Esmé could hear her friend's thoughts clacking like a word processor's keyboard. "You think you could introduce me to him, then?" Veronica asked. "He looked kind of, you know. Nice." "What happened to Perry?" Esmé asked. "Who?" Veronica asked. "Oh, never mind," Esmé said impatiently. "Morse is in love with a beautiful black woman named Mariana." "You think it's a political statement, a black woman?" Veronica asked. "I mean, preferring one of *them* over one of *us*?" "I don't think it's politics at all," Esmé said. "Not that I know the man that well."

Twenty-four years was much too long for a friendship with a woman like Veronica, Esmé thought. Maybe with anyone.

Soaking in a hot tub, her head against the hard porcelain rim, her eyes shut, Esmé felt a peculiar tingling sensation in her—uterus—as of ovulation. Was such a thing possible? (For a woman of her age, education, and sensibility, Esmé knew remarkably little about female biology; the thought that she, a quirky individual, shared *a biology* with an entire sex, filled her with indignation.) She shifted uncomfortably in the tub, and there again was the sensation, unmistakable, as of tiny bubbles rising to the surface of the water and popping.

And later that night, as she was undressing for bed, she heard downstairs a muffled cry, as of *Tin? Tin!*—and the sound of someone banging a door. Quickly Esmé slipped on her terry-cloth robe and hurried out, on the stairs hearing more clearly a woman's aggrieved voice, and the spirited rapping of knuckles against the door, "Damn you, Kin! You open this goddam door, you hear! I know you're hiding in there!" Esmé stood on the stairs, thrilled by what she saw: a gorgeous spiky-haired black woman pounding on Morse Kendrick's door. She was about thirty years old, and obviously quite intimate with the man; she must have been calling him "Ken"—a heavily accented "Ken"—for "Kendrick." The woman was perhaps six feet tall, very dark-skinned, and very exotic, in a raincoat of some slippery fire-engine red material, knee-high kidskin boots, diamond-patterned black tights. Her eyes were enormous, her lips brightly crimson. Gold hoop earrings swung from her earlobes. Tight-braided black hair lifted from her head like Medusa's. Seeing Esmé, she said, "H'lo! I'm looking for this damn K'ndrick! He lives here, I know he does, and he ain't man enough to open the door!" She banged again with her fist. Esmé winced, clutching her terry-cloth robe about her. She'd run out of her apartment barefoot, and was shivering in a cold draft. Weakly she said, "I don't think Mr. Kendrick is—home tonight." The black woman stared at her and snorted. "'Mr. K'ndrick'! Now, *that* is a laugh. He ain't home, where is he?" Esmé said apologetically, "I'm afraid I don't know where he is. I—don't know him very well." The woman's eyes dropped to take in Esmé's pale toe-curled feet, rose frankly to her face. "Nah, you wouldn't," she said. "Well—you tell 'Mr. K'ndrick' that Opal was looking for him, and none too happy he's out. Will you?" "Yes," Esmé said, "I will."

Esmé stared as the black woman strode magnificently away, gleaming red raincoat, sharp-heeled boots, quivering braided hair. She'd shut the foyer door so forcefully it swung open again in her wake.

But when Esmé relayed the message to Morse Kendrick the following night, Morse just shrugged and said, "Okay. Thanks."

Esmé said, disappointed, "'Thanks'—that's all?"

"What d'you mean, 'that's all'? That's enough."

"You're not going to tell me who Opal *is*?"

Morse leaned back, teetering dangerously on two chair legs. Raked the ceiling with his eyes. Crinkled his face, bemused. "The woman is who she *is*. She's only one of my problems right now."

"Who—are the others?"

"Try 'what.'"

"All right, then. 'What'?"

"Ain't spying on me, girl, are you?"

Esmé said sharply, "Of course not."

It was nearly one a.m. Esmé had heard Morse returning home at last and she'd gone downstairs and he'd invited her in, with surprising readiness considering the hour, his bloodshot eyes and stubbled jaws and general look of distraction. They sat in Morse's tiny kitchen drinking beer and picking at the remains of a cheese-and-pepperoni pizza that happened to be on Morse's table. Esmé seemed to recall that this pizza had been on Morse's table the last time she'd been in his kitchen, but this was not a thought she cared to pursue.

Through a doorway Esmé could see Morse's shadowed living room. Mismatched pieces of furniture, murky shapes of clothes, books, and papers strewn about. The way a man lives, alone, a man's secret life among his things—this fascinated Esmé. On a far table sat Morse's word processor, its screen never switched off; ghostly glimmering with faint green figures, like an alien consciousness made domestic. Morse was complaining, as if to change the subject, that he was stuck on a major paper for his genericity-analysis seminar. Esmé nodded as if knowing what genericity analysis was, and asked when the paper was due. Morse said, "Last Monday. Fu-uck." He laughed, and dug at his chest with his nails. His smooth eggplant skin, his wiry chest hair just discernible through his white T-shirt. Tight-muscled shoulders and upper arms. His brown eyes rolling in their sockets in that way of genial mockery. "Uh-huh!" he drawled. "White folks is after my ass."

Esmé sighed. "I bet."

"*You* wouldn't know, Esmé."

"I wouldn't. Almost nobody is after my ass."

Gallantly, Morse let this pass. He got up, a bit unsteadily, to fetch them two more beers.

He'd bought a case of this Chinese-import beer, in squat

bottles, with a fiery-maned horse on the label. It was Morse's opinion that when the beer got warm it tasted— and sure did look—like Chinaman piss; but when it was icy cold it took the top of your head off, didn't it?—Esmé laughed, and agreed.

There was this tension between them, which laughing wasn't going to dispel. A tension of the quality that, in old black-and-white TV movies, you could *cut with a knife*. Esmé said neutrally, "I thought you were involved with Mariana, Morse. Now there's Opal."

Morse shrugged, chewing pepperoni sausage. He'd taken to picking the coin-sized slices off the pizza and leaving the rest. "That's a problem with you?"

"Not with me but possibly with you."

"Not jealous, eh?"

"Jealous!" Esmé's heart was beating so rapidly she'd be- gun to vibrate. It was fascinating, actually—she stared at her trembling hand, her fingers gripping the perspiring beer bottle. "You know I am, damn you." Then she laughed. How like Esmé Pick to sabotage a romantic moment by laughing. And it came out wrong—a low nervous snicker, or snigger, such as a junior high schoolboy might make.

Morse seemed not to have heard any of this. Washing down his pepperoni with large mouthfuls of beer. *Isn't he going to look at me? Even in pity?*

Esmé pondered, "I've always wondered—what's the difference between a snicker and a snigger?"

"Between a what and a what?"

"A snicker and a snigger."

Morse thought for a moment. "One's a candy bar, the other's a bug."

They laughed. Just a little too loudly. Morse peeped at Esmé slyly. "One's a *sssss-nigger*. The baddest kind!"

They laughed even louder, and for too long. Esmé had a sense of glassware vibrating.

It was 1:12 A.M. Esmé knew she should leave, her alarm was set for seven, but now they were laughing it was hard to stop, like children sliding down a hill. And Morse seemed to want her to stay, offering her another beer. Esmé heard herself speaking rapidly, with many a quick compulsive brushing of her *burnished-gold* hair off her forehead, telling an *entertaining anecdote,* in one of those incandescent states in which her mouth ran ahead of her thoughts, like a Pomeranian straining at the leash. Morse laughed for a while, then said abruptly, "You know, Esmé, you don't always have to amuse people. We could just sit quiet, for five minutes. Collect our thoughts. Then go to bed."

Esmé wasn't sure she'd heard correctly. She felt faint, the base of her skull numb, tingling. Could you ovulate there? It is known that the central sexual organ in *Homo sapiens* is the brain. No, she knew better. She knew what Morse Kendrick meant. That man, that stranger *of another race* sitting across the dinette from her, a distance of perhaps two feet. An arm's length. His skin exuded a briny smell, he'd been in some harried state sweating and had not showered for a day or longer. Faint film of oil on his face, the broad wings of his nose. That flattish nose and a short, swollen-looking upper lip. Dark perfect skin. And paler, pink brown skin on the insides of his hands—and on the soles of his feet, too? Esmé realized she had never seen Morse Kendrick's naked feet. Nor any private part of him naked. She stared at his arm leaning on the table amid the beer bottles, pizza crust. If this man was going to make love to her, Esmé reasoned, wouldn't he touch her, at least? Soon? Esmé Pick's mollusc-pale hand, slender white-girl fingers within easy reach. Why wouldn't he look at her? She could feel the heat lifting from his skin,

and she could hear his breath. She downed the last of her
beer and said, as if it were a bright discovery, "I think I
need a baby." She heard the words and was aghast and
quickly amended, "I mean—a bath. I need a bath." Morse
said blankly, "A bath?" Esmé said, "To help me sleep.
Otherwise . . ." Morse was looking at her now, fully in the
face. Esmé could not imagine what he saw. He was saying,
almost stammering, "Huh, well—what time *is* it?—Jesus!—
going on two. Aren't you ready for—to—sleep?" Esmé
said, confused, "Oh, no. I mean—should I be? I mean—
are you? It's been a long—day, or whatever—"

Morse loomed above Esmé, on his feet suddenly. The
dinette table rattled. He was at the sink then, faucet on full
blast, as if an emergency sprinkler system had been set off.
Esmé gathered it was time for her to leave, her host was
tidying up. She stood unsteadily, clutching at something.
Her head *was* buzzing and tingling strangely. She thanked
Morse for the Chinese beer and the pizza and said "Good
night" in a reasonably sober voice, but her legs did not
move, stationary as concrete pedestals. She joked about
these legs, trying to lift one with her hands, and Morse was
saying from the safety of the sink and the gushing faucet,
in a quick, embarrassed voice, the whitest-white-man's
voice she had ever heard issuing from his mouth, "Esmé,
you're too good for anyone to take advantage of. You
know what I'm saying?" Tugging at the collar of his grimy
T-shirt as if something was itching there. Esmé said, "Nobody ever takes advantage of me. I mean—nobody I'd
want to. You know what I'm saying?" She laughed again,
soundlessly. The Chinese beer was coursing wildly and
gaily through her bloodstream.

Morse let her talk. Shut off the faucet. Turned, frowning. Face like a mask. *An aboriginal mask.* "It's just,
things are kind of fucked up enough the way it is. Not just

in the world, but, hell, in me, too. I got this, you could say this kind of attitude problem. Neurotic fixation. Soul twisted like a pretzel. You know what I'm saying?"

Esmé shut her eyes and plunged. "No, Morse. What are you saying?"

"I got this kind of attitude problem about white folks."

"*I'm* not 'white folks.' I'm not that unified."

Morse paced about the cramped kitchen, gesturing and throwing his fists, speaking in an odd quick-clipped way as if for the record. Esmé realized he'd been drunk but was no longer, he'd surfaced, leaving her flailing and gasping behind. "It's no big deal, it's just it happened to *me*. Kendrick Morse. Who'd always thought of himself pretty hot stuff, not just another black face. That's it, and I know it, but it doesn't alleviate the—" He groped about, wanting to avoid a word, and Esmé knew what the word was: *pain*.

"Kendrick Morse—? What?"

"A few years ago, I was twenty-two, going out with this girl, white girl from Shaker Heights, and we went home to visit her folks at Christmas and that was okay 'cause she'd given them warning who I was. But we went partying, visiting friends of hers, and one night just walking on a sidewalk there I had this incident, a police squad car pulls up and two white cops jump out and ask me for my ID and fire these questions at me where was I earlier that evening and I'm telling them, and my girlfriend is telling them, and they don't listen, next thing I know they got me leaning against a car and they're frisking me—ever had anybody's hands run over your body?—some cocksuckers who hate you?—so I lose it, I'd been drinking and kind of belligerent thinking *This shit ain't happening to me! this shit ain't happening to me!*—like I'm a special-category nigger, you know what I'm saying? And I'm shoving these white cops who're both of them bigger than me and they sure do shove back and next thing I know I'm facedown on the sidewalk and somebody's knee is between my shoulder blades and my wrists are being handcuffed and let me tell you I'm screaming, I ain't no tough-guy suddenly *I am screaming* 'cause I never felt anything hurt so bad. And it kept on hurting just like that all the way to the Shaker Heights station house."

Esmé said faintly, "Oh, Morse. My God. How could they—do that?"

"Easy. Learned the technique in police academy. 'Disarming and taking custody of suspect.'"

"But—why?"

"They were looking for a black kid who'd held up a convenience store that night, kid with a .22. And I fit the general description. And I was walking in a white neighborhood, with a white girl. That's why."

"You mean they arrested you? Like that?"

"They sure did, honey. Like that. And any time I go out, even here, even here it's mostly 'integrated,' the same thing can happen to me, or worse."

"But—an arrest like that is in violation of the Fourth Amendment!" Esmé said. "The police can't simply arrest a person for—for being who he *is*."

"Sure I raised hell, and so did my girlfriend's family, who got me a lawyer, but—the 'arresting officers had probable cause.' Under the circumstances, I was 'suspicious.' That's how it went down, and that's how it is."

"Because you're black? Just that?"

"Nah, not just black, but I fit the profile of the wanted man—*he* was black. Turned out he was *coal* black, the baddest kind of nigger, didn't look anything like me, or me like him, but it was white folks gave the cops the description, and white folks making the calls. And, hey: I *was* where I didn't belong, and for sure with who I shouldn't have been with."

"Wait," Esmé said. "The police arrested you, mistreated you—because you're black, that's all. That is in violation of the—"

"Fuck the Fourth Amendment! In the dark, every nigger looks alike. The cops didn't take me in 'cause I'm black—that would've been 'discriminatory'—but because I fit the profile of the wanted man, as described to the police. So my rights weren't violated. Just my pride, and my ass that got pretty banged up." Morse was rubbing his wrists, grimacing. He looked tired suddenly. He said, not looking at Esmé, "So, see, I got this attitude problem."

"Oh, Morse. I'm so sorry."

"Yeah. Me, too."

Esmé was too sober. The kitchen lights glared. She would not believe afterward how, at such a moment, she'd uttered such a banality. *Oh Morse I'm so sorry* in a weak reedy voice, put out a trembling-pale hand which the man pointedly did not see; would not believe that Esmé Pick had performed so inadequately—she who, in fantasy, was the quick shining heroine of romance. Yet it was so. And it was time to leave.

This, then: Esmé was halfway up the stairs to the second floor when Morse called after her, as an afterthought: "Uh, Esmé—one more thing? My name isn't exactly 'Morse Kendrick.'" Esmé stammered, "It isn't?" Morse said, "It's Kendrick Morse. My friends mostly call me Ken." Esmé swayed staring down at the man working her lips like a dull-normal child upon whom too much information has been too quickly thrust. Morse said apologetically, "See, in my mailbox slot I put a card, 'MORSE, comma, KENDRICK,' and you must've read it wrong, without the comma. So I let it go, you know? No big deal."

Going upstairs to her apartment, where the door stood ajar as if its occupant had flown out gaily, recklessly, bravely not long before, Esmé began to cry. But stoically, silently. Like a statue, rolling cold marble-tears out of her eyes.

Next morning, Esmé checked the mailbox slot for 1C. Yes, the name printed on the card was clearly MORSE, KENDRICK. The mistake had been hers from the first minute.

Five months, and her friend had never troubled to correct her.

Kendrick Morse. My friends call me Ken.

Outside there was a familiar malaise of morning fog. In career-girl checked linen suit and high heels Esmé went into the side lawn before leaving for the institute, looking at the neglected rose garden in which, six years before, new to this place, she'd volunteered to weed, trim, tend the roses. She was a woman who in another life, or in another tale, would have been mistress of a garden. Beds of sumptuous roses attached to a house. A house of romantic, substantial dimensions. *And who would be inside the house? Who, watching her from a high window? cherishing her for all that was special in her, unique and never again to be replicated in all of the universe and all of time?* She stared at a fist-sized multifoliate rose, petals puffed, crimson faded to sepia, on the brink of being shattered by the next strong wind. Did she imagine it, or was the rose facing her, too, in the pose of Edvard Munch's *The Scream*?

A Place for Nathan
by *Nancy Taylor Rosenberg*

April walked out of her molecular biology class at UCLA, climbed into her Volkswagen Jetta, and drove toward her home in Malibu. For many of her classmates the commencement ceremony scheduled for Monday night marked the end of their formal education and the start of their life as an adult. While her friends were celebrating, arranging job interviews, and planning weddings, April was preparing to enter medical school in the fall. Glancing out her window as she drove past an isolated stretch of beach, she decided to park and take a walk.

It was a glorious day. The sun was high in the sky, and the temperature was in the mid-seventies. The beach was deserted, though, and April wondered where all the sunbathers had gone. Once she locked her car, tossed her shoes into the backseat, and scurried down the embankment to the sand, she saw the answer to her question. A sign proclaimed the beach was restricted and swimming was prohibited. A sickly looking seagull stood beside the sign, balancing itself on one leg. Black tar was clumped among its feathers. At first April thought the gull had its other leg tucked underneath. As the bird hopped off, though, she saw it possessed only one leg. She had driven to the beach to lift her spirits, to enjoy the beauty of nature. Nature was not always beautiful anymore, however, and

April felt an overwhelming sense of sadness. They were killing each other, killing the environment. What the future might hold for her generation was frightening. Long dormant diseases had recently resurfaced. Nature was fighting back with formidable weapons, but for pathetic creatures like the seagull, the war had already been lost.

Walking near the water's edge, April saw another gull soaring over her head. The gull seemed to be examining her, almost as if it were trying to communicate with her. Was such a thing possible? Could a bird distinguish her as something other than a mound of garbage from such a distance? She was familiar with human anatomy, but she had never studied animals.

"What a day, huh?" a cheerful voice said.

April jerked her head around, startled. Standing beside her was a tiny old man, his skin wrinkled and gnarled. "Where did you come from?" she asked, her eyes scanning the empty beach.

"Over there," the man said, smiling. "I walk to the pier and back every day."

April squinted in the direction of the pier. The man was in his late eighties. Using a piece of driftwood for a cane, he seemed too frail and unsteady to walk such a long distance. His legs were skinny, twisted twigs, pale and hairless. The tissue around his knees was inflamed and swollen from arthritis. On his head was a fishing cap, and he was wearing baggy blue shorts, a white polo shirt, and a red nylon parka. The look in his eyes seemed vaguely familiar. "Do I know you?" she asked. The previous summer she had worked as a volunteer in a nursing home. Could that be where she had seen this man?

"You know me now," he said. "Nathan's my name. Want to walk a piece with me? Gets pretty lonely out here this time of day. Wouldn't mind a little company if you're game."

"I can't," April said, wrapping her arms around her chest. She took a step forward, but the man's gaze held her in place.

"Ah, come on," Nathan said, his eyes roaming up and down her tall frame. "How tall are you, if you don't mind me asking?"

April's shoulders slumped. Although she was an attractive young woman, with long brown hair and almond-shaped eyes, her height had always made her feel self-conscious. "Almost six feet," she told him. "I guess in your day there weren't as many tall girls around. My father says people are getting larger due to better nutrition. I inherited my height from my parents, though. My mother and father are both tall."

"Nothing is the same today," Nathan said pensively. He turned in the direction of the pier, then glanced back over his shoulder. "Pleased to make your acquaintance, Miss April."

As the old man shuffled off, April hiked up the embankment to her car. She removed a bottle of Evian water from the seat and took a swig. When she glanced back at the beach, the old man had vanished. She scurried back down the embankment to see where he had gone. All she saw was the same one-legged seagull, pecking in the sand for scraps of food.

The house was starkly contemporary. The floors were marble, and the furniture was upholstered in white fabric. April thought the decor her parents had selected resembled the cold sterility of an operating room. Seated at the long oak table in the dining room, she pushed her peas around with her fork.

"You're going to Baylor tomorrow, right?" Dr. Stephen Markel said. A tall, slender man, he had dark hair and fair eyes. Over his lip was a neatly trimmed mustache. "If you don't get down there right away, April, all the apartments near the campus will be taken. There's a flight leaving at three o'clock tomorrow afternoon. You can go straight to the airport after your last class. All you have Friday is the rehearsal. Getting your housing situation taken care of is more important."

"She can't go tomorrow," Elizabeth Markel said, frowning. "She has to see Ruben first and clear up that other matter, remember?"

April dropped her fork on the table. "Dad knows I'm having an abortion," she snapped. "It's not like I'm erasing a mistake on a paper or something. That's the way you make it sound, Mother."

Her father's face flushed in annoyance. "Don't talk to your mother with that tone of voice."

April slouched in her seat, sullen and silent.

"Let me tell you something," her father continued, leveling a finger at her. "You came close to screwing up your entire future, young lady. I never intended for my daughter to go to Baylor. If you hadn't been so emotional when you took the entrance exams, you might have been able to get into a better school."

"Stop it, Stephen," Elizabeth said, narrowing her eyes at him. "Baylor's a decent school. April worked hard this past year. She's graduating in the top ten percent of her class."

"Can I be excused?" April said. "I'm not hungry."

Her parents exchanged frustrated looks as April rushed out of the room. "That boy," her father said. "I know he's dead, Liz, but I wish he'd kept his hands off my daughter."

"He wasn't a boy, Stephen," she said. "He was a twenty-three-year-old man, and your daughter was in love with him. April could have easily been in the car with him at the time of the accident. If nothing else, we should be thankful our daughter is alive today. Of course she was emotional when she took her entrance exams. Pete was killed only three days before."

"There's no reason for a girl as bright as April to get herself pregnant," Dr. Markel said, a disgusted look on his face. "I guess that's what annoys me the most, that she was so reckless. What if this man had been infected with AIDS or some other sexually transmitted disease? How can my daughter be a physician when she acts so irresponsibly?"

April sat on the window seat in her room and gazed out into the darkness, too distraught to sleep. She had seen pictures of a fetus in the first trimester of pregnancy and could imagine its minute features. In the photos it looked like a tiny seahorse. If she concentrated, though, she could imagine Pete's features taking shape inside the dark waters of her womb. Did her unborn child understand why she had to end its life?

Many of her friends had already had abortions. It was nothing, they told her. Having an abortion was similar to having a tooth pulled. Her friend Sarah Johnson had undergone three abortions during the past five years. Birth-control pills made her gain weight, so the girl relied on abortion as a form of birth control. Pete's death had been devastating, but April was mature enough to know that life went on. She would give birth to other children once her medical training was completed and she found another man to love. The spark of life inside her was Pete's child, though, the one thing he had left behind. She wondered what his parents would say if they knew the truth. Wouldn't they want to see their grandchild?

Something fluttered outside her window. April saw a seagull sitting on the outside ledge, balancing itself on one leg. Hoisting the window up, she reached out thinking she could grab it, but the bird quickly took flight. It couldn't possibly be the same gull from the beach, she told herself. Their home was ten miles from the stretch of beach where she had seen the old man and the one-legged gull. Nathan's parting comment played over in her mind: "Nice to make your acquaintance, Miss April."

Was she going insane? She was certain she had never told the old man her name.

Instead of driving to the UCLA campus the following morning, April returned to the beach. The sky was overcast and the air was chilly. A storm cloud loomed on the horizon. She stared off into the distance at the pier, then walked toward the water's edge. After listening to the weather report, Nathan must have stayed home.

"Decided to come back, huh?" a voice said from behind her.

"Where were you?" April asked, grabbing the edge of his parka. "I looked for you when I got here. I didn't see anyone."

"Same place as yesterday," Nathan said. "I was up there in the sand dunes. We walking or not?"

"I can't walk all the way to the pier," April told him, falling into step beside him. "I'm supposed to be in class right now. I don't know why I even came here this morning. It looks like it's about to pour any minute."

"It's okay if you have to leave," Nathan said. "Don't apologize. Stay in school. Get an education. Are you in college?"

"I graduate UCLA on Monday," April said. "I'll be attending Baylor Medical School in the fall." As she watched,

Nathan strode out into the surf, soaking his tennis shoes and the bottom of the khaki pants he was wearing. "You shouldn't go in the water," she cautioned. "When a storm is moving in, the currents are too strong. Besides, you'll get chilled."

"I like it," Nathan said, giving her a toothy grin. "It's refreshing. The colder the outside air is, the warmer the water feels. Today might be a good day to take a swim."

April saw frothy whitecaps churning in the ocean. She was certain Nathan would be swept out to sea the moment he entered the surf. He bent down and placed his hand in the water, then flicked the drops at her face. "Pretty funny," she said, kicking sand at him. "Promise me you won't go in the water after I leave. This beach is posted. Swimming isn't allowed. Didn't you see the sign back there? They must have had an oil spill or something."

"I don't really have to worry about those types of things," Nathan said, arching a bushy white eyebrow. "That's one of the nice things about growing old. I could swim in sewage and it wouldn't be a problem."

As April watched, he dropped the piece of driftwood he used as a cane, waded out into the surf, then placed his palms together in a diving position. "Stop," she yelled, racing into the water with him.

Nathan slowly turned his head to her and smiled. "Got your feet wet, at least," he said. "See, it isn't that cold."

April sighed, then headed off toward the pier. The old man was crazy, more than likely senile. She wondered if she should notify the authorities. He might have walked away from a nursing home. Nathan appeared beside her, both of them sloshing through the shallow water near the shore.

"Can I tell you a story?" he asked, steadying himself with the piece of driftwood again. "It won't be a long story. Then you can tell me a story. That way our walk will be more meaningful."

"I don't know any stories," April said.

"Sure you do," Nathan told her. "Everyone knows stories. Just make stuff up if you can't remember all the details. That's what I do when my memory fails me."

"Where do you live?" April asked, her concern deepening. He had mentioned the sand dunes. Was he homeless? Homeless people sometimes lived in cardboard boxes high in the dunes. "Is there someone you want me to call for you, a relative or something?"

"Shucks, no," Nathan said, chuckling. "My family is dead. You can call all you want, but no one is going to answer."

"I'm sorry," she said.

"Let's not talk about sad things," Nathan said. "My story is about a boy by the name of Francis Carol Rutherford." He cleared his throat. "Francis contracted polio and had to wear braces on his legs. In addition to being crippled, he was what you might call a pretty boy. Blond hair, delicate features, the clearest blue eyes you've ever seen. All this might have been beneficial if the poor bloke had been a girl."

"Is this a true story?" April asked, glancing at Nathan's twisted legs. His eyes were amazing. The skin around them was crinkled and loose, but instead of being dull, the color was a vibrant shade of blue.

"I knew Francis quite well," Nathan said. "His father was a rugged man, a commercial fisherman. His son was an embarrassment to him. Back then a man had to have a little brawn to earn a living, and boys who were too pretty were considered sissies. If Francis had lived today, he might have been able to earn his living like those male models who pose in their underwear."

April laughed. "A lot of those models are gay," she said. "Was your friend gay? Francis is an unusual name for a boy."

Nathan smiled mischievously, but he didn't feel her question required an answer. "His mother decided the only solution was for Francis to become a man of letters. Every day she insisted he stay in his room and read. Once the doctors removed the leg braces, Francis wanted to run and play with the other boys. The bout of polio had left him with a limp, but he had learned to get around pretty good. His mother wouldn't hear of it. Francis had to have an occupation. He wasn't big enough or strong enough to become a fisherman like his father."

April shook her head. Why was she listening to silly stories from a man old enough to be her grandfather? "I have to go now," she said. "With graduation and all, I have a lot of chores to do."

"Please," Nathan insisted, "just a little farther and the story will be told."

"Another five minutes," she said, "then I really must go."

"Francis wanted to prove himself to his father," Nathan continued, "show him he was as strong as any other boy. He devised a little system. While he read one book, he would hold another book in his hands and lift it up and down. Every day he did this. I mean, Francis was religious about his exercise. He soon started asking his mother to get heavier books from the library. She was pleased that Francis had become such an avid reader, and had no idea the boy was building up his body."

April heard something behind her and turned around. A family of seagulls was following them, walking single file in the sand. "Look," she said, "we have company."

"Don't mind them," Nathan said. "They always tag along. They get a kick out of my stories."

"I saw this unusual seagull the other day," she said. "It had only one leg, and the look out of its eyes was peculiar. I'm almost positive it was the same gull that landed on the ledge outside my window last night. Do you think that's possible? Could a seagull follow me home? I live a long way from the beach."

Nathan said softly, "Would you like to hear more about Francis?"

April sucked in a deep breath. "Okay," she said. The walk had lulled her into a state of tranquility. She could see the pilings for the pier up ahead, and decided she might as well continue and let Nathan finish his story. He was a lonely old man, desperate for companionship. It wouldn't hurt her to extend a little kindness. A person couldn't go through life just taking and not giving.

"When Francis started swimming," Nathan went on, "he found that in the water his girlish appearance and the weakness he carried in his legs was not a problem. With his strong upper body and small trunk, he could propel himself through the water at lightning speeds. He tried out for the swim team at school and soon became the captain. Then a few years later, Francis decided he wanted to swim the English Channel. That was quite an accomplishment for him."

April became even more convinced that Nathan and the man he was talking about were the same. The twisted legs, the refined features, the piercing blue eyes. He was an extremely small man; his head reached only a few inches above April's waist. She wondered if he had always been this short or if he had shrunk with age. She turned and glanced behind her. From a distance, Nathan probably looked like a child walking on the arm of his mother. "You swam the English Channel?" she said. "I'm impressed."

Nathan thrust his shoulders back. "I'm sorry if I led you

to believe this story was about me. My name is Nathan, not Francis." He paused, gazing out at the surf. "Anyway, something strange happened as Francis swam the icy waters of the channel. His body was racked by exhaustion, his lips cracked and bleeding. What carried him was not the strength he had developed lifting books, but the stuff that was inside them. The great stories he had read were his companions. They carried him all the way across the channel."

"What happened to him after he swam the channel?" April asked.

"He became a poet," Nathan said. "He didn't make a lot of money, but he was highly esteemed in the town where he lived. He died, of course. Everyone dies eventually. Birth and death are the only certainties of life."

Without thinking, April placed her hand on her stomach. "Death is certain, but I'm not so sure about birth."

Nathan stopped walking. "What do you mean?"

"We have planned parenthood these days," April told him. "No one should bring a child into the world unless they have the necessary maturity and resources. And there are other factors to consider. My father says children with birth defects will be extinct one day. Think of all the suffering that will be eliminated through genetic screening."

Nathan's face blanched. "Genetic screening, huh?" he said. "Isn't what you are talking about called genetic engineering?"

"Not necessarily," April argued. "I don't think you understand. Genetics is a fairly new field. Since both of my parents are physicians, I've been talking about this kind of thing all my life."

"Ah," he said. "And you're going to be a doctor too?"

"That's the plan," she said, releasing a long sigh. "Medicine is fascinating. I'm just not sure I want to be a doctor.

What I'd really like to do is teach school. I love children. Mother says it's because I'm an only child."

"And you don't agree?"

"No," April said. "Children grow. Patients die. I don't think I'm going to be a very good doctor. Every time I walk into a hospital, my stomach turns upside down."

"So, be a teacher, then," Nathan said. "Don't your parents want you to be happy?"

April cut her eyes to him. "I don't think they've ever considered what I want."

"My, my," Nathan said, scratching the gray stubble on his chin. "Guess we're going to have to change some things." He poked the sand with his piece of driftwood. "This genetic stuff you were talking about. Think of poor Francis. If he had been born today, he might have been considered defective, and never had a chance to swim the English Channel or write all those lovely poems. As I understand it, scientists can isolate certain genes now, tell if an unborn child will develop a specific disease."

"Well," April said, surprised someone his age was so well informed, "maybe your friend would have preferred not to have been born if he knew in advance what he was facing."

Nathan grimaced. "I don't believe human beings should play God. There was another man who wanted to engineer a perfect race, but you're probably too young to remember him. His name was Adolf Hitler."

"That's not a valid comparison," April said, shaking her head. "No one's trying to engineer a perfect race, Nathan. The medical community's only goal is to prevent needless suffering."

Nathan reached down and clasped her hand. April resisted the urge to pull away. His touch was not what she expected. She had seen his craggy fingers, but his hands were as soft and warm as an infant's. "I'm glad I met you," she said. "I want to help you if I can. I hope you don't mind me asking, but are you homeless?"

"In a way," he said, "but not the way you mean. I've outlived my usefulness. My only son died two years ago. My lovely wife has been gone for many years. All my friends are dead. But me, I just keep on living, a miracle of modern science. I live when all I ever knew and loved has died."

April's face softened in compassion. "Don't you have grandchildren?"

"My son and his wife were career people," Nathan explained. "They elected not to have children. That's exactly what my son said to me, 'Dad, Joy and I have elected not to have children.' I was mighty disturbed by that statement. I know we elect congressmen, but a child is different." He pushed the fishing cap back on his head. "If I had elected not to have my son, then he elected not to have a child and so on, things could get really strange. There might be no one to elect anything, even a president. I have to tell you, this particular word is not one of my favorites." He knocked a seashell out of his path with the piece of driftwood. "Perhaps it's time for you to tell me your story."

Once they reached the pier, they turned and headed back. "I told you I don't know any stories," April said, thinking of the abortion scheduled for the following day. A man of Nathan's age would not be able to understand why she had to terminate the pregnancy. They were not just one generation apart but several. If she became a physician, she could save lives. Her father pointed out to her all the time how lucky she was that he had the funds to put her through medical school. Many of her friends were not as fortunate.

A commotion erupted behind them. The seagulls were flapping their wings and making strange sounds. "Stop that this instant," Nathan said, shaking his finger at them. The gulls immediately fell into an orderly line again. "April's going to tell us a story if you guys will quiet down." He smiled at her, squeezing her hand. "Go on, now. They'll behave themselves."

"There was this girl," April said, deciding any topic would be better than the one they had been previously discussing. "Her parents were intelligent, successful people. They didn't laugh much, though. The only thing they found funny was when someone did something stupid."

"These people don't sound very nice," Nathan said.

"Their daughter met this man at a party," April continued. "He was so handsome that just looking at him made her feel dizzy. He had black hair, black eyes, olive skin. She didn't fall in love with his looks, though. It was the way he treated her, the way she felt when she was with him." She stopped speaking. She saw Pete in his blue Mazda backing out of her driveway on that fateful evening, smiling and waving. So many things had been left unsaid. If only they'd had more time together, she might be able to accept his death.

"Aren't you going to tell me the rest of the story?" Nathan said.

"They date," April said. "The man was different from anyone she had known before, and not just because he was a few years older. He was romantic and affectionate. He brought her flowers, composed songs for her, wrote her love letters." Tears gathered in her eyes. "There's nothing more to tell."

"You're sure?" Nathan said. "That wasn't much of a story. I thought you were going to tell me that this couple got married and started a family."

"No," April said, sniffing. She gave Nathan a quick peck on the cheek, then jogged back in the direction of her car, leaving him standing alone with the family of seagulls gathered at his feet.

April sat on a bench on the UCLA campus, the morning sun beating down on her. She had stopped by the library before her first class, finding a book of poems written by Francis Carol Rutherford. She had looked on the back cover for a photograph, but there were only a few sentences stating the poet had grown up in Maine. The poems she had read thus far were wonderful, and she was eager to share her discovery with Nathan. Did he know his friend's book was still available in the library? The way Nathan had told the story, Francis Rutherford had achieved only a moderate degree of success, basically at the local level. If the poet's work was in the UCLA library after all these years, Rutherford must have been a widely acclaimed poet.

A slender blonde stepped up to the bench. "Where the hell were you yesterday? Are you going to eat lunch with us today?"

"I met a new guy," April lied, slipping the book into her backpack. "I'm meeting him for lunch in thirty minutes."

"I thought you were still in the dumps over Pete," Sarah Johnson said, a puzzled look on her face. "Where did you meet this guy? Do I know him?"

"No," April said. "I'll call you tonight. If I don't hurry, I'm going to be late. Nathan hates it when I'm late."

"Didn't you tell me you were going to the clinic today?" Sarah asked. "I only have one class this afternoon. If you want, I can cut and go with you. Everyone else is cutting anyway."

April dropped her head and continued walking. During the time she had been reading Rutherford's poems, the abortion had disappeared from her mind. Her appointment was scheduled for three o'clock. It was only noon, though, and if she didn't get stuck in traffic, she would still have time to stop by the beach and show Nathan the book.

Parking the Jetta in the same spot, April removed her shoes and took off toward the sand. The only people on the beach were a couple walking hand in hand. She jogged in the direction of the pier, then heard a voice calling to her. "Over here," Nathan shouted. "If I was a snake, I would have bit you."

Nathan was sitting Indian-style under a small umbrella, partially obscured by a large sand dune. He had on the same clothes as the day before, the khaki pants, the red parka, the white fishing cap with the floppy brim. A checkered tablecloth was laid out on the ground, with two paper plates piled high with fried chicken, mashed potatoes, and cold slaw. "Where did you get all this, Nathan?" April asked. "Kentucky Fried Chicken?"

"Sit down," he said, motioning to a spot beside him. "I've got some iced tea in the cooler. As to the food, well, I cooked it myself. Live long enough and you learn to do everything. Let's eat. I'm famished."

"How did you know I was coming today?" April asked, dropping down next to him. "And how did you know I would be here in time for lunch?"

"Lucky guess," Nathan said, winking. He reached over and placed a napkin in her lap.

April sank her teeth into a crispy chicken breast and sighed in pleasure. "This is great," she said, "but how can you eat this? You're going to have a stroke, Nathan. Fried food is loaded with cholesterol."

Nathan laughed, then tilted his head toward the heavens. "Got any room for me up there yet?" A few moments later, he fell serious. "A lot of people don't understand how the world works. The reason people like me are living so long is that there is no place for them to go. There aren't as many babies being born as there used to be, and a lot of couples are waiting a long time before they start their families."

April felt a lump form in her throat. "Are you implying that abortion is the problem? You think aborting a baby is immoral, right?"

"Not necessarily," Nathan said. "I agree that a woman's body is her own. I remember the days of coat hangers and butchers. If a woman doesn't want a child or is unable to care for one properly, then she has no business giving birth. It's the word convenience that gives me heartburn."

April's muscles tensed. "You think women are turning to abortion for selfish reasons. Is that what you're trying to say?"

"No matter," Nathan told her. "If my theory is correct and there are only so many souls in the universe, an old goat like me would have to find a mother before he could be allowed to leave this world. I don't mean literally, of course. Souls must have somewhere to go, though, don't you think? I've had my bags packed for almost twenty years now, but the ticket doesn't seem to be forthcoming." He stopped and chuckled. "I'm afraid I might live to be a hundred. Can you imagine how boring that could be?"

"Just keep eating fat and you won't have that problem," April said, tossing her bones into a paper bag Nathan had brought along for that purpose. "Why would you want your life to be over? You seem to be in fairly good health. If you were sick, I might understand."

Nathan rested his back against the sand dune. "Today would have been my fiftieth wedding anniversary," he told her. "That's why I decided to make a nice lunch, have a little celebration. I'm pleased that you came along to keep me company. Joan would have liked you."

"You didn't answer my question."

"Oh," he said, "why I want to die, right?"

"Right," April said. "Most people are afraid of dying."

"What's to be afraid of?" Nathan told her. "I'm ready to trade this old body in for a new one. Can you imagine how marvelous it must be to be an infant? Whimper a little bit and you get fed." He yawned. "All this waiting is getting tiresome. I always thought I'd die around the same time as Joan. That way we could hook up together in another lifetime. By now Joan's probably already got herself a new man. Shucks, if I had passed on about twenty years ago, I might have come back in time to be your fellow." He removed a toothpick from his pocket and stuck it in his mouth. "Interesting thought, huh?"

While April stared out at the ocean, contemplating his statements, Nathan placed another piece of chicken on her plate. "I'm not really that hungry," she said, handing the plate back to him. "I have a lot on my mind right now."

"Medical school, huh?" Nathan said. "You must be a very smart girl. In my day, women didn't worry about making a career for themselves. All they worried about was getting hitched. I admire an ambitious woman, but there is only one problem."

"What's that?" April asked, glancing at her watch and seeing it was almost time to head out to the clinic.

"Who's going to raise the children?"

"Parents share the responsibility these days," she said. "It's not how much time you spend with a child anyway, it's the quality. I don't think a career should keep a woman from being a good parent. Women have to work today. The cost of living is too high for single income."

"I see," Nathan said thoughtfully. "But answer one question for me? Are these women working to put a roof over their head, or are they working to buy a bigger house or a fancier car?"

"Maybe a little of both," April said, an uncomfortable sensation in the pit of her stomach. When her father discussed his work, the emphasis was not on saving lives but on building a financial empire. Wealth brought power, he had always told her, and power was the key to success. "Look," she continued, "women want to make something of their lives too. Can you really put them down for that?"

"My mother didn't have a career," Nathan told her. "She brought four children into the world. She fed them, rocked them, nursed them. We were dirt poor, but we were happy. Mother didn't care about fancy cars or big houses. As long as she could place a healthy meal on the table, life was good."

April stood and dusted herself off. "I have to go," she said. "I probably won't see you after today. I have graduation next week. Thanks for the lunch. I hope things work out for you."

Nathan smiled. "Same to you, pretty lady. What happened to that guy, by the way, the one you mentioned in your story?"

"H-he was killed in a car accident," April stammered.

"Too bad," Nathan said. "Should have been me, huh? Think someone made a mistake?"

April rushed up the embankment to her car. She had only twenty minutes to make her appointment. If she was late, she would have to reschedule and her parents would be furious. Her father had not forgiven her yet for making such a foolish mistake. She could not afford to miss her appointment.

* * *

When April pulled into the parking lot of the clinic, she saw a lone seagull perched on the electrical wires strung over the parking lot. She quickly looked away, but her curiosity pulled her back. When she saw the bird perched on only one leg, the hairs on the back of her neck prickled. She looked down at the ground as she walked to the entrance of the clinic, thinking her imagination was playing tricks on her. Tripping on her own feet, she sprawled face first onto the sidewalk. The gull hopped around right beside her. For a long time she stared into its beady eyes. "Leave me alone," she snarled. She felt like a lunatic, talking to a stupid bird as if it were human. She tried to shoo the gull away with her hands, but it refused to leave. The bird would hop a few feet away and then stop. Was she going to have to get a restraining order on a seagull? She had subjected herself to the idiotic chatter of a senile old man. Now she was being stalked by a one-legged bird.

Pushing herself to her feet, April reached the door to the clinic, then saw a handwritten note taped to the glass. Tears gushed from her eyes. Why hadn't the clinic called the house to let her know the doctor was out of town? Her parents were close friends with Dr. Ruben Fielding. She wanted to have the abortion today, prior to her graduation and the trip to Baylor. Because of exams she had put it off until the last moment. Now she would have to make other arrangements right away.

Instead of taking the freeway, April used the surface roads to drive to her house. When she drove past the beach, she realized she had forgotten to show Nathan the book of poems and turned around. On the same stretch of road where she had parked earlier, she saw a fire truck and an ambulance. Pulling over, she leapt out of the car and raced toward the sand. A group of people were standing in a small circle near the water. "Please, God," she cried, "don't let it be Nathan."

"Step back, miss," a lifeguard said. "There's been an accident."

"Is it an older man wearing a red parka?" April asked, her voice trembling.

"Yeah," he said. "Are you a relative?"

April nodded, and the lifeguard stepped aside. Nathan's small body was being lifted by two paramedics onto a gurney. The fishing hat was gone, and his silver hair sparkled in the sunlight. The expression frozen on his face was almost joyful, not at all the tortured mask of death she had seen on other corpses. "Did he drown or did he die of natural causes?"

"Drowned," the paramedic answered. "The lifeguard saw him swimming out to sea. He tried to swim out to him, but the guy was too fast. The coast guard found him floating facedown in the water halfway to Catalina Island." He glanced out at the horizon. "Why would a man his age think he could swim to Catalina?"

April wiped the tears off her face with her hand. "I think he was suicidal," she said. "He told me he had outlived his usefulness. That wasn't true, though. He was a wonderful man."

"Guess he got what he wanted," the paramedic said. "Can you give us some information about him?"

"His name is Nathan," she continued. "He never told me his last name."

"I think you've got the wrong guy," the paramedic told her. "Are you really a relative? Seems like you don't know much about this man."

"We were just friends," April said, dropping to her knees beside the gurney.

"We need to notify his next of kin," he said. "The Social Security card we found in his pocket listed his name as Francis Carol Rutherford, but we couldn't find an address or phone number."

"I don't think there's anyone to notify," April said. "He told me all his family was dead." She reached into her pocket and handed the paramedic a card. "This is the number to my father's office. If you can't find anyone to claim the body, call and ask for me. I'll take care of the funeral services."

"Move aside," the other paramedic said. "We've got to transport the body now."

"No," April said, clasping Nathan's cold hand. "Just give me a few minutes to say good-bye, then you can take him."

The two paramedics stepped aside and began conversing with the lifeguard. As April stroked Nathan's hand, it was almost as if she could hear him speaking to her. "I knew it was you," she sobbed. "I even brought the book of poems to show you. Why didn't you tell me your real name?"

Nathan's other hand suddenly opened, and an antique silver locket tumbled out onto the sand. April snatched it before the paramedics saw her and quickly pried it open. Inside was a photograph of herself that appeared to have been snapped from a distance. Her first assumption was that Nathan had taken the picture from his favorite spot in the sand dunes. The photograph was not recent, though. The long white dress she was wearing in the snapshot hadn't been out of her closet since Pete's death. She had worn the dress on their last date, the night they had made love.

April's fingers trembled on the locket as she read the inscription: "To my beloved mother, April." How could it be possible? She had never been to the beach in that particular dress. The whispery voice snaked through her mind again, and she leaned closer to the body on the sand. "I'm here, Francis," she whispered, closing her fingers on the locket. "I hear you loud and clear. Nathan is a fine name for a boy. I promise, I'll only name the baby Francis if it's a girl."

"Are you finished here?" the same paramedic asked.

"Yes," April said, patting Nathan's hand before she stood and drudged off through the deep sand.

Once she reached her car, she patted her stomach. "Things are going to be better this time," she said, a feeling of warmth spreading throughout her body. "I promise, Nathan. And in case I didn't tell you, your father was tall and muscular. He might have been handsome, but no one would have ever considered him pretty. I told you I didn't want to go to medical school. That was my parents' dream, not mine. After you're born, I'll go back to school and get my teaching credentials. That way we'll have every summer together. I'll take you to the beach and teach you to swim as far as the eye can see."

As April turned the key in the ignition, a flock of seagulls passed overhead. She stuck her head out the window, searching for the one-legged gull. Not seeing it, she waved anyway as she pulled from the curb and drove off.

The Unsung Song
of Mary Gallinger
by Linda Lay Shuler

The events that made such a scandalous change in Mary Gallinger began on a day like any other. September 6, 1968, time exactly 7:20 A.M. when, as usual, Mary closed the door of her apartment, locked it with the extra locks the landlord had installed at her insistence, and walked to the elevator.

She paused at the small mirror there and glanced into it, making sure the drab brown hair was neat and tidy and the scarf was properly arranged. Then she pressed the button for the elevator and waited.

As if on cue, old Mr. McTavish hobbled down the hall with his four-footed cane and greeted her with his wan smile.

"Good morning, Miss Gallinger."

"Good morning, Mr. McTavish."

That was the extent of their daily discourse. The elevator came and she held it open for him so he could enter without having the door close too soon. The elevator coughed and rattled on the way down, as it always did, and she held the door open for Mr. McTavish as he stepped out and nodded his thanks. The day had officially begun.

The sun was bright and clear. She walked briskly to the bus stop as she had done for twenty years. She was fifty-two now, but she felt as capable as ever.

The usual group was waiting at the corner: the pretty young thing with long, slim legs, long, straight hair, and long, shiny fingernails. Mary's own nails were plain and short to assure more accuracy on the keyboard. The pompous young man with the briefcase was there, discoursing, as always, upon the day's news to chubby little Mrs. Perry, who worked at Adrianne's, an exclusive boutique. She had orange hair which did nothing to detract from the wrinkles and flab, but which did give her a spirited air. She tartly disagreed with the young man's opinions, and they usually argued all the way to town, where they parted, to resume the argument with gusto next morning.

She knew the group at the office would greet her briefly and then ignore her. She was accustomed to this and prided herself on her ability to be inconspicuous. Her boss, Mr. Worger, expected her to be part of her desk, chair, telephone, and word processor, a quiet and efficient working unit. She performed admirably and each year she received a week's salary as a Christmas bonus, for which she was grateful; it enabled her to pay her Christmas bills.

It was September, time to begin thinking about Christmas. Mary made it a point to shop the sales for bargains: nice things for her sister, Estelle, and Peter, and their brilliant teenage son. Who would have been hers—if Peter had married *her* instead of Estelle.

But she didn't think about that, not anymore.

Mama was dead and buried now, and she was alone.

But hadn't she been alone always?

No, of course not. She had her job, the people at the office, and Mr. McTavish at the apartment. She had become better acquainted with Mrs. Perry, too. Sometimes they sat together on the way to or from work. Her friends. She had good health, she wasn't bad-looking for her age, she supposed, just not conspicuous, and she had a little saved in the credit union toward retirement. It had been more, but Mama's funeral was expensive. Peter and Estelle hadn't paid their share of the funeral expenses yet, but they would, and when they did Mary was going to take that trip to Mexico she and Mama had planned before Mama got sick—the trip they had always wanted—to see the ancient splendors and the picturesque colonial towns.

Mary had pored over travel brochures, books, and attended the Ballet Folklorico from Mexico. The music, the dramatic re-creation of ancient dances, the brilliant colors in swirling display, echoed like the clang of a gong in a secret place within her, the place for special dreams.

It was 7:45 when the bus reached her corner. She had all of fifteen minutes to walk two short blocks, get an elevator to the eighteenth floor, freshen up in the powder room, and check her desk for any speck of dust the cleaning crew might have overlooked. Mary's desk was an extension of herself—orderly, neat, everything properly in place.

Mary tucked her purse in the bottom drawer, uncovered her keyboard, and waited for Mr. Worger's call. He always called promptly at eight.

"Are you ready, Miss Gallinger?"

"Yes, sir."

"Good. Come in, please."

He was a big man with a beak nose. Sometimes, as he sat hunched over his desk, he reminded her of Snoopy being a buzzard; he had that look. But he was a good man, of course.

She sat across from him, pad and pencil ready to take notes on his plans for the day. She prided herself on keeping all his appointments straight and taking care of countless details. She waited several minutes, but he did not begin, and she glanced up. He was looking at her in a curious way, almost as if he were uncomfortable.

"Ah, Miss Gallinger . . ." He paused and looked away. She waited silently. After a moment he looked at her again, and she saw with astonishment that he was blushing. That had never happened before.

"Miss Gallinger, I have valued your services during your years here."

She felt a warm glow. "Oh, thank you, Mr. Worger." How nice of him.

"As you know from correspondence, we have been negotiating for a company merger."

"Yes. I hope everything works out well."

"Ah, yes, of course." He paused and looked away again for a moment. "Actually, I am happy to say that it has worked out very well, and the merger will take place on November first."

"Oh, that's wonderful, Mr. Worger. I am so happy for you." He had worked hard for it.

"Well, thank you." He seemed to be having difficulty with his tie. He adjusted it and continued. "At the meeting of the board yesterday there was some discussion about our present personnel."

Mary experienced a small pang of hope. Could it be a promotion? She had expected it for a while now.

"We are being forced to reduce our workforce, Miss Gallinger. I have to let you go. I am really very sorry." It came out in a rush, quite unlike him.

There was a long silence as he looked at her. "Did you understand what I said, Miss Gallinger?"

She nodded, unable to speak.

His blush deepened. "You will receive severance pay, of course. Friday will be your last day here."

Mary placed her pad and pencils upon the desk, making it a point to arrange them neatly. Then she rose.

"Mr. Worger, I have been here twenty years." Her voice shook a little.

"It was not my doing, Miss Gallinger. I am truly very sorry. Now, about the board meeting—"

"Mr. Worger, you will have to excuse me. I'm afraid I . . ."

She turned and left the room, closing the door quietly, as always. She went to her desk, took her purse, and walked quite calmly to the powder room, where she sat and looked at herself in the mirror.

"Friday will be your last day here," she said.

The face in the mirror began to crumble. She watched as it made crying noises. Tears streamed down, but still she sat there, watching.

In his office, Mr. Worger picked up the phone.

"Mrs. Jeffrey? You can come in now."

The door opened, and Mrs. Jeffrey entered with style, as she did everything. She smoothed the dress over her slim hips and sat down.

"Was it very difficult?"

"Well, yes. She has been a good employee, after all."

"Couldn't you have put her in another department?"

"No. I told you we are cutting down. I had to let her go." She gave him a glance from under her lashes. "Me, too?"

He answered her, look for look.

"Never," he said hoarsely. "And that's a promise."

It was Friday morning; Mary had not been at the office since Wednesday, when she left, pleading illness. Today was the final day. She must empty her desk and pick up her check—her last check—and decide what to do now.

She locked her door and went to wait for the elevator. Old Mr. McTavish was already coming—on time. He was always on time although he was only going for breakfast. At eighty, mealtimes were his only excuse for a schedule, and he had to have a schedule, Mary knew. She understood things like that.

"Good morning, Miss Gallinger."

"Good morning, Mr. McTavish."

She held the door open, they entered, and the elevator began its creaking descent.

"How are you, Mr. McTavish?"

He glanced at her in surprise at this breach of routine. Pale blue eyes peered into hers with pleasure, and he smiled his wan smile.

"I am very well, Miss Gallinger, thank you."

They parted without further conversation, but Mary felt comforted somehow. Old Mr. McTavish appreciated her holding the door for him.

At the corner, the man with the briefcase was declaring, "I don't care how old she was. Some women never age that way, if you know what I mean."

"You speak from experience, I assume," Mrs. Perry said tartly, her little brown eyes snapping under the orange bangs.

"It's scientific fact. Furthermore, a woman in her position should be like Caesar's wife, above reproach. No wonder he shot her."

Mrs. Perry sniffed. "You have a butcher's sensibilities, dear boy. That woman had cause."

"What cause?"

"Unsung songs. Too many unsung songs."

The bus came, and Mary found a seat by the window. She looked out at the passing scene but saw none of it. Today was the last day.

The bus stopped at her corner and she walked briskly toward the office, where her desk awaited, but something slowed her down. How could she face everyone? How could she tell them she had been fired? How could she say good-bye?

Well, there would be others fired, too. They were all in the same boat.

As usual, she entered the powder room for her pre-work check-up and found she was not alone. Mrs. Jeffrey was there, applying lip gloss with a brush. Mary had never used a lip brush in her life.

"Good morning, Mrs. Jeffrey."

The brush paused briefly. "Hello."

Mary sat and took a comb from her purse. As she touched her hair here and there to tidy it, she noticed how many more gray hairs there were than there used to be. Mrs. Jeffrey's shiny blond head had none. She had finished her lips and was watching.

"You can always get a touch-up," Mrs. Jeffrey said.

"Oh. Well, yes, I suppose so," Mary said, embarrassed.

"You have a whole new life opening up, you know."

Everyone knew, then. Well, good; she wouldn't have to explain.

Mrs. Jeffrey continued, "That's the way mergers are. Some people always have to go."

"Yes, I know. Are you going?"

"Well, no." Mrs. Jeffrey busied herself with her eyelashes. "As a matter of fact, I have your job now."

The lump in Mary's stomach gave a heave. "Oh?"

"Yes. Mr. Worger took me from the reception desk. The merger, you know." Sea green eyes turned to gaze into Mary's. "Somebody has to do what you did, keep his appointments straight and all that."

"I didn't know—" Mary's heart was pumping fast, and she was confused. "I didn't know you could use a word processor . . ."

There was a glint in the green. "Oh, I process just fine."

Mary replaced the comb in her purse, pulled the zipper, and stood up. Something wrong was happening, had happened. Why hadn't Mr. Worger fired a receptionist, which would not be needed after the merger, and kept her? After twenty years?

She left the powder room with her heart jerking, and headed for her desk, her haven. But something was wrong there, too. Her wastebasket was placed on top of the desk, and all her things, her personal things, were in the basket. Someone had already emptied the desk. *Her desk.*

Mrs. Jeffrey had followed; she came and stood beside Mary.

"I thought I'd do it for you, to make it easier, you know." She sat down in the chair, Mary's chair, and opened a drawer. Mary could see that everything was arranged differently from the way it used to be.

Mrs. Jeffrey said, "Shall I call a boy from the stockroom to bundle your things up for you?"

Something inside Mary gave way; a dam broke. Blindly, she picked up the basket and turned it upside down on Mrs. Jeffrey's head. The contents tumbled down, spilling over and around the shiny hair, and banged to the floor. Hand lotion poured on Mrs. Jeffrey's forehead to her cheek, down her chin, and upon her silk blouse, carrying an eyelash with it.

Mrs. Jeffrey gasped and screamed.

The office buzzed with shock, but Mary was gone. She ran down the hall to the elevator; it was waiting. She stepped inside; it closed upon her like a coffin, lowering her swiftly and quietly to the netherworld. She stepped outside, unaware of bright sunshine and a blue day, unaware of everything but the storm raging inside her.

The traffic signal said, "Don't Walk." Automatically she stopped at the curb. She didn't know where she was going, but it was necessary to stay in motion. When the light changed, she hurried across.

She walked a few blocks more, nearly running. The storm within was tearing her loose from emotional mooring. Resentments and frustrations of years, disappointments . . . loneliness, loneliness.

Peter . . .

Forbidden emotions pounded at the door.

Again the signal said, "Don't Walk," and she found herself at Adrianne's. She would go inside, have a cup of tea, and calm down. She *must* calm down.

In the sanctuary of the women's world she assumed more control. Sipping her tea, listening to soft music, she relaxed a bit; the pounding subsided and she was able to think.

She had to look for a job. It was twenty years since the last time, and she wasn't sure how to begin.

Two women shoppers bustled in and sat at the table next to Mary. One of them had hair nearly as orange as Mrs. Perry's.

Mrs. Perry, of course! She worked here, at Adrianne's; perhaps she could help Mary get a job here, too. Mary paid her check and took the elevator to the second floor, domain of the designer's room and Mrs. Perry. After searching among the racks, she encountered her emerging from the fitting room with an armload of garments.

"Why, Mary! What a nice surprise!" The little brown eyes peered into hers. "Anything wrong?"

Mary nodded. "Yes, as a matter of fact."

"I'll be right with you, soon as I've finished with this customer. Sit down over there." She patted Mary's arm and scurried away.

Mary sank into the velvet sofa. A coffee table of peach-colored onyx on a white wrought iron stand held a bouquet of silk flowers and the latest issue of *Vogue*. A saleswoman passed, carrying a long evening gown of gray chiffon embroidered with shimmering crystal beads. There was the odor of luxury, a tangible fragrance.

Mary rose to saunter among the racks. She paused to admire a dress, a soft beige two-piece costume, tailored and chic. She glanced at the price tag: $1,875.00.

What must a women be or do to own such things? To Mary they were a foreign race. She could envy and admire them but never be one of them. She would always be on the outside looking in, an invisible wall between.

Again, forbidden emotions began an assault. And then, as if stirred and aroused from the depths, a new emotion surfaced.

Resolve. At last.

At long last, she, Mary Gallinger, was going to ask— no, *demand*—something of life. She was going to accomplish something.

Be somebody.

Have someone . . . and go to Mexico.

Mrs. Perry touched her arm. "There you are. Come over here. Now tell me all about it."

"I got fired. After twenty years." No tears; a statement only.

"Oh!" Mrs. Perry shook her head, frowning in shock and sympathy. "Why?"

"Because of the merger." Mary paused, and blurted, "Actually, I think he just wanted to get rid of me so he could have Mrs. Jeffrey." Mary was surprised at herself; usually she was not so blunt.

"I see." Mrs. Perry leaned back, considering. "Who is this Mrs. Jeffrey?"

"A receptionist. Very attractive. Sophisticated. Oh, you know . . ."

"Not Mrs. Lorraine Jeffrey, by any chance?"

"Yes. You know her?"

"My gawd!" Mrs. Perry's bosom heaved. "Do I know her!" She leaned forward and lowered her voice, glancing around to see if anyone was listening. "Honey, everybody at Adrianne's knows that bitch, believe it. Always returning things and blaming the store. She seldom buys anything unless some man pays for it, which they usually do. You wouldn't believe—" She stopped and leaned back again. "But that's not what you came to see me about."

Mary took a deep breath. "I need a job. I wondered—"

"But of course!" Mrs. Perry nodded vigorously, her orange bangs astir. "Want to try your luck here?"

"Do you think they need a secretary? I'm good on the word processor . . ." Her voice trailed off.

"Never know till you ask. Go to the office and see Mr. English and give me as a reference, hon. I'd go with you, but I can't leave the floor."

"Thank you," she said gratefully. "I'll try."

"Good luck." As Mary turned to leave, Mrs. Perry whispered, "Don't let English intimidate you, hon. If he gets high and mighty, just picture him sitting on the pot." She chortled and gave Mary a little push. "Go tackle him, now."

The girl in the office was quite nice. Soon she was seated across from Mr. English, a tall, thin autocrat with opaque gray eyes and large, shiny teeth frequently displayed.

"Ah. Miss Gallinger." Smile. "I see you are applying for a position as secretary. We do not have any such opening right now. However, I'll be happy to keep your application on file." Smile.

The other Mary, the one who used to be, would have meekly thanked him and departed. This Mary just sat there, looking at him. Sitting on the pot. She heard herself say, "Mrs. Perry suggested that I see you, Mr. English. Perhaps there is some other way I may be useful?"

He looked again at her application. "Yes, so I see." Obviously, he had not given her application much attention. He cleared his throat. "Uh . . . yes." Smile. "We have a high regard for Mrs. Perry." He looked at Mary through gold-rimmed glasses as if seeing her for the first time.

Mary tried to appear indifferent, as if it did not matter what he saw. Or whether she had a job. She swallowed hard as she rose to go, pretending indifference.

Again, Mr. English cleared his throat. "Would you be interested, perhaps, in selling?" Smile.

"Well, I have never . . ." Mary hesitated, then sat back down.

It was over. She had a job selling lingerie at Adrianne's. Her income would be enough to pay her bills if she was careful.

She was on the bus, going home, watching the passing scene. Nothing had changed. Yet all of it seemed different somehow.

A middle-aged man with a paunch sat beside her, reading avidly from a paperback. Her eye wandered to the page.

> *His mouth crushed her silky breast, seeking the*
> *rosy nipple. She moaned as he closed upon it eagerly,*
> *hungrily. He curled his tongue around it, caressing,*
> *sucking, as his hand slid down over the curve of her*
> *lovely belly to . . .*

Mary turned away as if stung. Good heavens! How could they print such things? Imagine reading something like that! In public! She edged closer to the window.

Against her will her head turned and again her eyes found the page.

> . . . she was a thing gone wild, a tempest tossing
> him in a storm. He felt the flood rising in
> his loins, a tremendous wave breaking, crashing,
> as she gave a savage cry and . . .

The book closed and the man rose to leave, but not without glancing at her first. He knew.

Mary jerked back to the window, aflame with embarrassment.

Later, in the sanctuary of her bedroom Mary looked at herself in the mirror. She stripped naked and stepped closer, staring. Deliberately, she cupped her breasts in both hands. She remembered what she read on the bus. Was it really like that?

The breasts were not as firm as they used to be, but they, at least, were not old.

Again, she watched the face crumple, again she listened to the horrifying noises it made. Because of Mr. Worger. Mrs. Jeffrey. Her desk. Her life.

Peter.

And finally, because of the real, the secret, the most bitter reason: at the age of fifty-two Mary Gallinger was still a virgin.

It was mid-December. Mary had been selling lingerie at Adrianne's for three months, and she was surprised at what was happening to her. Dealing with customers in the intimacy of the fitting room gave her assurance and confidence. She found that her age was an advantage; women trusted her and were at ease in her quiet presence.

Mrs. Foreman, the head of the department, had complimented Mary several times on her progress. She was making money, too, more than she had made as a secretary. Her commissions added up to a nice sum each month.

Most of all, she was learning something about herself. Frequent exposure to the figures of other women made her realize that her own figure was good, indeed. Every day she learned more about how to embellish it. Undergarments to enhance her curves. A different hairstyle with highlights instead of gray. New makeup to enhance her lips and her hazel eyes. In her fifty-second year she bloomed.

The old longings of her youth bloomed with her, dreams unfulfilled and abandoned. Until now.

Eagerly she absorbed romance novels, studied love scenes on TV and movies, and dreamed of how it would be when her time came at last.

It would be in a beautiful place with flowers and fountains and singing birds. A handsome man (like Peter) would take her there. She visualized their lovely sipping of wine with music playing . . . soft, sweet, loving words . . . leisurely embraces. And finally . . . ah! . . . the tender, glorious ascent into ecstasy . . .

Days passed. Mary's dreams persevered, and she prepared for them. A drawer in her bedroom accumulated lacy things—a secret hoard to take with her when she had saved enough to go to Mexico. There the new, the other Mary would wear beautiful—yes, sexy—things. There, in that magical place, surely she would *have someone*.

Meanwhile, she enjoyed lunching with her spirited friend, Mrs. Perry. Occasionally, they joined the other employees for lunch and conversation. There was always much talk, especially by the indomitable Mrs. Perry, who always had a great deal to say and said it nonstop.

". . . and as I was saying, Mrs. Gerald is a *lovely* person.

Always remembers me at Christmas. Last year she slipped me a fifty, probably because I called her when that pink Norell evening gown came in, remember? I knew she would adore it."

"It pays to remember your best customers, all right," somebody said.

"And then there is Mrs. Jeffrey," Mrs. Perry continued, glancing at Mary. "She likes real sexy things, you know. The DeVere line, anything with fur. Says that fur turns men on." She snorted. "She turns 'em on, all right. But Mary here put her in her place. Tell 'em, Mary."

The faces at the table turned to Mary with interest and surprise. "Yes! What happened?"

"Well, Mr. Worger fired me after twenty years. And gave her my job."

"Son of a bitch!" somebody said. "What did you do?"

They listened avidly as Mary told what had happened.

"Wonderful!" There was laughter. "I never could stand that Jeffrey woman," somebody said.

"What happened then, Mary?"

"I don't know. I went home and haven't been back since."

"The rat! What did you say his name was?"

"Worger. Andrew X. Worger, Vice President." Mary had typed that thousands of times.

"Hm-m-m." Mrs. Perry frowned in concentration. "Andrew X. Worger. That name rings a bell."

"I wonder what the X stands for," somebody said.

"X marks the spot," somebody else said.

"Say!" Mrs. Perry exclaimed over the giggles. "Isn't he the one who makes such a big deal out of marabou? You know, who always phones and orders the L.B."

"L.B.?" Mary asked.

"Lecher's Basic, hon. Sheer black gown and peignoir

with loads of marabou. Not a woman alive wants to sleep in that crap, but it's not for sleeping, actual sleeping, that is." Chortle. "Anyway, Mrs. Foreman was telling me about this character who has a standing order to send a set to his latest love. I'd swear his name was Andrew X. something-or-other." She peered at them thoughtfully. "This Andrew X. has a standing order at Adrianne's to remember his wife on their wedding anniversary. The date is some time just before Christmas—the twentieth, I think. He leaves everything up to Mrs. Foreman; she has to select something and send it in case he forgets, which he usually does."

Everyone was silent, waiting for Mrs. Perry's next revelation. There was an air of conspiratorial expectancy.

Somebody said, "I wonder if—"

"The orders got mixed up?"

"Happens every day," somebody else said.

"It would serve him right," Mrs. Perry nodded. "But somebody would be in trouble. *Bad* trouble."

There were murmurs of agreement.

"It's a man's world, baby."

Then it happened. Ten days before Christmas, Mr. Worger called, asking for Mrs. Foreman. However, Mrs. Foreman was upstairs in a staff meeting, and Mary had to take the call.

"Mrs. Foreman?"

Mary recognized the voice at once. For an instant she felt panic, but then she swallowed and said in what she hoped was a disguised voice, "I am sorry, but Mrs. Foreman is in a meeting. May I help you?"

"Who is this speaking?" Mary knew that irritated inflection very well. She visualized the frown and pursed lips.

"This is Mrs. Foreman's assistant. How may I help you, sir?"

"Your voice sounds familiar. But very well, I'm in a hurry. Please get the order correct."

"Yes, sir."

"Your best black gown and peignoir. Sheer, you know, with those fluffy feathers like I always order. Size ten. Mrs. Foreman will know. Send it to Mrs. Lorraine Jeffrey, that's J - e - f - f - r - e - y at the Royal Scot on Turtle Creek. Do you have that?"

"Yes, sir." You son-of-a-bitch bastard.

"And include a gift card that says—are you getting this?"

"Yes, sir." You bet I am.

"That says, 'From your own Andy Pandy.' Got that?"

"Yes, sir. 'From your own Andy Pandy.'" Mary kept her voice impersonal. "And may I make a suggestion?"

"I suppose so."

Mary could not quite believe what she was doing, but she relished it. "Would you care to include a jeweled panda pin? We have some lovely ones, just in. Gold, with jet, really beautiful." And an extra bonus if she sold some.

"That's not a bad idea, Miss—what did you say your name was?"

"I know she will be impressed. Would you like this charged?"

"How much is the pin?"

"Eight hundred and fifty dollars plus tax."

"Oh." Brief pause. "Very well, go ahead and send it, and don't forget the card. Gift-wrap it, of course, your best wrap."

He gave his name, office address, and account number, and that was that. Mary was elated. She had handled it admirably and increased the sale as well. She was the first in her department to sell a panda pin. It was a beautiful pin, but Lorraine Jeffrey would not receive it. No, indeed. Nor would she receive the Lecher's Basic. Mary—or rather the stranger within Mary—would see to that.

Hardly believing what she was doing, Mary made out the sales slip for the package to be sent not to Mrs. Jeffrey, but to Mrs. Andrew X. Worger at the Worger residence.

When Mrs. Foreman returned, Mary felt she should say something, so she announced "I sold a panda pin."

"A panda? Well, congratulations! Really, Mary, you surprise me sometimes. Who bought it?"

"Mr. Worger. To go with the black peignoir he ordered at the same time."

"Oh. That reminds me. It's time to send his wife an anniversary gift. Pick out a robe, will you? Size forty-two." She hurried away.

The stranger within Mary gave a silent yelp of glee. What a beautiful coincidence! It took awhile to make a selection. Most of the robes were beautiful. Too beautiful. Surely, there must be one. . . . Ah, yes, there it was, and in a size forty-two. Mary ordered it gift-wrapped and sent to a Mrs. Lorraine Jeffrey at the Royal Scot with a card, "How could I forget? Love, Andrew."

Getting the addresses mixed up would seem a natural mistake. As somebody said in the lunchroom, "it happens every day."

The repercussions were immediate.

Bertha Worger was at home when the package arrived. She had known for years of Andrew's infidelities, but she had persevered for the sake of the children, her social position, and the hope, long held but forgotten now, that he might reform as he grew older, less attractive, and less demanding physically. Besides, she loved him.

She sat for a time with the package on her lap, being happy that he had, at least, remembered their anniversary.

Should she plan a little dinner to celebrate? With champagne? No, whiskey sours, that's what he liked. And so did she, especially lately. In fact, she had just had one, or was it two?

She opened the package and experienced a surge of emotion. A black negligee! Such a stunning surprise! Could it mean . . .

She lifted it from the box tenderly, as if it were a bouquet. The feathers rippled caressingly against her fingers. Then she noticed the size, saw the pin, read the note.

At the office, Mrs. Jeffrey informed all callers that Mr. Worger was in conference. Actually, she knew he was at the club having a rubdown. Getting ready for that evening; he said it stimulated the circulation.

She was growing a bit weary of his demands upon her time and upon her. As a lover he left much to be desired, and she found his attentions increasingly distasteful.

However, she was going to have to find a way to taper it off; she had to make time for Ernie. Plenty of time. He was Ernie Klamath, Jr., son of the chairman of the board. Tall, handsome, young, charming, dissolute, and oh, so rich; she had every intention of marrying him.

The phone rang and she answered it musically, as usual. "Mr. Worger's office."

"This is Ernie."

"Oh. Well, hello!"

"Hello, yourself, sweet thing. How about tonight?"

She was in the mood, all right, and the thought of another of those evenings with Andrew was not what the doctor ordered. But better to let Ernie dangle a bit.

"Darling, you know I'd love to, but I can't. Not tonight. Could you make it tomorrow?"

"Why not tonight?"

"Because I just can't, that's why. Look, someone is on another line. Wait just a second while I put you on hold. I'll be right back."

She let him wait a good, long time, and when she got back on his line, he had hung up. She smiled; things were progressing very well.

Andrew was, indeed, at the club. Fresh from a rubdown, he stood before the mirror. Nothing like a good rubdown to stimulate the circulation. He patted his paunch; the workouts at the club were beginning to show. But his waistline still needed a little shaping up. Now, if only his hairline . . . Maybe he should consider a hair transplant. And a face-lift, too. Hell, why not?

He visualized himself with hair as it used to be, face as it used to be. It could be that way again, almost. Lorraine would be impressed. She had changed a bit lately. But no, that was his imagination. He was so afraid of losing her that he imagined things. He had never been this gung-ho about anyone before. He could hardly wait for tonight when she would be wearing that transparent black thing with the fluffy feathers. He saw her walking across the room to him, aglow with pleasure at his gift, with the soft, transparent black floating against her skin and her lovely body inviting him.

Dispensing a largesse in tips, he left for home. On the way he pondered what excuse to offer to explain his absence later that evening. He wondered guiltily if Bertha really believed the excuses he had given during the many years of their marriage. And then, with a shock, he remembered. This was their anniversary! Good Lord, not tonight! He hoped that Adrianne's had remembered; they hadn't failed him yet.

He recalled talking to that woman on the phone at Adri-anne's. And then, like a delayed explosion from a depth charge, the truth hit him. He knew that voice! It couldn't be, but it was! He should know; he had listened to it for twenty years.

In a flood of foreboding he entered the house. It was quiet. Too quiet. No odor of dinner cooking, no television, no radio, no talk on the telephone, nothing. Something was wrong, wrong.

"Bertha! I'm home!"

No answer.

"Bertha!"

Silence.

In a cold sweat he began to run upstairs. He stopped, gawking.

Bertha stood on the upper landing. She was naked, to-tally, except for a pin, a panda pin, nestled in the luxuriant black triangle between her bulging thighs. She began to descend, large breasts bouncing with each step.

"Here's my darling Andy Pandy," she cooed hoarsely. She was very drunk. "How do I look, Andy Pandy?"

Andrew watched, horrified, as she took a few more stumbling steps and then collapsed in a heaving bulk on the stairs, sobbing.

"You goddam son of a bitch! You goddam son of a bitch!"

He turned and ran from the house, jumped into his car and zoomed from the drive. Sweat trickled into his eyes and down into his shirt collar; he wiped his eyes with his sleeve.

The doorman at the Royal Scot knew him and nodded briskly. "Good evening, sir."

Andrew mumbled a reply and hurried to the elevator. He arrived at her door and paused a moment before knocking.

Was there laughter inside? *Someone else there?* He put his ear to the door and listened. Silence. Vastly relieved, he knocked.

The door opened and a young man stood there. A tall, handsome young man with a mop of beautiful hair and a flat belly. Ernie Klamath, Jr.

Andrew stood riveted and speechless as Lorraine appeared. She wore a caftan, lacy and white with fur, and she had never looked more beautiful. She held something out to him as though it had a contagious disease. It was an enormous bulk of dung-colored quilted robe.

"I won't be needing this."

Andrew managed to croak through his nightmare, "It was a mistake—"

"It certainly was," the handsome young man said. He took the robe and shoved it at Andrew. The door closed.

Andrew could not leave. He stood clutching the robe, staring numbly at the closed door.

Mr. English was unable to muster his usual shiny smile. The man seated across from him at his desk was Mr. Andrew X. Worger's attorney, and he was threatening a suit. Nothing like this had happened before in all of the years of Mr. English's employment, and he found himself at a loss. Spread before him were the sales slips, each with the identification of the saleswoman, Mary Gallinger. The same Mary Gallinger who had been fired by Mr. Worger. Lorraine Jeffrey was the one who had taken her place. The obvious could not be ignored, but he must find a way to ignore it.

"I assure you," Mr. English said with great sincerity, "it was a natural mistake, a human error. We shall make every effort to correct it."

"You mean, you can put the pieces of my client's life back

together again, like Humpty Dumpty?" the attorney said coldly, rising to leave. "You will hear from us again."

After the attorney's departure, Mr. English called in his secretary. "Get Mary Gallinger in here. Right now."

Mary had expected the inevitable. She had gone about her duties as usual, knowing that it would be the last time. At any moment Mr. English would call her to the office and that would be that. She would remain calm and wait for the guillotine. It was not easy; she enjoyed her job and could not afford to lose it. But the stranger within her gloated, relishing revenge.

The call came, and Mary looked about her at what she was leaving.

What have I done to myself?

Mr. English came to the point immediately.

"Miss Gallinger, I hope you realize the damage you have inflicted upon Adrianne's—and upon your professional reputation." Cold eyes bored into her. "I believe I am entitled to an explanation."

"It was a mistake. I am sorry."

He leaned back, gripping the arms of his chair with both hands. "You have good reason to be sorry, Miss Gallinger." A chilly smile allowed his teeth to glisten. "You are fired. Furthermore, be assured that no other store will subject itself to your unprofessional, underhanded, sneaky behavior. In short, Miss Gallinger, should anyone ask me to recommend you, I shall certainly refuse to do so."

He dismissed her with a gesture and reached to open a drawer and remove a document. Mary visualized him reaching for toilet paper.

"I am being sentenced on circumstantial evidence? How disgracefully unprofessional." Mary paused. *Had she really said that?* "You're violating my legal rights."

Mr. English stabbed her with a lethal glance. "Are you leaving or must I call security?"

The stranger within Mary made her smile. "Call by all means. You will need security—in court."

She gathered inner forces to strengthen her knees, then rose and departed, closing the door quietly behind her.

Subsequent days passed in a wretched haze. What had she done to herself?

Who said revenge was sweet?

December was bitterly cold. Mary spent much time wrapping Christmas gifts. She had spent too much; how would she pay for these beautiful things for Estelle and Peter and their son?

Mexico . . . but a dream.

Christmas Eve approached. She was always invited to the family celebration, and she always attended. Estelle and Peter and the boy were the only family she had now that Mama was gone.

For comfort she watched movies and television, studying the love scenes, passionate and tender. *Was it really like that? How wonderful!*

Secretly she hoarded romance novels, carrying them home in her purse so nobody would know. She absorbed them avidly, comforted somehow. At least she was loved in her dreams.

Christmas Eve came at last. Mary was in the shower when the phone rang. She wrapped herself in a towel and padded to the bedroom.

"Hello?"

"Merry Christmas!"

Her heart gave a jerk. It was Peter. "Merry Christmas to you!"

"All ready for Santa?"

"Yes, indeed!"

"Good. I'll pick you up in a half hour."

"I'll be waiting."

Of its own accord the telephone receiver slid caressingly over her naked body, lingering where she had always wanted Peter to linger. His voice, his beautiful voice, so much a part of him, had touched her.

But he was Estelle's. Always Estelle's. He would be there in a half hour; better be ready.

She would be alone with him all the way there and back.

At least she would look good. Peter had not seen her since she began work at Adrianne's; he would be surprised. A final touch: she sprayed her body with perfume and returned to the living room, walking about so that the fragrance from her warm body permeated the room. Maybe Peter would realize what he had missed when he married her sister.

So many unsung songs.

The door chime sounded. Peter was there! She snatched her old bathrobe, wrapped it tightly around her, unlocked the door, leaving the chain on, and peeked through. Peter made a motion to enter.

"Peter, I'm sorry. I'm not ready."

"Well, all right," with a hint of impatience. "I'll wait. Open up."

"I'm not ready. Just wait in the car. I won't be a minute."

"It's cold out there."

"I'll be just a minute. Please."

With irritation, "All right, if you insist."

Peter returned to the Mercedes. Easing into the front seat, he pondered. There had been perfume in that room; he recognized it. Expensive stuff. A man in there? It couldn't be, not Mary. What the hell was going on that she wouldn't let him in as she usually did?

Peter was uneasy; things were not going as he had planned. He had always been convinced that Mary yearned to get him to bed, that she was crushed when he married her sister, and that she had never wanted another man when she couldn't have him. If Mary had been more of a looker, he might have done something about it sooner. As for now, he would enhance the warmth of Christmas season with a little display of affection. Suitably timed, of course. The matter of the loan would have to be played by ear.

He wondered how much Mary had salted away. He needed eight thousand. Ten, really, to get those damned accounts squared away, but eight would get him off the hook for the time being.

He adjusted the rearview mirror. Thank God he still had all his hair! He was combing it when Mary came.

"Sorry to keep you waiting, Peter."

"That's okay." She looked different, disturbingly so. And a hint of perfume lingered.

There had to be some man involved. Mary, of all people!

Peter gave her a sideways glance. "Did I come at an inconvenient time?"

"Not really."

She seemed preoccupied, disinterested even. Not touchingly grateful to be in his presence at all. No lingering glances at his profile as he drove, no little sighs of contentment. Nothing. His feeling of unease increased. They were on the freeway and would be home soon. Better get the ball rolling.

"I say, Mary, how are things going with you, dear?"

"Well, frankly, I'd just as soon not discuss it."

"No?" This wasn't like Mary at all. She loved to confide in him. "Why not?"

"I'd rather talk about you. How is everything with you, Peter?"

He wondered if maybe he should bring up the matter of the loan now. But no, the mood wasn't right. She was gazing out the window, not really interested.

"Look, Mary, after dinner and the tree and all that, I'll take you home and we can have a talk and get caught up on all the news. You know how it is at our place on Christmas. Bedlam. I want to talk to you."

"About what?"

"I just want to talk, that's all." He reached over and patted her knee.

Mary looked at him. She saw the aquiline profile, still firm, the well-groomed russet hair beginning to gray, the dark eyes under heavy brows, the mouth she had, yes, starved for. She saw the solid body in expensive clothes, the hands on the wheel. She turned back to the window. He must not see, he must not know, that she *needed* him still after all these years. When she was fifty-two. And a virgin.

Fifty-two and no job. No future. No husband, no child, nothing at all.

It was over. The dinner, the distribution of gifts under the tree. "Oh, it's just beautiful, Mary darling!" She had dipped into her small savings for gifts this year.

Mexico would wait.

"I'll take you home again, Kathleen," Peter sang. The rum punches had been strong; Mary felt engulfed in a misty haze. Peter sang more on the way home. He had a good voice, and Mary liked his way with a song. She liked his way, period. She found she was glad they would be alone together in the apartment and wondered what he wanted to talk about.

Did it matter?

She felt a little drowsy and beautifully content. She snuggled into the seat and sighed. Why worry about a job? Everything would be all right, and she was with Peter.

Peter reached over and touched her knee again. His hand lingered a moment. "What is that perfume you're wearing?"

"Candide."

"That's what I thought. Smells great."

"Thank you." She smiled at him. "I feel great."

Peter was elated. She was more than a little drunk! Things were going as he hoped; they would be at her apartment soon, and he felt damn good himself.

"Well, here we are, home again home again jiggity jig," Peter sang.

Laughing, they took the boxes and bundles from the car—things the family had given her for Christmas. Peter dropped one at the door while she fumbled for the key, and they laughed again. Mary opened the door, and they entered into a faint fragrance, infinitely alluring. The gifts were deposited on a chair. They removed their coats and stood looking at one another.

"Well," Peter said heartily, "now we can talk." He sat on the sofa and patted the seat beside him.

Mary complied in a joyful haze. He put his arm around her and pulled her close to him. She was completely happy.

"What did you want to talk about, Peter?"

Peter found he was becoming aroused. This was not the Mary of other days, not this sexy woman who he knew damn well had the hots for him. He had watched her covertly all evening in her soft green dress that concealed but enhanced beautiful breasts and a seductive curve of hips—a come-on. Well, he was ready. A good erection. The rum punch, of course; he always reacted this way to rum punch. But he *must* get on with the business at hand. They would play later.

He caressed her shoulder. "Well, the truth of the matter is, business has been bad lately."

"Oh, I am sorry to hear that." She wasn't sorry about a thing. Being pressed to him was intoxicating. She awaited sweet words.

"I'm in sort of a financial bind." He caressed her neck,

slipping fingers under the neckline of the dress. "I need you, Mary."

His need was all she heard. He needed her! Ah! Resistance dissolved and she leaned her head back against his hand. Of their own accord her eyes closed and her lips parted in an involuntary invitation.

Peter was triumphant. She was asking for it! He turned her head to his and kissed her on the mouth. Her arms went around his neck, and she clung to him.

"I need you, Peter. Oh, I need you!"

Peter exulted; she was ready! The money was as good as his.

They lay on the sofa in a passionate embrace. She made little sounds, moans, as he fumbled at her clothes.

"Take these damn things off!"

She rose, hurried into the bedroom, and closed the door. Her heart thumped crazily as she removed her new green dress and hung it carefully in the closet.

Standing before the mirror in her bra and panties, the reflection was hazy. It began to clear.

The rum punch haze dissolved.

She saw Estelle.

She *saw* herself.

No! No, that could not be she, that stupid half-dressed creature! That floozy!

Mortified to the bone, Mary reached for her bathrobe as the door opened and Peter entered.

He had undressed. She was in the presence of a naked man for the first time, a man in full erection.

She was shocked.

It was not like the books said.

It was ludicrous, that big meaty thing sort of wiggling as he moved. He was hairy from the neck down, and he had a pot belly.

He grinned widely. "Hey, you've got killer tits!"

She backed away and he reached to grab her. She whirled, ran to the bathroom, and locked the door. She leaned against it to keep from falling, burning with shame and humiliation.

He followed her and yanked on the doorknob.

"A teaser, eh? Come out!"

"Go away!"

He banged on the door. "You want it! You know you want it!"

"Go home!"

He pounded on the door again. "Who the hell do you think you are?"

"Your wife's sister. There's a phone in here. You leave right now or I'll call her to come and get you."

A pause.

"You do that," Peter growled softly, "and I promise you will regret it the rest of your life."

Mary huddled against the door, waiting to hear the hallway door close. She was shaking. Was he hiding in there? She waited a long while, then carefully opened the door a crack, ready to slam it shut again.

He was gone.

It had rained every day since Christmas. Mary sat in her old robe, drinking coffee, reading the want ads—anything to forget.

But there was no release from acid humiliation; flashbacks of the scene with Peter replayed again and again. Searing anger and shame roiled in her stomach.

How could I have made such a stupid fool of myself? How could I think I loved him?

How dare he do that! How dare he!

Mary rose and paced the room. Thunder growled

distantly and rain lashed the window. Mary sobbed, but tears could not wash away anger and grief and humiliation.

She would forget about wanting to *be somebody*. Or *have someone*.

Finally, she went to the bathroom, splashed cold water on her face, and confronted herself in the mirror. "Welcome to the real world, stupid. About time."

From the closet she gathered all the romance novels to donate to Goodwill for some other dreamer.

The wail of a siren, demanding and close, stopped outside. In a moment there were hurried footsteps in the corridor. Mary flung open the door as two men passed carrying an empty stretcher. They stopped at Mr. McTavish's door.

"Oh, no! It's Mr. McTavish!"

An anxious little group assembled, murmuring.

"What happened?"

But nobody knew. Mr. McTavish had always kept to himself. The men knocked loudly on the door, but no one answered.

"Get the apartment manager, and quickly! We have to get in there!"

Then the door opened slowly, and Mr. McTavish stood, wavering upon his cane. Mary was shocked at his appearance. He was haggard and disheveled; his thin face was drawn and flushed. A wrinkled robe hung loosely from bent shoulders and was fastened with a safety pin. But he bowed slightly with his old dignity.

"Thank you for coming." A convulsive cough bent him over the stretcher so that he nearly fell upon it.

The men placed him upon the stretcher and tucked a blanket gently around his thin frame. As they approached Mary, his pale blue eyes brightened a bit.

"Good morning, Miss Gallinger."

"Good morning, Mr. McTavish."

Impulsively, she took his bony hand and trotted beside him as they carried him hurriedly down the hall.

"Is there anything at all I can do?" she asked him.

"The flowers, lassie. Water the flowers."

"I will, Mr. McTavish."

"Thank you kindly." He smiled faintly as they carried him into the elevator and the door closed.

Mr. McTavish had been in the hospital for several days; pneumonia, they said, and no visitors. Each morning before she left for job hunting, Mary unlocked his door with the key entrusted to her by the manager, and entered Mr. McTavish's private world.

It was a world of books, maps, strange clay bowls, small clay figures, and stacks of magazines and papers, all neatly arranged. Three pots of brilliant pink azaleas were set on the window sill. Mary inspected them daily and watered them carefully when they seemed to need it.

It was a world much different from her own, and Mary found herself strangely at home in it. She liked the clay figures, the strange little men in their exotic garb, their aquiline faces. She liked the bowls with incised designs and faded colors. She held them carefully in both hands, turning them about, wondering who had made them and when, wondering about Mr. McTavish. He must have had an interesting life. More so than she.

So many unsung songs.

A man's photograph stood on a bedside table. Middle-aged, with graying hair, a lean, craggy face and blue eyes. He had a look about him that reminded her of Mr. McTavish. His son, perhaps. Mary picked up the photograph in its silver frame and looked long at those eyes. Intelligent. And something else. She would ask Mr. McTavish about him.

One evening when Mary telephoned the hospital to inquire about Mr. McTavish, she was told that he could have visitors. "But only five minutes, please."

Mary went to visit him, taking one of his pots of azaleas to keep him company.

Cautiously, she looked into the room. The narrow elongation under the sheet was motionless. His eyes were closed; his pale face and thin white hair seemed to recede into the pillow. She tiptoed into the room and stood beside him.

"Mr. McTavish," she said softly.

The eyes opened and the clear, pale blue came suddenly alive. He smiled and reached out his thin hand.

"My flowers!"

"I thought you might like to have them with you." She held the pot while he touched the blossoms. "I watered them as you asked me to."

"Thank you, lassie."

She placed the pot on the stand beside the bed, and sat down. "I am so glad you are better!"

"Aye." His eyes searched hers. "What do you think of my collection?"

"It's beautiful. Really beautiful."

"You have read my papers?"

"No. I have only cared for the flowers, Mr. McTavish."

"I would like you to read my papers, lassie. My manuscript." A hint of pink tinged his cheeks. "As a favor."

"Yes, of course I will be glad to. Your collection is so interesting—the bowls, the little men. Is your manuscript about them?"

"You will see." His eyes closed wearily, and Mary rose to leave.

"Good-bye, Mr. McTavish." She touched his hand, but he did not open his eyes. She tiptoed out.

Riding home, Mary thought about Mr. McTavish and the

inner force he seemed to retain, a generator that continued under its own power regardless of age and illness. She remembered the touch of his thin hand, the light in his pale eyes when he saw her, and she felt a surge of compassion and tenderness. She would read his manuscript to please him, and she would take care of him when he came home. He needed her. She wondered what he must have been like as a young man. Gentle, that would be it.

Not like Peter.

At home, Mary lingered only long enough to remove her coat and get the key to Mr. McTavish's apartment. She would read his manuscript now and would be ready to discuss it tomorrow.

Entering Mr. McTavish's world, she was reminded again of how much she felt at home in it. The books, the papers, the strange little men, seemed to welcome her. She leafed through the papers. Bills, modest ones and most of them past due; his rent was unpaid for two months. She wondered if he had insurance.

Under the bills were file folders filled with notes in his precise, spidery handwriting, and under the folders was a cardboard box. Opening it revealed a hand-written manuscript titled *Ancestral Memory: a Hypothesis.* She sat down to read.

Suddenly the words came alive.

> *The experience of being completely at home in*
> *a foreign place, the inner conviction that one*
> *has been there before, lived there before, is*
> *not infrequent. It is an echo in the subconscious,*
> *the voice of ancestral memory.*

Was that what she heard when she pored over the books and brochures about Mexico? That longing to be there?

Suddenly, Mary remembered Mama, who had yearned all her life to go to Mexico and never had.

"Mary, I can't explain why I want to go. I just feel I should, that something is waiting for me there. Maybe it's because your great-grandfather, Grandpa Conrad—you remember, who married three times—his first wife was Elena de Alba from Mexico, and we are descendants of that first marriage. Grandpa Conrad used to talk all the time about Mexico when I was growing up. He loved it so . . ."

Mary had forgotten, until then, about her great-grandmother, who had died long before she was born. She vaguely remembered having seen an old photograph of a dark-haired little woman with smoldering eyes, but it was only a quaint old photograph from a distant past. Until now she had felt no kinship.

We are descendants of that first marriage.

She had Latin blood! She remembered the photograph of those dark eyes smoldering for a hundred years.

She continued to read. Angus McTavish took her to Mexico, to Guatemala and Panama, to Bolivia, Ecuador, Brazil, and Peru, searching for knowledge of ancient races, knowledge to be discovered in the subconscious, the ancestral memory of living descendants.

Hours passed. At last she turned the final page and lay the manuscript aside with regret; it was unfinished. But she looked around the room with new eyes: the books, the bowls. The strange little figures looked back. She walked slowly to a table where a clay musician sat cross-legged, playing a flute. She picked it up gently as though it were alive.

What music did her brother play?

A key turned and a door opened.

Mary gasped in surprise. A man stood there, a tall man with graying hair and blue eyes in a craggy, tanned face. He shot her an encompassing glance. "May I ask who you are?" His voice was low but demanding, with a slight accent.

Mary swallowed shocked surprise. "I am Mary Gallinger. Mr. McTavish—"

"Of course. Forgive me. My father spoke well of you."

He shut the door and stood looking at her. He wore jeans and boots and a cotton shirt open at the throat. "I am Alexander McTavish."

Mary managed to say, "His son, of course." She indicated the photograph. "I recognized you." Under his gaze she felt exposed. She still held the clay musician and set it down carefully. "How is your father?"

He looked away without reply. He went to stand by the cluttered, small desk where the manuscript lay. He stood with his back to her, head bowed. "They got the pneumonia under control. But then he had a stroke. He . . ."

Mary went to stand beside him. He turned his head away, but not before Mary saw his eyes shiny with tears.

"Your father . . . Is he . . . will he be okay?" she asked softly, touching his arm. "I saw him—"

He sat down, put his elbows on his knees, and buried his face in his hands. "He has never let me help him. He always refused . . . lives alone . . ."

Mary knew he was grieving. She wanted to comfort him but didn't know how.

"He is proud. I should have insisted on bringing him home. This might not have happened . . ." He took a large handkerchief from a pocket, wiped his eyes and blew his nose. "I should have insisted, but he is my father. Proud." He stuffed the handkerchief back in his jeans pocket, stood and looked at her, pretending there had been no tears.

"My father told me about you—before he had the stroke. He is paralyzed on his right side."

"Paralyzed? Oh, I am sorry. So sorry." Suddenly, she could

not remain standing, and she collapsed in Mr. McTavish's comfortable old chair. His cane was propped against the wall beside her. Mary visualized him coming down the hall, smiling. "Good morning, Miss Gallinger . . ."

"I am sorry, Mr. McTavish . . ." Her voice broke.

He stood looking down at her. He took an old straight-back chair, turned it around, and straddled it, facing Mary.

Mary looked into the craggy face and saw Mr. McTavish in his son. She *knew* him.

He said, "I must take my father home. He will probably object as usual, but—"

"He may change his mind. He needs you."

"He thinks he needs no one. Always has."

"But it is different now."

"Perhaps."

He rose and picked up the little musician. "These are valuable—my father's collection." He paused, turning the clay figure in his big hands. "They belong where they originated, in Mexico. My home. I will bring them when I take him back where he was born. Where I was born . . ."

"Oh." Mary could say nothing more.

He set the musician down. "These things must be packed. I must stay with my father. I don't know anyone—"

Mary heard herself say, "Let me do it. I would love to!"

He looked at her. Something in that intense blue gaze made her feel vulnerable. He said, "I understand why my father feels as he does about you."

"Mr. McTavish, your father—"

"Call me Alex." He smiled suddenly. "I accept your generous offer. Packing materials will be here in the morning, Miss Gallinger, if you are sure that—"

"Call me Mary. Yes, I am sure. These things are beautiful; I will be careful."

"Very well . . . Mary. I thank you."

He shook her hand briefly. "Until tomorrow."

He closed the door; Mary listened to footsteps fading away. How like his father Alex was! Already she missed his reassuring presence.

She slept little that night; Peter intruded brutally in her dreams. She woke and thought of Alex; it eased the grip of painful memories.

Mary rose early. She was in Mr. McTavish's apartment gathering the artifacts to be packed when a deliveryman arrived with packing boxes and plastic sheets and bubbles. Mary was sitting on the floor, materials spread around her, when the door opened and Alex stood there. He was in jeans and boots and wore a different shirt that looked as if it was new.

"Good morning, Mary."

She liked his voice, calm and deep. "Good morning to you, Alex. How is your father?"

"Holding his own." He handed Mary a bowl and sat on the floor beside her, watching as she wrapped it. "I told him I was taking him home."

"What did he say?"

"The usual. But not as forcibly as before." He smiled. "That's a good packing job, incidentally."

"How about handing me some more?" She liked his proximity and the clean male smell of him.

Alex brought several small figures cupped in his big hands. "I told my father you would pack these. What he wanted most to know was about his manuscript. I know he has been working on one for years. What is it?"

"A book about ancestral memory. Quite remarkable. But unfinished. There are voluminous notes—"

"I did not realize he was still working on that. I'll take it home with the rest of his things."

If he took everything away, if he left with his father,

Mary knew she would never see either of them again. She said, "It is an important book; he will want to complete it, surely. His life's work—"

Alex shook his head. "I saw him this morning. He can't write. The stroke—"

"Oh. I am so sorry."

For a time they sat side by side on the floor, packing in companionable silence. He handed her the more delicate objects while he wrapped the bowls and larger items.

Mary thought, *I feel I have known him always.*

Finally she said, "The manuscript should be typed. I'm good at that." She smiled. "If your father can dictate, I could help him finish the book. And help him with his notes. I was a secretary for twenty years, you know."

"Not now?"

"No. I was fired. A merger."

He sat back on his heels and regarded her. She pretended not to notice. Abruptly he said, "I'm hungry. Have you had breakfast?"

"No, but I have the makings at my place. We can—"

"I would like you to meet a friend of the family's. We can eat there."

She glanced at her jeans and shirt rumpled from the packing. "I would like that, but I should change—"

He rose, pulling her up with him. "It is unnecessary, I assure you." He smiled. "Besides, you will be riding in a dusty pickup."

Mary laughed. "It won't be the first time."

She snatched a coat from her room and walked with Alex down the hall to the elevator.

"Good morning, Miss Gallinger." She felt Mr. McTavish's presence—in his son. A comforting and, yes, exciting feeling.

He led her to a pickup that was dirty, indeed. "I grabbed the first vehicle that was at hand. Got two tickets on the way." He helped her into the high seat. "My plane is in Brazil, so I drove. Didn't know I would be asking a lady to ride in this thing." He swung into the driver's seat. "A pretty lady, at that."

A plane in Brazil.

Who was this Alex McTavish, anyway?

A pretty lady.

No one had called her that before. She did not know what to say. She looked at him as he drove, hands easy on the wheel. His hair was an unruly thatch, like a boy's, but his profile was that of a man accustomed to the elements.

Something was happening to Mary that had never happened before. She felt beautiful. She felt *protected*. By a man she had just met and did not know at all.

It made no sense.

Was he married?

The "friend of the family" turned out to be the owner and manager of Alfonso's, an elegant little restaurant in a solarium. He greeted Alex warmly, bowed low over her hand, and urged them to dine as his guests.

They sat near a fountain surrounded by fragrant flowers, and looked at one another across the table.

"You deceived me," Mary said.

He laughed. "I was afraid you wouldn't come if you knew." He leaned forward as if to absorb her answer when he said, "Do you really like my father's manuscript? I mean, in a business sense."

"Yes. I think a publisher will, too. Once it is finished."

He leaned back in his chair and looked at her in silence for a moment. "My father's work is urgently important to him. He needs help. Obviously."

The waiter returned with a laden tray. The food was delicious, but Mary could eat but little, waiting for him to say the obvious—that they needed her.

"You understand I have to take my father to the hacienda."

"Of course."

"Could you come as his assistant?" He paused. "Professionally, of course." He glanced away. "I am being clumsy about this. The fact is that we need you. I need you."

Mary looked at him. She heard herself say, "Why do *you* need me?"

"Because my father needs you for more than work on his book. Because my wife is dead and my two sons are grown and gone. Because you are kind. And efficient. And beautiful." He leaned back. "Does that answer your question?"

She smiled over her coffee cup. "For the time being."

The fountain sang musical water notes, rejoicing. Mary listened to what it was singing.

You have always been somebody. You just did not know it.

Mr. McTavish's son would take her to Mexico! He needed her! Mary rejoiced with the fountain.

Maybe . . . maybe . . . I will have someone.

About the Authors

Lisa Alther was born in Tennessee in 1944 and now lives in Vermont. Her first novel, *Kinflicks,* was published by Signet in 1976, as were *Original Sins* (1981) and *Other Women* (1985). She has written two other novels, *Bedrock* and *Five Minutes in Heaven,* as well as many articles and short stories.

Lawrence Block's crime novels range from the urban noir of Matthew Scudder (*Even the Wicked*) to the urbane effervescence of Bernie Rhodenbarr (*The Burglar in the Library*). Signet published him first in 1970 (*Such Men Are Dangerous,* under the name Paul Kavanagh) and now publishes his Chip Harrison and Bernie Rhodenbarr series. He says it's good to be back.

Larry Collins is a native of West Hartford, Connecticut, a graduate of Yale University, and served with the U.S. Army at SHAPE (Supreme Headquarters Allied Powers Europe) in Paris. There he met Dominique Lapierre. After working as a foreign correspondent with the United Press and *Newsweek,* he joined with Lapierre to produce five international bestsellers, among them *Is Paris Burning?, O Jerusalem,* and *The Fifth Horseman.* Since then he has produced three novels of which the first, *Fall from Grace,* marked his debut as a Signet author.

Jeffery Deaver is the author of fourteen suspense novels. His most recent are *The Bone Collector* and *A Maiden's*

Grave. Winner of the Ellery Queen Readers' Award for best short story of 1995 and twice nominated for the Edgar award, he makes his home in Virginia and California. His first book for Signet was *Praying for Sleep.*

E. L. Doctorow is one of the most celebrated writers of our time, author of such bestsellers as *The Book of Daniel, Ragtime, World's Fair,* and *Billy Bathgate,* and winner of virtually every major American literary award. His first book to be published by Signet, *The Waterworks,* was a *New York Times* bestseller.

Joy Fielding is the author of twelve novels, including *See Jane Run* and *Missing Pieces.* Her first major success was *Kiss Mommy Goodbye,* which Signet published in 1981, followed by other Signet paperbacks *The Other Woman, Life Penalty, The Deep End,* and *Good Intentions.* She and her lawyer husband have been married for twenty-three years and have two daughters. They divide their time between homes in Toronto and Palm Beach.

Stephen Frey is thirty-six and lives in Princeton, New Jersey, with his wife, Lillian, and their daughters, Christina and Ashley. During his finance career he worked in the Mergers & Acquisitions Department of J.P. Morgan & Company, and most recently in the Corporate Finance Department of Westdeutsche Landesbank. Stephen writes full-time now, and his first book, *The Takeover,* was published by Signet in June 1996. His other books include *The Vulture Fund* and *The Inner Sanctum.*

Eileen Goudge, a distant relative of novelist Elizabeth Goudge, draws on her own rags-to-riches life story in creating romantic novels she describes as "dysfunctional family dramas." Starting with the bestselling *Garden of Lies,* all four of Eileen's titles were published by Signet. Her other titles include *Such Devoted Sisters, Blessings in Disguise,* and *Trail of Secrets,* all of which have sold millions around the world. She lives in New York and is married to talk-show host Sandy Kenyon, whom she met over the phone while being interviewed on the radio.

Joan Hess, winner of the Agatha, McCavity, and American Mystery awards, is the author of two highly acclaimed series, including ten mysteries featuring Claire Malloy and nine Maggody mysteries featuring Arly Hanks. She lives in Fayetteville, Arkansas. Her first book for Signet was *Mortal Remains in Maggody.*

Wendy Hornsby is the author of seven mysteries, including five Maggie MacGowen novels, *A Hard Light, 77th Street Requiem, Bad Intent, Midnight Baby,* and *Telling Lies.* She won an Edgar award for her story "Nine Sons," which appeared in *Sisters in Crime IV.* She lives in Long Beach, California, where she is a professor of history at Long Beach City College. Her first book for Signet was *Telling Lies.*

Erica Jong is the author of six bestselling novels, including *How to Save Your Own Life, Parachutes and Kisses,* and *Fear of Flying,* which marked her Signet debut; seven books of poetry; a children's book; *The Devil at Large,* a memoir of her friendship with Henry Miller; and most recently, her autobiographical *Fear of Fifty.* She lives in New York City and Weston, Connecticut.

Stephen King, the world's bestselling novelist, is the author of over thirty novels, most recently *The Green Mile,* published in monthly installments, and *Desperation.* He lives with his wife, the novelist Tabitha King, in Bangor, Maine. His first book to be published by Signet was *Carrie.*

Tabitha King is the author of seven novels, including *Caretakers, One on One,* and *The Book of Reuben,* all of which are set in the fictional world of Nodd's Ridge. She lives with her husband, novelist Stephen King, in Bangor, Maine. Her first book published by Signet was *Small World.*

Ed McBain, a pseudonym for Evan Hunter, began writing mystery fiction in 1956. He has written more than sixty crime novels since, many of them about the 87th Precinct or featuring the character of Matthew Hope. *Cop Hater,* the very first of the 87th Precinct novels, was late reprinted by Signet.

Sharyn McCrumb is an internationally known Appalachian novelist whose works have won wide critical acclaim as well as five of the major awards in crime fiction, and the Best Appalachian Novel awards in 1985 and 1994. She is the author of the Ballad series, including the *New York Times* bestseller *She Walks These Hills* and *The Rosewood Casket.* Her first publication with Signet was *The Hangman's Beautiful Daughter.*

Joyce Carol Oates is the author of a number of works of fiction, poetry, and essays, including *We Were the Mulvaneys, Will You Always Love Me?, Zombie, What I Lived For,* and *Heat.* She has been a William Abrahams author at Dutton Signet since the publication of *Solstice* in 1985. She has been a member of the American Academy of Arts and Letters since 1978 and is a recipient of the National

Book Award and the 1996 PEN/Malamud Award for Achievement in the Short Story. She teaches at Princeton University, where she is the Roger S. Berlind Distinguished Professor in the Humanities.

Nancy Taylor Rosenberg is a former deputy probation officer. Signet published her first novel, *Mitigating Circumstances,* in 1993, as well as subsequent titles, *Interest of Justice, First Offense, California Angel,* and *Trial by Fire.* Her sixth and most recent novel is *Abuse of Power.* She lives in New York.

Linda Lay Shuler is a former Dallas writer-director-producer of radio, television and film spots, dramas and series. She retired to Brownwood, Texas, where she wrote the first novel of the Time Circle Quartet, *She Who Remembers,* published by Morrow in 1988 and by Signet in 1989, where it became a *New York Times* bestseller. She has also written *Voice of the Eagle* and *Let the Drum Speak.*